RABELAISIAN REPRISE

RABELAISIAN REPRISE

JAYGE CARR

DOUBLEDAY
NEW YORK
1988

All of the characters in this book
are fictitious, and any resemblance
to actual persons, living or dead,
is purely coincidental.

Library of Congress Cataloging-in-Publication Data
Carr, Jayge.
    Rabelaisian reprise.
    Sequel to: Navigator's syndrome and The treasure
in the heart of the maze.
    I. Title.
PS3553.A7629R33   1988   813'.54   87-24648
ISBN 0-385-24436-3

To teachers, and especially English teachers, without whom no one would be able to read or to write. Most especially, to two of the finest English teachers ever encountered, Miss Ruth Hickey and Professor Ralph Ciancio, just to prove that bread cast on the thickheaded waters does eventually come back . . . wet.

One by one, Rabelais drew them back.

Rabelais: the world with no laws, no morals, no government, no ethics, no anything to hold the fabric of humanity together but an abiding faith in the sanctity of contracts. The world that proclaimed ultimate freedom and employed ultimate slavery. Nonetheless, one by one . . .

Estaban Xavier, Navigator: For him, Rabelais was only a routine stopover; until he discovered, the hard way, the difference between contracts and honor.

Jael the Navigator: Years ago she had almost been the spark to blow up a world; now she was older, and wiser . . . but just as explosive.

Brine the ex-enforcer, the contract-breaker: On Rabelais, contract-breakers die slowly and painfully in Agony Square.

Golden Singh: Once the most powerful—and most feared—c'holder on Rabelais, would his sudden arrival topple the usurpers—or Rabelais itself?

Freighter-master Rowan Reis, Navigators Alizon and Spyro, Sister Victory, and the blind spacer Will—all came.

Rabelais was waiting for them.

RABELAISIAN REPRISE

ONE

Navigator Estaban Xavier shifted restlessly on the narrow cot. He had not been beaten or abused, food had been shoved through the slot in the door at reasonable intervals, but he had nothing to do and nothing to do it with—except think. Regrettably, three standard days (approximately) as a prisoner had brought him no closer to the reason for his abduction.

He consulted his mental chrom, that inner sense of time passing that some people have, and decided he had about eight more stimmits before he could start pacing again. Not that he was being coerced into pacing or lying on the anonymous hard cold surface—Wheel, he had awakened alone, and the only communication since had been the trays of food—but it was one way to pass the time, to split it into fixed intervals, pace for a half stour, rest for ten stimmits. And think all the time.

For the nth time he glanced around his tiny prison. One room; walls, floor, and ceiling smooth, their surfaces dungy beige in the dim light. (Glow-paint on the ceiling and upper walls, old enough that part of it had peeled, leaving leprous patches of darkness in the fluorescent green.) Whatever they were made of, the surfaces were impervious to his bare hands, which was all he had to attack them with. He had been stripped to the skin before being thrust in here. Now he had only his fingers, and his brains. And whatever was in the small, almost bare room.

Item: one cot, made of a single piece of metal or plas, top and bottom bent at ninety-degree angles to form legs, welded or otherwise rendered undetachable from the floor.

Item: one thin sheet of foamed synthi to cushion the hard surface of the cot. The synthi was probably flammable, but without something to start the blaze it remained simply a piece of material to lie on.

Item: one chem-pot, like the cot welded or otherwise nondetachable from its corner. It worked, it achieved its purpose—with no more than a faint raw-alcohol tang that he couldn't smell unless he was standing right next to it—but so far he hadn't been able to pull it off, break into it, or break anything off of it, to use as a weapon or for any hypothetical useful purpose.

Item missing: windows. There was a row of vents running around the boundary between wall and ceiling. If he stood on tiptoes on the cot he could just reach his fingers into the nearest one. Not that it did him any good. All he could feel with those straining fingertips was the smooth bottom lining the vent and the emptiness of the narrow hole. He couldn't reach far enough to tell if it was a deep groove, a pipe or what. Just that what he had his fingers in was a hole and not a dark stripe. He was pretty sure it was a vent, though, because if he held his breath and listened hard, he could hear the faintest of hisses, moving air for sure.

Item: one door, locked. At its base was a small slot with a hinged flap through which his food was pushed at intervals. Standard spacer emergency rations, dried unpalatable bricks that tasted like clay, to carry out the metaphor. Water came in similar spacer packs, cellophane wrapped mini-pillows with a tear-off corner. He was collecting them as he emptied them, though what he could do with a dozen limp tubes of thin synthetic he didn't know yet.

Ten stimmits up. He rose from the cot in one easy controlled flow, began pacing up and down the longer stretch of the room. Ten paces up. Ten paces back.

His bare soles made the softest of chuffs striking the slightly yielding synthetic. Ten paces up to this wall. Turn, an almost military about-face that was a dead giveaway—had people been watching with any understanding of what they had imprisoned—of the great control he was exercising, or the strength held tight-leashed. Ten paces back. Turn. Ten paces. Turn. Ten paces—

He saw himself in his mind's eye, a muscular, athletic man with silver-gilt hair and tawny-amber eyes, who looked much as he had at twenty-five, at forty. Pacing sentry-quiet in his featureless cell, the green glow with its dark patches sliding over his skin . . . His mind sailed up and back, searching the nooks and crannies, the ins and outs of his life.

Had he felt the slightest of premonitory twinges when he accepted the berth that had landed him here? No. Just another berth, this world one of a dozen on the circuit.

True, he hadn't liked the world on his first, long layover here, but that wasn't unusual. Few worlds came up to the high standards of his own, his home world. But this one . . . His lip curled, a thousand generations of breeding, of standards, of honor, judging those who had none.

Rabelais.

The world with no laws, no morals, no government, no ethics, no anything to hold the fabric of humanity together but an abiding faith in the sanctity of contracts. The world that proclaimed ultimate freedom for its inhabitants and employed ultimate slavery.

Rabelais.

On his first layover on Rabelais he had seen the workings of their "free" society at first hand. He snorted, remembering.

What had happened when the cruel and powerful contract-holder called Golden Singh tried to pirate away the Navigator Lady Jael by accusing her of contract-breaking, the one sin on a world where there was no other sin, the only crime on the world where even murder was not considered a crime, unless it involved breaking one's signed word on a contract. He snorted again.

Honor that needed a written bond to uphold it was no true honor.

Muscles flexing and relaxing in easy rhythm, ears registering routinely the soft plats of his feet falling, the regular sound of his breathing, and the Silence—was the cell soundproofed?—he had gotten used to in three days, his body moved on automatic while his mind probed again the riddle of his imprisonment.

He was a Navigator, one of the necessary few who guided the ships through the mazes of hyperspace, the ones who led them from world to world, binding humanity together. Navigators were sacrosanct. On any world but this, they were lionized, cosseted, protected.

And even this one had learned its lesson.

So the Navigators' Guild had thought.

Could his abduction have anything to do with that years-ago attempt to enslave the Lady Jael? It seemed unlikely. He had been merely one of the bystanders in that, one of a dozen Navigators who had stood behind their threatened sister. He went over again the events of a dozen styears, more, in the past; had he acted in any way less than befits a man of honor?

No.

True, he had rewarded treachery in that one instance as it should have been, but he had known what none of his fellows had. It had not pleasured him to exact punishment.

He could remember no details, except a thin, frantic pleading. It had been distasteful; he had shut it out of his mind as soon as he orbited out, and time had done the rest. He could remember the rest of it, the Lady Jael herself, tall and lithe and charismatic, a woman in a thousand, a woman who understood honor without being bred to it, a challenge to any man who considered himself a man . . . His mouth curved into a very male smile.

Lady Jael. Tiger-striped hair and slanting, intelligent gray-green eyes. Eyes that had seen too much, knew too much, suffered too much. He would have liked to have done what he could to ease that suffering. He would have liked—

"Man." The first sound in three days not made by himself sounded loud and harsh in his ears.

"Man." He froze in mid-stride, a neoleopard of his native jungle poised to strike.

"Man," the muffled voice repeated for the third time, "go and lie on the bunk."

He turned slowly, faced the door. Unconsciously, he folded his arms on his chest—and waited.

"Man, if you do not go and lie on the bunk, we will gas you unconscious and put you there." The voice, muffled as it was, had a terrible triumph bubbling through it.

Estaban ground his teeth. That voice's owner meant him ill. He knew it, and the unknown knew he knew it. And was enjoying his futile knowledge.

"We can do it, man." The light in his cell was dim, but he could see the flap in the door slowly rising and a thin nozzle poking in. "We will, if you don't obey."

He whirled, dropped to his knees to where he had neatly piled the wrappers of his water containers.

"Those silly bits will plug out the gas for less time than it takes me to tell you that they won't protect you. Get on the bunk."

He hesitated, then, with a glint in his eye that promised repayment sooner or later, lay on the bunk.

"Feet up, hands at your sides. Don't even twitch again until I say you can, or you'll wake up in a couple of hours with a monstrous headache."

He believed the voice. He turned his head so he could see what was going on at the door, but kept his hands and feet totally still.

"This won't take long." The voice was amused. Estaban wasn't.

There was a squeaking noise, as though something heavy was being drawn past thin metal. Estaban could almost see a thick plank being pulled away from metal brackets.

A thud, as the—plank?—was laid aside.

Clicking and shuffling.

He lay, poised for action, holding still by an effort of will no one but himself was appreciating. When the door opened . . .

But the door didn't open, not for several seconds. There were sounds of a scuffle, then it was suddenly shoved open, and a single figure staggered in, propelled from behind. The door slammed too soon; a flutter of gauze got caught and tore. There was a clicking, and the sound of the heavy plank—or whatever it was—being hastily slid back in place.

Estaban felt his eyebrows rising. "Well, well." He chuckled softly.

"You can move now," said the voice, with a very nasty undertone. "Do whatever you please."

Estaban pleased to sit up slowly, assessing his new companion from the crown of night-black curls to the bare, pink-toed feet. "Well, well," he repeated with a soft chuckle. "*All* the amenities."

"Please." It was barely a whisper, forced out through a tight throat.

Estaban leaned back, twining the fingers of both hands together and resting his head on the cradle formed thereby, elbows up and the rest of his body relaxed. For a second time he surveyed his new fellow prisoner, draped rather than dressed in black lace and chains of brilliants that drew attention to instead of concealing.

"Well, well, *well.*" He drew a deep breath and almost choked on heavy musk laced with jasmine. "All the right trimmings," he murmured.

The girl (she was a long way from being a woman, but her clothing—embellishments—proved beyond doubt that she wasn't a child, either) took a step toward him and held out an appealing hand. "Ohhhh—" It was more moan than word.

He lifted a foot and planted it, heel down, sole stiffly facing her, a symbolic barricade. If he had sunk his toes into her midriff, he couldn't have made his "Keep Off" clearer.

"Now, why," he said, very softly, but quite firmly, "do I have the suspicion that you are not here just for the benefit of my well-being?"

She sank to her knees, held her hands out pleadingly, then bowed her head. "Please." He could hear strangled sobbing.

"Please yes, or please no?" he asked, curiosity the only noticeable emotion in his voice.

"What—whatever you want." Another strangled sob. "You're a man, aren't you."

"Um." He considered it. "You have eyes, don't you. I am used to considering myself such."

She grabbed the foot he was using as a barricade, planted a wet and clumsy kiss on the big toe. "You spacers sometimes," she got out then, frantic: "Me. Choose me."

"My dear child." In one easy movement he had scooped her into his arms and sat back down on the bunk, stroking her hair in a comforting, paternal manner. "My poor infant, don't you know that a prisoner's first rule is never do what your captors want?"

She was crying in earnest now, gulping and gasping in terror, trembling and shivering, and he set himself to soothe her, thinking that they would have to try some far less obvious ploy than this to ensnare him, since that seemed to be their goal.

Though the cell was empty but for the two of them, he seemed to hear again the "Do whatever you please," with its undertone of nasty laughter.

TWO

Most days, Agony Square in the city of Pantagruel on the world of Rabelais was remarkably thin of people. Especially if there were no contract-breakers currently on display, moaning. If there was punishment scheduled, the square would be jammed, as most contract-holders liked to have lessons well rubbed in, and insisted that all their contracted not on duty be present to witness the reprisal for breaking the one unbreakable commandment on Rabelais.

This day the sun was beaming down on an empty row of stakes and chains; nonetheless, when the ornate palanquin made the turn toward the square, it stopped abruptly. The two women inside were rolled against each other. The older giggled, and the younger spat a curse. "Those clumsy—"

"We're not moving." The older woman was puzzled.

"You're right, we're not." The chair carriers had righted their burden almost immediately, but it was beyond their power to move from the fringes of the solid mass. "I'll have them whipped." She moved lithely toward the side curtain. "No, that's too easy. What do you suggest, dear Medee? Slow flaying? Emasculation? Hot irons?"

"My dear girl . . ." The woman lying flat on the heap of fur-and satin-covered cushions fanned herself languidly. "There are eight men carrying this chair. If you eliminate a useful team every time one of them makes a mistake, you'll run out of carriers eventually."

"Oh, not all of them, aunt." The girl twitched aside her curtain and looked out. "Just one; but I'll make the others watch. I'm sure there's a glint of rebellion in the eyes of the freckle-faced one who's left rear." She twitched the curtain again. "I can't see much, but it looks like people. A mass of unwashed, blocking the way."

The older woman, supine on the musk-scented pillows, giggled again. "Then you can't blame the carriers. Still, if there is a problem, the guard captain—" At which point the tinkle of a discreet bell on the inside of the palanquin interrupted her.

"Speaking of guard captains," the younger woman said slyly, "this one must be quite . . . efficient in his duties. He's lasted longer than most."

The older woman snickered happily. *"Most* efficient, product of—" She swallowed her next words hastily, as she realized she was about to tell the girl something she'd prefer she not know—yet. "Never mind." With jovial generosity: "Still, one occasionally longs for . . . newer, younger, bolder. Would you care to try him out, Emerald child, if I feel like replacing him?"

"Too muscle-nose for me. But if I haven't anything better—" The girl twitched the curtain open just slightly and said impatiently, "Yes, Guard Captain?"

"Beg pardon, c'holders." The guard captain was a tall, beautifully built man with a shock of russet hair and hard, shallow blue eyes. "Beg pardon, but the way in front of us is blocked. It would take quite a while to force a passage through. Request permission to retrace our route, until we can go around."

"Retreat." The younger woman sniffed. "Before a mob of unwashed contracteds. Never."

"But, m'lady c'holder—"

She snapped her fingers at him, pixie hazel eyes alight with mischief, and turned to lie back in the luxurious palanquin. "You're a guard. Do your duty. Take us through. Or—" It was a threat, delivered in a malicious, sweetly knowing tone. "Do you tire of the responsibilities of your position? Perhaps your contract can be renegotiated." She flicked him an up-and-down glance of contempt. "I was just remarking to the Lady C'holder Medee that I might soon need to replace one of my bearers that's clumsy."

The guard captain bowed, his back stiffly straight. "We'll take you through. Beg pardon for disturbing you for so trivial a decision, ladies." He took a step back, the guards behind him blocking off what little view the girl had through the slit in the curtains.

"Wait." The cold, clear young voice stopped him. "I was not aware that punishment was scheduled today. Why are so many crowded here?"

The captain glanced sideways over his shoulder, then turned back. "There's a madman perched on the gallows, haranguing the crowd. He'd best pray that he's not keeping any of them from their contractual duties."

"Oh." The girl called Emerald leaned back, yawning. "Some merchant trying to dispose of uncontracted-for goods, no doubt. But what an odd place to choose to try for contracts." She let the curtain fall shut, as a single reply of the guard captain came through.

"No."

Emerald cuddled into the luxurious heap of furs and synthisilks with the slow sensuousness of a well-fed cat. "Merchants are boring," she said with a yawn. "Though"—a happy, reminiscent giggle—"desperate ones can be amusing."

Medee was chomping desultorily on a nut-crusted sweetmeat. She swallowed the last morsel, licked the tiny dribbles of pink frosting off her fingers, and sniffed. "Not a merchant."

"No?" Emerald reached over, sampled the icing off one from the pile of goodies with a questing finger, and grimaced. "Too sweet. You like your nibbles far too sweet, Medee. And you've forgotten to tell your cook I'm back, so he can include some of my favorites in your trays."

Medee yawned. "I didn't forget. If there's nothing you favor, I'll have him whipped. Lightly. He's too skilled in what pleases me to destroy his usefulness. Do you wish to watch?" She started on another treat.

"A whipping? Light? Thank you, no." Emerald was well aware that her aunt had forgotten; but if the cook was too stupid to keep track of his owner's whims and guests, that was his hard luck, and a light whipping was less than he deserved. She frowned in thought. "Is he skilled in other areas?"

Medee picked up a brown treat cunningly shaped like a long-furred, bushy-tailed cuddle she sometimes amused herself by petting. "Altered. Before I obtained him." She gave the treat a long slow lick.

"Ech." Emerald cocked her brow, eying the treat suspiciously. "What is that brown stuff all over that, Medee? It looks like—"

Medee's tongue slowly cut a long swath in the brown coating before she answered. "Off-worlder stuff." She licked around her lips. "Chocolate." She swiped the tiniest possible bit off on the end of her finger and offered it. "Want to try it?"

Emerald shook her head, her mouth pursing in disgust. "Not I. Who knows what the off-worlder worms put in their boxes."

Medee licked her finger and took another swipe from the sweet, which was rapidly losing its tail as she licked. "More for me, then."

Emerald stared at the embroidered hangings of the palanquin without seeing them and drummed her fingers on the covers. She had not her aunt's interest in food, and she was bored, bored, *bored*. Maybe she ought to order the guard captain to come inside and amuse her. Or replace the freckle-faced bearer, and *he* could come in and— Then she remembered something her aunt had said.

"What did you mean, Medee, that the man out there isn't a merchant? What else would he be? Why else would someone wish to address a crowd, except in hopes of contracting out something?"

"He's one of them," Medee said, around the body of the shaped treat, on which she was now sucking.

It took Emerald a second to translate the rather garbled words. Then, idly, after sampling another of the treats on the piled tray: "One of which them?"

"*Them* them." Medee was now crunching her treat.

"Aunt Medee—" Emerald called her "Aunt" only when she was irritated with her, and Medee sniffed. She had told the child time and again not to do it, because it *aged* her so. Although there had been *years* between her and her sister Esme. Of course, the older Emerald grew, the more years younger Medee claimed.

"*Dear* Medee," Emerald cooed. Then, with an impatient snap: "What them?"

Medee licked chocolate off her fingers and searched avidly for another brown treat. "Sandmen," she mumbled.

"Ooooooh!" Emerald sat bolt upright and clapped her hands eagerly, looking for once like the not-much-more-than-child that she truly was. "Oooooooh, *dear* Medee, I heard all about those delicious almost anti-Cs even on m'lord's estate in the far Gargantuas." She jounced up and down in her excitement, causing the palanquin to sway and her aunt to complain querulously. "And now, now, dearest"—she chortled—"I'm going to actually see one myself!"

"Emerald."

Too late. The girl had pulled the embroidered cord. In seconds, there was a discreet tapping on the body of the palanquin and a low-voiced "M'ladies?"

"I'm coming out." Emerald thrust her legs through the curtains, fully expecting that someone would hurry to break her fall. And the guard captain did, though even his impassive mien was startled. He placed her carefully on the ground, his men forming a little wall between him, the girl, the palanquin, and the mass of people.

Emerald's nose twitched at the thick scent of people tight-packed. "I've mud on my shoes," she accused, holding out her foot, encased in gilt and scarlet satin. "Clumsy. I'll hold you accountable later." A small, nasty, knowing chortle. Then, changing the subject with a child's short attention span (though the guard captain knew her well enough to brace himself for the inevitable): "Is that truly a sandman there?"

The guard captain hesitated, then nodded. "Yes, m'lady."

"I wish to see him. I wish to hear him. Now." She tilted her head and smiled up at him; it wasn't a pleasant smile, and promised him much, none of it nice, if this little spoiled-rotten scion of power didn't get what she wished, immediately.

"M'lady," he dared to protest, "many of these are lower contracteds. Their presence alone would be displeasing to your sensitivities."

She stamped her dainty little foot. "I shall ask my Aunt Medee for you. We'll see if you refuse me when you are contracted directly to me."

"M'lady," he said on a sigh, "if you are sure . . ."

She awarded him her best smile. "I'm always sure. Obey me. Now."

"Aye, m'lady. Hosephus." He spoke to a guard near him. "I want Almaric's platoon to form a guard ring about me. We will take the Lady C'holder as close as we can get to the gallows and the man on it. You close around the palanquin, continue to force it through this mob. I'll meet you on the other side, as soon as the Lady C'holder has seen and heard enough. If, m'lady"—he bowed—"that suits."

She stamped her foot again. "We have to get closer."

"We will. As close as is safe." His men had formed around him, and they began cleaving their way through the mob, not hesitating to threaten with hands on hilts, as they shoved and pushed.

She dug her nails into his arm. "I want to *see.*"

"When we get a little closer, I'll raise you onto my shoulders," he said, "if you'll pardon the presumption."

"Oh goody," she exclaimed. Then, "Can't we go any faster? Pfaugh, they smell!"

The captain didn't say anything. It was all he and his men could manage to move at all through the tight-packed crowd, but no use telling the spoiled little madam this. She was accustomed to getting whatever she wanted immediately, if not before. Typical of a powerful c'holder, which she was, even if she was a half-grown girl.

"Almaric, close in," the captain ordered. On an almost inaudible sigh: "M'lady." He held out his hands.

"Ooooh, yes!" she agreed, and he picked her up as if she weighed not much more than his shield, and held her high until she could wriggle into position on his shoulders. Since he was a tall man, she had a good view.

The man standing on the platform of the gallows, his voice reverberating out over his audience, did look rather as if he were made of sand. His skin was sun-browned to darkness, his hair almost the same shade, flowing in dunelike waves down past his shoulders. Even his eyes were a sandy-brown hue.

For the rest he was tall but oddly ill-fleshed, as though nature had intended him to be as brawny and broad as the captain, but something had burned away the muscles covering the big bones. His arms moved as he spoke—there was something a little odd about the way one of them gestured—and he was holding his audience absorbed in a way that no one single man, no matter how charismatic, ought be able to.

"—obligations," he was saying. "Do obligations begin and end only with the words on a contract? They could, and sometimes they do, but when a contract is fulfilled there may be obligations left. What do obligations not determined by contracts consist of? Are they similar in type and kind to contractual duties? No! A contract may involve many, many people, but a person's own obligations are unique to themselves. In the ultimate judging, each individual person must be responsible for himself or herself and only that one's self! I am not responsible for you, or you, or"—his desert-sun-burning gaze fixed on the sylph perched on the broad shoulders of the man in the guard's uniform—"or you! There is, to my knowledge, no contract between us, and without a contract I can never obligate you without your consent, pretty one, now, can I? Though I would muchly enjoy it if I could!"

"You would indeed." Emerald giggled loudly. "But would I?"

He chuckled, seeing only a mischievous child, on her—father's?—shoulders. "I'd see that you would, pretty one, for you deserve no less." He held out his hand, long-fingered, each knuckle prominent. "But the best, the best, pretty one, is if two enjoy freely, of their own will."

She ignored that last, asked pertly, "Are you really a sandman, tall and ugly?"

He frowned. "I'm *the* Sandman, pretty one."

"The Sandman." She bounced up and down. "Aren't you afraid, preaching anti-C?"

"What I preach, pretty one," he said, still frowning, "is the true sanctity of contracts. Of true contracts. No one respects the sanctity of contracts more than I. But to be a true contract, a contract must be based on truth, total and complete truth. If there is a lie, a mistake, an omission, or a misunderstanding involved, it must be corrected, before the contract can be a valid one. I but preach—"

"Is your contract available?" she interrupted.

"My contract . . ." He had completely lost his argument. Automatically: "I am not under contract."

"Oh." She made a moue. "You're a c'holder." A sigh. "I've not heard of you before now. Are you a c'holder from foreign parts, or perchance—"

The grinding of his teeth was audible. "I am not a c'holder, I would not enslave—"

"Not a c'holder!" She stared at him. Then, gleefully, clapping her hands, a child who has seen a promised treat withheld and then dropped in her lap: "Captain!"

He clamped a warning hand on her leg and hissed. *"Not here!"*

She glanced down, her mouth pursing into a disappointed pout, her eyes narrowing. He nodded at the mass pressing close around them, faces angry at this interrupter who had disturbed the Sandman, and she understood. There were hundreds jammed into the square, and if they got angry enough to forget contracts . . .

C'holders had been killed in mobs before, even unarmed mobs, trampled by sheer numbers. Later, many of those involved would be punished for c'breaking, but that would not bring the dead back to life. "Later," the guard captain hissed. It was a promise.

She gave the tall, lean desert-eyed man an assessing look. Yes. Later. He would pay for the delay by being even more amusing. That is, she would be amused. He would not. She seldom had to wait for what she wanted; she didn't like it. It boded ill for the Sandman.

She awarded the guard captain with another kick in the ribs. "Let's go now," she ordered petulantly. Loudly, with a sniff: "He's *boring!*"

The guard captain was not displeased to get his responsibility out of this seething but—for now—controlled mob. He turned immediately.

The Sandman, realizing what he had been talking to, smiled thinly. "I guarantee, Lady C'holder," he said softly, "that boring will not be the word you use about me—soon!" Then he raised his voice and resumed his interrupted monologue, again holding his large audience enthralled with his charisma and logic.

Getting out of the mob was not much easier than getting in, but the guard captain persevered. Emerald, enjoying this novel form of transport, giggled and continued to kick his ribs. She then discovered that leaning down and tugging his moustaches caused him to grind his teeth and muffle groans and curses *most* amusingly. She didn't realize that rubbing her pert young breasts against his cheek and the ears exposed by his helmet—as she had to to reach his thick moustache—was causing another sort of reaction. Luckily for the guard captain, she remained unaware until he could control himself.

The palanquin was big and clumsy, much harder to move through the masses of people, but its bearers and escort had been content to work around the thinner fringe of the mob, and so they were free of it and able to continue on while the guard captain and his men were still mired in the mob.

"Stop!" Emerald suddenly shrieked, grabbing both ears of her mount and pinching painfully. Her head was twisted behind them. "I want to go *back.*"

"Back, m'lady?" He kept his voice even with an effort.

"Yes, oh, *contracts.* They're going."

"Going? Shall we re-join the Lady Medee then?"

A fretful whine: "Yes, since you couldn't obey me in time. Ummm." Thoughtful: "but he's beautiful."

"He?"

"Yes. A stranger. But he won't be as soon as I find out who has his contract. Ummmmm . . ."

He had been beautiful. A tall man, one of a group, his arm around the shoulders of a lithe woman Emerald was not fool enough not to realize was the sort that men, given a choice, would fight to the death for. There had been other men, too, men and women, but it was the one man she wanted.

The beautiful man, all golden, hair, eyes, skin, body tautly muscled and the creation of a sheer genius. She forgot—no, not forgot, just shoved aside until she was again bored—the Sandman; all she wanted now was the beautiful man who looked like a perfect statue come to life.

"Medee," she was coaxing a few minutes later, "Medee, I've just seen the most delightful toy; and you're going to help me locate his contract and obtain it."

"Of course, m'dear." Medee fanned herself languidly. "Of course. Whose insignia—"

"If I knew that, I wouldn't need your help," the girl whined. "If he was wearing insignia, I couldn't make it out at the distance I saw him at. But there can't be two like him in the whole city, soooo lovely."

"If he's that spectacular, his contract will be prominent." Medee reached for another sweet. "I'll be pleased to make arrangements for you, dear child. After I try his paces myself."

"I don't want to wait. You can have him after, dear Medee."

"After." Medee swallowed a bite and choked for a second. Then: "After, dear child, if he *was* any use, he *won't* be. You know that."

"I'll leave plenty for you." Emerald slithered back into the luxurious synthis and furs, her eyes glazed, her hand gently stroking her own skin. "I'll take care."

"He must be quite something, for you to make such a promise." Medee giggled.

"Oh, he is," Emerald murmured. "He's all gold, dear. Golden hair, golden skin, even his eyes—"

"Aiieeee!" The lazy Medee sat up with a screech, revealing herself to be a grossly overweight woman with a crown of frizzy hair, much becrumbed. "What," she demanded hoarsely, "did you say?"

"I said he was gorgeous." Emerald tugged at the chain that held her namestone—an emerald—precisely over her bare navel. "He is. All gold-colored, everywhere. And the most beautiful—"

"Even his eyes?" Medee almost couldn't force the words out.

"As gold as my bracelet." Emerald held up the wrist to display a broad yellow-gold band.

Medee collapsed back, moaning softly. "It can't be him, he's long dead. But if it is him—"

"Him who?" Emerald propped herself up to stare at this uncharacteristic behavior.

"Golden. *The* Golden. Golden Singh. The most powerful c'holder of them all."

"What *are* you saying? The most powerful c'holder is—"

"Golden Singh—you know who he is . . . was, idiot child—left Rabelais before you were born, and died. But if he didn't die—if it is him—"

Emerald sniffed. "He doesn't look that old."

"He wouldn't. His family were GAed, from the old time. If it is him—" She sniffled. "We're *doomed!*"

THREE

The man with the golden skin stood in a room in the fortified building that was the Navigator's Guildhall on Rabelais and gazed out at the world that had belonged to the man he no longer was.

The woman watching him chewed her lip in uncharacteristic hesitation.

Gaze flicking from one to the other, a rather homely man sat tailor-fashion on the bunk, shrewd eyes narrowed, rubbing an occasional hand through his shock of thick gray hair.

The woman broke the silence. "Never should we have come."

The homely man grinned, the gleam of even white teeth bringing an odd attraction to his mismatched features. "You think you, or I, or both of us together, could have stopped him." He jerked a thumb at the man standing by the window.

"Mam could have."

"Mam." His face softened into love, for a second beautiful in the fugitive way that love can transfigure the most ugly. "Mam could. But never when it was his choice, freely made."

"To come back into such danger." Her gaze assessed the bunched muscles in the tense, golden back.

"You're in danger here. I'm in danger here." The ugly-faced man stated the obvious.

"I know." She sounded angry. "And why Mam forbore tying you up and plunking you in the bottom of her garden until after we left—"

"It's my world, this," the ugly man reminded, "just as it's his. Not yours. If there's one of us who should have stayed behind—"

"Brine!" she burst out. "You didn't—"

Even in the dimness, the red burned under his leathery bronzed skin.

"You did!"

His flush deepened and he had trouble meeting her gaze. Suddenly, some embarrassment in the way he was hunching his shoulders got to her, and she chuckled. "Obvious it is she refused. What happened."

He sucked his lips in, as though to swallow the answer she was demanding. He was so brightly red she was sure he would glow in the dark.

"Brine." She changed her tactics, voice soft and coaxing. "Tell me you may as well. Mam will, once I ask her, and you know it."

He sighed and dropped his clasped hands between his legs, looking down at them. "She read me a lecture. Her favorite. About free choices for responsible adults. Then she—" He swallowed, then went on. "She said that if I could even ask, it proved I wasn't as far along as she thought. Then she walked away. I thought—I was afraid—"

"Oh, Brine," the woman commiserated. She had had plenty of experience with Mam's for-your-own-good tactics herself. Mouth tight, she held out a hand toward the man gazing at the window, and then let it drop helplessly. "Oh, *Brine*," she repeated, in a completely different voice.

"There's nothing either of us can do," he said roughly.

"I know." For her, at that moment, there was no one else in the room, no one else in the world. "But—he hurts so."

"I know." He echoed her statement. He hurt, too, for different reasons, but he knew the two hurts did not compare, and that was why the woman was focused on the other man. He swallowed jealousy, finding it, once again, as bitter as bile.

"Oh, Brine," she said a third time, smiling at him for a few seconds, and the bitterness was gone. She didn't have to say the obvious: He needs me *now*. He knew it, she knew it. It helped, mostly. Sometimes, he muttered to himself, being an adult on Mam's terms wasn't . . . He sighed.

"Have you been able to . . ." She nodded toward the stiff, unyielding back.

"No trespassing, even for me." He frowned in concentration, then sighed, relaxing. "Even for me." The smooth, golden-skinned back might have had KEEP OUT tattooed on it a foot high.

Again she stretched out a hand toward the unmoving man, and let it drop. "Try."

"I just did."

"With words."

He sighed, unfolded his legs, and slid off the bunk, walked the couple of steps to the unmoving man and laid a hand on those broad shoulders. "Golden," he said.

No response, not even a quiver of muscle.

Louder: "Golden."

Nothing, except the sound of three lungs breathing.

Softly: "Son."

Slowly, the man named Golden turned. His eyes were haunted. "I wish I were your son, Brine," he said softly.

"Sorry that Mam helped you to regain all your memories, are you, Golden?" The woman moved to stand next to the two by the window.

Golden grinned, an oddly boyish grin for a man in his prime. "I much prefer you as my contemporary than my mother, love," he said, catching her hand and pressing her fingers to his lips in a soft kiss.

She slipped her hand from his grasp and patted his cheek with it. "Strange. Now, I preferred those halcyon days when a thwack on the rump was enough to make you do as you were bid."

Brine snorted. He remembered halcyon days—evenings when a man tired from working outdoors all day sat by a roaring fire, the woman opposite him, her hands busy with spindle or embroidery, and a man-sized boy curled at their feet, playing with a carved toy and chattering six to the second, his golden eyes sparkling and childishly innocent. He also remembered boyish pranks, and boyish mischief, and more than once administering a well-deserved spanking, not easy to do when the spankee is half a head the taller.

Golden's grin broadened, spread to include Brine as well as the woman. "Not easy being a father, is it, Brine?"

"No," Brine said shortly.

"Ahhh." The woman, knowing exactly what he was thinking, patted him on the shoulder.

He smiled, including them both. "My choice."

They both knew it was true, and not true. It had been Golden's choice originally, to come back. Brine would have let him go cheerfully, but she would not, and since she had to come, so did he, and they all knew it.

"My thanks, though, for that choice." He laid his hand on Brine's shoulder, and the woman laid hers atop. For an instant they stood, joined, and then the woman shook herself and said practically, "Make plans we needs must. You both heard him today. The reports are correct. The Sandman is incredibly dangerous to Rabelais."

Golden laughed, an easy chuckle. "The old I would have said it was simple. Three inches of steel, and that dangerous voice is silenced forever."

The woman was dressed in navigator black, quasi-military trousers and boots, an epauletted jacket. But the jacket was unfastened to reveal a soft rose-pink ruffled blouse that was certainly not regulation. Now she seated herself in one of the chairs haphazardly set around the small table and propped her booted legs, casually crossed, on the corner of the table. With a brow high cocked, she said, "Now, I never thought you that stupid, Golden."

"Past easy measures, isn't it." He caught a chair, turned it around, and plumped himself down, arms crossed on the back, chin resting comfortably, the chair creaking protest as he rocked back and forth, balancing on the two back legs.

"Before we got the news, I'd say." The man Brine resumed his favorite posture, tailor-fashion on the bed.

"Long past." The woman shifted slightly. "Hard to get accustomed to these again," she muttered, sotto voce.

"Hard to get used to . . . a lot of things again," Brine agreed.

"Freedom." Golden nodded, meaningfully. They knew each other so well that they understood what was not said as well as what was. "Sorry you came?" he added.

Brine snorted, flicked an eye to the woman.

She shifted her shoulders uncomfortably. "Too tight."

"You can go back," Golden offered, eyes downcast, not meeting theirs. "I'll go back with you, if you wish."

"And stay," the woman said softly.

The slightest of hesitations. "And stay," he agreed, low-voiced.

"Gol—" Brine started, and then stopped, seeing the expression on the woman's face.

"Tear your soul in two to go back now, would it not, Golden," she said, not a question.

He shrugged, not meeting her eyes. "What can one person do, or three, or all of us, if the word gets through to the others in time."

"I thought I'd taught you better."

He looked up. "But you—and Brine—"

"Brine worries, and he misses those we left behind"—a pause—"as do I. But dearest"—a brilliant smile—"this is the way it must be. Made our choices we all have. So come, tell me why the old Golden would have felt three inches of steel sufficient."

He shrugged. "The old Golden would not have heard him except by accident, would not have realized the danger. Three inches of steel silences a voice; it cannot silence ideas."

"Precisely," the woman agreed dryly. "Native here, you two are. Are his ideas as dangerous as I perceive them?"

Golden looked at Brine. "Probably more so," he said. "Fifteen years ago, the Navigators' Guild threatened to blacklist Rabelais, so that no new ships would arrive, and all off-worlders leave forever—or until the blacklist was rescinded. The Navigators claimed then that such a change in this world would topple its society in a bloodbath. Most c'holders laughed at the threat." He was telling them what they already knew, but they let him, to allow him to build to his conclusion. "But some looked at the strange equations and believed. I do not have your off-worlder thinking-machines, I do not know these relationships you call equations; but I listened to that man today, and I heard in his words, his ideas, the end of my world as I knew it, as it exists today." He paused.

"All societies evolve over time," the woman said gently. "Just as people start from babies, grow up, grow old."

"And die." He nodded. "Some age gracefully, though, and some—"

Brine finished it for him. "Are murdered in their beds. That is what I heard today. The change the Navigators predicted fifteen years ago, for a different reason. Bloodbath, dissolution, destruction."

"Soon?" the woman asked.

Golden shrugged. Brine frowned.

"Very soon?"

The two men communicated without words. "Perhaps, perhaps not," Brine said slowly. "But—inevitable."

"Well . . ." The woman bent one leg, ran an easing finger inside the rim of the almost knee-high boot. "Well, the problem we have established. Next, gentlemen, comes the—"

A hesitant tapping interrupted her.

"What the . . ." She frowned, looked at her two companions. "I gave orders."

The tapping came again.

"Someone—" She was all regal in an instant. "Someone is going to—" She slung her legs to the floor and strode toward the door, every inch of her stiff, a promise that *someone* was going to regret—

"Prime emergency," a voice hissed through the closed door.

"Prime." She looked back at the two men, face pale under bronze. "It can't have started already." Both men soared to their feet, ranged themselves protectively at her side.

She hauled the door open, stared at the quivering apprentice, who promptly babbled out, "Prime emergency, lady, do forgive me, but your communicator was turned off, I had to—"

"You did correctly, child. What is the emergency, and what is to be done?"

"Thank you, lady." The slim girl relaxed. "The Guildmaster has called a meeting, in the main auditorium, as soon as those outside the Hall can get back. A stour, I mean"—she glanced down at her chrom— "a stour less some ten stimmits. I tried to get you on your comm, then I ran up the stairs."

"Good. We'll come down immediately."

"We? But, lady—"

"These are two intelligent adults who were once natives of this world. They may not share my skills, but they speak with my voice on any other subjects. If the Guildmaster objects . . ." She frowned, with all the weight of her maturity.

"I would not be so impertinent to say you nay, lady. Only 'tis never happened, outsiders at a Senior Navigator council."

"It may be necessary. I repeat, what is the emergency?"

"A Navigator has disappeared."

"What!"

The apprentice nodded. "A message came through on secret-wave. They landed here with two Navigators, took off with one. The captain told the remaining Navigator that the other had gotten a plush berth and would be replaced at their next stop, since they were already behind schedule. But the youngster had received no message directly, as one Navigator would send another in farewell. So she sent back a message of her own, to Guildhall, to be sure that the other Navigator had indeed received such a berth. No other ship took off in that period, and the Navigator is not at Guildhall or aboard any of the other ships in port."

The woman in Navigator black, hastily fastening her jacket, whistled.

"He never reported to Guildhall," the child informed. "Seemingly, just got off the ship—and vanished."

"Is the other Navigator sure he went off the ship?"

"Yes. She saw him leave."

"But never made it here." The woman whistled again. "What class?"

"A. Class-A Navigator Estaban Xavier."

"Estaban—no!"

"You know him," Brine asked.

"I've met him." She frowned. "Were there anybody in this universe I'd say could take care of himself, it was Estaban Xavier. And anybody less likely to embroil himself in local politics."

"Oh," said Brine, suddenly realizing when she must have met the missing Navigator.

" 'Oh' is correct. Our oath he took, and would defend all those protected by that oath to the death. Other than that . . ." She frowned.

"Other than that?" Golden prompted.

She gazed at him with troubled eyes. "Estaban despises this world. His own world is based on the concept of honor. He has a special word for it . . . pundonor, or something like that. His people believe that a man's word alone should be sacred, that nonsense written on a sheet of paper is just that."

Golden nodded slowly. "A dangerous attitude, in these troubled times."

"But never was he overt about it. He thoroughly believed in minding your own business." She bit her lip.

"Honor," said Brine slowly. He had been an adult while Golden was going through childhood, and had done much talking with spacers. "If his . . . honor demanded something, something dangerous, would he do it, no matter what the cost?"

She nodded.

"To himself—or to others?"

Another nod.

The three looked at each other, almost if all three were thinking with a single brain. Then Golden spoke for them all. "Every explosion," he said slowly, "starts with a single spark to set it off."

Jael the Navigator, once almost such a spark herself, finished it. "And Estaban Xavier might be that spark."

FOUR

Estaban Xavier was in a temper. Not that most people could have told it from just looking at him. He was standing, arms at his sides, hands held loosely, breath coming in and out at a slow, controlled rhythm. His aquiline, saturnine face was smooth, his tawny-yellow eyes staring straight ahead.

Only a very knowledgeable observer would have been aware of the minute tremors that wracked that seemingly relaxed muscular body, the way twelve bare toes dug into the synthi flooring, or the meaning of the single word in his native tongue that he spat out, before setting his teeth firmly together.

He was alone, once again, in his cell. They had removed the girl the same way they had thrust her in, by ordering him flat on his bunk, and her to stand by the door, on threat of paralytic gas, the nozzle thrust into the cell like the tongue of a snake, and he had obeyed, seething but helpless, waiting for the chance that might never come.

He had lain down, flat, well away from the door, and watched, as it opened, as she was jerked bodily out, as the door was once more slammed shut and secured. Then he had sat up in his bunk, fingers interlaced, and thought.

He had still been sitting, almost unmoving, his thoughts his own secret, when the first desperate scream split his ears.

He had spat one single word as he hurtled out of the bunk and ran to stand next to the door, panting and listening.

The second scream had followed within seconds.

All he could tell was the screamer was probably female, and in acute pain.

He was straining his ears when the third scream came, and with it a wet thunk, a sound like cloth tearing. It was all he needed: They used whips on this world.

Three more times it was repeated, the thunk, the scream.

Then there was a short pause, except for muffled broken sobbing, interspersed with desperate, hysterical "Please"'s.

Odd shuffling noises, as though people were moving about.

Seconds passed.

"No!" High, frantic, earsplitting with pain and terror. "Not that! *Please!*"

Muffled laughter.

"PLEASE!"

Muffled words, none of them intelligible.

"Yes, yes, I'll do anything you say! Anything!"

More laughter, very loud, nasty and triumphant.

"No! Please! I said I'd—nooooOOOOO! AyiAAAAAHHHHHHHH—"
The screams went on and on, howls of pain and more than pain, wordless
don't-stop-helps! that proved whatever punishment was occurring, it involved
more than simple physical pain.

It seemed to go on forever, but eventually the screams dimenuendoed into
silence.

"Slap her with the vibrator," a cold voice ordered loudly. "The slut's
shamming."

Estaban ground down on the scrap of lip caught beneath his teeth. The
vibrator was a spacer toy; it stimulated the nerves directly. Like having all
your teeth aching, and a migraine, and being bathed in molten metal and
every other pain imaginable all at once. Anybody who kept silent under a
vibrator was truly unconscious. He wondered if the vibrator was what had
been used all along, but he doubted it. A vibrator was total agony while it was
being applied, yet left nothing but the ghost of pain after. Whereas the whip
left bleeding sores that hurt for hours, days—scars, mental as well as physical.

There was silence from the outside. Whoever had been tormented was
mercifully unconscious—or dead.

He waited, breathing slowly and carefully. There were again movements
outside, then a slithering noise, as though a large limp body were being
dragged down the corridor outside his cell. Some low-voiced comments.
More movements.

Then nothing.

They put the girl back in his cell some three hours later, using the same
technique as before.

He waited until the door was resecured and the sound of footsteps had
died away before slowly sitting up, feet dangling over the side. He looked his
fellow sufferer up and down, apparently casually.

If she had been dressed like a high-class courtesan before, now she was
displayed like an expensive whore. All the gauze and lace and cloth were
gone; instead, circles of brilliants emphasized her nipples, her breasts, her
navel, while innumerable chains clanked and jangled and covered absolutely
nothing.

"What happened?" he asked, his voice apparently calm.

Without a word, she turned around. Her back was decorated with a similar
display of chains, tinkling as she breathed, caressing her and then falling
away.

Estaban cocked his eyebrow, repeated, "What happened?"

A single finger curved over her shoulder to point at her back.

"Um." He rose, took a couple of steps for a closer look.

He had thought her back smooth under the chains, but it wasn't. He bent closer. Six stripes. All raised. Some just welts, others covered with a thin strip of insta-skin, proving that skin and flesh had been cut.

"Doesn't like scars, does she," he commented.

"The clients don't—most of them," the girl said, in a tight controlled voice.

"And the ones that do . . . are not preferable to the ones that don't," he said, dryly.

She shuddered, a small shudder that only his fingers on her shoulder felt, it wasn't visible to the eyes.

"And you'd rather avoid them, as long as you can, correct?"

Fiercely: "Yes!"

"My deluded child, it is inevitable," he said, his voice almost paternal. "If nothing else, you will get older."

"That's then. This is now."

"You're younger than I thought, even." He turned, went to sit on his bunk again.

"Please." She dropped to her knees. "Please—she threatened. If you don't —the next time, it won't be the whip."

He drew up his legs tailor-fashion and eyed her straightly. "I told you. I won't do what my captor wants."

"She'll punish me."

"That has nothing to do with me. Cruelty is inevitable as long as you're in her power. Do something for yourself, child, because I shan't do what your mistress wants."

"She'll"—she mumbled it; it sounded like "punchello" to him. "Like Esta, today."

"That wasn't you doing all the screaming?"

"No." She caught her arms around her childish self and shuddered. "Poor Esta. When she recovers, she'll go on the other side."

He didn't say anything.

"It'll be me next."

He still didn't say anything, just gazed at her out of night-darkened eyes.

"I'm frightened."

He sighed. "Come here, then, child. I'll give you what comfort I can." She almost leaped into his outspread arms. "Short of what your mistress wants," he finished dryly.

They talked. There wasn't much else they could do, locked together in a cell ten paces at its widest. Not much else but what he refused to do, and she quickly discovered that he meant it, that his strength was greater than hers and his control almost equally immense. She pouted, begged, pleaded, wept all over him, and finally, sullenly, gave in—for the moment.

He knew, and was amused by, precisely what was going through her head, but had infinite faith in himself. Faith that, as time went on and she ran out of ploys, proved justified.

So they talked.

He was a Navigator, and had seen many worlds, could talk of them for hours. But he quickly realized that she was bored by his talk, though she had been trained to hide it, and turned the conversation back to the only world she knew.

Which was even more constricted than he'd supposed.

Her name was Brandy, given her because of the color of her eyes. She was somewhere in her early teens, and she knew little more than the house she'd grown up in, the nearby market, clothes, and how to please a client.

Politics, history, economics, poetry, religion, other worlds and other occupations were not even words to her, they were so outside the narrow path she knew that she couldn't even imagine anything else.

Most of what she said did not surprise him—he could feel pity, even compassion for the waste of such potential—but occasionally she shocked, even stunned him. As when she said—

"She's your *mother!*" He had been pacing up and down, but on hearing her words he froze, one foot poised to come down, so that she giggled and said he looked like a stwork ready to tuck its leg under its wing.

"Your mother?" he repeated, totally incredulous.

"It's unusual, I know, for a contracted wench to keep her get, to control a contract on her own output, but she was already rising when she had me, and was able to append my contract to her own. As she rose further, she took me with her."

He stood, big and square, and faced her. "Couldn't she have found you a better place than this?"

"Better than this? For a contracted?" She laughed. "Why, the possibilities are limitless. A powerful c'holder may desire me, contract for me. Or if I please my clients well enough, I may eventually earn enough in extras to clear my own contract and rise, as my mother has. She started out as an inn-slut, you know. And look at her now."

He had recovered himself. "I haven't had the pleasure, as yet. But be assured, if we do meet, I shall certainly look."

She was not stupid enough to misunderstand what he hadn't said. She pouted. "But I haven't pleased you?"

"On the contrary." He had reached the end of his mental half-stour of pacing, and so went to sit beside her on the narrow bunk. "You have pleased me excellently well. You may tell your . . . mother so."

"But you haven't—"

He shrugged. "I have told you why I haven't. If your mother asks, say I've not the need."

"I daren't." She dropped her eyes, but not before flicking him a quick, sly glance—which he didn't miss. "She'll know it for a lie. All you spacers, why, that's all you do, once you've come aground."

"Some spacers," he corrected. "But naturally, that's the ones you see here."

"If you say so," she said, doubt in her voice. "But she's long experience with spacers, and she says—"

"I don't doubt she's had long experience with spacers." He noticed a tear in one toenail and began slowly pulling off the flap.

"She says you black ones are the worst. It's well known that you must be kept satisfied, or your mind suffers. Then you cannot guide your ships, and so are no longer of import."

"Black ones?" The nail tore down into the quick, and a spot of blood appeared. He licked a finger and rubbed it away before saying, "Black ones? You mean Navigators?"

"You proud ones dressed in black. Only"—a childish giggle—"you're not dressed in black now. Does that make you less than you were?"

"Not hardly," he said dryly.

"You've a lovely body," she said shyly, running her fingers across his broad, hard-muscled chest. "It seems strange, when you spend so much of your time cooped up in those tiny rooms aboard your ships."

"Isometrics," he explained. "If you haven't space or equipment, you can make your muscles work against each other. Like this." He put the palms of his hands together and pressed, so that the muscles in his arms and upper torso flexed.

"Ohhh." She ran her fingers down his arm. "Ohhhh. That's all it takes. And such a—a marvelous result."

"Not hardly." He was old enough, and wise enough, to recognize another, not-so-subtle ploy. He could also realize that there was some truth in it, too. She did admire his body. His lips twitched. "There are exercises you can do, using a floor, or the wall."

He slid down, positioned himself. "This is a simple one, called a push-up." Still breathing steadily, he did ten neat push-ups.

"It doesn't look hard." She thrust out her lips in a childish pout. He grinned.

"Come and try it."

Five minutes later, she was sniffing sullenly. "Well, it didn't *look* hard."

They were both sitting sprawled on the floor, he chuckling and she rubbing her shoulders aggrievedly.

"You have to work up to it," he told her. "I'll figure some simple ones for you." Grimly: "But it isn't muscles you need or want, is it?"

"No." She sighed. "But I'm glad you have them just the same." She ran a hand down his shoulder to his chest again.

He cocked an eyebrow at her and then went back to what she had been saying earlier. "Your . . . mistress put you in here, didn't she, because she's afraid I'll lose my value if I'm not kept"—he winked—"healthy."

She sulked. "You think she tells me anything, except who to please?"

"It makes sense," he mused. "Though what madness made her think she can hold the Guild for ransom, I can't imagine. She's far more likely to find herself in a punishment pit than gloating over riches—contracts, here, correct."

"She's smart. It'll be contracts."

"So she thinks. I'd not count on it, were I you."

"You don't know her. I do."

"You don't know the Guild, I do," he answered calmly. Then, firmly: "I doubt you're old enough to remember what happened the last time someone on your world tried to savage away a Navigator. I was there."

"Oh?" She was tracing circles in the hair on his chest and apparently paying no attention, but he wanted her to know, to understand what kind of risk she was running.

"The Navigator in question was a woman, not beautiful precisely, but I imagine there were few men who saw her who did not feel—"

"I know what you mean," she murmured.

"The man who actually attempted her died, ugly. Your own people did it. Gladly. The powerful man he claimed urged him to do it lost what he prized most. He left your world soon after. Those involved peripherally . . ."

She had finally put it together. "Are you trying to warn me?"

"Yes."

"You do like me!" She flung her arms around him and nuzzled into the hollow at the base of his throat.

"My dear child." He pulled her away, held her gaze with his own. "Listen to me. I would not see anyone hurt unnecessarily, and you are not much more than a babe, after all. Your mistress's course can lead to nothing but disaster. If you can, convince her."

She was shaking her head.

"Well," he said, sighing, "if you get the chance, try. Not for my sake. For yours."

"You're in danger, and you worry about me?" she said, wondering.

"I've taken care of myself for a good many years. You're young and vulnerable. Do try to remember what I said, and act on it if you can."

She wriggled slightly in his lap, and gave him a glance of pure mischief. "For a kiss," she coaxed pertly.

"A—"

"Just one." She fluttered thick lashes at him, and he burst out laughing.

"You little—"

She gave him a look through her long lashes, and held out her hand, finger and thumb a fraction of an inch apart. "Just a *little* one."

"You . . ." He caught her shoulder, shook her slightly, then sighed and laughed together. "All right. A little one. Bargain sealed."

She nodded, with such the hopeful look of a sparrow watching a worm stick its head out, not *quite* far enough to grasp, that he had to bite his lip to keep from laughing again. "A contract it is, if not written."

"On my world we never write them down." He tucked a finger under her chin, tilted her face up. She obediently shut her eyes, pursed her lips with such innocent naïveté that he frowned. Well, she wouldn't keep that long, he decided, and framed her face with his hands to put it at just the right angle, lowered his own face for a long and exquisitely gentle kiss.

When he lifted his face, she stayed just as she was, eyes shut, only her mouth moved slowly opening to an O of surprise.

"Shut it." He tapped the fullest part of her lower lip. "Before something flies in and makes itself at home."

"Oh." Her eyes flew open and she stared at him. "I liked it."

His brows went up. "That's the general idea," he said.

"But I never have before."

He snorted.

She thought it over. "Maybe it's because you're my first *important* client," she concluded.

"My girl . . ." He popped her lightly on the rump and withdrew himself to rise lightly to his feet. "You have a great deal to learn."

"I know." She heaved a large sigh, reminding him how young she was. "But I try," she confided, looking up at the full height of him standing.

"Commendable," he said. He reached down and drew her up to stand beside him.

She smiled, a child's glowing but transient, unalloyed happiness. "Thank you."

He raised silent brows skyward, then remembered what else he had meant to say to her. "Listen, child, there's something you must know. Your mistress is both right and wrong about Navigators."

"Oh?" She fluttered her lashes, and he suppressed a chuckle at her artlessness.

"She is correct, if we are not kept . . . healthy, especially mentally serene, we cannot fulfill our duties. However—" He held up a finger, thus
stopping her interruption. "However, not all of us require the same . . .
treatment to stay healthy."

"So?"

"Some of us require what you have been ordered to provide. Some require
pure solitude, to be left alone whenever they're not working. Others—"

"Yes?"

"Others require simply to be provided with precisely what they wish, at
any particular time, and of course, what they wish varies, with their own
particular condition. I, for example, require—"

She bit her lip, staring at him with such an expression of hopefulness that
he again swallowed a guffaw. The worm had come out another fraction of an
inch, not quite enough to get a grip on, but if it ventured out just a *tiny*
fraction more . . .

"Someone of sympathetic temperament to talk to."

"Ooooooh!" It was a childish wail, a child who has had one lick of ice
cream and then had it snatched away.

"You have a sympathetic temperament," he pointed out.

She pouted.

"It's not common among your kind," he said gently. "Why, I'd be very
surprised if there were two here that would suit my needs."

Wheels turned. "You like me best?"

"How could I not?" *You're the only one I've as much as laid eyes on.*

The wheels turned faster. "And later . . ." she prompted.

"I make no predictions," he said stiffly. He had gone as far as he dared to
protect her, as far as a man of honor could. He had told no lies, and would
tell none. He did need someone to talk to; any other needs he could and
would control. No man of honor cooperated, in any way, with a captor,
except in exigencies that didn't apply here. But a man of honor didn't throw
innocents—well, children—to the wolves, either, without making some effort
to protect them. He had balanced his responsibilities, delicately, to come up
with this compromise, this careful telling of selected truths that added up to
at least one big lie. It was as much as he could do.

"I don't think she'll like hearing this."

"If she has your world's equivalent of ransom in mind," he said smoothly,
"I don't think she'll appreciate having nothing of value to trade with."
Which I intend to see is what happens!

"Ummmm."

"Understand this, child." He caught her chin and held it, his gaze boring
into hers. "Make her understand it if you need to, and you might. If she

stood with a knife at your heart, and I could stop it with a word, and that word besmirched my honor, I would not say it."

"You'd let her kill me when you could prevent it easily. You'd be responsible—"

"Listen carefully, my child. Each person is responsible for his own acts. I for mine, you for yours, she for hers. Yes, if I saw someone about to be hurt or killed, I would do all in my power to stop it. I would risk my own life, if need be. But not my honor. That must come first. If she holds a knife, ultimately it is her hand, her responsibility. If she would have my chest for yours, she may have it. Honor does not permit a man to let a child hurt in his stead. She may have my life, if she chooses. She has had that option ever since she took possession of my body in that underhanded way. But not my honor, never my honor. That remains mine alone."

"She'll kill me!"

He shrugged. For both their sakes, both the girl and her mistress would have to be convinced that, regarding his honor, he had spoken the plain and simple truth. As long as she hoped to manipulate him by working on the child, both of them would endure hell.

He shrugged again.

They had no choice, no choice at all, either of them.

Except endure.

FIVE

Several months before Estaban Xavier walked off his ship on the world of
Rabelais and disappeared, a slender woman with lavender skin and pale pink
hair that reached almost to her knees sat up abruptly from a sound sleep,
stifling a scream with a clenched fist ground into her mouth.

Her husband, who had the red and blue mask of a mandrill monkey tattooed over his face and depilated head, stirred and rolled over on the bed
they were sharing, sinking slightly into a force-field-restrained mass of opales-
cent bubbles that served as mattress.

His wife, her amethyst eyes wide, continued to stare into nothingness,
whimpering, until she brought her emotions under control. Then she sighed,
staring down at the block of muscle and fierceness that was her husband.

Slowly, her eyes narrowed, and she made a decision, and then several
others. Cautiously, so as not to wake the sleeping man, she slid off the bed
and padded over the blood-warm synthi floor to the comm. Leaving the
vision part of the comm off—on her home world, modesty was long forgotten, but her husband was product of a different milieu, and she preferred
deferring to him to arguments or hurt feelings—and putting up a shield so he
wouldn't be disturbed, she began making a series of comms.

It was over a stour later that Spyro began to stir and groan with returning
wakefulness. His tattooed face went through a series of grimaces that would
have scared babies into hysteria, but would have made his wife, as she had
many times in the past, smile gently and begin to kiss the frowns away.
Automatically his hand went out to his wife's familiar softness; when it flailed
through nothingness, he became fully aware on the instant.

He sat up and looked around, blinking. Almost immediately he spotted his
wife, stark naked as they both slept, standing at the comm and using it.

He frowned (an expression that had sent more than one grown man fleeing
in fear) and slid off the bed to stride over to the woman at the comm, the
irresistible force crashing toward—all too often, when it was his wife involved
—the immovable object. He was at least half a head shorter than Estaban
Xavier, whom he had known, off and on, for many years, but outweighed him
by better than ten kilos, and not a gram of it was fat. In his natural state,
once he had reached his full growth, he had been a juggernaut of destruction.
But that had been years ago, and his natural fighting ability and brute

strength had long since been honed and trained in a variety of martial arts. Now he was a fine-tuned engine of destruction, only one thing unchanged: his hair-trigger temper.

"Alizon," he roared, as he charged across the room, "how many times—"

"Excuse me, Guildmaster," she said politely, as she flicked the speech circuit on hold, while stopping her own personal rampaging bull with a kiss on the cheek. "I'm so sorry, dearest, I didn't mean to disturb you," she said sweetly.

"—letting anybody and everybody see—" he bellowed.

"I'd hardly call the Guildmaster anybody and everybody, dearest," she interrupted calmly.

"—see you as stark as—" he got out and stopped abruptly. If the forefinger of one hand was on the hold button, so that Guildmaster, frowning, was on the screen but couldn't hear them, the forefinger on the other hand was poised over the Visual blank-out button, and it was down. The Guildmaster wasn't seeing anything. "Oh," he said, on a breath of air.

"I love you." She dropped a kiss on his ear, watched with unalloyed pleasure the tide of red that flowed on the patches of un-tattoo-colored skin.

"Good." He recovered his amour propre quickly. "Finish your call and let's . . ." He kissed her, and she smiled and turned to him. He kissed her again, more enthusiastically, then paused, frowning. "Why did the Guildmaster call?"

"The Guild—*oh!*" She turned back, hurriedly flipped off the Hold. "My apologies, Guildmaster, a slight emergency here."

"No problem, m'dear, no problem. I believe I have all the necessary, anyway. I'll let you know as soon as a route—" He paused, cocking a brow. "Are you sure? I thought you and that walking temper of yours are taking a well-needed vacation?"

"Emergency, sir," she replied.

"Well, in that case—" he started, but Spyro's bellow overrode him.

"Emergen—"

Soft as her voice was, it cut through her husband's easily. "Yes. Red alert, but personal. I'm sorry I can't tell you more, sir, though if it grows and involves the Guild—as it might—I will keep you informed."

"Of course, m'dear," he humphed. Then, with a sly smile: "Take care not to let that husband of yours go off half-cocked." Spyro growled. The Guildmaster's smile broadened. Marriage was uncommon among working Navigators, because of the difficulties of their profession, and the amount of traveling involved. But most Navigators had a world they considered home base, and it wasn't uncommon for the Guildmaster of that world to have an arrangement of some degree of formality with one or more of his or her Navigators. Or want to.

"Just what—" Spyro started, but the Guildmaster went on with a frown. "Are you serious, m'dear, about taking a commercial cabin if I can't find you a berth?"

"Yes," Alizon said firmly, before Spyro could interrupt again.

"As you choose. I'll be back when I have some news."

"Make it soon," she muttered. Then, louder, more formally: "I thank you, Guildmaster."

"Anytime, m'dear. Anytime. That's what I'm here for. I'm just sorry"—his smile gave his words a double entendre—"that I couldn't do more for you."

Spyro snarled and ground his teeth together, but Alizon gently stepped on his bare toes and said all that was polite.

Once the Guildmaster had switched off, Spyro turned his wife to face him and growled, "Now, what's all this about? I thought we agreed—"

"Spyro." She cupped her hands, cradling his face, and said softly, "I have to go—somewhere. I'd hoped you'd want to come with me."

"Try to stop me," he snapped. Then, with a thoughtful rather than ferocious frown: "But why? An emergency? Did we get a message and—" She was shaking her head.

"I just know."

"Eh?" he asked, puzzled. Then: "Oh!"

She nodded.

"You must?"

Solemn, she nodded again.

"I see." And he did. Alizon was a psychic. Mostly it was small stuff—he knew better than to play any gambling game with her. Her clairvoyance and psychokinesis were erratic, but enough to give her quite an edge. She was telepathic, too, now and again, which smoothed their marital life in many ways—and had led to one or two wall-bangers of arguments; though when two such strong personalities came together, a wall-banger now and then might be expected. But by her expression, this wasn't small stuff.

"Tell me, please," he said.

"While we eat, though there's not much I can tell." She turned toward the little autokitchen. He followed her in, watched her scan the supply console, frowning. "I'm not really hungry, but we must eat. What do you want?"

He didn't say a word, but she *was* psychic; though plenty of nonpsychic wives would have known equally quickly. "Later," she said firmly. "What do you want to eat?"

He shrugged. "Anything. Whatever. Do we have any of that lean left?"

"For breakfast?" She made a face, then sobered. "How about your lean, with brangles and a scoop of chillies."

"No chillies for me, thanks, not with lean." He thought a second. "Hot choc and sardies."

Her fingers programmed the console. "Got it. Would you get the table."

"Um." He strolled over, pushed some buttons, and watched as a table-height platform and two matching chair-height ones slid out of the wall, stopping when there was space for one on each side.

He sat down, and she was almost behind him, setting the table with the lean for him, a thin-sliced local meat, smoky gray in color. The brangles were a local grain, insta-cooked into amber disks. She added to her bowl a generous scoop of chillies, a pale-strawberry slushy liquid full of crunchy bits whose origin Spyro preferred not to speculate on. She topped her concoction with half a dozen sardies, a tiny fish cooked tail into mouth, the resulting ring no bigger than a thumbnail. She poured herself a mug of hot choc and passed the pitcher and a second mug to him. He poured for himself and reached for the sardies, which he sprinkled over the several slices of lean he had set on his side of the table—the extruded surface was guaranteed sterile, no need of plates—before shoving the second bowl for the brangles aside, merely adding more lean to his pile.

Alizon took one look at the lean heaped with sardies and shuddered, then began eating with her eyes anywhere but at the food opposite her.

"Now." Spyro took a bite, chewed and swallowed, then went on. "Now, what is all this about?"

She took a sip of choc before answering. "I wish I knew. Only—" Another sip. "Bad. Very bad."

"And where are we going, by commercial cabin if necessary?"

She reached over, put her hand over his. "I alone am needed. You—"

For once, he didn't lose his temper. "You think I'd let you go into Wheel-know-what danger alone?"

She smiled. "No. At least, I hoped not. Only . . ." He waited patiently. "I think—I think it may be worse, with you."

"For you, or for both of us?"

"For both of us."

"Too bad." He reached over, took a single brangle out of its bowl and crunched it loudly. "Where?" he repeated.

She smiled. "Rabelais."

"Rabe—" He rose out of his seat, a human volcano on the verge of eruption.

"We must." It was said with very little emphasis, but he subsided.

"Why?" he asked, almost calmly.

"I don't know. I only know what's at risk." His mandrill-monkey-mask face wrinkled in a question. She held up her hand, one finger pointing skyward. "The world of Rabelais itself."

He snorted, mumbled, "It couldn't happen to a nicer world."

Two fingers. "Our Guild."

"Ahhhh." He sounded as if someone had kicked him in the diaphragm.

"And—" She hesitated. "Estaban Xavier."

He pursed his lips in a thin whistle.

She patted his hand again. "He is our friend," she reminded, "as well as one of us, one of those we took our oaths to defend and protect."

Their gazes held for interminable seconds, before he nodded, slowly.

They were wandering around the busy port. Arrangements had been made, but Rabelais was not a popular port of call and it would be a couple of weeks before the first ship of the three they would need to reach Rabelais took off. They had just left a rather convivial "breeching party" for a young Navigator who would be making his first solo trip. Spyro, who had a capacity large even for someone his size, was rollicking along, roaring out an ancient space chanty about an incorrigibly macho spacehand named Vic and his various adventures with his lib captain Hannah, when Alizon grabbed him and pointed, "That man, Spyro! Stop him!"

"Huh?" He choked off the shanty. "Who? What?"

"The redhead. That one!" She had already started to run. *"Grab him before he—"*

Spyro, with a muttered curse, started after her. Broad-shouldered as he was, he couldn't slither through the moving mob of people the way she could, and though he could keep her proud coil of pink hair in sight, he was falling farther and farther behind.

Their quarry, unaware of the commotion behind him, was trotting toward a very small freighter, the kind that specialized, because of its size, in equally small if precious cargos, drugs, high-T devices, frozen embryos, and seeds and DNA of all kinds.

He was at the very ladder to the cargo port of his vessel when Alizon panted up and grasped his arm. "Oh, stop. *Please* stop."

He turned, and asked politely, "May I help you, woman?" He frowned slightly. "Navigator?" He was of average height and a few years, perhaps, younger than Spyro, early to mid-thirties. Yet if his body was young, there was an expression in his eyes older than time, and he waited with the patience of true maturity.

"I must speak to you."

"If you wish." His aquamarine eyes were clear and serene. "I am due to take off shortly, but if it is some emergency, perhaps—"

But she was staring at him with a mixture of horror and hope. "Jael!" she burst out.

"What!" Spyro had run up just in time to hear that last.

The red-haired man merely frowned. "You know the Navigator Lady Jael? You have a message?"

She flicked a glance around her, where several of the people had stopped and were frankly staring. "Privacy?"

He nodded. "Inside. If you would. May I offer you hospitality?"

Alizon didn't bother to nod, merely started up the ladder. The red-haired man, his brows rising, bowed slightly to Spyro to follow her up.

Inside, seated and with hot kaffee poured for three, he introduced himself. "I am Freighter-Master Rowan Reis. And you are . . ."

"Navigator A-class Spyro Hirohito," he growled. "My wife, Navigator A-class Alizon DeBeaumarchais."

"Navigators." Rowan Reis nodded. "Friends of the Navigator Lady Jael?"

"Reis." Spyro was frowning. "I remember—only you're too young. But he was a redhead, too, darker."

"That's right," Alizon exclaimed. "The freighter-master who testified at the Lady Jael's trial, wasn't his name Reis?"

"My brother." Rowan Reis leaned back. In the artificial ship's light his hair did not flame as it did in the sunlight, but it was still a dark red unleavened by brown. Once it had been a clear red in all lights, so most who saw it thought it was gene-altered, which it wasn't. But the years that had matured him had cooled the flamboyance of his hair.

Alizon and Spyro exchanged glances. "Could you get a message to the Navigator Lady Jael?" Alizon asked softly.

Rowan shrugged. "A possibility. At least, I could leave it in my next ports to be passed on."

"Is Jael mixed up in this?" Spyro asked his wife.

She gnawed a knuckle, briefly. "I don't know."

"Not directly." He was thinking aloud. "She'd never, ever go back to Rabelais."

Rowan Reis didn't jump, but something changed behind the polite impassivity of his face.

Alizon wasn't unaware of the change. "Freighter-Master Reis," she said softly.

"Yes?"

Spyro leaned back to let his wife take over this delicate fencing. Everybody has secrets, as he well knew, and this young man with the maturity and authority of a Guildmaster three times his age seemed to have more than most.

"You mentioned your next port of call."

"Star-Roads," he said with a nod, mentioning the largest, most advanced world of the next quadrant over.

"Star-Roads." Alizon made it a question.

"Medical emergency. They want—" But she was shaking her head. He smiled, still calmly. "It is my stated destination."

Alizon smiled back. "So it is." Then she placed a hand on his arm and her smile broadened. "You're Lady Jael's friend; so are we. We are working toward the same goals, and should compare notes to be sure we are not getting in each other's way."

He nodded. "If you say so, Lady Navigator."

She just left her hand on his arm, while her eyes glazed slightly. Then she blinked and murmured, "Maze . . ."

Rowan Reis became so still that Spyro knew instantly his wife had hit a nerve, a raw one. Then he smiled. "Mace is not a part of my cargo this time. However, I believe that a Captain Riverez of the *Flying Dutchman* has a cargo of spices, which may include mace."

Alizon turned to her husband. "Have you ever heard of a world called Maze, love?"

"No, not I. Not anything like it. A local name? Perhaps a port, not a world?"

"No. The world is Maze." She frowned. "Not a world, exactly. A—a—"

Rowan Reis laughed easily. "A world that isn't a world. If your emergency, Navigators, is simply to propound useless riddles, I'm afraid I must ask—"

"You're from Maze." Alizon was laying her cards out. "And it's a place to live that isn't a world."

"Artificial satellite?" Spyro suggested.

"Yes. No. I don't know." A breath. "The Lady Jael is there."

"Is she?" Rowan Reis was back under control.

"You think she is. Only—"

He was still blocking neatly. "If you say the Lady Jael is on this world which is not a true world, I will not contradict you," he said politely. "I only remind you that I am traveling under a medical emergency and—"

"You think she is on Maze. But . . ." Suddenly: "Where's your Navigator?"

He neither paled nor flinched. "Upstairs. Computing."

"Did your Navigator check in at Guildhall?"

"Due to the nature of our layover—"

"A comm, registering, takes only a few seconds. You have a comm, I can check." He didn't move. Softly, she went on, "But I don't have to, do I? There is no Navigator aboard, only you."

"What!" Spyro soared up, only to have his wife stop him with an upraised hand.

"You are trained, but not a registered Navigator." It wasn't a question. He simply stared at her. "You weren't trained in a school."

"Lady." He relaxed back, laughed lightly. "You pile riddle upon riddle. First a world that is not a world, then a trained Navigator who cannot have been trained."

"I wish I could convince you to trust me. We could help each other."

"I have a medical emergency."

"Jael would vouch for both of us. By then it would be too late."

"If you say so." Disbelief flavored his calm voice.

"I won't report you."

"Report what, Lady Navigator?"

Spyro lost what patience he had. He clenched his fist and shook it under Rowan Reis's nose. "Look, you, a Navigator is in danger, and—"

Something in the aquamarine eyes stopped him. "Who from?" he said softly.

"I can't know," Alizon replied, equally softly. "I only know soon—and on Rabelais."

"The Sir Navigator is right, though. The Lady Jael would never return to Rabelais."

Spyro may not have been psychic, but he was a man deeply in love; sometimes that makes a man sensitive to the same symptoms in another man. "Are you sure?" he said, in as soft a voice as his bull-bellow could produce.

"Absolutely," Rowan Reis said firmly. But he bit down on his lip, and his eyes glazed slightly. Spyro opened his mouth, but his wife signaled silence with a quick finger across her own. Both the Navigators watched the man, as he turned around in his own mind what had been said. Suddenly Alizon's eyes widened and she gasped.

Rowan's eyes focused, and he smiled wryly at her. "Caught some of that, did you?"

"Only—but it's impossible."

"What is?" From Spyro.

"He—formed a link—across light-years!"

"You're the psychic, not I. Is it possible?"

"No. But he did it."

Rowan Reis grinned, for the first time looking his age. "If you say so, Lady Navigator. But I will tell you this, and it is truth." He stood up, calm and casual and at the same time a tornado of energy about to be unleashed. He glanced at his comm. "This ship is taking off in five stimmits. For Rabelais. You have four stimmits and some steconds to decide whether you want to stay aboard for the voyage or get yourselves off."

"Stay, of course. We'll have to comm Guildhall."

He was already heading for the door. "Come'n. Nearest outside comm is in the control room."

Alizon was right behind him. "It won't take me a stimmit. Is Jael on Rabelais?"

"Heading there. Beat us there, can't say by how much." His voice echoed down the level spiral he was speeding up. "What comes of giving our idiot son his head."

"Your son?" Spyro had followed them into the control room, where Alizon was already on one comm to the Guildhall while Rowan was at another, preparing the ship for takeoff.

"Ours." He was punching buttons, barking phrases into various comms and controls. "Mine. Jael's. Brine's. Hann's. Damask's. Ferine's. Mam, of course. Morocco's. Prax's."

Alizon and Spyro gazed at each other. He shrugged, she nodded. "Advanced," he said.

Rowan, for all his concentration, caught and understood the single word. "No, not gene-jangling." He grinned. "Long story."

"Interesting," Alizon said.

"As in the old curse," Spyro muttered.

Rowan had jacked himself into the console for faster control, and the two Navigators hurriedly began strapping themselves in, as the ship trembled preparatory to actual takeoff.

"Maze is interesting," Rowan said, as the ship roared upward, the vroom of the engines almost drowning out his last words. "It's Rabelais that is the curse."

SIX

The Sandman talked the day through, his audience ever-changing, as some listeners drifted away to necessary business while others approached to take their places. Occasionally a squad of enforcers worked their way through the mob, but each person they questioned turned out to be either a minor c'holder, an independent contractor, or a contracted on a legitimate errand for his or her owner, trying to squeeze through the mob, or, rarer, a contracted on a free day, earned by extra service or whim of a c'holder.

When the Sandman had first started making his speeches, there had been many in his audience who could not justify their presence away from their duties. The punishments their c'holders used quickly stopped that. But by now the Sandman—and many other people—knew that for every man or woman actually standing there, a dozen or more, working stolidly, would hear the words repeated within hours. Contracted had their duties, but all contracted also had their sleep periods. If they chose to use them listening to one of their number murmuring repetitions of words spoken by a tall, sand-hued, fanatic madman, there was not much their c'holders could do about it, except punish them for any derelictions caused by lack of sleep later.

Besides, many of the c'holders were unaware of just how much damage simple words could do.

The Sandman knew. The Sandman was a product of Rabelais at its hypocritical worst. He knew exactly what he was saying, and what the spread of his ideas could do. A spacer friend of his had once told him a saying that went, "Hell hath no fury like a woman scorned." Having known that kind of woman, he believed it. But he knew himself, and he knew that there were worse. The c'holders, many of them, abused their privileges over and over. It was almost surprising that it had taken so long for the worms to turn.

The Sandman smiled, trotting through the gathering dusk toward the simple tent he called home.

He had been called a worm himself, by the powerful c'holder who had tormented and abused him. Tormented and abused and then shipped away across the great desert, because others, friends, would have rescued him, protected him.

Worm.

But this worm had escaped, and the desert had hardened a beaten, humiliated boy into a savage, powerful man.

This worm had turned, with a vengeance.

For vengeance.

Between one step and the next, the Sandman's eyes slitted, and he sucked in his breath with a sound like a cobra about to strike. Then, without breaking rhythm, he turned, began weaving his way sideward instead of straight toward his goal. Most of the people around him, contracteds scurrying to finish this errand or that before dusk fell, paid little attention to the man who had been heading toward the city wall and was now circling around, casually altering his course completely.

If there was one thing the desert had honed to a fine edge in him, it was a danger sense, that sixth sense some people have always had, that warning instinct that sets the body on full alert for no apparent reason. The Sandman smiled to himself, an ugly expression that made those who noticed it shudder and increase their pace, to be out of range when the inevitable explosion came.

Looking without seeming to look, the Sandman suddenly turned right into a narrow space between two smallish buildings. The gap connected two major thoroughfares and, despite the slippery footing and stench from piles of rotting offal, was often used as a shortcut between them. Had people noticed, they would not have thought it odd for the Sandman to go in.

It was distinctly odd, though, that nobody came out.

Grinning thinly to himself, crouched over so that nothing showed—were anyone to look—over the rim of the roof, the Sandman scrambled across the gravel roof of the low building.

Just the merest edge of sandy-haired head showed over the rim of the opposite side of the roof. Patiently he waited, then, abruptly, made the jump to the next roof.

Silent as a desert cat, he pattered across the gravel, his feet so precisely placed that he made no sound, disturbed not a single pebble.

And over another and another. It was much slower than walking, and the ring was already rising when his patience and stealth were rewarded. Below him, hidden from the road in a narrow alcove, was a small squad of armed men.

The Sandman looked over, noted the insignia on their tunics, and nodded to himself.

The man the little witch of a c'holder had been riding had been wearing the same insignia.

He frowned. In fact—there. Even in the dimness, didn't that head gleam with a hint of red, short locks escaping from the polished helmet?

The Sandman smiled. Had the half dozen men below him been able to see over the rim of the roof, soldiers or no, they would have quailed at the dreadful promise in that smile.

The roof was flat, ringed with a wall that was a hangover from older times, when most buildings needed defenses. The Sandman sat himself comfortably down, to wait, to listen. If it took all night, he would stay all night.

It got dusky, and then dark. The ring rose higher, shedding its opal glow. The six armed men waiting in ambush were well disciplined. All the Sandman heard was an occasional rustle of skin against wall or tunic, a chorus of muffled breathing, once in a great while a ting, as a metal brassard on tunic or greave brushed against similar metal. Until—

"Capting." It was not a whisper, but a very low-voiced tone.

"Hush."

"He ain't comin'." The speaker had the faintest of lisps, as though one or more of his front teeth was missing.

"She wants him." (The Sandman nodded to himself.)

"She's done forgot him," the same voice grumbled. "She wants the gold one." (Above, the Sandman stiffened, froze in his comfortable curl against the low wall. The Gold One—could he have come back at last, the Gold One, just in time for his worm's revenge?)

"A spacer." The captain bit it out. "All we could find out. Getting him will take some doing. The sand one has no contracts to protect him. She can play with him tonight." A rasp of laughter. "Let her practice on him. We'll paint him gold if that's what she wants."

"He ain't coming." Lisp-voice had a one-track mind.

"He'll come." The captain spoke with certitude. "Like as not he just stopped off at a chophouse for something to eat."

Muttered, but desert-sharp ears caught it: "Wish I was eatin'."

"Warn him off with your babble." It was said in a cold, calm voice more threatening than bellows. "And you can eat the uselessness between your legs and report as a harem guard."

No one even breathed for a second, and then a third voice said soothingly, "Chamel's right about one thing, Captain. He shoulda been past here long since. He either came another way, or he's getting drunk in a grog-'tractor's by now."

"Doesn't drink, from what I could find out." The captain was thinking aloud. "Could have taken another way, but . . ." Firmly: "More like he was just delayed. We'll wait until the ring has spread both wings across the walls."

"And if he ain't showed—"

"He's not contracted." The captain had been busy, finding out about his quarry, like any experienced hunter. "He and some of his followers shelter out in the rock scarp east of the city, the badlands no one has ever contracted for."

"Quite a walk, every day." It was the older voice, thoughtful.

"Big place to search, by ringlight." Lisp hadn't been quite squelched.

"If we must." Again the cold, calm voice that threatened without naming a threat this time.

The Sandman had heard enough. If these six armed men went combing through his people, in the temper they were in, blood would flow. One-sidedly. These all had contracts; touching them would be cause for c'break-ing. His own people, on the other hand . . .

He eased himself into a crouch, began slithering back across the roof. Knowing where his enemies were—he paused, thought. Knowing where *some* of his enemies were—he himself would not have relied on a single squad, ambushing the likeliest route. There might be—almost certainly was—at least one more somewhere. He began speeding across the roofs, using them as a second roadway. Like any other hunted animal, he had long since devised alternates, hidey-holes, escape contingencies.

When twelve armed and angry men tromped out and began combing the scarp, they found nothing but some scraps of garbage and a blind, ragged beggar who was sound asleep at least ten minutes' fast trot from where several people had obviously been camping out.

At that point the captain was furious—and worried—enough to have slit the crippled contractless's weasand just to relieve his own tension, but he wasn't stupid enough to silence the only clue he had.

Instead, he shook the snoring man awake, set a knife to his ear, and hissed, "Unless you want to lose your ears as well as your eyes, contractless, you'll answer some questions."

"Ah-huh-huh." The gaunt man came awake whimpering. Then, auto-matic, in a practiced, keening whine: "Crumbs for a blind man, crumbs for a blind man. Stale crust, bitter rind, scrap of bone. Pity the poor blind one, crumbs for a blind—"

The captain twisted his ear viciously. "Shut up. Listen to me, old fool, and answer me straight, or I'll give you your own blood to drink. Do you hear? Do you understand?"

"Crumbs for a blind man—"

"Perhaps he's deaf as well as blind," suggested one of the younger guards, pity in his clear tenor.

"Crumbs for a blind—" The voice choked off, as the captain gave his captive a hearty shake.

"Perhaps he's a fake." The captain glared down, assessingly. The beggar was dressed in ragged, ancient scraps, stiff with ground-in filth, that left no doubt, even in the dim light of the torches the guards carried, that crippled or not, this was a male. His eyes were covered with a swath of bandage, and the captain got his knife under it and cut through, not without difficulty, as the bandage was tight and as hard with dirt as the clothes.

"Fake," he muttered again, sawing and tugging.

"Crumbs for a blind—don't—don't, please," the beggar, realizing what was happening, began to wail.

"Fa—" The captain stopped in mid-syllable. The bandage still shaped itself to the head beneath, but he pulled it away and stared. The lids revealed fell in instead of curving convexly. The captain used the hand not holding the knife to peel away one of the sunken-in lids.

The ringlight was dim enough to haze the worst, but what was revealed was a scarred cavity.

"Blind," said the young guard, even more pity in his clear voice.

"Blind," the captain agreed, disgusted.

"Eyeless in Gaza, treading corn," the blind man said on a whine, interspersed with odd almost-giggles. "Crumbs for a blind man, pity from those safe under contract, crumbs for a blind—"

"Here." The young man knelt, put something wrapped in oiled cloth in the blind man's hand, then carefully unwrapped one corner. "It's a comb, blind one. There's not much in it save a little sweetness, but suck it anyway."

The captain caught the thin wrist halfway to the open, eager mouth. "No. Not yet. When I'm through with him."

"Dark, dark, dark amid the blaze of noon. Is it noon now? It's cold. Tom's a-cold, Tom's a-cold."

"Cold," the captain bit out. It was cool all right, with the double sun down, but not cold. Yet the withered limbs were trembling, a sort of Sayntvitus dance, and he decided to change his tactics. This was the only clue he had, and it wasn't all there. If he scared it to death before it could help him . . . He tried to moderate his voice from its normal rasp. "Cripple, blind man, if you tell us what we want, you can have the sweetness, and a fire." There was dried brush about; it wouldn't take long to gather it. "And—" He looked around, his glare an order.

The youngster who had proffered the honeycomb shook his head. It was all he had.

One by one, the captain checked out each man. The lisper hesitated, then reached into his breastplate and pulled out a thin slab of cheese, warm, almost runny from its proximity to his chest.

Another man produced a thin strip of porg rind, a third half a dozen segments of norange. (The captain filed that away. Noranges were off-worlder delicacies. It was ill-got somehow. He'd find out later.)

"Smell you these, cripple." The captain held his booty piece by piece under the blind man's nose. "All yours, for a few answers."

"Winged words, winged words. Crumbs for a blind man. Words mightier than the sword, he, he, he." He had been sitting up; now his hands groped out, and the captain put some of his booty in the hands, some in the lap that was more hairy thighs than cloth. But he held both wrists, keeping the hands away from the trembling mouth. "Words first, old man."

His nose sucked in the scent of the food, trembling like a dog fenced away from his bone. "Ooooooooh. How sharper than a serpent's tooth, he, he, he. Ask away, kind one. What are words, but whispers on the wind, the cold wind doth blow, we soon will have snow, and what will poor robin do then, poor thing."

"All right, Robin—"

"Who killed cock robin? I said the sparr—"

The captain's growl cut him off. Through his teeth, the furious man growled, "Where are they? The people who were camping here? Where are they?"

"They who camped here? They come, they go, they come like water and like wind they go."

"A straight answer, beggar!"

"I paid for my contract with my eyes," the blind man said suddenly, in a sane voice. "The off-worlders put my eyes in my master's son's head. He saw and I did not. I paid off my contract, but who wants to make a new contract with a blind man. My master kicked me out, to beg or starve. You wish to know where the people who speak of the sanctity of contracts are?"

From between clenched teeth: "Yes."

"I told you. They come and go. Here for a few nights, then off, I don't know where."

"When'll they be back?"

"I don't know. Wish I did. They've always crumbs to spare for a blind man." Then, sliding back into his mad whine: "Crumbs for a blind man, scraps, tittle, a bite to spare." In a confidential voice: "I had blue eyes once, true blue, leaf blue. The c'holder's favorite looked at my blue eyes and liked them. That's why he choose me, when his son's eyes got the mule-spit disease, all covered with scum, and he couldn't see out of them. But I thought he'd at least care for me, after, when I was blind, blind, blind, none so blind as them that will not see, but I could not, cannot, never will. Blind, blind, crumbs for a blind man, pity a blind man, help—"

"Rot you!" The captain's hands gripped the old man's wrists, but his second-in-command, a gray-haired man just past his prime, said calmly, "Let him have the food. He's told you what you want to know."

"He has not." The captain heaved, and the old man wavered, half standing, half kneeling, wailing, "Blind, blind, crumbs for a blind man, pity—"

"He has." The second unclamped the taut hands from around the blind man's wrists, and the beggar collapsed back into a sitting position. "He has, as much as a mad cripple can. D'ye think they confide their plans to a wabble-mouth like that, with not enough brains to know who to tell and who to keep silent to?"

"I'll kill—"

"And warn them off, when they camp here again. Think, man. These folk are contractless. Our mistress isn't the only one looking for them for one reason or another. In their shoes, would you boldly camp in the same spot night after night, like leaving a sign out, 'Come and get us'? No, you'd do what they do. Have several places to hide out in, camp a few nights, move on."

"You're right." The captain turned away from the beggar, who had immediately begun wolfing down the cheese in one hand, alternately with the rind in the other. Keeping an eye on the captain and his second, now pacing angrily as they talked, the young man who had supplied the honeycomb in the beginning knelt and hurriedly gathered the other small bits of food and put them on the hairy thighs, where the man could feel them and have them. Then he patted the blind man's shoulder and hurried to join his companions, trotting along behind their two leaders.

"—birds have flown. What good?" the captain was saying.

"Think. They can't have that many hideaways. Leave a man or two here as lookout, while we search out their other bolt-holes. If we don't find them sooner or later—"

"Sooner or later will be too late!"

"We'll be looking—" Their voices were drowned out by metal soles on rock, as they stomped away. Single-mindedly, the beggar kept chomping.

Like the soldiers, the Sandman and his lieutenants—twelve in number and carefully chosen, though only nine were with him in the narrow cave—were having a council of war.

"If the c'holders are after us, openly . . ." A woman was saying. As she spoke, her pendulous breasts and flabby belly, evidence of the dozen children she'd borne, flopped. She wasn't yet thirty, and she was fighting for the most basic female right: to keep and decide the destiny of her children. It hadn't dawned on her yet to claim the right to choose the fathers, too. She couldn't stay much longer; someone would have to help her go back and sneak into the wool shed she lived and worked in, along with the two children young and not yet contracted away from her.

The Sandman's lip curled. "Not us—me, I think. The little witch just wants a new play toy."

"From your description . . ." An older man stirred. He had been an enforcer, until he lost an arm in a practice bout to a scratch that had infected. A one-armed enforcer was useless, but his intelligence had been recognized and he had been trained as a clerk. It had been the opportunity he needed, and now he was a small-time independent contractor, dealing in goods but not contracteds. "I'd say it was the Lady Emerald Oriflamme."

"Oriflamme?" The Sandman's mouth dropped open. The others blinked at this totally uncharacteristic amazement.

"Oriflamme. She's the daughter of—"

"I'd forgot, it's been so long," the Sandman murmured. Shaking his head as though to clear away memories, he went on, "Of course. The Lady Medee."

"No, her sister. The Lady Esme."

"I don't believe it!" They were sitting around a small fire, and the Sandman had been about to throw another branch on the blaze. Now he froze, the branch poised in the air.

The woman took it out of his hand and tossed it in. "It's old story now, but it's true enough. The Lady Emerald Oriflamme is the daughter of the Lady Esme Oriflamme."

"Impossible." The Sandman's desert eyes were looking inward, remembering. "The Lady Esme wasn't that kind of c'holder. She was sweet and gentle and—"

"Died in the birthing of her daughter, or so it was claimed." She took a sip from her flask. "With so many contracts involved—and the Lady Medee what she is—who knows what really happened. And with the Lady Medee raising the child, what else could you expect."

The Sandman sighed. "Lady Esme's child."

"Your enemy," the ex-enforcer reminded.

The Sandman rubbed the scar on his arm. "I can't see the Lady Esme leaving her child to be raised by her sister. She knew what the Lady Medee was like."

Servants, as anyone who hears their whispers knows, are privy to all their masters' secrets. "She didn't. She left the child to the regency of the Lord Karolly Zarkos. But when he decided to go off-world to visit his bonded's family—he was bonded to an off-worlder woman—the Lady Medee screamed to the Adjudicators about him taking her contracted heiress off-world, and the Adjudicators refused, so the child was left with the Lady Medee at a tender age. By the time the Lord Karolly returned . . ." She shrugged. "The Lady Medee, who has no direct heiresses, demanded the child spend a portion of her time with her, to accustom her to her future contracts, and the Lord Karolly was forced to give in, despite the contracts he and the Lady Esme had entered into." She hesitated. "I believe he had other problems at the time. Of course, when he died—"

"We're getting away from the main problem," the ex-enforcer pointed out. "I think we've agreed it was the Lady Emerald. If so, all we have to do is

keep you out of her clutches for a few days." His lip curled. "Her attention is
. . . very short."

The woman nodded. "Little." A snort. "If she does get you, all you have to
do is survive a few days. She's a user and tosser—"

"Thanks," the Sandman said dryly. "Enticing as the witch is, I have a
feeling that her idea of pleasure and mine might not jibe."

A man halfway around the circle snorted. "Lady Medee had me under
contract for a while. Don't ask. And *don't* let yourself get caught."

"I don't plan—" There was a commotion at the mouth of the cave, and a
tall figure was limned by the firelight in the oval of darkness without. "Will!"
The Sandman jumped up and almost ran to the figure, hand outstretched.
"Will! It's about time!"

The blind man, very tall now that he was upright, stumped into the cave
and knelt, hands outstretched toward the fire's heat. "Crumbs for a blind
man," he whined, "pity a poor blind—" Then, abruptly, in a precise, strong
voice that fitted the easy way he moved, blind or not: "They're off back to
the city, but they plan to have someone watching the place, starting tomorrow night. I hope you crooks have left a crumb for me."

"Deli." The Sandman raised his voice over the murmur of the folk in the
cave.

"I'm coming." A young girl who hadn't been part of the conference appeared, her hands holding a large tray, all of the several dishes on it cut into
neat, bite-size pieces. "I saved your supper, Will. You—they didn't hurt you,
did they?"

" 'At's my girl." His left arm went around her hips in a hug, while his right
probed the tray. "No, they didn't," he answered her question after chewing a
cube of meat. "Almost, though. I could feel that knife in my weasand more
than once." Another cube. "But they swallowed it. Mostly. The scarp won't
be safe from now on. They plan to leave a guard."

A young man spat out, "One. We could take him."

The ex-enforcer sighed. "Of course. But if I were doing it, I'd have my
men change every few hours. And if one didn't report back . . ."

"All we have to do"—Will stopped both eating and talking to nuzzle the
curve of Deli's hip—"is keep Sandy here away from the scarp."

"Will." The Sandman began pacing, up and down, in a tiny ellipse. Automatically, the others moved to give him room. "Will, long as you've lived on
our world, and losing your eyes via a contract, and you still don't understand.
If I'm what they want, but they can get one of the others—Deli, say, not
protected by a contract, they can do anything to her—torture, rape, whatever, to get her to talk. They can torture her to death—it's happened—and
nobody else would or could punish them for it. We couldn't because they'd
all be protected by their own contracts."

Will muttered something under his breath. Then, louder: "What are we going to do then?"

They all looked at each other, but nobody answered him. They all knew what they could do: nothing.

SEVEN

Estaban Xavier was blindfolded. His hands were bound behind his back, and he was seated in a hard chair that dug cruelly into his unprotected skin. A muzzle ground into his left shoulder blade, and a knife blade caressed the hollow between his neck and right collarbone.

Nonetheless, he was infinitely dangerous.

Potentially.

For now, he waiting patiently for the chance that might or might not come.

"I have decided to inform you of your probable fate," the woman's voice was saying. Estaban, blind, was trying to fit a face, a body, to that voice.

He had seen literally no one on this world. He had exited his ship, stretching his muscles in the pleasure of real gravity, strode a dozen paces—"

There had been a hiss, a prick, and a feeling as if something had slapped his arm, lightly. He had bent down, puzzled, stared at the arm, but there was nothing visible against the smooth black of his Navigator's uniform. He frowned, wondered if he should return to the ship, started to turn—

And woke up in his cell, naked. It must have been an anesthetic dart, he decided later. Whatever it had been, he had not seen whoever shot him, or whoever hauled him away. Nobody.

"We are negotiating." It was the nasty, triumphant woman's voice. In the same room with her, he could add a little to what he already knew. Female. Not a girl-woman like Brandy, probably not even young woman. But not old, probably not even middle-aged. In styears, somewhere between thirty, say, and sixty.

At a guess, since Brandy was in her early or mid-teens, and this was almost certainly her mother, somewhere between thirty and forty-five. On advanced worlds, people lived longer, stayed fertile longer, but this was a prim world, with a thin scum of imported technics spattered here and there over neo–Bronze Age peasants.

He tried to analyze the voice. Not pleasant, not pretty, but he'd known lovely women with voices like crows. This one sounded as though it had been ruined by years of screaming and screeching. No telling what it had been like before.

"You might be going free soon, if your people cough up the proper contracts."

He said nothing. Honorable men did not cooperate in any way with their captors.

"You might even be allowed to take along that contracted wench you seem to favor, if you don't cause us too much trouble."

He didn't say anything, but his body language was eloquent.

She cackled. "You've not much choice, either way. But be a good boy, off-worlder, or I'll punish her in front of you this time."

He had to speak. "Madam, that is not a threat that will affect me. You have the girl in your power; you may abuse her as you choose. If you are the type who will abuse, then you will, sooner or later. My actions cannot affect your actions."

"I said, you be good, or I'll—"

The segment of face showing under the blindfold, especially the carved jaw, could have modeled for a statue titled "I Shall NOT Be Moved." "Now or later, time is a circle. What will be, will be. If you want to abuse, you will. If any actions of mine anger you, so you abuse now instead of tomorrow, I cannot blame myself. You may do what you choose, whatever you choose, to those in your power, and your evils are on your conscience, if you have one, and your honor. Not mine. Never mine. No matter what. My honor demands that I act however I can to counter you, and I will. No matter what threats you use, against me or anyone else, that girl, or anyone."

"Stubborn," she muttered. Then, louder: "The chit's right, you have a beautiful body. Perhaps I will be kinder to her if you're kinder to me. What do you say to that, off-worlder with the muscles rippling even as you sit there?"

He stiffened, then relaxed, knowing that she could see every muscle twitch. He knew that he wasn't conventionally handsome, but his looks—or lack, by most standards—had never hampered him. He produced a calm smile, with just a hint of shark underneath. "Madam, I have said that I would not cooperate."

Again she muttered something. Then: "If I decide, you will do as I want. We have ways."

He raised his brows over the blindfold. "Madam, I doubt it not; many worlds do. But I tell you, and I do not lie, the only way you will force your will on me is if you have one of those high-T nerve-binders that takes control of a man's body totally away from him and awards it to whoever is running the binder. If so, you may do as you choose—I cannot stop you—my honor will not be besmirched whatever you force my body to do. It would be as if you do it. There is no other way you can force me. None."

"We'll see about that later." It was a promise—not nice. "For now, what is Navigator's Syndrome?"

He kept his mouth shut.

"Does the cell bother you?"

He said nothing, but his mouth got a fraction tighter. Like most Navigators, he suffered from Navigator's Syndrome in a mild form. The cell did bother him, and it was getting worse. But she could rack him until his legs tore off before he would admit it.

"Another secure place is being prepared for you. You'll be moved into it as soon as it is ready."

He thought about what he would do if he had her in his power, instead of the other way around. A man's honor made a lot of demands; so did machismo, and vendetta. The nasty-voiced woman was piling up quite a score.

"You might at least say thank you."

"Thank you, madam," he said obediently, but with such a sardonic inflection that her breath hissed in on a gasp.

"You had better pray your people choose to be cooperative," she gritted.

"I will pray," he agreed, and nobody was fooled about exactly what he intended to pray—and work and sweat and scheme and devise—for.

"A taste or two of the whip would lick some of that sass out of you," she said, and he shrugged. "Now, about your health," she went on. "You do prefer women, don't you?"

He didn't pretend to misunderstand; he simply shrugged again.

"Or am I wrong? Do you want a boy?"

"No."

"A more experienced woman? You may have to wait; my skilled girls are in high demand."

"Madam," he said slowly, "if I feel the need of a female, any female will do, though I prefer spontaneity to . . . training. At present, I do not need."

She made a comment, the gist of which, shorn of its obscenities, was that all men needed.

He said nothing again.

"Do you or don't you want the girl again?" she barked abruptly.

"Her prattle amuses me. For now. If you have others, of whatever sex or age, who can hold their own conversationally with me, I shall be wherever you put me and unable to thrust out what you have put in. If they bore me, I simply shall ignore them."

"She doesn't bore you?"

"She hasn't yet." He left it at that.

"I'll consider it."

He shrugged yet again, wondering how long it would be before his muscles stopped protesting. Shrugging while your hands were tied behind your back was uncomfortable, to say the least.

She wasn't in his cell when he was thrown back into it.

But when he pulled off his blindfold in his new cell, which he had been moved into the same way as he had been moved the other times, blindfolded, hands bound—they were cut as he was thrust in—and prodded with weapons every step, she was hurling herself into his arms.

He caught her easily and looked around, assessing his new berth away from his berth.

Besides the door he had come in, which was already closed, with a very solid-sounding thunk, there were two others.

Catching her against his chest with one arm, he stalked easily to the nearest, opened it.

His brows raised.

Inside was a sybarite's bath, walls and ceilings mirrored, furry carpeting underfoot, all fixtures coated with gleaming gold, including the man-size tub, big enough for him to lie flat.

His brow went higher; with a frown he opened the taps and inserted the round gold stopper into the drain at the bottom of the huge tub.

"It won't work," Brandy said.

"What won't, my child?"

"Drowning yourself. There's something in the tub, it won't fill more than a little."

He watched the water pouring into the tub.

She was right. The water poured in freely then stopped, though he hadn't touched the taps. He glanced down at the three centimeters of water. "Not very effective for cleaning purposes," he commented.

"If you want to be clean, pull the plug and use the upper taps."

"Ah." He looked up and saw the second pair of taps. "I do feel the need of cleansing."

She nodded, reached onto a shelf just below the upper taps, and offered him a pair of bowls of sky-blue ceramic, filled with thick milky liquid.

"What . . . ?"

"Cleanser," she informed. "There are several up there, but most men prefer—" She extended the bowl in her right hand directly under his nose and he involuntarily flinched a little.

"Ach. Too strong. And near solid musk."

She shrugged. "Many men like it. On their women, too."

"The other." He leaned over and took a cautious sniff of the bowl in her left hand. "Sea wind. Odd for a city so far from the salt sea. Not bad. What else is there?"

Being taller than she, he could inspect the shelf directly. "Floral. Sicky-sweet," he pronounced. "Spice. Not bad. This one." He hesitated. "I can't identify it."

She took a sniff. "From a tree sap. It's called jewelwood, because you can carve a bracelet or necklace pendant out of it, and it gives off that scent for years."

He grinned at her. "I don't suppose they supplied one that simply does its task without leaving a smell behind?"

She didn't smile, but mischief gleamed in her brandy-colored eyes. "They make your skin soft, too. Though yours . . ." She returned her bowls to the shelf, ran a finger down his arm. "Plush over"—she thought about it—"a whipstock. Flexible yet hard."

He chuckled. "Never give up, do you. For now, I intend to scrape several days' dirt off my skin. You needn't—"

Eagerly: "I could scrub your back."

He laughed, but let her.

The bedroom was, if anything, more sensuous and sybaritic than the bathroom. The floor was furred, the furniture piles of silken or fur-covered cushions, and walls and ceiling were mirrored, except for one wall, which was a huge window.

Or seemed to be. Estaban strolled over, and stared out into a panorama of rolling plain and mountain that existed nowhere within a hundred kilos of the city of Pantagruel.

"Do you like it?" Brandy's voice throbbed with pride.

"A trompe l'oeil view-window," he said, voice expressionless. "Unusual on this world."

"It's the only one," Brandy bragged. "And it has lots of views." She skipped over to a corner, where a tiny gray-blue panel was hidden behind a pile of cushions. She tapped something, and the mountains were replaced by an underseascape, fishes and underwater animals playing hide-and-seek in an intricate structure. Estaban took a step closer and pursed his lips thoughtfully. If he remembered correctly, Apricot Honeycomb was a quasi-coral indigenous to the world of Romanza. It didn't mean that the view-window came from Romanza, but knowing where its views came from might make it easier to identify later. And when it was identified, its owner might also be.

In rapid succession, Brandy displayed in the view-window what Estaban recognized as The Grandest Canyon, of Never-Say-Die; a forest; a room filled with people, including a buxom belly dancer; a desert, with magnificent wind-carved structures; a lake dotted with rainbow-hued floating flowers; a formal garden with slim plants bending slowly in the wind; another room with people, this time a naked pair; a jungle so fierce he could almost smell hot wet death.

"Enough." He knelt beside the girl. "How many are there?"

"I don't know. I've never been allowed to play with it before."

"Can you make it go back?"

"Umm." She nodded. "This button changes, this one goes back."

"Right." He pushed until the lake with flowers was back. "This is soothing and tranquil. Besides, it reminds me of a pond not far from where I grew up."

"Oh. I thought you spacers lived in those funny big moving space-wagons of yours, or on temporary homes on each world you visit."

"Do you think people and space-wagons spring up out of nothing?" He lay back on the cushions. "So many other worlds." He sighed.

She pouted. "You sound like you like those other cities—worlds, whatever —better."

He tapped her lip. "Your world has some pretty sights—and lovely people." He made her a seated bow. "But your society is the ugliest I've ever encountered."

"Society? You mean our city?"

"No, I mean the way your people act. I can't explain it to you, child." He held out his hand. "Come, let us see what else has been provided to make us forget we are prisoners in a cell."

But he had seen all he really needed. The lady who pandered for her own children, those children who ought to be her ultimate responsibility, was going to find out what a mistake she'd made, giving him the tools to bring about her downfall.

EIGHT

Power is an interesting concept. In any society, there are those who officially have power, those who have power in the eyes of their fellows, and those who truly have power. Title, appearance, and reality. On some worlds they coincide, on some worlds never the trains shall meet. There are even subsets involving those who think they have power and do not, and those who think they do not, but do. Influence, intelligence, ingenuity can make mock of official and even unofficial standings.

On Rabelais, it was even more complex, because Rabelais had no official powers, not any. No government, no organized religion, no laws, and thus no lawmakers. Nonetheless, there were c'holders—contract-holders—who controlled large amounts of property, wealth, and human destinies, i.e., contracteds. There were also Adjudicators, who decided how those contracts would be interpreted, whose word was final thanks to a clause universal in all contracts. And there were, increasingly, off-world merchants, who supplied high-tech tools and medicines that could be literally life and death.

Medee, a contract-holder of influence, knew exactly whom to gather for a council of war. The evening of the day that Emerald had seen a man with golden skin and eyes in Agony Square, an oddly assorted group of people assembled in one of the rooms in the Oriflamme mansion.

"Medee, my pet," complained an older man, laid out on a lounge and being fanned by a buxom, jasmine-scented female contracted. "I had the most amusing entertainment planned for this evening. I do hope that whatever you have to say justifies its delay. Sour, my dear, sour; timing is everything."

Medee, on a pastel chaise that supported her back in a half-sitting, half-lounging position, a male contracted caressing her bare legs, looked as stern as an overstuffed bolster pillow of a woman can. "Is losing half your contracts sufficient cause to delay whatever amusement you had scheduled for tonight, Genesis?"

He opened his mouth, and a second contracted hurriedly popped a blue ovoid in. He bit down, and a sharp citrus scent stung the nostrils of those nearest him, while a stream of greenish drool trickled out of the corner of his mouth. He chewed thoughtfully, then smiled. "If our discussion is to involve someone losing contracts, my dear Medee, it will not be me."

"It may be all of us, Genesis." She nodded over to a thin, depilated-bald any-aged man sitting quietly in a corner, in a carved wooden chair softened only slightly by a thin cushion on its seat.

He looked, saw, and pursed his mouth. "An adjudicating matter, Medee?"

The others also looked, but only the bulldog-jowled man dressed in a flowing yellow sarong rose and bowed slightly, murmuring a greeting.

"I don't know." Medee was uncharacteristically blunt and forceful. "It may come to that." She hesitated, then added, "It may come to us pushing for it to come to adjudication."

The man called Genesis sat up. "If we are talking about my contracts," he said coldly, "the only adjudication I'll allow is one that ends in my favor." Both the contracteds shuddered, and tried to melt back away from his gaze.

Medee reached over to the tray set on the arm of her chair, picked up a sweet without looking and stuffed it in, crunched loudly, and looked a little surprised. Hastily swallowing, she said, "It's to prevent trouble that I called for consultation. Perhaps this is all nothing, perhaps a bitmouse is bellowing like a mountain-fang, but with what is at stake, it's better to check all clauses than to wind up with a voided contract."

"What case, madam?" asked the bulldog-jowled man.

Instead of answering, she frowned and snapped her fingers. To the contracted who immediately bowed, she barked, "Where's the Lady C'holder Emerald Oriflamme?"

He bowed lower. "She sent a message that you are to act for her in all ways, that she is—"

"Take six contracted." Her voice was sharp. "Eight or even ten if you think it necessary, and bring her here, will she nill she. Tell her she will be carried if she won't walk of her own accord."

He bowed, but he had paled. "Yes, Lady C'holder." Then, hesitant: "Lady C'holder, the Lady—"

"Obey me."

Genesis snickered. "Won't like that, the brat."

"Indeed, Lady C'holder." The contracted bowed even lower. "The Lady Emerald—"

"Obey me!" It was a fierce hiss. "Or I'll see how you look without your skin—and a few other things!"

He bowed, trembling. "Yes, lady."

"Is the Lady Emerald truly necessary?" The bulldog-jowled man frowned. "I thought you acted for the pair of you."

"I do. But it was not I who saw the man who—"

Genesis snickered. "I didn't think there was a male in this city you hadn't more than seen, Medee."

"This is— May I begin at the beginning, merchant?"

He smiled, rearranging the jowls. "That's usually wise, Lady C'holder."

"Then the beginning is Golden Singh."

"Yes?" The merchant was merely puzzled, but the other c'holders present leaned forward.

"Golden Singh had more contracts, and more important contracts, than any other c'holder in this city or anywhere." Medee started with what they all (but the off-world merchant) knew. "Fifteen years ago, Golden Singh went off-world. He left his contracts to be administered by a consortium of fellow c'holders, chosen by him, with little power except to keep things running as they were."

The merchant nodded.

"He made no provision for what would happen if he failed to return, or died."

"Golden wouldn't," Genesis drawled. "He always acted like he would live forever."

The merchant nodded again. It was a not-uncommon attitude among the more powerful c'holders.

"But as time passed, decisions needed to be made, which the consortium was not contractually empowered to make." She eyed the merchant straightly. "Others of us were affected, you understand."

He indicated that he did.

"Had Golden chosen an heir, that heir could have made those decisions. Or a council of regency, had the heir been too young."

The merchant smiled. "I think I understand. He had not chosen an heir, so you did. A child. The consortium then made major decisions instead of minor ones."

"Yes."

"I should have guessed. I've contracts enough of yours signed in the last years as Regina for—"

A curtain was jerked open. "Aunt Medee!" Emerald stormed in. "I told you already, I didn't want to tend to ol' contract-business tonight. I'm punishing the most delicious male contracted."

"How?" Genesis asked, sitting up slightly.

"I have him up on a couple of rings suspended from the ceiling, well above his head height. He's clinging to them now, with his chin hooked on the top of one of them and his legs drawn as high as he can."

"What's on the floor?"

She giggled. "Guess. But as long as he keeps his chin hooked and his legs up, he's safe. He's getting tired, though. Maybe it's better you called me. I had him taken out safely, and they'll let him rest. It's more fun if he starts fresh again. Maybe I'll play with him tomorrow, too. Watching his face as he strains and tires is more fun than what'll happen if he drops."

"Emerald." Medee sounded more tired than angry. "You and Genesis may discuss punishing contracteds later."

"I have a female that displeased me," Genesis said. "I've devised the most ingenious new way—"

"Genesis."

"Tomorrow, at noon, if you want to watch, Emerald."

"Goody." She clapped her hands. "I'll bring the male, and you can play with him, too. Use him on her, if you like. He's amazingly enduring."

"Emerald," Medee interrupted again, "I want you to tell these here about the man you saw today."

She shrugged and pranced to the only empty seat, a lounge, which she jumped on like mounting a horse, bouncing a little as she talked. "He was beautiful."

"And golden," Medee prompted, and the other c'holders gasped or cursed.

"All over," Emerald agreed, "even his eyes."

"Golden Singh," Genesis said. He looked gray under his face paints.

"He was wearing . . ." Medee prompted.

"Spacer clothes," Emerald said. "Couldn't see but his shirt, but it was spacer all right. Sky green, bright and pretty, open at the throat—what a neck he has." A little shiver. "And one of those caps, you know, with all the stuff on it." Her fingers sketched headphones. "And a little sun-shield for the eyes, only it was up."

"Jewelry?" Genesis had recovered from his shock enough to ask questions.

"No. His throat was bare."

"That doesn't sound like Golden Singh." Genesis looked to the others for agreement. "No jewelry, and spacer clothes."

"No clothes, especially not spacer stuff—he hated them—and lots of jewelry sounds more like Golden," agreed an older man who had been quiet up to this point.

"Right." Genesis nodded.

"If it is he, he's been in space for fifteen years. He might well be wearing spacer clothes," Medee pointed out.

"If it is Golden—" said the quiet man.

"It isn't, Festus." Genesis was certain. "If his ship had landed, we would have been informed. Would Golden leave his affairs in our hands a second more than necessary? Would he be wandering around like any eyeballing spacer, instead of contacting us to take back what's his? No." He shook his head aggressively. "You know that skin of his is a gene-altering that one of his grandsires bought as a joke from one of the earliest contract-spacers. Perhaps it's common among spacers, or if not common—that's it—" He was convincing himself as much as the others. "It comes from some faraway world, and this spacer is simply one from such a world. A spacer, and not Golden. What did he look like, Emerald?"

She spread her hands. "Handsome. Big. Muscular."

"My age? Older? Heavy? Overweight?"

She frowned in thought. "Grown, but not—not much more, I'd say. I wasn't that close, but his face looked smooth as a young man's. There was an expression in his eyes. . . ."

"He could have gained or lost in fifteen years, as far as the weight goes." Medee, too, was thinking aloud. "Was his face flabby-looking, child?"

"Oh, no, Medee." She smiled dreamily. "Beautiful. Not at all flabby." She flashed a gleam of pure mischief at the off-world merchant with the bulldog jowls. He didn't say anything, knowing that the jowls were a racial characteristic, not a sign of dissipation.

"I'd wager almost anything Golden would be flabby, more than flabby by now," Genesis said smugly. His own small-boned, delicate build had resisted forty years of abuse to stay lean.

Another man had thought of something. "Was he alone, or with people?"

"How can I know who he was with or who he was just standing next to?" Emerald said with a pout. "The two closest were dressed in spacer clothes, too. A woman all in black, and a man in olive green."

"Spacers." Genesis laughed. "That settles it."

"A woman in black." Medee was thoughtful. "That means a Navigator. You hadn't mentioned her before, child."

"You didn't ask." Emerald sniffed.

"That does make a difference. I hadn't thought. If he is simply a spacer who looks like Golden Singh . . ." She turned to the Adjudicator, who had kept silent. "If this is Singh . . ."

He shrugged. "I would suggest turning over his contracts to him as quickly as possible. If not, and he demands, the whole affair may go into adjudication, and you know what that could mean."

They all did. Years of squabbling and negotiating and acrimony.

"But how could we be sure?" Medee murmured. "Suppose this is a spacer, but he learns that he resembles Golden, and tries to take what isn't his?"

"He may fool the child who never knew Golden," Genesis said, "but I'd say, from her description alone, it isn't. Some spacer, mayhap from the world the process came from in the first place."

Emerald dropped out of their conversation and, a few minutes later, slid out of the room entirely.

The man who had managed to keep his legs high enough for safety might be *very* enthusiastic about earning a reprieve. It was a boring way to spend the rest of the night, but desperation did lend spice to even the most over-well-known of activities.

Genesis's novel punishment involved chaining the female contracted by the waist well below the surface of his garden pool, and sliding in with her, equipped with an off-worlder breathing mouth that he shared with her. If she pleased him enough.

He evidently enjoyed it, because he shared the mask with her quite often during the first few minutes, but Emerald yawned behind her hand. Borrrrrring.

It stayed boring, even when Genesis got so engrossed in what he was doing that he forgot to keep sharing the mask, and the woman's struggles got increasingly frantic.

Until she stopped struggling at all.

"Curse," said Genesis a few minutes later, being dried with loving care by a trio of contracteds, all extremely solicitous to even his unspoken needs and whims. "What a waste. She turned out to be quite superior, after all."

"Boring," drawled Emerald.

"If you're bored now"—a flick of a finger indicated to the blonde what he wanted—"what will you be when you're my age?"

"Old." She giggled.

"Old." He glared at her. "Watch this!"

"Boring," she said, but not loud enough for him to hear, had he attention to spare for listening.

NINE

The meeting of the powerful of Rabelais decided about as expected. Most of those present agreed to wait and see. Those who did not dismiss the whole thing as space fluff, that is. But one of those who had been there, mostly silent, entered her palanquin to return to her home with a very thoughtful look in her intelligent eyes.

Rabelais wasn't her world, so perhaps she saw things that those close to it missed for very familiarity. Her guard captain handed her into her palanquin with all the gentleness of unrecognized (he thought) unrequited passion. (She knew, but had not decided what to do about it.) Then he barked orders, arranged his men, sent out an advance guard, and—

There was movement in the shadows. A man only doing his job would have missed it. The man achingly aware of the vulnerability of a desirable woman even on, especially on, Rabelais, charged, sword out.

The shadow froze, and the guard's sword pricked a throat.

"I mean your mistress no harm," a deep voice said out of the darkness.

"No?" The guard captain dug his sword a trifle deeper. "Those who mean only good always lurk in the dark, instead of approaching openly, announcing themselves, and requesting a meeting?" He dug the blade in a little more, deliberately using the duller edge, inflicting pain but—as yet—drawing no blood.

"Is something wrong, Ramesis?" came her voice from the palanquin.

"Nothing to worry about, mistress," he called back.

"I cannot approach her openly. The danger is great, more hers than mine," the man said in a low voice.

"Approach her at all and I'll—"

"Hush," the man commanded fiercely. In the dimness, he was only a shape, tall and, from the way he moved, young. "Her danger may be greater than she or you or even I know, and my help necessary. Take her a message, as she rides." The man's left hand came out, slowly, so the guard could see that something was in it, but not a weapon. "Give her this. Tell her the man who received this from the hands of Karolly Zarkos would stand her friend, render aid if needed. Tell her that a message to the Navigator's Guildhall, care of the Navigator Lady Jael, will always reach that man, and his hand, his sword, his blood stand ready to defend her. Tell her—"

A low growl. "Who are you?"

"A man who is not what he was, whose name proclaims him enemy but who would do anything in his power to make up for the deeds that once made him an enemy."

"I'll not—"

"Give it to her, guard. If I survive, I knew the Lord Karolly, man and boy. If nothing else, she'd like to hear those tales I can tell. But that's for later, when there's time for such luxuries."

He draped whatever was in his hand over the fist clenched on the sword, and added, with a flash of bright teeth in the darkness, "Go. She waits, *guard.*" There was such amused knowledge in that, that the guard felt heat flooding his cheeks. He retracted his hand instinctively, and the man took a step back, his masculine approval as obvious as the flashing grin.

"Where—"

"Ramesis." His mistress's voice came out of the palanquin.

"Go!" Low-voiced as it was, it was a command. The man took another step back, and the guard, torn between duty and a mixture of emotions he himself couldn't have put a name to, let him disappear into the darkness.

The woman was coldly angry. Between her fingers, held accusingly, was a handmade pendant, gemmed and carved. "He gave you no name, no way to reach him directly, only this message?"

The guard captain licked sweat off his lip. "He said it was dangerous."

She slammed the pendant into her palm, winced at the sharp pain. "Too much goes on in darkness," she said slowly. "Ignorance is the greatest danger of all."

"I can run to the Guildhall, mistress," he offered eagerly. "I can leave him a message."

With an effort, she smiled. "I would you had detained him, but if that is the best you can do . . ." He was already turning.

"Ramesis." Her voice stopped him in the very doorway.

"Yes, mistress?" He turned, alert, poised.

She smiled. "Be careful."

"Always, mistress." He nodded, turned, muttered to himself, but her ears were sharper than he thought. "You may need my protection greatly."

"Ramesis." His name spoken in commanding tones for the second time in a few minutes stopped him in mid-stride.

"Ramesis." Softer, from the shadows to the left. Drawing his sword, he approached cautiously. "It's I," said the man who had given him the pendant. "After you left, I thought her unassuaged curiosity might be a danger, too."

"She wants to see you."

The darkness nodded. "I want to see her. Only—" A slight hesitation. "Can you be sure you can smuggle me in?"

Ramesis had enough honesty to consider the matter fully before replying. "Yes."

"Not just so that no one sees me. No one besides you and she herself must ever suspect I've been more than in the same city with her, for her sake."

Ramesis ground his teeth. "You should not have—"

"I had to," the man said gently. "Call it"—his voice softened—"contractual obligation, though there was never a contract. Karolly—"

"You knew the Lord Karolly?"

"Yes. He . . . tried to do something for me once, no contract, no obligation, but—"

"Yes." There was hero worship and more in the guard's rough voice. "Yes, he was like that."

"So you understand. I must protect his lady, if I can."

"I understand. Only—"

"I know. My protection may be the greatest danger of all. But I had to."

"A friend of Lord Karolly's. That makes a difference." Ramesis was thinking aloud.

"Not a friend," the man in the darkness said sadly. "I wish I had been. But don't you see, that makes my obligation all the more."

Fifteen years ago, the guard would not have known what he was talking about. But the Sandman talked a lot about obligations. He nodded. "The Lord Karolly," he said, as though that explained everything—which it did. "The thing is, lord," he went on, laying a confidential hand on the arm half shrouded in the cloak, noting that it was well muscled and firm. "I could likely smuggle you in and out, without anyone seeing enough to recognize you, but ensuring that no one suspects you've been there. That's another sort of contract."

"Not in the habit of using anonymous contracteds brought in to warm her bed, is she?" There was a note of cynicism that hadn't been in the voice before.

"You—"

"Sorry," the man apologized, the compassionate self back. "I should have known Karolly would never bond to one of that sort. But you realize how much more difficult that makes my entrance."

"Ah. I see. Yes. If she had a series of contracteds in to entertain her, one more wouldn't stand out. As she does not . . ."

"You know," the man said softly, "you and I are much of a height. . . ."

Tamilee eyed her visitor up and down, a very female, assessing look. "You came to give me a warning, spacer. I make you one in return: This world is very unhealthy for you. Leave it as soon as you can."

He slid out of the concealing cloak completely, and Ramesis couldn't contain a gasp. Ever since the rediscovery, there had been Gas, especially in the port area, where a spacer might leave more than his credits behind. But he'd never seen anyone as completely altered as this man, who was golden from head to toe.

"I know. Even though I'm not a spacer."

"You're not truly." She took a step back, and Ramesis instinctively went into guard position.

"I told your man the truth," the golden man said sadly. "I owe Karolly far more than I can ever possibly work off. I assume you know who I am, and remember what he has said about me."

She looked down at the pendant. "You are Golden Singh? But Karolly said you were his greatest enemy."

"I was the greatest enemy to all including myself, lady." He spread out his hands, open and empty. "But I have learned, and now I am back. Be warned by me. The bloody changes Karolly thought were coming are here."

"I . . . see. You are working for those changes, but you felt you owed something."

He was shaking the golden mane. "No." A smile. "I am not as I was. I am working against blood. Rabelais needs change—I think Karolly would have agreed on that—but not the terrors that may well accompany it." He began pacing restlessly up and down. "Karolly spoke once to me of his well-fortified home in the Gargantuas. Is it still a sanctuary?"

It was Ramesis who said, "Yes. We keep it as it was when the lord was alive."

"Good." A sudden smile. "I can't order you to return there to safety, but if words of mine can persuade you—"

"Golden Singh? You are truly Golden Singh?" she asked.

"Yes. I am."

"Why? You and I never met, but Karolly spoke of you. I know—"

"What I was. I told you, I have changed muchly. Space was—say it was an education to me."

She smiled suddenly. "As your world of Rabelais was an education to me."

"Will you retreat to the Gargantuas?"

"Can this terror Karolly spoke of be prevented?"

He shrugged. "I and others work to that end. But . . ."

"And you would have me run away, and allow others to do what I could and should be doing, fighting for what's best for the world my children will inherit?"

He made a face. "I might have known. Karolly's choice. No." He raised a hand to silence her. "I know well it was mutual. In fact, knowing Karolly's excessive conscientiousness . . ." He awarded her a grin so roguish she had to smile wryly back.

"You're quite right," Tamilee admitted. "I had no choice but to put him in a position where he had no choice."

"Congratulations."

"Luck."

"Whatever." He sobered. "Whatever, Karolly's chosen lady would not be one who could turn her back when her help was needed. Even at her own risk."

"I wish you hadn't come!" Ramesis burst out. Then, aghast at what he had done, he clapped his hand over his mouth.

The old Golden would have had him tortured to death, exquisitely, for having an opinion of his own, let alone expressing it. The new one merely cocked a brow to Tamilee and murmured, "Loyalty beyond contracts. I trust you appreciate your prize."

Under her breath: "Quite." Louder: "Ramesis, you wished to say . . ."

He was sweating, though the night was cool. "Lady, if there is danger—"

She smiled. "You're quite correct, Ramesis. Lord Singh, I thank you for your warning. The children start for the Gargantuas at dawn; their baggage can follow. Have you children of your own, Lord Singh?"

The reminiscent glow on his face was answer enough. What he said aloud was, "You could say so."

"Then you know. I will be able to work with an easier mind, if mine are safe."

He nodded.

"I would there were two of you, Ramesis," she said thoughtfully.

"Mistress?"

"Protecting the children is far more important than protecting me." However softly spoken, it was an order. His lids dropped to veil his eyes for just a second. Then he looked up, his crude-cut face with the out-thrusting stubborn chin serene.

"Yes, mistress."

"A very good man," Golden said softly. Then, louder: "Did you know I tried to suborn your contract from Karolly once?"

"No!" For a second she looked again the very young girl in love who had crashed innumerable barriers to convince an older stubborn man of the sincerity of her emotions. "You tried to get my contract, and he refused?"

"Most emphatically. Though I offered him something he desired most desperately. I dangled peace instead of revolution for Rabelais before him. You're an off-worlder, you know what revolution is; you probably taught

Karolly. There was something I could do that would have secured peace in Rabelais's immediate future, instead of almost certain destruction. Karolly came to beg me, to urge, plead, cajole, offer anything." Another smile. "Almost anything, I should say. I asked for the one thing he would not give up, even for the sake of Rabelais and all its people. I asked for you."

"And he said—"

"That he would not contract his greatest enemy into my hands, much less the woman he prized over his own life. He said he hoped I lived long enough to regret my decision." He frowned. "He was right in that hope. I have many times regretted my own actions. Yet . . ."

"Yet?" She prompted this odd tie to the man she still mourned.

"Through the evil of my actions, came eventually good. I am not as I was. Others have found themselves, their lot, improved." He was almost thinking aloud, expressing a philosophy that had been slowly evolving within. "We cannot see the ultimate consequences of our own actions, only the immediate ones. Sometimes not even then. If the obvious consequences look good, and we do what we think will lead to good, and it leads to suffering instead—or it leads to good but in the long term, evil comes . . . So how can we choose?"

She patted his arm, much as she would have her own young son, puzzled why the ailing nestling he had tended had died instead of getting better. "Carry that argument to its ultimate conclusion," she said, "and we would none of us do anything, ever. Yet doing nothing is a choice in itself, and has consequences. We can do only what seems best at the time we do it, with all the knowledge we have at that time. And the bigger the decision"—a smile —"we both agree that bloody revolution will do little more to Rabelais than cause a lot of distress without improving anything. Another time we can argue what level of distress, if any, is permissible for a good end, but for now . . ."

"Yes. We need to do."

"Yes." She sat herself, fanned languidly with an elaborately painted fan. "You were the topic of discussion tonight."

He froze in mid-stride.

"You, or the spacer with some appearance of Golden Singh."

A number of expressions flickered across his face. "I see."

"The consensus was that you were a spacer with similar GA to Singh. Most favored dismissing any problem you might represent. A minority worried that a venal spacer might discover that he resembled a powerful native and would try to grab what he could."

His lip twitched. "Yes, that would be the second line of defense."

"If anyone thought you were truly C'holder Singh returned, they didn't say so. It was agreed that Singh wouldn't wander around, would not delay a second in putting his hand out for the power he left behind."

"The man I was when I left would not have delayed; they are right in that," he muttered. "So they decided to adopt a wait-and-see attitude," he went on.

"In essence. However—"

He shrugged. "No one said so, but there are those who decided that a dead spacer now was much cheaper than a possible claimant to Singh's contracts later."

"You know their minds well."

"Intimately. They reason as I once would have."

"Do you miss," she asked, curious, "the . . ." She searched for a word, then went on: "The single-mindedness you once had?"

"In a sense. He didn't agonize over his decisions, his actions."

"Maturity has its price."

"Yes."

"And its prizes."

"*Yes!*" His face smoothed into youthfulness again, though the too-old eyes held sadness under serenity. "Thank you."

"As Karolly said many times, Pass it on."

His gaze flicked to the guard, leaning with elaborate casualness against a wall. "I will." Then, gathering his thoughts: "We need to make what plans we can, though there may not be time. Not because of me, though I am taking careful steps to regain what was weaseled away while I was gone. But." He caught her gaze, then said bluntly, "There is a possibility that a Navigator has been savaged away."

She whistled.

"Yes." A nod. "You understand. His captain may have slain him, concealed the deed. He may have gone aboard another berth and neglected to inform the Guild here, or the message went astray, though either is much unlike him, as he is known to his fellows. But the greatest possibility is that—" A shrug. "He is known to be a virile, strong-willed man in his prime, older than many would prefer, but to certain tastes—"

"The lord of the sea preserve us!"

"You understand why I had to warn you, despite the risk."

"Yes. Your arrival will topple towers, but if a sacred Navigator has been secreted away here . . ."

"Yes. He is being searched for, even as we speak. I myself should be aiding. I quiet my conscience on this score"—a flicker, as they remembered the previous philosophical discussion—"by asking you if you have heard anything of this Navigator, Estaban Xavier by name. I have a holo of him." He displayed it, and Tamilee looked and gestured Ramesis to look likewise. "This was taken some years ago, but those who have seen him more recently say he has changed little. If you see or hear anything of him . . ."

She nodded, mouth tight.

"I'd best not leave this with you; you want no tangible evidence I was here. But tomorrow you can think up an innocuous reason for visiting Guildhall, if you need a copy to keep."

She shook her head. "That man has his own face. I'll remember."

"Good. But on second thought, I will leave you one small item." He reached into a pocket, handed her a small communicator. "Conceal this about your person. Don't use it unless you must. Its transmission is shielded, but someone else may pick it up, know you are transmitting scrambled, and wonder why. Your safety—"

"It is well known I am an off-worlder, though holding contracts here now."

"Yes. But suspicious ones look for the slightest deviation from norm, any little change which feeds their suspicion. You live on Rabelais, you live much like other Rabelaisians. Have you used such communicators recently?"

"No." She shook her head, the gills on her neck flaring slightly. "I use regular communicators often enough, to friends of mine. But never any attempt at shielding what I've said."

"I thought not. So if you start shielding now, it might be a danger." He chewed his lip in uncharacteristic hesitation.

"Perhaps an unshielded, seemingly innocuous message."

"If you can and feel it necessary, do so. Send the message openly. But if you need urgently, in secrecy, use the comm— But there's something else about this one. It's hooked to several others, and they're all dead-manned."

"I see."

It was Ramesis who cleared his throat.

"A dead man," Tamilee explained, "is a comm set to ring a general alarm if it is removed from the proximity of the person it's tuned to."

Golden took the comm back, balanced it in his palm musingly. "This one rings the alarm if the owner is unconscious, or dead also. It differentiates between unconsciousness and natural sleep, but don't get sick and fall into a coma unless you must. Shall I set it for you or him?"

"Him."

"Her."

"Her," Golden decided. "It looks like a piece of jewelry. You'd be more likely to wear jewelry than he," he said to Tamilee.

"Right," the guard captain said with a grin, nodding vigorously.

She gave him a look that said he shouldn't have been so smug at his victory.

They discussed ways and means, ploys and possible counterploys, what might be done to locate the missing Navigator for another hour before Golden sighed and said, "That had better be it. I'm not going to be able to scan my assigned territory tonight as it is." He had already told them that his group had devices that homed on Navigator's Personals, and were sieving through the city, hoping for a blip. It was not a likely method, because it was quite possible whoever had snatched the Navigator had destroyed his Personal and anything else of his technics that might help locate him.

At the entrance to the room Golden turned and grinned. "I came part of the way inside your defenses by flying belt, the rest because Ramesis here cleared a passage by implying that you and he wanted total privacy."

She got that one instantly. "Ramesis," she started in a truly awful voice.

"We couldn't think of anything else," Golden defended the luckless guard, who was standing frozen, knowing what happened to contracteds who disobeyed their owners, or infringed on what the owners considered their rights. "So you are going to have to go along with it."

Wait-till-I-get-you-alone burned in her eyes.

"It's my guess that, like Lord Karolly, you allow your contracteds to conduct themselves however they mutually choose in their free time."

"Yes." She was only a *little* distracted from her anger. "But what has that to do with—"

"And that, if so, Ramesis here has a fair reputation among the female contracteds."

He blushed bright red under the helmet's rim.

"Thought so. In which case, neither of you had better show your faces past where he cleared my passage for a while yet."

The prospects for Ramesis didn't look very good. Tamilee was a proud woman, who had enjoyed her own way for quite a while.

"Do you know how to play Backgimon?" Golden was apparently oblivious of an atmosphere that could have been packaged by the slice and sold to the arenas.

"Yes." Tamilee blinked at the abrupt change of subject.

"Thought you might. Spacer friend of mine taught me. It passes the time, and you don't need any more equipment than a few markers, and a pair of dice. And if any guard captain doesn't have dice in his pouch, I'll eat his helmet, plume and all."

Tamilee finally understood, and burst out laughing. "Men. How you stick together. It's the largest little boys' club in the universe."

"Precisely." Softly: "Your choice, of course. And his." He made her a formal salute, laughing, swirling his cape, looking young and vital and astoundingly attractive, in an oddly impersonal way.

"Take care, newfound friend," she said soberly, as he turned to be escorted back to where he could use his belt to fly safely away.

"I always do." And he was gone, and the smile she had waved good-bye with faded.

Sometimes all the care in the world wasn't good enough. Many worlds' mottos might have been "Buyers beware." On Rabelais, it was *"Everybody beware!"*

TEN

Estaban Xavier was playing. Brandy was humoring him, though her expression said plainly that she was far too old for children's silliness. First he took off several of her chains, knotted them together to make one long strand, and taught her how to play ship's-cradle.

Watching him frown in concentration with his fingers tangled in a Gordian knot of chain made her suppress giggles. Though the giggles stopped and her eyes widened in amazement when he deftly wove his fingers in and out, untangling the maze in seconds.

When the ship's-cradle finally started to bore him, he switched to calisthenics, in which he made Brandy, despite her complaints, join him, as long as she could.

When *that* palled, he decided he wanted to lift weights. Unfortunately, the only detachable object in the room that weighed more than a few grams was Brandy herself. First she kicked and squealed, then she used her closeness to him, to play a few games of her own. Which only made him grin and, without warning, grab both her wrists and swing her around like a living banner, as he spun in the center of the room.

There was nothing in the room that could be used as a weapon or a battering ram, but he showed a remarkable ingenuity in adapting what was there to toys.

"You know what's the matter," he said, some interminable—to Brandy—time later. They were in the bathroom, both wet, because Estaban was demonstrating a historical water battle he called Veirtal's Bay in the tub, with soap bowls as ships.

"You need more ships," Brandy drawled. She was sitting sprawled on the chem-toilet, with its lid down, wriggling her toes and noticing that one of the nails had chipped paint.

"If you aren't careful, I'll decide we need to have Catastrophe Mount about here." His finger pointed to a position near one edge of the tub. "If you were to scrunch yourself together, head down and rump up, you'd be about the right configuration. No." He studied her carefully. "No, perhaps not. The Mount is far more generously rounded. But we could use our imagina—"

"Are you saying I'm too skinny?"

His brows rose. "Perish the thought, my child. The Mount is simply more rounded than you are." He held his hands, curved, palms upward, at least ten centimeters apart, and juggled them, as though he was estimating the weight of a pair of imaginary globes. "Much too much." He said with a decisive nod.

"Thank you," she said between tight-clenched teeth.

"My pleasure," he replied, rather absentmindedly, as he gazed discontentedly at the assortment of soap bowls, perfume bottles, unbreakable statuettes, and pendants off her chains that he had distributed in the half inch of water.

"If you were to be satisfied with a land battle," Brandy said with a sniff, "you could have all the rug in the other rooms to use, instead of that tiny tub."

He looked up with a frown. "One of my ancestors, Commodore Alphonzo Xavier de Medina, distinguished himself in the battle of Veirtal's Bay. Thus, I'm quite familiar with it, and it's such a clear demonstration of pundonor. . . ." He continued to squat, chewing his lip thoughtfully. Then, springing up: "I know! We'll do both!"

"Both?" Brandy shut her eyes, a long-suffering "why me?" expression on her young face.

"The naval engagement"—he was in the main room, tossing pillows about with abandon—"now known as Veirtal's Bay was only the climax of a long combined effort, sea and land. We can do it all."

"Dandy," Brandy grumbled as she slowly stood up, the long-suffering look more exaggerated. "I hope you're enjoying all this."

"Superstition Heights here—yes, that's about the right distance," he was muttering, "Glory Crevasse here—pfaugh!" He stood up, glared around himself.

"What's the matter?"

"Those cursed mirrors. How can I set it up properly when everything I do is duplicated so many times."

"Well," she said, a whine in her frustrated young voice, "they're here aren't they, so there's nothing you can do about—*Estaban!*" She finished on a shriek. He had stalked over to a low table—like all the others, bolted to the floor—and picked up a statuette, a voluptuous female figure, a quarter of a meter high. It was made of a softish, yielding synthetic. Hit a person with it, and very little damage would be done. But hit a stiff, inflexible, thin object . . . He hefted it, flexed it a minute to get the feel of it, and then, a determined grin on his face, stalked over to the nearest mirror. Statue in hand, he made a couple of practice swings, seeking the vulnerable center of the mirror.

They were true mirrors, silver-backed glass, hideously rare and expensive in their beveled perfection.

"*ESTABAN!*" She leaped, held his arm back.

"I don't want the mirrors here," he said, calmly and sanely—and determinedly.

"She'll kill us both!"

"She probably will anyway." He was still calm, sane—and as obdurate and unmoving as the distant Gargantuas.

"Terribly." He was as much stronger than she as an adult than a toddling child. If he wanted to destroy the mirrors, she couldn't stop him. And if he did—she shuddered.

"That, too," he remarked, in the same tones he might have said, "The sun will set later today."

"Ten times as terrible." She was almost literally swinging on his arm.

"My dear, past a certain point, there are no comparatives." He smiled. "I know that, if you do not. That is your mistress's disadvantage with me, you understand." He looked at the mirrors, as though seeing for the first time the worth they might have in this primitive culture. "Well, well." The smile broadened, and she shuddered again. She knew that smile, even if she'd never seen it on *his* face before.

"Estaban!" It was moan, plea, she knew not what.

The smile only glittered brighter, and he swung his arm with the soft but clublike statuette playfully, watching her face. "Prizes her pretties, does she? Can you give me one good reason why I shouldn't take pay in advance for what she intends to do to me, to say nothing of what has already occurred?"

"She has done *nothing.*" She got it out through a throat almost choked closed with sheer animal terror.

"My dear child." She was still clinging to his muscular arm; he pulled, and she bent over in front of him, so that he could see her back. The welts had faded, and the stripes were healing, but still visible. "Your back says different."

"I didn't do what I was told," she choked, tears streaming out of her eyes, both from fear and the awkwardness of her bent-over posture, putting strain on the stripes.

"You mean *I* refused to cooperate. Child, I will continue to do so, and you will pay the price for being in the wrong place at the wrong—" His voice softened. "Do you fear the pain so much?"

Fervent: "Oh, *yes!* Oh, Estaban, *please!*"

He jerked his arm up and broke her grip, so that she was upright, facing him, as his arm swung slightly, his face smiling. "I can kill you now, if you wish," he said gently. "Break your neck before I break the mirrors. Then you needn't fear the pain, ever again." He offered it like the gift he felt it was.

"Estaban!" she gasped.

"I can." He brought his free hand up; it went better than halfway around her slender neck. His fingers bit in just slightly, and he positioned the thumb hard against the corner of her jaw. "One-handed. Now if you want. Snap it like a dry twig." He smiled. "If someone is watching, and I'm sure they are, they couldn't possibly do anything in time to stop me, no matter what weapons they have or can bring to bear."

"Estaban!" Frantic, knowing utter truth when she heard it: "I don't want to die."

"Despite the pain." His fingers tightened, almost imperceptibly.

"That's sometime, this is *now*. Estaban, I'm so young."

"That's right, I had forgotten just how young you are. Well . . ." A gentle smile. "You can help me pick up the pieces, then." He glanced down at his bare feet. "You've sandals, but I'd hate to—"

"Estaban—" In one step, she had moved between him and the mirror, twirled to face him, hands lightly on his wrists. "Estaban, if you break the mirrors, it won't be just you and me she punishes. When she's angry, everyone here suffers. Children, Estaban. Young children. You said once your honor wouldn't permit you to stand by and let children be hurt if you could prevent it."

In a control room watching a screen, a slim young man called Dandro with full, painted lips was chewing those lips and hesitating. He had been told to monitor, but never to let his surveillance be known, unless he had to prevent the prisoner from hurting himself. Never. Even if he killed Brandy. But Dandro was sure that his mistress would be far more furious about the destruction of the mirrors than the destruction of Brandy. He chewed his lip, his fingers hovering over a board with buttons on it.

"Children, Estaban," Brandy was saying. "Pitiful, innocent, young children. How can you—"

Better to let Brandy handle it, Dandro was deciding. But there was a trickle of blood dribbling down from where his teeth had cut his lip.

"You're right," Estaban mused when Brandy had run down a little. "I shouldn't take my small satisfaction of breaking what she prizes at the price of those children out there." He made a vague gesture. "But I can't"—his eyes were clear, his voice filled with calm reason—"can't reenact my battles with all those mirrors around. As I said at the beginning."

"They can be covered," Brandy informed him eagerly.

"Can they?" He looked around. "I hadn't thought of covering them." He frowned. "There's nothing here."

"They can be brought. Not all clients like to see . . . everything." She was almost babbling. "There are—like curtains on a window. All the walls, even the view-window."

"Oh, I want that." Innocent anticipation. "I saw a landscape a while back, while we were playing with it, that would make a perfect backdrop to all this."

"Fine." She patted his massive, smooth-muscled shoulder. "Just fine. Now you be patient." Another pat, with all the tentative, stiff-lipped bravado of a sacrifice in the arena with a snorting but not yet furious bull. "For just a few minutes, while I call out through the door for the curtains."

"All right." He put the statuette back on its table, seated himself on one of the low lounges, hands folded, legs neatly disposed, a child patiently waiting for the birthday cake to be brought in.

Anyone who knew Estaban Xavier would have known exactly when he was most dangerous. Brandy herself should have realized the peril in his change of persona. But she was, after all, very young—and very, very worried about the menace she had known all her life. She just couldn't see this half-client, half-prisoner, a single, if muscular man, as a threat.

Her mistake.

Several hours later, if Brandy had thought he'd made the bathroom a mess with his water battle, he had turned all three rooms into utter chaos for his land-and-sea display.

Cushion mountains, piled high or individual, were everywhere. Twining around among them were chain roads. Soap bowls of water—lakes—nestled in cushions or cuddled to the floor; there was even one perched on the view-window control.

(The extra cushions had been brought in the same way the curtains were. By her screeching out through the slot in the door, and then both of them retiring into the bathroom with the door closed while their "supplies" were brought.)

Estaban was humming happily as he continued to arrange and rearrange his insane diorama. Brandy, exiled to a couch—*Pity I can't move that, it's entirely too far west for the Dogskills*—to keep her out from underfoot—*Curse you, child, that's the third time you've kicked something out of place!*—was pouting and playing ship's-cradle with the only length of chain he hadn't commandeered for his roads, her feet carefully tucked up underneath her not to disarrange the pile of statuettes and dangles that he called "The Black Army."

Finally he rotated slowly, in the middle of the room, finger tapping his lip as he considered. Then he turned to her with a merry smile. "All ready. I think we shall do a quick run-through, just to see that everything is placed properly, before we start a formal reenactment." A roguish smile. "The original battle took over three days, you know."

Brandy moaned.

"Um." He was now facing the view-window and frowning. "That landscape isn't quite what I wanted. I can make a better." He strode over, squatted, and punched the control, his head turned slightly to watch the window. Views flicked past, and he continued to watch.

Brandy rolled her eyes ceilingward and sighed.

Views flicked.

Suddenly he growled, "None of these is right. What I think I'll do . . ." To her surprise, he put a finger in his mouth and did something. Then he held up whatever it was triumphantly. "I'll just stick this into the control to wedge it shut, and I can be watching the views while I get the rest of it ready. I know I saw a coast and mountainscape that will be just perfect, and it has to come up sometime." He inserted the little scrap of wet fingernail into the button and remained squatting, hands away from the controls.

Views continued to change.

He smiled at her. "Perfect," he said, and started to rise. As he came up, one of his legs brushed the "lake" perching precariously on the small control panel.

"Blast," he spat out, as the water spilled into and around the panel. "I'll have to refill it," he grumbled, picking up the fallen bowl and trotting into the bath.

"Does one silly lake matter?"

"Of course. Lieutenant Hammurabi's forces were delayed circling the lake for several crucial hours." He came in, carrying the full bowl. "Timing is everything, you know, Brandy. Well . . ." A grin. "Knowledge helps, too. You should always reconnoiter your—Owwww!" he jumped, the bowl flying, and half knelt, half sat to examine the sole of one foot.

"Estab—yeeek!" She jumped and screeched in her turn. "Those uncontracted armies of yours—I stepped on one! Owww!" She flopped back into her couch in her turn, to look at her own foot.

"I had to use what I could get." He rose, looking suddenly very tall and *very* muscular. He smiled. "It's not my fault that whoever designed those pretties had a corner fetish. We'll just have to watch where we step."

"You watch *your* step," she said sullenly, drawing her feet well under her. "I intend to be pure audience, until you clean up this—this booby trap you've made."

"Tsk," he clicked his tongue. "I thought you were supposed to do anything I wanted."

She looked him up and down, gave him a smile that showed at least fifty teeth, or seemed to. "Getting everything you want spoils people." She nodded. "So, for your own good . . ."

He burst out with a roar of laughter.

"Besides," she added, "if I've learned one thing in the last few days, it's that you won't make me."

He took a step toward her. "Sure?"

She nodded.

"You have matured," he admitted with a wry grin. "You're right, about this at least. I know where everything is—should be. I'll refill the lake. Again."

"Good." She picked up the ship's-cradle she'd dropped and began to straighten out its tangle, while he shrugged, picked up the bowl, and went back into the bathroom. In seconds, he was back.

"You left the water running."

He shrugged. "It'll shut itself off."

"Of course." She continued untangling.

He set the bowl on the panel, glanced at the view. "You know, I think the view I wanted was in this series. It should be coming soon." He continued to stand still, watching the view, until suddenly he wrinkled his nose. "How odd. Do you smell anything, Brandy child?"

"Wet carpet."

"Perhaps you're right." He continued to watch the view-window, muttering, "I'm sure it was in this sequence."

Brandy snorted. She was down to one rotten, pulled-tight little knot.

Suddenly he sniffed again. "That smell," he murmured, and looked around, face puzzled, sniffing, sniffing.

"I don't smell anything."

He took a step back, sniffed, another step back, sniffed again, then moved back close to the view-window. "It's here." He sniffed again, baffled. "Right here. By the view-window."

She heaved a sigh. "Honestly, Estaban, you don't think. That's where you spilled the water, isn't it? You used the soap bowls, they must have had perfume still in them. The water would have smelled, too."

He turned to face her, his face puzzled. "It did. It does. I can smell that, too. This is something else, something—I can almost recognize it."

"Oh, for—" She put her feet down carefully, and began to mince over toward him.

Abruptly he jumped back, thrust out an arm to block her. "Smoke! That's what it is! Fire! Must have shorted something when I spilled the water. See, there's smoke rising, Brandy."

"Fire! I don't see—"

"Stay back, I'll get some water." He galloped into the bathroom, came out with two bowls of water, hurled them toward the screen, turned himself around, was back almost instantly with two more.

"Estaban—"

"Brandy, help me, you little fool! Do you want to burn or suffocate before they get this door unlocked? All these synthetics, they'll go up like rocket fuel!" He gave her a shove toward the bath, tossed the two pitiful bowls of water, and was suddenly behind her again, hurling her into the bathroom.

"Fire!" he bellowed. "Fire—fire—*fire!*" He grabbed another pair of bowlsful and raced out into the main room, roaring louder as he hit another "soldier" in the room, hopped and limped, but kept going. "Fire!" he thundered as he tossed the water.

He met her coming out, "Smoke's worse," he panted, shoving her back in, into the tub, turning the water on from both taps full blast, jerking the plug so it would continue to run. "Stay in the tub, that's safest. Keep low, there'll be poisonous fumes."

"Estaban—"

"Stay here," he barked. "I'm going to do what I can to put it out, and to get attention, help. You keep low, but if I yell 'Door's open,' you zoom out of here. Keep your head low, more people die of the fumes you can't see than the flames." He refilled his bowls, charged out.

Brandy, her eyes wide, sure now that she could hear flames crackling and smell smoke, dived into the water, screaming, "Fire! Fire! Fire!" like a berserk air-raid siren.

In the main room, Estaban's bull-bellow was echoing her. "Fire! Fire! Fire!"

It seemed to go on for hours, but it was probably less than a stimmit when Estaban shouted, *"Door, Brandy!"*

For a second, so frantic was she that she couldn't remember what "door" meant. Then she realized—Freedom! Safety!

Soaking wet, she leaped out of the tub, charged into the room—

No smoke. No flames. Estaban was flapping frantically at the base of the view-window, dripping with water, with one of the curtains.

It was the expression on his face that stopped her. He was bellowing "Fire!" again, but his eyes—

Caught hers. Laughing.

Some men reacted to danger that way. She charged on toward the opening door.

Tangled with two men with buckets coming in. And—she realized later— one of Estaban's chain roads, somehow held tautly at ankle height.

Then he was there, one blow—she winced at the solid thunk—two blows, and the bodies she was tangled with went limp.

Then she was pulled from the pileup, as easily as he'd untangled ship's-cradles, dumped over a firm shoulder hard enough to drive the breath out of her, and sailing upward as he rose.

Estaban, grinning, wrapped the folded curtain around his waist several times, scooped a knife from each of his victims and stuck them in his improvised sash, scooped up a pile of "soldiers" that had been placed carefully for exactly that ease of grab, and hurtled through the now open door, bellowing "FIRE!" louder than an arena announcer.

He didn't know—and wouldn't have cared if he had—that behind him in the bathroom a thin thread of real smoke was rising. One of his chains, draped around a metal tap, had landed its other end in the water, caused a short with the circuits that controlled the water, and the resulting spark had caught some of the dry wood splinters inside the wall.

All Estaban cared about was that he had caused mass confusion, and was out of his cell!

For now.

ELEVEN

Golden Singh, Navigator Jael, and Brine the ex-enforcer stood at the base of the steps leading up into the Hall of the Adjudicators. Jael shivered slightly, and Golden, ever sensitive to her, put an arm around her shoulders.

"I can take it from here, love. You needn't have come."

"No."

Brine was staring up at the massive façade, with its murals and relief carvings, lip caught between his square, slightly yellow teeth. Now he turned, saw her face, and caught her hand in both of his. "He's right, Jael love. This is too much for you. We'll both take you back to Guildhall and—"

"No." She straightened her shoulders and smiled. "No, we agreed, my name would get the quickest cooperation. Even were we to use Golden—and I would rather not, until we know the lay of the land—it will take some time to establish his bona fides."

"Bona—" Brine frowned. It was not the first time she had used a phrase he didn't understand.

"True identity. Fine I am now, loves. It was just . . . memory, for a second."

Golden hugged her. "If you're sure," he said, doubt tingeing his deep voice.

She tapped his nose. "Sure I am," she said, her own voice firm. "And now —" She nodded toward the double doors. "In the words of the Immortal Bard: 'Once more into the breach, dear friends.' "

Brine glanced down at himself, puzzled. "Breeches," he murmured. But the other two had already started up the long flight of steps, and he trotted after.

It took a certain amount of time, but finally the three were escorted into a small but elegantly furnished sitting room, where a slight, anonymous older man with intelligent gray eyes was rising and saying, "My esteemed Navigator, how may I serve—" Then his eyes went to the two men behind Jael, and he exploded, for the first and probably the only time in his life without thinking first, "Sanctity preserve us, C'holder Singh, you've signed your own death-contract coming here so openly!"

Sometime later, Aristide the Adjudicator was rubbing his forehead wearily, ignoring the coaxing coils of jasmine that were tantalizing his nostrils from the untouched cup of hot tay on the table in front of him.

"It's hard to know where to start," he said with a sigh.

"With Navigator Estaban Xavier." Jael was firm.

"You Navigators." Aristide sighed again. Then, with a smile of odd sweetness that changed his cypher-face into something more than charming: "Did you know, I was involved the last time a Navigator ran afoul of our freedom, Lady Jael."

"You—" Brine started. As an enforcer, he knew who had sat on the bench during Jael's adjudication; but he couldn't know what had gone on behind the scenes.

Jael's hand on his wrist silenced him. "You were not, I remember, the Adjudicator who actually ruled."

He bowed from his sitting position. "I am honored you recall my colleague so well. True. I did not sit. But—" The smile of infinite charm again. "I was involved." His shrewd gaze flicked to the man who was and yet was not, could not be, the Golden Singh he'd known. He had offered to kill the Golden Singh of fifteen years past, to protect the Jael he had barely seen— and his own people and hers. Except that he had known that killing the golden man would only make matters worse, and not protect Jael at all, or stop what her crash would mean to his own world.

"Past history cannot affect our current problem," said Golden, truly believing it. Aristide, who knew better, said nothing. Jael caught the glint in his eye and nodded, almost imperceptibly, her mouth twitching.

The boy will learn. Give him time, he's bright.

Aristide blinked. He couldn't have just heard— He frowned at Golden Singh. The boy? Singh was five years younger than he. Yet this strangely rejuvenated Singh was an odd mixture of maturity and—and youthful impulsiveness. "I would suggest," he said, "that the first step is to ensure that the Navigator isn't still aboard his ship, despite what the other Navigator has been told."

"Can't," Jael said. "They're out of range."

"You've no way of knowing he's truly on our world, then."

"No. But the Navigator Miramne Sung-Kenyatta would not have risked using the comm unauthorized were she not sure of her facts. Navigator Estaban Xavier is not aboard that craft."

"His corpse may be," Aristide pointed out. "It won't be the first time, I suspect, that a contract has been abrogated so very permanently."

"And secretly." Golden frowned. "Jael, who would know? The crew think the second Navigator found another berth aboard another vessel, and no one on the ground is thought to know that he was aboard, much less that he came ashore, or supposedly came ashore."

Jael chewed her lip.

"Lady Navigator," Aristide said gently, "though it seems to me most probable that your Navigator is the victim of a venial captain—your Navigators's contracts come very high, do they not?—nonetheless, we will proceed as though he did come aground and is on this world now. We will search this city to the last crevice and brick. But—"

"But . . ." Golden put a comforting arm around Jael's shoulders, and Brine caught her hand between both of his.

"You off-worlders wear wealth worth a dozen human-life-contracts about yourselves, and there are unscrupulous and uncontracted scum who will risk all for less than a pair of boots. Your Navigator, if he is alive, may be lying bound and stripped of all identification in a caravan hold, while his possessions go in an opposite direction."

"But think you that his corpse is buried somewhere."

"That is most likely. People do not simply disappear, Lady Navigator. Especially not important people, such as a Navigator. Words rustle in the very winds."

"But you will look," Brine rumbled.

Aristide spread his hands. "Of course."

"As though you knew he was alive to be found, not a perfunctory search for one you believe is a corpse, and most likely a corpse on a ship long gone," Jael said grimly. It wasn't a question.

Aristide frowned. "He is a Navigator. We have not forgotten the import of Navigators."

"It's more important than you think," Brine insisted.

"Spacer"—Aristide took Brine's clothes at their face value—"have you a reason for saying all this? You're not one of us, not a Navigator either by your lack of their uniform."

Brine had once been a contracted, had run out on that contract. He was safe now, Golden was not the menace he had once been, but the penalty for contract-breaking—and he was guilty of that—was a long session in Agony Square. "I'm a citizen of the world Maze," he informed with truth, "but I'm bonded to the Lady Jael. And we're both—all three—on this world now. If it goes up in fountains of blood . . ."

Aristide rubbed his lower lip thoughtfully with a finger, remembered the cooling tay, and took a slow sip. "Your spacer equations again?"

"Worse," said Golden. "Equations." He nodded to Jael. "Instinct." He tapped his own chest. "Intuition." Brine.

Aristide took another sip of tay, his face as pursed as if it were straight lemon juice. Then, with a sigh: "And your own contracts, C'holder Singh?"

Golden shrugged. "I left them under the administration of proxies." Proxies with little power to change anything. The old Golden had been suspicious, almost paranoid, but very intelligent. "Those proxies are naturally void, now that I am back. There will be formalities, of course."

Aristide cocked an eyebrow. He didn't have to say, "If you survive to complete them."

The old Golden had had unlimited self-confidence; the new one merely nodded.

Jael wasn't stupid, either. "You were not surprised to see him; just to see him here."

Aristide nodded. "He has been seen, and recognized. His coloring—"

"Not uncommon, in the Nucleus. But here . . ."

A nod. "Precisely. In the port, he's just a spacer with coloring like a long-dead c'holder's. But once he has come here . . ." A smile. "I'll do what I can. Like pass around the simple truth: that two spacers escorted the Navigator Lady Jael to inquire about the missing Navigator."

Jael smiled. "Simple truths are the best lies, are they not."

He smiled back, his glance flicking to all three of them. "Who should know better than you, Navigator Lady Jael."

Brine stiffened, wondered if he had paled under the bronze he had never lost.

Aristide the Adjudicator's smile broadened to include all three of his guests; he knew when an idle foot while walking kicked up a pebble to reveal the glitter of something valuable. Even if he didn't know what yet, or under whose, if any, contract.

But Brine was no slouch in the brains department, either. He put together secrets concealed out in the open, and his knowledge of the world that had once been his; his eyes narrowed. "Golden . . ." Very much the father: "You knew that you'd been recognized—or at least, suspicions aroused." Very stern: "Why didn't you tell us?"

"I didn't want to worry you."

"Oh, Golden," Jael said, half sighing, half grinning. "Too bad you grew too old to spank so quickly."

"Love." He spread his hands, saying it all in one word, one gesture. Then, with a roguish twinkle: "If it would make you feel better to spank me—or anything else . . ."

Aristide covered his mouth to hide a grin. If nothing else, the sight of Golden Singh wooing instead of grabbing . . .

Brine was not amused. Nor soothed. "Golden."

"I talked with one who was there," Golden admitted. "She's no danger, and from what she said of the conclusions they drew, they planned nothing, overtly, anyway. So I thought, What difference? I knew you were unlikely to come in contact with any of the c'holders involved yourself." He licked his lips, for one second very much small-boy-with-hand-in-cookie-jar. "How was I to guess they had the common sense to consult with an Adjudicator on such a delicate matter?"

You wouldn't have, Aristide thought shrewdly, *back then. And perhaps not now, but for different reasons.* Aloud: "Speaking of common sense, best the formalities be started, as quickly as possible. You will need a number of witnesses to swear to your identity." He meant c'holder witnesses, of course. A contracted was not considered a witness, since a contracted must say whatever his or her c'holder ordered. "They had best be chosen wisely. There are some who would find their contracts improved if you were not Golden Singh."

Golden nodded, wheels obviously turning.

"Then there is the complication caused by whatever further contracts have been entered into on behalf of your heir."

Golden was startled. "I named no heir." Unlimited self-confidence.

"I know. Foolishness. Yet as time passed, certain decisions had to be made, but the proxies had not the authority."

Golden said nothing, but his lip curled, and for a second he looked very like the man who had once cut such a swath through Rabelais.

"So the Adjudicators examined all your contracts, and an heir was assigned."

"An heir." The old Golden was more and more in evidence. "Who was the lucky c'holder to win the toss?"

"Your child of course. The one conceived—"

Pssssssss! Golden had been taking a sip of tay. He sprayed it all over the table, mouth and eyes wide in shock.

"Your child conceived just before—" Aristide tried to go on.

"You transferred my contracts to a chance-chosen contracted's spawn, that might have been mine or the product of—"

"Not a contracted. A c'holder. Oaths were sworn."

"I dare swear they were." Golden was still furious.

"It's your own fault, son." Aristide couldn't have said why he said it, or why he was feeling more and more paternal toward the man who was his own age but didn't look it and, mostly, didn't act it. "You left no assigns. You left us to clean up the mess your carelessness caused. And if you don't want to see it happen twice, make a contract of heirship and have it witnessed before you leave this hall!" He glared back, one brow rising, half mockery, half command, half—he wasn't sure what, himself.

Brine couldn't help a snigger, at the two faces glaring at each other. "He has a point, Golden," he said, placatingly.

"He does," Jael agreed, patting the trembling broad shoulder.

Golden relaxed, which made Aristide—when he had time to consider it more fully later—very suspicious. Golden angry, he recognized. Golden Singh had been notorious for his temper—and what it made him do. But a Golden controlling himself . . . If it weren't ridiculous, since Golden Singh had been into middle age when he left, he would have said that the man had finally grown up. And somehow—how?—gotten younger at the same time. "All right," he agreed. "I'll do it. And whom shall I name as my heir? How about it, Brine, you want to be target number two?"

"No!"

"Not you, Jael love," he said, thoughtful.

"Nobody vulnerable," she warned.

He was still frowning. "I knew who wasn't vulnerable fifteen years ago. But—"

"May I suggest—" Aristide began, but Brine interrupted him, grinning.

"Not a person, Golden. Split it, three ways. One part to the Navigator's Guild, eh, my Lady Navigator Jael, one part to the Off-Worlder Merchant and Spacer Association, and one part . . ." The grin widened.

"Clever," Aristide admired.

Brine spread his hands. "Where else? The Adjudicators' Unity."

"But, Brine—" Jael started to protest.

"It's like your Guild, you know. Apprentices, long years of training, contractual commitments of the strongest."

Golden was nodding. "A beautiful solution. Thank you, Brine."

"Anytime, son. Anytime."

Aristide blinked. The man in spacer clothes introduced as Brine looked about the age that he knew Golden Singh was. Son?

"A long story," Jael murmured.

Aristide had a feeling that he wasn't going to hear it, either; his curiosity would remain unassuaged.

Brine grinned again. "You wouldn't believe it if we told you, and swore it on a contract with witnesses."

Aristide sighed. *Spacers!*

Golden had remembered one tiny item. "My child by a c'holder? Which one?"

"The Lady Oriflamme."

Golden smiled. "Medee. Tsk. Got careless one time, did she."

Aristide shook his head. "Her sister, the Lady Esme."

"What!" Brine and Golden exploded simultaneously. But it was Golden who went on, "Not the Lady Esme. It couldn't possibly have been the Lady Esme."

"Are you sure?" Aristide frowned. According to Golden Singh's reputation, there wasn't a girl over the age of puberty—and some younger—who hadn't passed through his hands.

Golden nodded. "I'm sure." A wry grin. "In those days, it was easier to keep track of the ones I missed."

"How odd," Aristide mused. "I didn't know her well, but the Lady Esme had a reputation for—for—"

Golden was nodding. "Perhaps one of her own contracteds—"

But Brine interrupted him. "*Didn't* know her? Are you saying the Lady Esme is dead?"

"Died in childbed." Aristide was thinking aloud. "And the child was sworn as the Lord C'holder Singh's several years later, when it became . . ."

All sat and mused for a time, but Jael had caught something the others missed.

"Brine," she said, "you sound as if you knew this Lady Esme."

"No, I—yes. In a sense. We spent a night together, the night before I shipped out."

"Sacred contracts," Aristide swore. If the child Emerald Oriflamme was the product of the Lady Esme and a spacer . . .

"Brine." Jael laid a hand on his arm. "You don't have to say any more, if it pains you."

"Pains me." He smiled, and looked, somehow, despite his mismatched features, almost attractive. "I love you, Jael, but that hour—it wasn't any more than that—that Esme and I had, it was a—a moment out of time."

"You didn't"—Aristide was still boiling the consequences in his mind—"use force? She was willing, a stranger to her, a—"

"A stranger." Brine smiled. "Yes, we'd never met, never exchanged a word. But that night—" He hesitated, edited a little. "Force? A c'holder with all her guards about her? I was alone, in danger, desperate and frightened. Her men stopped me." He paused, shrugged. "C'holders do that. She was curious, bored a little. We talked. That was all at first. She had me set down, and I—I ran after. She was in a palanquin, alone in it, being carried, and she let me in, a second time." He stopped, stared at the Adjudicator, and said, his voice asking the question. "I shipped out on the freighter that carried the Lady Jael from here to Crossroads, that's how we met. So I would have been with the Lady Esme—"

Aristide calculated, then nodded. "At almost exactly the right time. Yes. I'll have to look up the dates to be sure, but it sounds right."

"She was—I wish you'd known her, Jael. She was"—his mouth twisted—"glorious."

"Was she?" Golden frowned. "I hardly remember what she looked like, hardly noticed her."

Brine was still in the past. "Most didn't. Those who knew her well, they thought, or anyone else. We were strangers, yes. All her life, though, she'd been looking, waiting, for the man who would see her as she was, as the woman she was, and not a—a c'holder of immense power. That's all she wanted. I wasn't wise enough then to have seen ordinarily, but that night I— I was stripped down to soul alone myself. I saw beauty, sweetness, gentleness, joy. Inside, outside, what did it matter. What she saw—"

"Strength and compassion," Jael suggested.

"Virility," Golden added, with a very male grin.

"Brine," Jael enthused.

"Whatever," Brine said. "We stole an hour, we loved. But I couldn't stay."

"Oh, *Brine.*" Jael's hand slid into his. "I know her through you, love. Her love helped make you what you are."

"Dead and cremated and ashes on the wind," he said with a sigh. "But you're right, she lives in my memories."

"Which won't be very long, if word of this reaches beyond this room," Aristide inserted dryly.

"What?" From Jael.

"The Lady Emerald Oriflamme enjoys the contracts of both the Lady Esme and, for now, the Lord Singh. The spacer Brine might have a claim to some of those contracts; through standard contingency clauses, he can claim himself the heir of the Lady Emerald."

"What a world." Jael shook her head sadly.

"You see further than most," Brine said. "Pity the Lady Esme never met you."

"I signed my contract with the Unity when the Lady Esme was barely a babe. But then, being a spacer, you wouldn't be aware. Once the contract was in force, I could never bond with any but a fellow Adjudicator." He smiled.

"I know." Brine sighed. "Pity."

"I did meet her, not long before the babe was birthed," Aristide said. "She glowed. I think, spacer, that she would not have changed a minute of her life —even had she known how short her happiness would be."

"An hour. She deserved more."

"Nine thirties," Aristide corrected.

"Thank you."

"My pleasure. But that doesn't solve our problems. Lord Singh, have I permission to start the various contractual procedures?"

He nodded. "Of course. And I'll send you a list in a day or so of those I wish the Adjudicators' Unity to contact, to serve as witnesses."

But only a few hours after the three had left the Adjudicator's office, none of them was in any condition to make such a list, much less send it.

TWELVE

Estaban burst out of the doorway to his cell bawling "Fire!" like a wounded bull-elk; Brandy, still draped over his shoulder, was letting off train-whistle shrieks that added to the verisimilitude.

There were at least a dozen people, either in the corridor or drawn within seconds by the commotion, some running toward the cell, some away, some merely frozen where they stood, mouths agape and eyes popping.

"Fire!" Estaban thundered. Then: "She's hurt, breathed smoke, help, *Fire!*"

Four men and a woman jammed into the doorway, while others ran to spread the word, bring buckets.

Estaban headed for the youngest person available. "She needs fresh air," he shouted. "Which way closest?"

The boy—he couldn't have been more than eight—pointed to a door.

Estaban took off, his long legs eating up distance.

"Stop him!" A voice cut through the screeches and screams of "Help!" and "Fire!" "Stop him, he's an escaping contracted, not a client!"

Estaban whirled, saw two men thundering their way through the bystanders. He smiled thinly, pulled a bangle from the assortment in his left hand, let fly. The lead man went down with a gilt triangle in his eye. Another throw, and the second man crumpled to his knees, gasping and choking and plucking at the bruise where a silver disk had crashed into his windpipe.

Estaban spun and crashed through the door and hurtled down a flight of steps, still shouting "Fire!" like an audio with a looped tape.

Estaban hit the bottom of the steps and saw a door, jerked it open, and realized he was out in a street.

It was night, late night judging from the position of the ring, and the street was almost deserted, except for a derelict or two huddled in doorways, and here and there guards standing erect under lighted lanterns.

Estaban took the distance to the nearest guard like a sprinter going for the gold. "Fire!" he bellowed. "Get your people out—Now! It's out of control, and if it spreads—"

"Wha—" The guard looked at him dully.

"Fire, you mudbrain! Fire! Get your people out and away before it—" He pushed the man into the doorway. "Fire!"

A few feet away, one of the derelicts had leaped to his feet. "Fire?" he screeched. Then, turning, ran.

So did Estaban. The next guard had heard the commotion, but not the words.

"Fire! Get your people out, warn the rest of the street, clear it before it spreads, get people to help!" Estaban got it all out on one breath, then ran on.

Within seconds he wasn't the only one. People, many of them naked or partly undressed, were pouring out of the two houses he had aroused.

Estaban, grinning, slowed his speed a little, although he continued to scream "Fire!" to every guard as he passed. Within a minute he was surrounded by a thin, running mob. Within two, it was thickening, several of its members, like Estaban, carrying some sort of treasure slung over their shoulders.

The Hallmaster regarded Estaban's sudden arrival, Brandy cursing and struggling in his arms, as a mixed blessing. The first thing he said was, "I'm Navigator Class-A Estaban Xavier. This girl is a testee. How long can we protect her from her contractual obligations?"

Brandy, who had been shifted to a cradle-carry, stiffened in his arms and wailed, not for the first time, "She'll kill me!"

The Guildmaster, pushing to the front of a growing crowd of Navigators, native assistants, and spacers using the Guildhall's hospitality, was not stupid, despite not having slept for over two days. "Inside," she snapped. Then: "Secretary. Record the admission of a native testee, identified as—"

"Brandy," Estaban supplied with a grin, marching in, naked and with the tear-grimed Brandy in his arms, as proudly as an apprentice in full array marching to the dais to be admitted to the Guild as Navigator.

"Brandy," the Guildmaster went on, "for full range of testing. Contractholders to be paid off in the usual method, for twice the standard rate for her time for a week for the testing, plus option to buy out her contract if testing succeeds." Then, dropping formality: "I assume the testing had better succeed."

"She'll *kill*—" Brandy started another wail, but Estaban rolled over her.

"She'll need *full* training."

"Ah!" Very low, to Estaban: "That bad?" Louder, shaking Brandy's hand vigorously all the while, "Welcome to the Guild, m'dear, welcome. Always glad to have a new potential Navigator, ranks too thin, far too thin, and now" —mouth twitching, though her female eye, running up and down Estaban, was *most* appreciative—"I think you both look like you could use a bath, some food, and some clothing, not necessarily in that order."

Estaban roared with laughter, and set Brandy on her feet—though keeping one hand gripping hard on her arm. Then he stuck out his own hand. "Navigator Class-A Estaban Xavier greets you and thanks you, Guildmaster." The Guildmaster was a woman who enjoyed challenges, which was why she had decided to stay and "whip Rabelais into shape"; and why Estaban, if he chose—it was all there, in her eyes—might find an enjoyable challenge of his own, on Rabelais.

"Glad to see you, Navigator." The Guildmaster put an arm around Estaban's shoulder. "We've been looking for you. For now . . ." She frowned around, and the non-Navigators melted away. The Guildmaster grinned.

"Testee," she said gently, "you look hungry and exhausted. Sister Victory, Sister Amelie, if you would show our new testee and soon-to-be-sister hospitality . . ."

Brandy whimpered, "She'll kill me," as the two Navigators stepped forward.

"Brandy." Estaban dropped to his knees, so that he and his fellow sufferer were eye to eye. "Brandy, you're safe here. The Guild protects its own. Always. You're safe."

"Oh, Estaban." A funny, high little laugh. "You don't know her."

"You don't know the Guild," he answered firmly. "You're safe now, Brandy child. Safe."

"Oh, Estaban," she wailed, flinging her arms around him and bursting out into a storm of sobbing.

With a sigh, he picked her up, and said to the two who had been detailed to take care of Brandy, "Sisters?"

The shorter one with the totally depilated head and the shrewd hazel eyes glanced at his burden, gave him an assessing female glance, and nodded. "Follow me, brother."

"With thanks and gratitude, sister," he answered, over Brandy's noisy, childish weeping. "Guildmaster, I need to discuss with you—"

The Guildmaster nodded. "My office, after you've eaten and slept, say."

Estaban was shaking his head. "Time, Guildmaster. Your office, as soon as I have Brandy settled."

The Guildmaster sighed but nodded. "My office. I'll be waiting, Brother Xavier." But by the last word, she was talking to Estaban's back. She looked around, said mildly, "Does no one here have duties?"

The Hall was empty by the time she reached the corridor leading to her office.

Someone had loaned Estaban a pair of sandals and a loose robe in an eye-catching shade of blue. He stood poised in the doorway of the Guildmaster's office for a second, then walked in, nodding. "Guildmaster."

The Guildmaster rose. "Brother Xavier. Sit. Make yourself comfortable."

As Estaban dropped into a chair with a heavy sigh, the Master gestured to the man on her left, "Guild Secretary, Memnon Hirimoto." And to the rather androgynous figure on her right, as ebony black as oiled silk from top to toe. "Grievance Coordinator, Ismay Mboya."

"Grievance?" Estaban's eyebrows went up. "This isn't a big enough post to warrant a formal grievance committee, is it?"

"On this world"—Ismay Mboya's voice was a liquid tenor—"a post of one would keep a grievance committee busy."

Estaban grinned. "Pity it's on so many routes."

"There's talk of building a station." The Guildmaster sighed. "A consortium of the largest lines— Well, that's not our problem now."

"Holding the Guild to ransom." Estaban nodded grimly. "I'd say not. Our problem is—"

"Ransom?" The Guildmaster interrupted. "We had no ransom demands."

"Wha—"

"No ransom. None."

Estaban bit his lip. "But you said—glad to see me."

"Yes. We knew you were missing. But not who or why. A ransom demand would have at least held hope you were alive and not—"

"Brother." The secretary shoved a tray toward Estaban. "Refresh yourself. I think we've got a long night yet ahead of us."

The Guildmaster's lip curled. "Understated, as usual, Brother Memnon. My apologies, Brother Xavier. Refresh yourself."

Estaban leaned forward, chose a couple of covered dishes, and had his cup filled with kaffee. When all four had at least a cup of kaffee, the Guildmaster said with a frown, "Does anybody besides me smell the distinct odor of rat in this?"

Estaban nodded, swallowed hastily. "They told me—no." Biting his lip, he went on, "She said—negotiations. It was I who assumed that the Guild was being held to ransom."

"Negotiations." The Guildmaster glanced at her two associates. "Not with us," she said thoughtfully.

Memnon Hirimoto pursed his lip in a soundless whistle. Ismay Mboya examined black nails filed into perfect ovals.

"A second party, who hoped to sell me back to you—or perhaps, simply for your gratitude," Estaban suggested, though he didn't believe it himself. He took a grateful sip of kaffee, often laughingly called Navigator's lifeblood.

"No." The Guildmaster didn't believe it, either. "Brother Xavier, you will think over carefully every word said in your hearing and give them to Brother Memnon to be recorded. As soon as we're through here, and while all is fresh in your memory. But for now . . ." She took a sip of her own kaffee.

"Brother Xavier, we knew you were in trouble because your fellow Navigator aboard your vessel managed to comm back a message."

Estaban froze with the cup to his lips and choked as a bit of kaffee ran down the wrong way.

"She had been told," the Guildmaster went on, "that you had accepted a berth on another vessel, and due to his tight scheduling your captain would not replace you until his next port. It was only that she felt certain you would have sent her some personal message, despite your hurry, that made her send us a message."

Estaban's lips narrowed. "Who told her I had accepted another berth?"

"The captain himself."

A curl of his well-cut lips. "Which explains why the captain did not report me missing, I think."

Ismay Mboya was still contemplating perfect almond nails, a dreamy smile on the smooth young face. "He registered here. Word will be sent. Sooner or later."

All his listeners knew what that meant. The FTL ships themselves were the fastest method of between-the-stars communication. A message would go out on each ship that lifted off from Rabelais, warning the Guilds on all its destinations about the captain who had betrayed, naming his current ship. He would then be blacklisted at those ports, and the Guildmasters would send out similar warnings, with all ships that lifted off. Like a runaway chain reaction, word would spread. Eventually, the unfortunate captain would land on a world that *knew.* If possible, he would be tried on that world. If not, he would never lift off of it. No Navigator would serve on a ship he rode. Even the wildest of criminal worlds, the slave-marts, the montes, whatever, depended on Navigators for supplies, for communication. The man was doomed, one way or another.

"That takes care of him." Estaban had recovered a little from the shock. "But—"

"Who here was part of the plot?" the Guildmaster finished. "We had hoped you could tell us."

Estaban laughed. "Except for Brandy, I saw no one, literally no one."

"Then they did intend to ransom you." Memnon Hirimoto drummed his fingers lightly on the Guildmaster's desk.

"Or something," Estaban agreed. "I follow your reasoning. They allowed me to see no one, so I could identify no one later." His face got very grim. "I wonder what they intended to do about Brandy."

Ismay Mboya was still engrossed in the curve of perfect black nails. "She's contracted."

The secretary frowned. "So?"

"I've had more contact with this world than you. It's very easy to . . . tear up a contract."

A snort. "I thought it was the most difficult thing on this world to do."

"Oh, no." Another dreamy smile. "Very easy."

Estaban stiffened. *"Madre de Dios!* You're saying they meant to kill her all along."

"I'd say her fate was sealed as soon as you laid eyes on her."

Estaban's hand clenched into a fist, fingers working. "Those—"

"Didn't you suspect that?" Mboya asked. "I thought that's why you brought her out, to protect her."

"Yes. But not from that. Just punishment—and the life she would have been condemned to, otherwise."

"As a contracted," the Guildmaster said.

"Whore."

Only Memnon was startled. "That child?"

"This is Rabelais," the Guildmaster said with a growl. On her home world, child molestation was a mortal sin, not a crime.

"That does limit the search somewhat." Ismay's smile was singularly sweet. "If all we have to search is the brothels."

The Guildmaster snorted.

"High-priced brothels," Estaban snarled in disgust. "Supplied with a view-window." Even Ismay's nonexistent brows rose at that. Imported luxuries were *very* expensive. "Mirrors even on the ceiling, furs and silks everywhere, gold taps in the bath."

Ismay smothered a snicker behind a polite hand. "One wonders how you could bear to tear yourself away from such hospitality."

"Take a look at the child's back," Estaban snapped.

"Rabelais." The Guildmaster said it like a curse.

"The child," Ismay said thoughtfully. "We are ignoring our primary source of information."

"Once she gets over being afraid."

"Curse!" Estaban hit his own forehead with his clenched fist.

"Brother?" The Guildmaster asked.

"I wasn't thinking. She was so upset." He shrugged. "Too late now, I'm afraid. Poor infant, she was hysterical. I told the sisters to give her a sedative as soon as she was bathed and fed. Sooner, if she seemed to need it. By now . . ."

But the Guildmaster was already punching her console. She didn't bother to switch on Privacy, so they all heard the crisp conversation.

"That's it, thank you, sisters." She signed off.

"My apologies, Guildmaster."

"My dear Xavier, after such an escape—you'll have to give us the details someday. But for now, I think we all agree, this has the earmarks of a well-planned plot."

Three yeses.

"And that our next step is to locate the person at whose brothel you were held."

Estaban muttered a single very uncomplimentary word in his own tongue. Louder: "Brandy's *mother.*"

The three Navigators stared at each other. It was Ismay who recovered first. "Mother?"

Estaban nodded. "So she says. Do you know, Brandy was actually grateful to her. She thought a brothel has the best opportunities for a contracted on Rabelais."

Memnon frowned. "We'll have to rethink everything. If the child's her daughter, then she isn't in such danger."

Estaban sneered. "She was chosen because she was less trained and so less popular with the clientele. I wondered about that at the time. But of course, she's the smallest loss."

"Then why . . . ?" The Guildmaster frowned.

"Navigator's Syndrome, would you believe. The old harridan feared I would lose my Navigatorial skills if I lost my health, and that . . . Brandy's services were a necessity to that health."

The other two snorted, but Ismay Mboya merely tapped perfect nails against the beautifully carved black lips. "Another indication of the ransom theory. There are Navigators who would have broken in any kind of imprisonment, and those who would break in such circumstances, without the use of such as the child. It makes a sort of twisted sense."

"Twisted is right," the Guildmaster agreed. "Rabelais."

"What we need to do now," Memnon decided, "is send to the Adjudicators, demand sufficient enforcers to check out brothels until we find your view-window. And then—"

"It's simpler than that," Estaban said with a grin. "I got out by raising a cry of fire. There must be hundreds of people this night who know of a brothel where a false alarm of fire was raised." He remembered the unclad folk fleeing through the night. "More than a hundred."

"That does simplify the search." The Guildmaster's hand hovered over her console.

"Lady." Memnon put a hand on her arm. "While you're calling, there's another who should be here, conferring with us."

"Yes?"

"Who else but our sister, the Lady Jael. If anyone would be able to unsnarl the ins and outs of this accursed world, it's she. And if not she, remember the suggestions those two companions—"

"The Lady Jael," Estaban exploded, then relaxed, muttering, "It can't be the same one—"

"As the Lady Jael who was once accused on this world?" The Guildmaster nodded. "It is she, returned."

"Impossible!"

"No. And you're right, Memnon. She can help us compose our message to the Unity of the Adjudicators."

Five minutes later, all four were staring at each other. The officer of the watch had been firm. The Lady Jael had checked out, no fixed time of return —and not only had not returned, but was not answering her comm.

THIRTEEN

Brine was paying more attention to his wrist screen than to possible dangers around him. A bad mistake. A mistake few Rabelaisians would make, even Rabelaisians who had been away from their native ferality for fifteen years.

But Brine had an essential innocence, a naïveté, a bone-deep faith in the basic goodness of humankind. Growing up on Rabelais, fighting his way to a comparatively shielded position had forced a shell around that inward belief. But his years in the freedom and goodness of Mam's world of Maze had slowly stripped that protection away from him. Now he was wary—but not as wary as he should have been.

They had split up, he and Jael and Golden, along with a dozen others worried about the fate of Navigator Estaban Xavier, each trotting rapidly through an assigned sector of the warren that was Pantagruel, trying to find a trace of the missing Navigator. They were going through dangerous territory, but they were protected by spacer arrogance or Navigator black, plus Rabelaisian uninterest and fear of consequences.

But somebody wasn't uninterested in the tall spacer with the golden skin and eyes. Somebody was very interested. That somebody spotted Brine, knew him as a possible route to their goal, first.

"Spacer," hissed a low voice.

Brine turned, blinking eyes that felt filled with sand. He had been on his feet for a full day, was swaying with fatigue, his reflexes slowed. For a couple of steconds he didn't see who had hailed him. The double sun was almost completely up over the horizon; there should have been light. But the buildings surrounding this narrow street cut much of it off. This was the fringe of the rookery, that might have been called a slum on other worlds. The rookery, filled with the pettiest of free-contractors, the scum of contracteds.

"Spacer," came again, and Brine saw a slight, fresh-faced youngster, standing in the shadow of a several-story building, beckoning.

A couple of strides, and he was cocking an eyebrow and asking, "What is it?"

A leer, incredibly ancient evil, incongruous on the young baby-fat-rounded face. "You lookin' for something, spacer? I can find most anything for you."

Brine's mouth twisted. "No."

The youth only winked. "You lookin'. I hear. You lookin' for something special."

Brine turned, started away. "Not that you can find for me."

"No." The unknown caught his arm, tugged. "I can find anything. You name it. Contracteds, any kind. C'holders who think spacers are amusing. Joyjuice. Anything."

Brine shook the hand off. "I'm busy. When I'm not, I have my . . . own resources."

"But you're lookin' for something special," he persisted. "I hear everything. I can help."

Brine hesitated. Then: "Maybe you can. Listen, fellow."

"My name is Halvord."

"Halvord. I'm looking for a man."

Hopeful, eyes agleam: "Oh?"

"A particular man. A man I . . . hope to contract business with."

"Oh." Disappointment. "I was hoping"—an up-and-down assessing look —"you liked 'em young."

This was Rabelais, where there was no sin or crime or immorality, so long as contracts were upheld; Brine wasn't shocked. Or surprised, even knowing how far his battered looks were from handsomeness. But he was dressed as a spacer, and everybody knew that spacers carried high-T portable wealth worth several life-contracts. "I said I had my own resources."

Halvord made a face.

"For now, I'm looking for a man I know of. He is not where he is expected, supposed to be. He may be held in defiance of contractual obligations. Those holding him are thus c'breaking, and will have concealed his presence and their own complicity well. But perhaps, if you hear all . . ."

Halvord made a gesture. "C'mon." Nodding into the dimness of his alleyway. "If you're talking c'breaking, maybe you oughtn't to talk out on the street, hey."

Brine nodded, followed. The youngster had a point. If word got around, then those who held the Navigator might be panicked into disposing of the evidence. Permanently.

"I'm looking for a man, a spacer like myself," he said, as they stepped into the dim alley. "A Navigator, he may be dressed in black, if he is dressed at all."

"Navigator? Aren't they the ones you have to be extra careful with?"

"Yes. This one's older than I, but he doesn't look it, hair shiny silver, not old-white but a natural platinum, skin space-treated brown, features— *annnnwh!*"

That should have been the end of it. The abductor sneaked behind the stocky, gray-haired man, clapped a cloth impregnated with a spacer knockout drug over his nose and mouth, and should have been able to catch a helpless falling body and drag it off.

Unfortunately for his attackers, nobody told Brine this scenario. The instinct when startled is to take a deep breath. The fumes of the liquid would have done the rest. But Brine had been a guard from childhood, and had spent the last fifteen years absorbing advanced defense training. When startled, he froze, held his breath—and exploded into a fighting fury.

In the first second he had bucked off his attacker and sent him smashing against a crumbling mud-brick wall. The man scrambled to his feet and threw himself on his larger opponent. Meanwhile the youngster had grabbed the cloth and was trying to clamp it back over Brine's face. A sharp elbow in the stomach discouraged him, while Brine laughed, a chest-reverberating chuckle of sheer joy. "Two on one," he caroled, almost grateful for the pure physical combat. "Have at you!" He dived onto the man half back on his feet, and the two barreled out into the street.

They rolled over and over, cannoning onto passersby. Women were screaming, someone was bellowing, "C'breaking, c'breaking!"

The youngster who had lured Brine into the alley had gotten back to his feet, gasping, furious on his own account, and had run behind them, a rock in his hand, waiting for the opportunity to settle his own score, orders forgotten.

Despite a split lip where a blow had landed, Brine's gleeful grin showed big square teeth. His eyes sparkled, he was returning blows with enthusiasm. He was a very physical person who had had far too little exercise lately.

Half a kilometer away from where Brine was beginning to enjoy himself, the golden man who was the heart of this abduction attempt spat out the vilest curse he knew, turned abruptly and started running.

A little farther away in a different direction, the Navigator Lady Jael slammed her fingers against her comm and bit out a curt message, as she, too, began to run.

The russet-haired, desperate guard captain temporarily—he hoped!—contracted to Emerald Oriflamme had quick wits. He was the one who was shouting "C'breaking!" It was enough to make most of the spectators disappear between one eye-blink and the next. When a charge of c'breaking was being flung about, most Rabelaisians preferred to be elsewhere. Instantly.

Brine's opponent went limp, and he sprang to his feet, fists clenched, a broad smile on his lips. "Next," he invited cheerfully.

"C'breaker," the russet-haired guard said firmly. "Come with us quietly, don't add to your c'break—"

Brine could have argued, but he knew when he was outnumbered, in a trap. He leaped toward the guard, his foot coming up in a straight-line kick carefully gauged not to break his opponent's neck but to put him down for the count.

If it landed. The guard dodged, and the fight was on.

It was an odd fight. Had Brine wished to, he could have left a trail of bodies and escaped. But fighting to leave opponents temporarily disabled took more skill and slowed him down that fraction between escape and capture. (And he was, he admitted to himself, a little out of practice. What he didn't want even to consider was that, for these sort of games, past a certain age the reflexes began to slow. But he wasn't that far along. Yet.)

His opponents likewise were fighting carefully. They wanted their prey alive, and minimally damaged. It made it, for a time, an almost even fight. Except that no one man, however skilled, can prevail for long against a dozen opponents. As long as they could hem him in by sheer muscle and numbers, the end was inevitable.

Golden Singh knew exactly when one well-timed blow slammed against Brine's jaw with just the right amount of force. He felt the blow, and the cessation of consciousness, but not the limp collapse that inevitably followed.

"HIIIIIIII—" he shouted, and slammed two opponents aside carelessly, to literally leap over Brine's falling body.

"Jackpot!" gloated the guard captain. Then, for a second, he quailed. The older man had been a formidable opponent, hard to take, as per orders, with little or no damage. The younger one . . .

He stood, feet straddling the limp body, tossing the mane of hair gilded by the rising suns, hands in an unfamiliar defensive posture—and he laughed. Not Brine's wry chuckle but a youthful peal of sheer animal joy. A young leopard, sleek and deadly. A golden god.

The guard captain decided to try the easy way first. "C'breaking," he said. "This man has been caught c'breaking, and if you assist him you, too, will be guilty."

"Liar." Golden smiled with no amiability whatsoever. "If there is c'breaking involved, it is yours. But if you wish to tell your tale to an Adjudicator, I am more than willing."

"You spacers bind yourselves to contracts, too," the guard captain bluffed. Two of his men were closing in from behind.

"We are Navigators' bondeds, the both of us." Golden told the part-truth with a grin. "Protected by Navigator contracts, which take—"

The guard captain flicked his gaze about. No one in sight but his men. "Take him!"

"HIIIIIIIIIII—" Golden spun around on one foot, the other foot and his hands lashing out. The faster-reflexed of his would-be abductors saved themselves by jumping back. The rest went down like so many dominos flicked by a careless finger.

The guard captain blinked. The older man had taken out three of his men in minutes; the younger had halved his force in seconds. But if he didn't bring back what his new mistress wanted . . . "Take him," he shouted, and dived toward the man who couldn't be simply killed. The survivors of his squad threw themselves onto the writhing melee.

Golden jumped again, and the guard captain dodged backward. While he was recovering, Golden again took his defensive stance over Brine's unmoving body. The squad retreated almost immediately when the captain went back, though several sported new evidences of the speed of Golden's reflexes and the precision of his blows.

"Take him!" the captain gritted, furious.

It was the signal the young man with the rock had been waiting for. He jumped, and though Golden flung up a defending arm, the rock crunched against his skull, just above his left ear. But the arm had done part of its work. He wasn't unconscious, just slightly dazed. In that condition, his training took over. The slighter man took a blow in the solar plexus that raised him up on his toes; as he came down, Golden landed a flush hit to his chin. He kept going down, and slithered into a heap.

Panting, more triumph than need for air, Golden unconsciously repeated his foster-father's joyous challenge: "Next?"

He should have known better. He should have grabbed Brine and charged, using his momentum to break out of the circle. That way, he might have had a chance. But Golden Singh had been a c'holder, a powerful c'holder, not insulated from Rabelais's savagery, but worse, controlling it, above it, powerful beyond imagining by anyone from a more civilized, gentler world. He had learned better than most of his c'holder ways, but that almost omnipotence had been his life for too long, and sometimes, instinctively he forgot his newer lessons and reverted to that former carelessness.

The captain advanced grimly, fists clenched. Golden beat off his attack with ease. But it distracted him for the necessary seconds. He was still laughing when bodies from behind flung him to his knees. Arms held him, thrashing and cursing, helpless long enough for another rag with knockout juice to be pressed against his face. His struggles accelerated from fierce to desperate, but whoever was clamping the rag down was equally desperate. He dropped to his knees, then collapsed totally.

The guard captain held the rag down for a further count of a hundred, before sliding up and flipping his victim over for a quick examination of the small lump near his ear.

"Get the palanquin," he snapped over his shoulder.

"He has courage." Halvord, the youngster who had lured Brine into range, stared down, furtive pity in his eyes despite his own mishandling. If it hadn't been so desperate a struggle—on his part—it would have been a fun fight, the two spacers opponents to admire, to stretch himself to meet.

"She'll like it if he has courage," said another guard with a sneer. Unspoken but obvious: The harder they are to break, the better she likes it.

"Better for him if he hadn't," growled the oldest of the guards, running a hand through the gray-streaked hair on his sweat-soaked forehead.

"Kinder to kill him now," muttered Halvord, putting on his own leather armor, eyelids lowered to hide his pity.

The oldest of the guards simply nodded and settled his helmet again.

The guard captain looked around. The street was deserted, and if there were furtive eyes at any of the windows, they were taking good care to be out of sight.

"Where's the palanquin?" the guard captain demanded impatiently. He had rolled his second victim over, and was busy binding his wrists together behind him.

Jael charged around a corner and skidded to a stop. The street before her was not empty, but the people moving along it were few enough that she could tell in a second's scan that neither the height and flamboyance of Golden Singh nor the stocky solidity of Brine was visible. She glared at the street that had to hold the two men she loved best in the universe. They *had* to be nearby.

The mind-link was nondirectional, but there was a sense of closeness as its sharers moved near each other. The men were close, very close, unconscious or no, and she knew it. Which meant they were in one of the buildings lining the broad street or—

She froze, intelligent gray-green eyes narrowing. There was a c'holder's palanquin swaying toward her, a powerful c'holder judging by its elaborate decoration. If Golden and Brine were inside . . .

The spacer weapon, the 'lyzer, was comforting in its insta-draw sheath on her wrist. All she had to do was flex her fingers in a certain way.

Mouth compressed, apparently engrossed in the readout on her wrist, she studied the palanquin carefully as it grew nearer. Unlike the men, she was not a native of Rabelais, could not read the insignia. But she could describe it later.

Her first plan was simply to play it for the men's safety, to observe, to follow circumspectly. But within seconds, as the palanquin continued its slow way toward her, she discarded it. She was certain without knowing how she knew that the insignia would be no help. It would probably prove false later, whoever it belonged to safe with an alibi, all his or her contracteds equally, demonstrably involved somewhere else. None of them could possibly—

This was a plot, a planned maneuver, and if she didn't get the men out now, she'd never see either of them again. Alive.

She took a step toward the slow-moving palanquin.

What she didn't realize was that not all the guards were immediately surrounding the palanquin, and that she herself was very memorable. The guard captain had gotten a poor look, but he remembered the vibrant woman standing next to the equally memorable—for different reasons—man, very well.

And Jael had, when she didn't know that somebody who had a fair idea of who she was and what she was looking for was observing her, a very expressive face.

Jael eyed the slow-swaying palanquin calculatingly, stepped back as though casually admiring a window box of jewel-toned night-singing plants, their voices dying to low murmurs as the suns rose. Her left hand went to the comm; a quick report and then . . . She snapped it on.

"Don't!" There was a world of imperative command in that single word. Jael's thumb flicked the comm open. She sucked in a breath.

Almost soundless, the comm would carry only garbage: "Obey, or the men die."

Jael measured the distance between herself and the palanquin, the number of armed men surrounding it. Then her thumb moved again. "It's off."

"Good. Turn. Smile."

She turned, the smile that broke across her face genuine enough to fool any but the man with hard blue eyes who had a look of comic surprise spreading over his own features. "Lady Amercy!" Surprise and joy mingled in his loud voice. "Lady Amercy!" He picked her up, boldly whirled her around. Almost a hiss: "Follow my lead!" Loudly: "How marvelous to see you again, after so many years."

"Judas my boy!" Her own joy was as convincing—and as false—as his. She flung her arms around his shoulders, planted a loud kiss on the cheek above the russet beard. "Who would have thought that the sweet child I once knew would have grown into such a"—minutest of hesitations—"man." The glint in her eye turned the statement into heart's-blood insult.

He smiled. He could afford to; he knew when he was the victor. In the short time he had watched her, he had followed her thoughts with almost telepathic accuracy. As long as he had the men, this woman with a fighter's instincts and the courage of a man would obey him. He let her slide down his body, enjoying the contact, until she was standing on her feet again. Then he threaded her fingers through his and tugged. "Come. I have some time contractually free. We can eat, and talk, and laugh."

"And catch up on the years that have made you what you are," she said dryly.

"And you." He used their entwined hands to turn her, until they were facing the direction the palanquin was moving. They would be ahead of it, all the way. "And you," he repeated.

"That would take more time than I believe we will have," she said, smiling up at him, her eyes sparkling in genuine amusement, as she obeyed the command of his hand and fell in beside him, matching her pace to his.

The smile hit him like one of the golden man's kicks in the diaphragm. He stiffened, understanding the phrase "women men die for." She was one of them. His mouth curled, denying his dream in the same second it was born. He was a contracted, always and forever. His eyes narrowed, as he noted what she wore. Black. Distinctive black. *We are both Navigator's bondeds*, the golden man had said. This Navigator? If she was truly a Navigator . . .

She mustn't be seen going into the manse.

But he was instinctively sure that his one chance of controlling her lay in keeping her well away from the men—until he had her truly helpless. "You're shivering, you're not used to our climate. Here." One-handed, a little clumsy, he draped his own cloak around her, carefully covering her betraying garb.

Her gray-green eyes said she knew precisely why he had done it. "Why, thank you, Judas my child-grown-into-something-strange. Your solicitude for my health positively overwhelms me."

"You'd best pray that I'm never the one to be allowed freely to unweapon you, space lady," he said softly, smiling.

"Better men than you have failed at that," she returned, equally soft, equally smiling.

"They were fools if they worried about what you carry, like whatever you are disciplining yourself not to use, in your hand."

She gave him a pure female smile that again made him gasp in air as if he had been kicked. "I could use it on you, my boy, at whim."

"You won't." He was certain. "Because you can't be sure what would happen to them if anything happens to me."

"Too intelligent to be trapped in this cesspool indefinitely," she muttered. Louder: "Fear you not my weapon, which could"—she lied without a flicker —"turn you into tiny particles too small to see, between one breath and the next."

There was a hood on his cloak, and he pulled it up, to hide the distinctive tiger-striped hair. He flicked a finger through that soft mass, so like the patterning on the hide of a local animal, as fierce as the earth tiger, though its actual earth prototype would have been an enlarged cross between rat and rattlesnake.

"You can, but you won't." He was totally certain. A smile, as he brushed a lock of the striped hair off her forehead. "You are a far more dangerous weapon than whatever you carry. Were I ever to disarm you"—he laid a finger across her mouth, the immemorial gesture of silence—"I would remove that tongue of yours before any less potent weapon."

She laughed merrily. "An astute observation, my man. To return the compliment, I suspect that the only way to defang you completely would be to brain-burn you and turn you into those particles I spoke of."

"I'll remember that," he muttered grimly.

"Why, my man"—another small trill of laughter—"you have me on a leash. What fear you?"

He cocked an eyebrow at her and shrugged. Yes, he had her under leash for now, temporarily, of her own choice, because she feared for the men, helpless in his power. But there are some ferals that can never be successfully kept on a leash for longer than a few seconds, a few minutes. She was one of them.

Emerald Oriflamme another.

It was going to be a clash of titans.

At least, once he had her inside the manse she was trotting so willingly toward, the carnage might be confined. Not that *she*'d have any chance at all.

He wondered if she realized how little chance she, any of the three spacers, had.

He looked down, their gazes met.

She knew.

She smiled.

He bit his lip, worrying about his own skin suddenly. She hadn't a chance, but the havoc and destruction the coming struggle would bring . . .

"I always did enjoy a challenge," Jael murmured.

"Lady," he said grimly, "if that's true, then you are going to get your wish to overflowing!"

FOURTEEN

Estaban Xavier had had a long, weary time of it. Most men would have collapsed way before it was over, begged off the council of war, told the secretary to wait for the recollections. But Estaban was not most men; he had strength of both body and will, and he stuck it out to the very end. Then he could rest. He was staggering as he entered the bedroom he had been assigned; he dropped the robe and sandals on the way to the bed and fell into it, asleep before he landed.

The young apprentice who had been assigned to "settle Brother Xavier in" gazed down at the sleeping man for a minute, in sheer admiration and envy. If only he looked half as good . . . Then he sighed, pulled a light cover over the oblivious sleeper, and tiptoed out, though he could have marched out wearing tap-dancing cleats on his shoes for all the difference it would have made.

Estaban's eyes opened and focused instantly, like a jungle cat ever alert.

The woman seated centimeters from his shoulder smiled. "Awake at last, Brother Xavier. Or would you prefer to roll over and sleep some more?"

"Ummm." He sat up, the coverlet sliding down to bunch around his hips. "I greet you, Sister . . . Victory?" She bowed the depilated head, smiling. "Am I needed?" He swung his long legs down. "I can be ready."

She put a hand on his arm. "You needed your sleep, so I waited. But—I believe—you are needed, badly, which is why I am here. However, the matter permits you to refresh yourself first."

He poised, bending over to reach for the nearest sandal. "Not the Guildmaster, then?"

"No. She is . . . pursuing inquiries. But"—she handed him the sandal by her own feet—"it's the girl."

"Brandy?" He reached for the robe, which somebody had picked up and draped over the end of his bed. "She's not tried to run away. She's not a fool."

"No." She paused, tried to choose her words carefully. "She's obedient, more than obedient. I've no fears she'll run away, only—"

"Only?" He cocked a questioning head toward the small refresher, draping his robe over his arm. She nodded.

"I'm not sure I can make you understand. It's sort of an instinct, a premonition, perhaps."

"Go on." He strode into the refresher, leaving the door open.

"I'm from Archimedes III." She tried—unsuccessfully—to tune the mourning out of her voice. "The Navigators' training school was on our sister planet Archimedes II. Both are T-norm satellites of a J-type. So it meant I could—rarely—visit my home. After I matriculated, I got a berth on a liner not leaving for some weeks. I made one last visit to my home." Her face tightened, in remembered pain. "There was a war. It started as a minor thing, between two island archipelagos. But as I was making my way to my parents it exploded, and half the world went up. I was caught in a missile attack and woke up, badly wounded, in a survivors' hospital. We were jammed in, there was little medical care." She took a breath, trying to shut away vivid memories of a dim, crowded room, filled with pain and stench, moans and cursing.

"You are your parents' gift to the universe." His deep voice echoed in the tiny refresher. "You should not lessen that gift by hurting yourself with what is done and cannot be undone."

"I thank you. I would not speak of it, only . . . Listen. I shared my bed with another girl; that was the only way they could manage. I, on heavy care, and she, burned and with a broken leg that needed immobility. We had both lost all we held dear, family, friends, possessions—everything. Except I had the Guild, and she had nothing, literally nothing."

The normal sounds of someone using the 'fresher continued, but she could almost hear him listening, see his ears, his whole attention, focused on her, what she was trying to convey.

"I healed, slowly. Her leg healed. Her burns healed. Only . . ."

"Yes." He walked out of the 'fresher, droplets left by his too-swift passage through the air drier glittering in his thick hair.

"She withered. She lay quietly, did as she was ordered, ate what she was given—and died."

"Of a broken leg?" He frowned, ran his finger down the pressure-sensitive seam of his robe.

"Of a broken soul. Of a broken will. Of"—a breath—"sheer terror?"

"Brandy's not like that."

"She reminds me of that other girl. A quietness. An acceptance. As if she's a child, frightened, ripped away from everything she's known. Tomorrow, the next day, she'll realize what a good thing has happened, but for now, she needs something. I think you're the something." He cocked an eyebrow. "The link between here and what was her home."

"Let's go."

He knew Victory was right as soon as he walked in the door.

It was a pretty room, personalized out of a carry-case, as Navigators had to, but nonetheless quite unique. Obviously, Victory had been worried enough about Brandy to share her own room, instead of simply popping her into a spare, as Estaban had been. He took one comprehensive look around, assessing the personality reflected in the elegant yet comfortable room. One wall boasted a gossamer embroidered scarf stretched across it, all cool sea colors, blues and greens and soft grays. Another was covered with holo pictures, smiling faces. Ribbons, plaques, and certificates finished off a third. The bed sported a cover in matching greens and blues—it looked hand-embroidered, though on a material delicate enough to fold into a small bundle—and the window had matching curtains, a thinner, almost gauzy translucency.

Brandy was sitting in a chair by the table, like a child waiting to be taken to the principal's office. Spine stiffly erect, legs straight, feet lined up, head high, face blank. A soldier snapped at by a general could not have been more at attention.

Estaban exchanged a wry look with Victory and strolled in, radiating casual ease. "Hello, Brandy my child, how do you like your new home?"

She had only to turn her head slightly to be facing him. "Hello, Estaban." Her voice was high and thin, but calm. "They have been treating me very well. I have all I need."

"Your back." He caught her shoulder, twisted her forward so he could see. She obeyed his hand's command, bonelessly, will-lessly. He looked down, frowning. "It looks all right. I was afraid I'd torn open the stripes, handling you so roughly. It was necessary, you understand. There was no hope for either of us, otherwise."

"I understand." Still the high, thin, accepting voice. His mouth jerked. "You did what you thought you had to, Estaban. You didn't hurt me. I'm fine."

"So I see," he said dryly. No flicker in her eyes. Then, with an easy smile: "Sitting and brooding's not the way, Brandy child. Why don't you let me show you around. The Hall will be your new home, until you can be put on a flight to a training school."

"Yes, Estaban." She rose, gracefully. Someone had trained all the awkwardness of adolescence out of her.

He exchanged a glance with Victory over Brandy's head.

"You may be here a while, you know," he said, tucking her little hand in the curve of his elbow and turning to the door. "Few of the liners that stop over here will have a spare cabin. We'll most likely have to claim Navigator's privilege, commandeer a supernumerary berth for you. Small rooms don't bother you, do they, child?"

Victory hesitated, then closed the door behind them instead of following them, rubbing her lip and wondering if she'd done the right thing. Not that she thought Estaban Xavier would ever do anything but what he thought as the best for the child he had rescued; she had gotten his worth in their initial meeting, would have known he had nothing but good in mind even if there hadn't been other Navigators who knew him, or of him, to tell her.

But sometimes a man, for all his good intentions, didn't know what a woman wanted, needed.

"I'll just be a minute." Brandy stood in the doorway where he had left her, while Estaban strode to the chair, dropped in, and began unbuckling the sandals. He inspected his foot and looked up with a wry grin. "They've rubbed a blister. I think I'll just take them off and leave them. These floors are smooth enough, and I'm better off without them."

"Oh. Yes. Whatever you say."

He had one sandal off and was unbuckling the second. "Should have thought to stop off at the slop chest. I need clothes and shoes." A snort. "Wheel knows where my luggage is. The hold of the ship I should still be on, or the bottom of your river."

She just stood, hands at her sides—waiting.

He sighed. Then, with a smile that was an effort: "We'll get you some spare clothing, too. Unless Victory already has."

"No. Just this." She was wearing a loose smock, white piped with black and scarlet, with full sleeves and an open collar, plus matching loose breeches and soft-soled ship-shoes.

"We'll have to get you more and replace it." He stood up decisively. "That's an apprentice's uniform, Sister Victory's or Sister Amelie's, no doubt, and likely has sentimental value."

It didn't seem to need an answer, so she stood, silent, patiently waiting for him to tell her what to do next.

He took her arm, hesitated for the merest instant, then drew her inside the room and shut the door.

"Brandy."

"Yes, Estaban?"

He winced, a little. He had a sudden mental picture of her replying to a client in just that "What do you want? I'll do whatever you want" tone. "Sit down, Brandy child. There's a few things we need to get straight, before we get some clothes and return you to Victory."

"Yes, Estaban." Obediently, she sat in the chair opposite the one he'd just gotten up out of.

"If you say 'Whatever you say' one more time, child . . ." He seated himself right across from her.

"What— Not if you don't want me to."

" 'At's a girl." He caught her hand in both his own. "Look at me."

Her eyes were wide, with all the suffering in the universe in their clear depths. He grimaced.

"Brandy child, you understand why I didn't, couldn't touch you, except in the most casual way, in the brothel?"

"A—" She licked her lips, tried to drop her eyes, but he put one hand under her chin and forced it up. "A little. You said that you couldn't cooperate with your captors, make it any easier for them."

"That's part of it. It didn't matter who you were—I couldn't cooperate. But that's not all of it. Had I taken you, had I shown any evidence of partiality or affection or liking, even the least scrap, it could have been used against both of us. A threat to you to ensure my cooperation. You could have been hurt, badly hurt, much more than that little she did. Whatever happened to Esta, or worse. In front of me, or in my hearing. Had I let even the least hint drop of how I really felt . . ."

The brandy-colored eyes widened. "Estaban."

He tapped the end of her nose. "You're a sweet child, mostly, and I've a fondness for you. But you're young, Brandy, far too young for me, I've been a man longer than you've been alive."

Something he said had broken through her shell. "You're lying!"

He stiffened, drew back. "I don't lie," he said coldly.

"Doing what you did to her. Telling part of the truth to add up to a lie."

"Brandy." His hand tightened on hers instinctively, and she winced. "I'm sorry, child." He released her hand.

She glanced at her hand. "I've known worse," she said, with sad acceptance. "But why don't you admit the truth, Estaban. You won't touch me because I'm a contracted and you're a c'holder."

"You think—"

"That you despise me, because I'm a contracted, a woman whose body isn't her own. I lived in a brothel, but it wouldn't have made any real difference—a brothel, a stable, a c'holder's kitchen, wherever. Work hard during the day and amuse my c'holder or his guests or whoever he points a finger to at night." She made a sad little shrug. "You think we don't know how you feel? Contractors, c'holders, they're people, and we—we're just things. Toys to use and abuse and break and throw away. *Things!*"

"Brandy." Voice throbbing with compassion, he flung his arms around her.

For a second, two, she clung back, her childish arms tight around his breadth. Then she drew away. "You're kind. Not many of them are." Her voice was sad, but accepting. "You don't want to—to make me feel bad, so you say things. But whatever you say doesn't change what is."

"I thought you understood. I could have done nothing else but what I did, in the brothel. I—"

"Not in the brothel. I understood that, all right. Here."

"Go on." Tight, hard voice of command.

"You shoved me away on those two women, and you left me. You got rid of me, quick as you could. You—"

"We had to make plans. You were hysterical, exhausted, you—"

She was sitting, centimeters away, yet an impassable gulf lay between them. "You're here, now," she said simply. "I'm with them."

"Oh, Brandy." He leaned forward, rubbed at the corner of her eye where there wasn't a tear, just a suspicious sparkle. "That was for your good, too."

She didn't say anything, but her eyes did. *So you say.*

"Listen carefully, dear. I'm a grown man, a mature man. I can form relationships and break them, perhaps not easily, but doing myself no damage." His mouth curved. "Being a Navigator makes it hard to form a true, permanent relationship, but it can be done, if you meet the right woman. I haven't yet— But I'm getting away from the point. Which is, I can—and walk away afterward. You can't."

She opened her mouth, and he laid a finger across it. "Don't tell me about clients and the brothel. There's no comparison, nothing like, in those easy-come, easy-go encounters, and a true, lasting, two-way, committed relationship." Loud voices outside, arguing, interrupted him. He waited, until both dispute and clumping footsteps diminuendoed down the corridor.

"If we came together now, Brandy dear, it couldn't be for long. One or the other of us would have to go, probably fairly soon. And you'd be hurt. I don't want that."

She took a breath to protest, and he squeezed her lips together, lightly.

"No. There's no way. I'm a Navigator, Brandy. It means I travel, go from world to world. Even if we left on the same ship, it would only put off the parting. I'd have to go on, you'd stay for training. It takes a long time, training. Years. A separation—"

She laid a hand on his arm. "Anything could happen an hour from now. You could die, I could die. If we both choose, why not enjoy the hour that may be the only one we'll have?"

"I just told you," he said patiently. "You're young, you're vulnerable. I don't want you hurt."

"Your rejecting me hurts me. If you don't want me, I understand. If you say you don't despise me for being a contracted, I'll believe you. But to deny us both, for—for—for—"

"Honor."

"I hurt *now.*"

"Brandy, you haven't had a chance to choose. There are younger men here, handsome young men. There'll be more at the training school."

"The training school is the future. As for the other men here, are they as good as you? As kind, as compassionate, as gentle, as caring? Will they laugh with me instead of at me? Will they blame me for what I couldn't help, didn't choose? Will they—"

"I want you to have your free choice!"

Her smile was the sun sparkling through a rainbow. "That makes it simple. I choose you."

Much, much later, they were lying together in the narrow bunk, she curled against his breadth, asleep but with a smug cat-smile curling her mouth. But Estaban stared into the dimness, puzzled.

"I don't understand," he muttered finally. "I just don't understand."

"What don' you unnerstan', love?" she mumbled.

"You. You didn't. You hadn't— In a brothel, how did you manage—"

"Oh." A luxurious stretch, as she rubbed against his bare chest sleepily. "That. Allus said she was saving me for a special. Powerful c'holder, I thought. All I ever got was the ones who wanted to fondle, or who wanted me to fondle them."

"I see." But he continued to frown.

"Thought you'd be glad. Thought men always liked to be the first."

"Technically, at least," he said dryly, still frowning. "But it . . . changes things."

"You're not angry, are you?" she asked anxiously.

"No, no, child. Go back to sleep."

"Ummm. Love you, 'Taban."

"I'm very close to loving you, too, Brandy," he said, incurably, precisely honest.

"Make it all the way soon," she said confidently, and shifted slightly and started to snore.

But he continued to lie, frowning. That Brandy was a virgin changed everything. Keeping him healthy by giving him a woman, that made sense. Giving him the woman it would hurt least to lose, just in case something happened, *that* made sense. Giving him a young and relatively inexperienced nonvirgin was the obvious choice.

But Brandy was a virgin.

Virginity, even slightly shop-soiled virginity like Brandy's, was worth a lot. Too much to waste.

So why . . . ?

He had a feeling he wouldn't like the why of it when he discovered it.

He was right.

FIFTEEN

Brine groaned his way back to consciousness. His tongue was bigger than his mouth, vilely colored fluorescent spirals were spinning in front of his closed lids, and an army of lead-booted insects were parading around on his skull.

Somewhere, not too far away, a familiar voice was saying wearily, as though repeating what had been said many times before, "I told you, I am a Navigator. These two men are affiliated to the Guild and protected by our contracts. Release us immediately, and nothing more will be said."

A high, sweet, childish giggle answered her. Brine flinched, it pierced his head like knives. "If you prove to be what you claim," the young voice proclaimed, and giggled again. "If you are, you will be returned to the others. But as for these two . . ."

Brine blinked. Dimness was starting to coalesce into—

"I want them. Both of them. The pretty and the ugly. Contrast. They will be mine." In a completely different voice: "You clumsy fool. There!"

Brine struggled to bring his surroundings into focus.

"They are under contract to your Guild. The Guild will release—"

"The Guild will not release them," Jael dared to interrupt.

Instead of being angered, the c'holder—a powerful c'holder, Brine knew, his instincts on red alert—only giggled again. "You must be a Navigator," she said when she was through laughing. "No one else on this world would be so bold."

"Your world has certainly learned to respect the power of the Navigator's Guild," Jael said dryly. Brine instinctively turned toward her voice. She was seated in a carved wooden chair—Brine recognized ryawood, prized among the people of Rabelais for its crisp, musky scent—and, except for a certain dishevelment, seemed all right. It was only when she shifted slightly that he saw that one of her wrists had been attached by a short chain to her ankle. Seated, she would be reasonably comfortable. But she would be able to walk only with difficulty, bent over, and running would be impossible.

Golden was sprawled on the floor not far from her feet. He was naked, and crumpled in such a way that Brine couldn't see if he had been similarly chained. He didn't think so, though. For what the c'holder obviously had in mind, that sort of restraint would be . . . limiting.

"Silliness." The childish c'holder sneered. "Your off-worlder play toys, we can get along very well without them." Brine turned his head slightly. She was lying on a fur-covered lounge, immature body revealed in swaths of sea-wave green threaded with gilt gauze, while a male contracted crouched over her, hands and mouth frantically busy. Brine pitied him. She looked bored, and if she stayed bored, the male would be expected to amuse in many more . . . painful ways than he was at present.

Jael stretched her long, black-clad legs in front of her, realized that the one with the ankle chained would go only so far, and brought it back. "Different your people have had proved to them, long since," she said, in a voice of sweet reason. "Believe you not me, check with your Unity of Adjudicators. They will tell you the importance of the off-worlders, and especially the Navigators' Guild."

"You just want to keep them for yourself." The girl sniffed.

Brine groaned to himself. Despite the torches pouring out clouds of scented smoke all around, he was still having trouble seeing. But there couldn't be that many c'holders of power this young. And she looked like an Oriflamme. Like his memories of the gentle Esme. And since Medee had no children, that meant she could only be Emerald Oriflamme, Esme's daughter.

And—very likely—his.

As selfish and self-centered and vicious a c'holder as ever tormented all contracted in his or her power.

He only hoped that Jael had learned enough about Rabelaisian customs to realize that the worst thing she could possibly do would be to tell Emerald that it was her father lying—he bit his lip; he was, as he had been so often on Rabelais, "the Ugly; the contrast"—helpless and naked at her feet.

"My dear child." Jael put her free hand behind her head and leaned back, smiling faintly. Only a child as protected and pandered to and obeyed instantly as Emerald would have failed to recognize danger on a very short fuse. "My *dear* child, *I* have never had to abduct a man who interested me."

Emerald sat up, eyes narrowed, mouth pursed. "What are you saying?" she said in a dangerous voice.

"It's always hard for a woman to see herself as a man does, isn't it?" Jael said sweetly. "You poor child." Her voice dripped pious solicitude. "Have you always been this way, or is it recent. Perhaps I can help—your makeup, for example. Has no one ever told you that most men dislike kissing a mouth made up like a fair-day clown? And your eye-black is smudged; it must be because no one would dare give such a powerful c'holder a black—"

Emerald leaned forward, breathing loudly through her nose like a bull pawing the earth. "I can have any man I want." She snapped her fingers loudly. "Just like that."

"By holding a contract and punishment over their heads." Jael laughed softly, mockingly. "Most folk would be willing to make love with a spaceslug, be it a choice between that and having the skin flayed off their backs with the whip your folk so enjoy using."

"Men beg for my favors," Emerald hissed.

"You are more attractive than being whipped to death, then, aren't you?" Jael examined her fingernails, and then looked up, awarding the furious child a thin smile. "Now, *I* have had men willing to risk a beating or worse, for me. For a smile. Risking punishment to be with me, not risking punishment if they were not with me, did not please me. There's quite a difference, you know."

Emerald spat.

Jael chuckled. "Never have I had to force a man into my bed, you poor little dear. Of course"—a long, level, assessing look, before Jael laughed again —"I can see why, even if a man I am not."

"Call the guards," Emerald screeched, jumping off her lounge and running for the embroidered pull. "Call the guards. I don't care if you're a Navigator or not!"

Jael laughed again, loudly. "Think you truly that silencing me will make the truth into a lie? Wipe your mother's milk off your mouth, girl, and see the world as it really is. You have not what it takes to attract a man's free choice."

Emerald whirled, her gauzy drapes swirling around her. "I do too!"

Jael only laughed, softly, knowingly.

Emerald stamped her foot, screamed it: *"I do too!"*

Jael only buffed her nails on the collar of her jacket, then looked up with a sly glint in her eye. "Say it loud enough, you might even convince somebody who knows not better. Somebody blind, deaf, and brainless."

"I'll kill—" The doorway drape swished aside, and a squad of guardsmen poured in. "Lady," their leader panted, "where's the danger?"

"Kill her!"

Brine didn't stop to think, he acted instinctively. Jael was threatened, was unable to defend herself. With her hands and legs free, he would have bet on her against any squad of guards, armed or not. As it was . . .

He surged upward, arms out in a protective pose. The guard captain hesitated for a second, sword in hand. The c'holder had ordered kill *her*, not this naked man.

It was all the time Jael needed. "C'breaking!" she shouted in a voice that reverberated in her hearers' eardrums. The guard captain froze, and she went on. "Touch any of the three of us, and it's c'breaking. Agony Square. Protected by contracts we all are."

Emerald stamped her foot again. "I *order* you to kill her!"

"C'breaking," Jael repeated. Then, quickly: "Navigator contracts take precedence."

"Kill her or I'll have you flayed by inches!"

"Lady," The guard captain said coaxingly, "if she is a Navigator, as she claims, then she is speaking truth about the contracts. Navigator contracts take precedence."

Emerald slithered up to stand beside him, her hands stroking his brawny arm. "Who would know?" she cooed.

The man's shallow blue eyes narrowed in thought. Obviously, he cared little for the sanctity of contracts, and a lot for his own advancement, to say nothing of his skin. Wheels turned. He was the head of the squad; the others would obey him.

"You don't listen, sweetie, do you?" Jael stood, a little bent, and leaned on Brine. "Think you we off-worlders trust the goodwill of such as you, when we have the technologies to protect ourselves? A while it may take my friends to triangulate our exact position, but they can *hear* quite adequately while they're doing it. The c'holder is young, perhaps fourteen standards, plain under paint. Estimate I her height at about one hundred sixty centimeters—"

"She's an Oriflamme," Brine interrupted, fearing they would both have their throats slit before she could make an adequate description.

"Thank you, dear. She's an Oriflamme. The guard is—"

"Wearing Oriflamme insignia."

"Wearing Oriflamme insignia, russet hair, a scar like a W over his left nipple—"

"Contracts!" The guard captain swore, putting his blade's point to her windpipe. "Are there two of you with such scars?" Jael asked with a sweet smile. "In which case, finish what you've started. You've merely one chance in two of screaming your lungs out in Agony Square."

"She's bluffing!" Emerald squealed.

"Of course." Jael nodded eagerly. "I'm bluffing."

The guard captain pulled back his sword a fraction, and Brine tensed, ready to make one last desperate try at knocking it out of his hand. Only her hand on him held him back, a *Don't! Let me handle this* as tangible as the bright blade flashing in his eyes.

"Are you?" the guard captain growled.

"You know," Jael said confidingly, "she is rather a spoiled, nasty little piece of filth, is she not? She will spread a lot of misery if she is allowed to keep on, and I considered that. I had rather decided that you people deserve what you get. Possible you made it for her to be the little vileness that she is, why should I interfere? But her for me, to say nothing of my men? Not fair. Gold for spit. And you." Her lip curled. "You don't really count. You are a nothing.

You let her be what she is, instead of turning her over your knee and spanking some sense into that rotten, spoiled little brain of hers." She frowned. "She does have a br—"

"*KILL HER!*"

"My, she does have a one-track mouth, does she not? A brain? I doubt it. Anyway, not worth it, she and you both. Not for my little finger breaking. So, for all our sakes, you better believe me. Yours the proof will be within stours, one way or the other. But if willing you are to take the risk . . ." She shrugged. "Go ahead."

"Lady C'holder," he said hoarsely. "That much makes sense. Wait and be sure."

"Think how much fun you can have with me"—Jael smiled—"*if* I am lying."

The guard captain pulled his sword back and sheathed it. "Lady, a few hours isn't much. And Agony Square—"

"She just wants to delay, so her friends can come and take her away."

"I said she had no brain," Jael told the guard captain. "Sweetie." To Emerald, in the voice one used to a very young—and very slow—child: "If I'm lying, how can my friends be coming to rescue me?"

Emerald's lip came out in a pout, then she too smiled, the smile of an ancient, evil dwarf. "All right. You later. Him." She pointed to Brine. "Now."

"No." Brine folded his hands over his chest.

Emerald giggled. "You think you have any choice." A threat.

Brine put his arm around Jael's shoulder. "Yes," he said simply.

"I told you all three of us were under Guild contract," Jael said. "Have you a brain, you obviously never used it. All three of us are protected." Slyly: "See if you can make him come to you willingly." A chuckle. "Now, that would amuse me."

Emerald stuck her lip out. "He's ugly. I don't want him," she whined.

Jael cocked an eyebrow at her. "You will learn, eventually. Beautiful Brine is where it counts."

Emerald flicked a glance downward. "Humph," she sneered.

Jael only laughed. "Inside, where it counts, child. And even outside—it is quality, not quantity, that matters." She gave the guard captain a slow, female assessment, which made him flush until his face was almost the color of his russet hair. "Trainable to acceptability," Jael finally decided. "Possibly."

He growled, and took a step toward her.

"Like you not the heat, stay away from the hearth," Jael told him coolly. Brine grinned, and leaned over to kiss her ear lightly, and she shivered with remembered pleasure, her free hand stroking up into the gray mane.

Emerald hissed in a breath through her nostrils, and then, plastering on a wide smile that wouldn't have fooled a two-year-old, slithered up to Brine and gazed up at him, eyes fluttering. "I could make it lots of fun for you," she promised in a voice that tried to be husky.

Brine looked down at her, face solemn, but Jael, who knew him well, knew he was laughing inside, even if the slight tremor of his shoulders wouldn't have told her. "Jael and I," he said, voice as solemn as his face, "go back a long way."

She rubbed up against him slowly, fingers playing with his neck and ears. "Then you know all about her. She's old and boring. I could show you"—her voice dropped even lower—"endless delights."

"You're prettier than Jael thinks," he said musingly. Over his shoulder, she stuck out her tongue.

"And I know"—she was still playing the vamp, her fingers stroking, and caressing—"how to make a man cry out for more."

"I'm sure you know how to make a man cry out," Brine agreed. Some of Jael's astringency had rubbed off on him in their years of association.

"Let me prove it to you," she purred.

Jael raised an eyebrow skyward, and caught the gaze of the guard captain, studiously stolid.

"If it was just a question of you and me . . ." Brine let it trail off.

"It is!" Triumphant.

"I know what I'd do. But not while we're all three prisoners."

"Perhaps there'll come a time"—her fingers played with the thick mat of hair on his bare chest—"when there's just you . . . and me. . . ."

"I do look forward to that!" Brine couldn't help saying. There was a sardonic glint in the guard captain's eye. He understood Brine exactly, even if Emerald was preening like a cat with yellow feathers on her chops.

"You know"—Jael stepped slightly away from Brine—"I can think of a way we can all amuse ourselves, without c'breaking, while we wait and see if I am telling the truth or not."

"You." Emerald pouted and turned away.

"If you want to be bored . . ." To the guard captain: "Hunger and thirst are damaging to the health. Is that c'breaking, too?"

He looked down at Golden, still lying unconscious, and frowned.

"Guarantee I can that you will not be punished for what you did in ignorance and under orders. But hungry I am."

"Don't give them a thing." Emerald had gotten back on the couch and was playing with the male contracted, who was sweating, eyes pleading but smothering his moans by biting his teeth hard on his lip.

Jael looked at what Emerald was doing, frowned. Then she shrugged, sat down. "It is only a few hours, anyway."

The guard captain wasn't stupid. "Lady," he appealed, turning Jael's statement around, "it's only a few hours."

"Oh, all right." A giggle, as the contracted writhed under her cruel fingers, unable to contain his moans. "Feeding them now will make them last longer, later. Take them away, Guard Captain. Take care of them—carefully. Don't bring them back until . . ." Brine heaved a sigh of relief.

But Jael wasn't through. "You must like being bored," she said sweetly, as two of the men picked up Golden's limp body.

"You," said the guard captain softly, "must like dancing on the sword's edge."

Jael looked up. She was seated beside a narrow cot, wiping Golden's forehead patiently with a damp cloth. Brine, who had been pacing up and down, had stopped in mid-stride when the door opened.

"Sometimes we have very little choice." Jael dipped her rag into the bowl on the table near her, and squeezed it out, and reapplied it.

"Yes" was all the guard captain said, but she looked up and nodded.

Brine had his own worries. "He's been unconscious for hours," he said shortly. "It's dangerous. Can you get any kind of medical aid for him?"

The guard captain shrugged. "I would if I could. At this point . . ." He shrugged again.

"Nasty dilemma," Jael said coolly. "Does he die, when medical aid could have saved him, in great trouble you are. But—"

He finished it. "If you have been lying, and getting medical aid reveals that you are here—"

Jael laughed, not humorously. "Think you that I am lying?"

"That Navigators' contracts have precedence? I know you are not. That your people know *who* has you, if not *where* yet? I think you are not."

She looked back to what she was doing, but said, "Interesting. What leads you to that conclusion, Guard Captain?"

"My name is Petrik. You are a handsome woman, and I would like to hear my name on your lips. As to what leads me to that conclusion: You are intelligent."

Jael exchanged a look with Brine. "So . . . Petrik?"

"You are intelligent," he repeated. "You must know that this is a cruel world to those not protected by contracts. Or to those to whom that protection is not—cannot be—applied."

Again, Jael spoke to Brine. "Petrik does not lack for intelligence himself. But there are accidents, bad luck, eh, Petrik. Even an intelligent person can . . . stumble."

He nodded, then realized that she couldn't see him. "Yes, but an intelligent person prepares in advance for as many contingencies as possible. You off-worlders do have many devices which seem to us as magic. I believe in one that makes it possible for those somewhere else to hear what we say. I broke all that I found of yours I did not understand. But"—a grim smile— "how long before we can expect someone to come looking for you?"

Jael looked up, looked at Brine, who shrugged, pursed his lips, then spoke. "At least six more stours—a quarter of a day maybe. Plus how long to go to the Adjudicators, and find out where the Lady Oriflamme is likely to be."

"So long."

"He's that far away."

A frown. "Not at the—what do you call it?—Guildhall."

"No. But, Petrik, does anything bad happen to any of us, you had best pray to whatever forces you believe in that your own people take care of you before Rowan gets his hands on you." She laughed suddenly, a girl's carefree young laugh. "For that matter—Brine, love, you've never met Spyro, have you? Were it me, I would pray Rowan before Spyro."

Petrik was chewing his lip. "A quarter of a day. I don't think she'll have the patience."

Jael shrugged. It was Brine who said, "She better had. You don't think it's just the three of us, and you two, at stake? Set off the Navigators' Guild, Petrik, and blood will run free in the streets before it's all over."

Petrik didn't want to believe, it was obvious by the way he was chewing his lip, but there had been such a note of unquestioning sincerity in Brine's voice. Then Petrik shook himself. "There may be blood before that. I almost forgot. She sent me to get you."

"Golden shouldn't be moved," Jael said grimly.

"Not him. Just you."

"Oh." Brine glanced down at the unconscious man. "He needs care."

"You can do it," Petrik informed him. "I didn't mean you two, I meant just her."

Brine didn't stop to think about it. "No."

"Brine." She rose, laid a hand on his arm. A thousand memories passed between them in a second.

"I don't like it," he said, but it was acquiescence.

"I am the safest of us three."

"Tell me that," he responded, "when that nasty little protégée of Medee Oriflamme is rubbing salt into where your skin used to be."

Jael cocked an eyebrow. "Think you she would be that trite?"

"She's stupid enough to be dangerous."

"Don't worry."

He muttered something under his breath, and she leaned over to kiss his ear.

"Wait." Petrik knelt, unfastened the chain at her ankle. "Hold on to this. We'll replace it just before we go to see her. We need to make up time."

"Take me to your c'holder."

"Don't worry." Brine addressed the closed door after they left sardonically. "Don't worry."

Jael and that little mistress of mayhem, Emerald Oriflamme. Not that he wouldn't have backed Jael under most any circumstances, but this time . . .

An outsider could never know Rabelais like a native. He bit his lip and turned back to Golden. It wasn't as if there was anything he could *do*.

SIXTEEN

She was a woman of perhaps forty, with a hundred years of hard living carved in her face, and a thousand years of cynicism glittering in her eyes. Her profession was blazoned from top to toe, froth of blood-crimson hair, painted face, body determinedly voluptuous, clink of chains, and strategic slits that opened as she moved to display her wares.

She was also Brandy's mother.

The nasty, triumphant laugh was just as he remembered it; the rest of her, no better than he'd imagined. She saw his lip curling, and she laughed again.

The Navigators stared, puzzled, at her: She should have been frightened, and she wasn't. Her surety, like her viciousness, shimmered around her like some evil aura.

Aristide the Adjudicator, presiding, saw it, too, and hid a frown behind his smooth, professional face. If the Navigators weren't satisfied, they would blacklist Rabelais, as they had threatened to do before. And Rabelais couldn't survive blacklisting. If anything, thanks to the Sandman and his disciples, their situation was worse than it had been.

At least, small mercies, this was a private adjudication; he had been able to close it to all not directly connected. Not the Navigators, of course; the front rows were black with them. And not the powerful c'holders or their representatives, who might have an interest in any adjudication which involved high-level contracting.

The Adjudicator glanced down at the Guildmaster. "Are any more of your people expected, honored Guildmaster?" he asked.

"No." The Guildmaster didn't use a title of honor, the Adjudicator noted, and sighed inwardly.

"Does anyone know of a contractor or contract-holder whose contracts are involved with the adjudication, who is not yet present?" He raised his voice slightly.

There was a murmur of dissent, and no one stood up to mention the name of someone expected who had not yet appeared.

"Something to be said for low-T societies, after all," drawled a male voice from the second row. "On a civilized world, a trial might be delayed months, if not years."

"Hush!" hissed a female voice. "This isn't a trial."

"A rose by any other name . . ."

The Adjudicator tapped the tiny gong suspended just to his left. Despite its small size, it had a surprisingly brazen clangor, echoing and reverberating and demanding silence.

As the echoes died away, the Adjudicator spoke. "The arguments for this private adjudication are now open. Navigator Lady Guildmaster, would you care to state the opening position of the Navigators' Guild, holders of numerous contracts with various independent c'holders and contractors of Rabelais?"

The Guildmaster stood up. "A Navigator has been savaged away," she said bluntly. "He has been imprisoned, held for a time in solitary, his possessions taken, his life and health threatened, until he managed to free himself. All those are contravened by the contracts signed between the Guild and your people. That woman there"—she pointed—"is responsible." She sat down.

The Adjudicator nodded. In some adjudications, accusers and defenders might go on at great length, citing obscure precedents, arguing over the interpretation of a comma, a single word. The Guildmaster had a major act of c'breaking to argue with; she stated it, and that was all that was needed. "Noted and recorded?" he asked.

"Noted and recorded," agreed the young clerk sitting just below him.

"Is that your complete statement, honored Guildmaster?"

"Yes."

"Free-contractor"—his voice was cold as he turned to the woman—"have you an opening position to establish, to counter the accusations made by the honored Guildmaster of the Navigators?"

"Yes." She had been standing; now she took a step toward him, the hem of her multiply slit skirt scraping on the flagstone floor like the hissing of a snake. "Yes, I do." She smiled, a showing of teeth. "I have only fulfilled my contractual obligations. I have abrogated not a jot or a tittle of anyone else's contracts. All that I have done has been contractually justified."

The Adjudicator took a deep breath, leaned forward. "That is your opening position?" he asked, incredulous. Then: "Do you wish to clarify, or add anything?"

"No." She didn't address him by title, either—a very bad sign.

He sighed. "Noted and recorded?"

"Yes, honored Adjudicator. Noted and recorded."

The next few minutes only revealed what everyone already knew, anyway. Estaban was the Navigators' main witness. He sat in the truth chair, immaculate in his Navigator's black, and described his adventures, succinctly, the screen behind him remaining a clear sapphire blue the whole time.

When Estaban was through, the Adjudicator asked a few questions, ostensibly to clarify what he had said, but mostly to satisfy his own curiosity. In

Estaban's position, there was a lot he would have done differently. Though he admitted to himself he would never have come up with such a deliciously subtle ploy to escape. "You say you were held for three days, alone in your cell. How can you know it was three days? Time might well drag in such a situation."

"Like many Navigators, I have an excellent, precise time sense. Would you like me to demonstrate it?"

"No, the screen shows that you speak truth."

"The screen"—Estaban was as precise as usual—"shows only what I believe is the truth. However"—a thin smile—"it can be proven by outside evidence that I was imprisoned for almost eight days. I believed myself to be alone for three days, Brandy was in my original cell with me for just over a day, and we occupied the larger suite for about three and a half days. It adds up. My internal estimate of the time may not be totally accurate, but it cannot be too inaccurate either. Within a few stours of three local days, one way or the other."

A little later: "You say that, in all the time you were imprisoned, you did not touch the contracted girl called Brandy, who was with you."

"No." Estaban answered the question as asked. "I touched her many times, in many ways. I hugged her and comforted her when she was crying, I held her away by force when she would have flung herself upon me, I caught her when she tripped and would have fallen, I escorted her by tucking her hand in the crook of my elbow, I moved her around when we were setting up the battle. I touched her many times. But I never, ever, touched her sexually, a lascivious fondle or caress, never did I use her sexually, with my hands or any other part of my body. I did kiss her, more than once, but avuncularly, as a man might kiss his own daughter, or the daughter of his brothers or sisters."

The Adjudicator was staring at both Estaban and the screen that remained an unvarying blue behind him. He sighed, shaking his head. "You were naked, she essentially so. It must have been . . . very difficult."

Estaban laughed. "She is very beautiful. It was not easy to refrain."

"Few men could have," the Adjudicator said honestly.

Estaban shrugged. "What is important is seldom easy. The more important, the more likely it is to be very difficult."

"Why refrain, when you had so many other difficulties to contend with?"

"Partly my own honor. On my world, we do not use children; honor prevents it, if family and law do not. She should be in a schoolroom learning her numbers, not entertaining one client after another." He held up a hand, as the Adjudicator started to protest. "I know, on your world it is different. A contracted may be used in any way her contract-holder sees fit, at any age. I do not denigrate your customs; they are yours and will remain yours as long as the majority of your people will it. This is the right of any free people, though the minority may be hurt in the course of it. My opinions remain my own, and while I am on your world, I have striven not to go against your customs. Which does not mean that I would acquiesce willingly in being imprisoned, of course. Or that if one of your people attacked me, that I would not defend myself first, and straighten out reason and contractual obligations, or whatever, later." A smile. "We Navigators learn to do this. We visit so many worlds, you understand, and each has its own 'proper' way of living, acting, reacting to other people."

"I see. It was your own world's contracts—customs, as you call them—that stopped you from using the contracted."

"No, not really. Circumstances must be taken into account. She wasn't that young, and she was pathetically eager." His lip curled. "Though it was painfully obvious that she was eager to avoid the punishment for failing to seduce me, not me myself. Still, I had no wish for her to be punished unnecessarily. I would have taken her, to prevent her being whipped again, except for one thing."

"Which was?"

"That my captors wanted it so badly. I had to fight them, in every way I could devise. I tried to protect Brandy as much as I could, in every way short of taking her, which my captors so ardently desired." He spread out his hands to the Adjudicator. "Look at it from my view. I know little of the intricacies of your world. But I know war, and strategy, and tactics, and methods of making a man do what another wills. For all I knew, once I had taken poor Brandy, she'd be tortured in front of my helpless eyes, to make me—I couldn't guess. Sign a contract of somewhat, that perhaps I would have died before signing of my own will. I told her, and it was the simple truth, that where my honor was involved, I would watch her being tortured to death and not stop it. But that doesn't mean I wanted to risk it happening."

"I see."

"On my world, on most worlds, men protect their women." He intercepted a glare from Victory. "And vice versa, of course. Bondings are important. Not just sexual, but friendship, loyalty. They make a strong tie, especially on a person who reveres honor."

"But without contracts?" The Adjudicator was struggling with the alien— to him—concepts. "Here, none of that would be of any import, without contracts. Did it not occur to you that that's how you think, but not how our people would think?"

Estaban laid a finger aside his nose, an ancient, knowing gesture. "Even one of your people with much contact with spacers? Who might be looking for a lever to use on a spacer?"

The Adjudicator nodded. "A point." He went on to other questions, most of them simply making this or that point clearer, except once. "How could you be sure your cry of fire would get help, someone to unlock the door, in time? It would not have taken long for your companion to realize that there was no fire. And once she did, since you had told her nothing, she might not realize to play along with the hoax."

Estaban shrugged, then grinned. "It was a risk. But I was fairly sure the room was monitored, at least aurally, if not visually. That might have been a risk, but smoke won't show on a small screen, unless there's clouds of it. I didn't think they'd wait; they'd send somebody to put out the fire while it was small."

After Estaban, several of the other Navigators witnessed briefly, mostly that he had charged into the Guildhall naked, panting, with Brandy in his arms.

A minor c'holder, much amused, witnessed to strolling out of a favored sweet-singer's house after a recital, and seeing streams of people screaming "Fire!" streaming past him.

A c'holder owner of a house of pleasure likewise witnessed, growling.

Brandy's mother, like Estaban, chose the truth machine. She sat down in the wired chair easily, confidently, and the Guildmaster chewed her lip. Either she was totally insane or there was something she knew that no one else did. She exchanged a glance with the Adjudicator, who cocked a judicial eyebrow.

The Guildmaster pursed her lips. If that woman thought to use her world's peculiarities to wriggle out of kidnapping and Wheel-only-knew-what, then she was either in for a shock, or . . .

The Adjudicator followed the play of expression on her face and winced. If the woman did have a contractual out, then the Navigators were going to insist—

He focused back on the woman, arranging herself so that the slits in her clothing best showed her. "Now, madam contractor, you averred earlier that you have done nothing not contractually confirmed. Yet the contracts the Navigators' Guild have with major c'holders protect their persons implicitly and explicitly. How do you reconcile—"

"I would like to have called and recorded into the record a sealed contract."

He reared back, then subsided. "You aver that you are one of the signatories, that you have the right to break the seal?"

"I do." The screen remained blue.

"Identify it and it will be sent for," he said grimly.

The name of "House of Pleasure Contractor registered as Lachesis" meant nothing to Estaban, but the other name did. He jumped slightly, surprise widening his eyes. The Adjudicator noticed.

"Navigator Xavier, is something wrong?"

But Estaban had already recovered. "Not wrong, perhaps," he answered calmly. "But that man is the captain who connived at my shanghaiing."

"A contract that breaks other contracts is no true contract," the Adjudicator said, more to himself than his audience.

Brandy's mother—Lachesis—smiled.

SEVENTEEN

"Take off your clothes!"

Jael stood in the doorway to the most decadent room she'd ever seen, and her experience in the love-marts had shown her decadence aplenty. Her gray-green eyes roved around, as her lips slowly curved up in a sardonic, utterly Jael grin.

Crimson velvet and passion-pink satin, ebony furs and flesh-toned cushions in suggestive shapes; the soft, alluring plaint of flutes counterpointed with the slow, seductive murmurs of sweet-string sitars; and over all, almost to the choking point, the smell of musk. Jael sniffed and gazed about, at lascivious statues and salaciously embroidered hangings, at a pool dotted with pink jasmine and peopled with slick, languid swimmers, at—

"That position"—Jael pointed to a statue—"is impossible. Unless both participants are hermaphrodites. In which case it is merely difficult and unrewarding."

"I said"—petulantly—*"take off your clothes."*

Jael stared at what was obviously meant to be the pièce de résistance in this harem/bordello garden of delights: Emerald Oriflamme. The girl was posed, naked except for a single strip of gossamer silver lace, running diagonally from one thin thigh to the opposite shoulder. A naked male was lovingly brushing out the ash-brown hair, a second was polishing already gleaming pink toenails, while a third massaged a white cream—probably musk, too, but who could tell in this hothouse, Jael muttered to herself—into soft, pale skin.

"Are you addressing me, girl?" Jael asked, in bored tones.

Emerald sat up, forgetting her pose as seductress, and the lace gathered in her lap. "I'm C'Holder Oriflamme to *you*, contractless slime. If you can't remember, perhaps a spike through your tongue would serve to remind you."

Jael turned to Petrik, who had entered behind her. "Are c'holders immune to the normal punishment for c'breaking?" she asked, in interested tones.

"No, Lady Jael," he answered.

"Don't you call her Lady again, you 'tracted," Emerald screeched.

"Yes, Lady C'holder. I will remember," he said servilely. But his eyes, fixed on Jael, said plainly who he thought the lady and who the slime. He bowed low to Emerald. "If you would excuse me, m'lady, I do have other duties."

She sniffed, her short attention span now totally on him. "More important than obeying my orders?" she asked sweetly.

"My prime contractual duties," he reminded, "are to your safety. For many hours I have not checked the guards while serving you directly. If you order me, I will continue to stay. But guards, even the best, tend to slacken if a superior's eye is not on them occasionally." He dropped to his knees. "Punish me, if you will, for desiring to do my contractual duty, to serve you, to make you safe. But the greatest punishment will be mine, being away from you even a moment." He grabbed what was nearest, a dangling hand, and covered it with kisses.

"Oh, pooh-pooh." Emerald pulled her hand away with a giggle. "When you return, you will prove how much you missed me."

"You smiled. You smiled at me. M'lady." He dropped flat, squirmed forward on his belly to lay his russet head under her dangling foot. "M'lady, I am like to die of sheer happiness."

Jael rolled her eyes skyward, but Emerald was too accustomed to servile flattery to take it as anything else. "Hurry back," she said coyly, "and I just might—"

"M'lady." He twisted his head up to rub his cheek against her instep. "A look, a smile . . ."

Another giggle. "We shall see."

"Please."

"You get boring, Guard Captain. I said, we shall see."

"Thank you. Thank you. And the sooner I go, the sooner I can return."

"Oh yes, go, if you must. Until then . . ." Her glance flickered around; she was pondering her next amusement. Petrik started slithering backward, never taking his gaze off her, keeping his entire body close to the floor. Suddenly she screeched in pain; Petrik froze, but her next words relieved him of responsibility, and he disappeared through the draped door.

"You clumsy fool! You pinched me with your nail. Klathur! Klathur!"

There were at least a dozen male figures, armed, lining the walls. One of them stepped forward. "At your command, m'lady." Jael saw that not only was he armed, but had a whip curled around his waist, and other odd tools attached to a belt. Other than that thick, brass-studded belt, which stretched from his lower chest to his hips, he was naked, his thighs as big around as Jael's hips, the rest of him proportionate, and every bit of it solid muscle, from the way he moved.

"His nail pinched me, Klathur," Emerald whined.

"You wish me to punish him, m'lady?"

"Yes, that's your contractual duty, isn't it. Make him scream, loudly, Klathur."

"Yes, lady. Have you a preference?" He picked up the luckless contracted who had been rubbing in the oil; the young man was fair-sized himself, but he dangled like a rag doll in the massive Klathur's hand.

"No. Something new. I'm bored, Klathur."

"Yes, lady." Still holding the man by one hand—his handsome face terrified—Klathur reached down to his belt. "Since he pinched you with his nails, lady, it might be amusing and ironic to prevent him from doing so again. Yet, since he is a rubber, losing his nails—"

"Losing his nails?" Emerald sat up to see.

"Quite amusingly painful." He had shifted his grip so that the man's thumb was isolated, sticking out from Klathur's fist. He brought up a tool in his other hand, got a good grip, and pulled.

The man writhed in that implacable grip like a beheaded chicken, screaming like an air-raid siren.

Emerald laughed delightedly, clapping her hands.

Klathur shifted his grip, ignoring the blood spewing from the denailed thumb and his victim's struggles. He got a grip on the second finger, realized his tool was slippery, and wiped it casually against his own hairy-pelted thigh. He put the tool on the imprisoned finger—then took it off.

"No, now, hurt him now!"

"He's in too much pain from the first one, mistress. Wait a little, until he's ready to feel."

The screams gradually diminished in intensity. When they had diminuendoed into helpless sobbing, Klathur again affixed his tool onto the man's nail.

"Noooooo! Please, *no—pleeeeee—*"

"Lady?"

"Yes!" She leaned forward, mouth open in anticipation, eyes sparkling like those of a child spotting a well-presented birthday table.

"AIIIIIIIIII!"

Klathur held his bloody trophy aloft, while the man, still suspended from his massive fist, thrashed and screamed.

"Again! Again!"

"As you wish, m'lady. But I warn you, he's in so much pain, he'll hardly feel any more. If you save him, by tomorrow these fingers will merely ache."

She pouted. "Oh all right." Her dissatisfied gaze flicked around. All the inhabitants in the room desperately tried to look busy, anything to avoid catching that spoiled, vicious gaze.

Except Jael. She stood where she had stopped when she first entered, her mouth curled in contempt. The unfortunate being punished had been allowed to slump into a quivering, sobbing ball, his mutilated hand clutched to his belly. She had taken one step toward them when the massive Klathur had first picked up his victim, but she had restrained herself. No one in this room except—possibly—herself had any protection from Emerald's whim, and anything she did to try to help would only make matters worse—if that was possible, and she suspected it was. So she stayed where she was, the only evidence of her reactions that sardonic, disgusted expression.

Which even a naïf like Emerald couldn't mistake.

"You." She pointed to Jael. "I told you to take off your clothes. You dared disobey me." On a high, vicious note: *"Klathur!"*

"Never made you clear that you meant me." Jael was as calm as if death and destruction weren't rumbling toward her, i.e., the massive Klathur. "You poor deluded infant, imagine you really that taking my clothes off will make me less than I am? *Klathur!"* The force of command in the last word, low-voiced but firm, stopped him, poised on the balls of his feet, towering over her, like an avalanche ready to fall.

"Punish her, Klathur!" Emerald screeched, while Jael cut through with the calm but firm threat she had already used to protect herself.

"C'breaking, Klathur. Touch me, even under contractual orders, and it's c'breaking. A Navigator I am, and Navigators' contracts have precedence over native ones."

It didn't take her as long to convince Klathur as it had before, mainly because half the guards present had been in the lounge when Jael had argued her way out of it the first time.

Jael, knowing she'd won, temporarily, and recognizing the storm clouds behind the sullen pout of the spoiled young face of her adversary, strolled leisurely over and plunked herself comfortably on Emerald's lounge, not far from where the unfortunate contracted had been kneeling. "You know, infant," she informed, her outside, unchained, leg swinging idly, "whether or not I wanted to take my clothes off, I would find the commission near impossible."

"You'd find it even more impossible if your arms and legs were chopped off," Emerald muttered, her mouth pouting mutinously.

"Dear, dear." Jael yawned. "How boringly your mind works. Intend you the giant Klathur to start with my fingernails and work his way up? If I scream loudly enough, will that make Agony Square worth it, for both of you? As well as whatever punishments the Adjudicators demand for all who watched and did naught to stop such blatant c'breaking."

Emerald gave her a sullen glare. "You're lying. You're not a Navigator, you're not contracted or c'holder or anything. I can order Klathur to do what I choose."

Jael yawned again. "You are slow, sweetie. Once already have we been through this. I thought you did not like being bored."

"I won't be bored watching Klathur work you over," she snapped.

"I would be. He is almost as remarkable for his lack of imagination as you are."

An angry titter. "You won't be bored, I promise you."

"Beg to differ," Jael said. "Worked on by experts I have been. I was going to suggest a more amusing way to pass the time than your dull ideas, but you have no brain to appreciate subtlety, so wasting my breath I would be."

"I can be twice as subtle as you." A snarl. "Take off your clothes."

"You are *boringly* dull, are you not." Jael tapped her finger against the apple-round and red cheeks. "Look you, bone-brain, in the first place, you have me so chained up I could not take my clothes off if I wanted. While it is a matter of sublime indifference whether I am clothed or no, I have no intention of strangling myself to provide you with amusement at my helpless struggle to do what cannot be done until and unless you have my chains taken off."

"When the desert freezes over," Emerald snapped.

"I thought not. You are a bone-brain, but that stupid you are not. Are you not even the slightest bit interested in *amusing* ways to pass the time? I thought that was why you had me brought here."

"No. I want you to prove how men adore you. Seduce one of my con-tracted."

"Which one?" Jael asked, mildly interested.

"They're all contracted." Emerald sniffed.

"Yes, dear, but some of them are attractive, and some are not. I see no point in wasting my time with some hopeless wretch incapable of providing me with sufficient pleasure to make it worth it."

A sneer. "You're just saying that to wriggle out of it."

"Oh no, dear. You are bound to have at least one male around here who is minimally acceptable. I am just establishing the ground rules, that he is my choice and not yours." A sly smile. "Surely you cannot begrudge me a paltry mere one, from all your many."

"Oh well." Emerald lay back down, and the contracted immediately started brushing her hair slowly. "All right. There's plenty here to choose from. Pick one and let's see if you were just boasting."

"All right." Jael was off the lounge and ambling over to Klathur, the nearest male except the two slaves kneeling at the head and foot of the couch, working on Emerald. "Klathur, now—a marvelous example of mus-cle." She started to go around, as though to examine him from all sides, and then stopped, her body between him and Emerald. "Have you enjoyed him yourself?"

"Ehhhh." Emerald made a little *comme ci, comme ça*, verbal shrug. "Too heavy," she added, though whether she meant she'd found him too heavy or she hadn't tried him because she thought he'd be too heavy, Jael neither knew nor cared. What she did know was that was fear mixed with desire in the male slate-gray eyes.

"I see." She meant it literally. "Magnificently muscled, though, and larger I am than you. . . ." She let it trail off, while watching sweat pop out on the broad forehead, desperation seep into the eyes that had so little pity for anyone else.

"Beautiful specimen," Jael mused, while Klathur stood, jaw clenched, eyes promising her that if he ever did get her into *his* power . . . "But you know," she went on lightly, "he distinctly smells of stale blood. I never could stand people who smelled, and I fear so very strong it is, that even if he washed . . ." Her light but double-edged mockery had done the trick. She could walk away, and he'd be safe. Others had seen his reaction to the thought of having Jael, but Emerald hadn't, and that was what counted. She tapped him lightly on the shoulder. "Better luck next time, Klathur." He knew, if Emerald didn't, exactly what she was saying. His teeth ground together, and threat made his eyes glitter.

She strolled up and down the room, bent over by the chain, giving each male a lengthy assessment. They were all at least attractive, but young or mature, blond or dark, they had one thing in common: fear as long as her gaze was on them.

If it had been written in letters of fire a foot high, it couldn't have been clearer. Whoever she picked was in bad, bad trouble. And if she did succeed in seducing the unfortunate . . .

Petrik came back while she was circling the room, to watch her mysterious —to him—antics with a raised brow.

In a light, amused tone, she informed him of all, finishing, "I really ought to choose you. I have a weakness for red hair, you know, but she has promised to consider you for herself this evening, and your disappointment would alloy my pleasure."

His mouth didn't move, but an almost soundless *Teasing bitch!* reached her ears.

She laid a finger by her lip and pondered. "It's a terrible decision, though. That's precisely the shade a particularly marvelous lover of mine had." Equally softly: "Did you *want* to be a sacrificial goat?"

The glint in his hard blue eyes was appreciative as well as angry.

"You know"—Jael strolled leisurely back to Emerald's couch—"this is dull. But I was thinking—want you truly to make this contest amusing?"

"This isn't a contest. You're proving yourself."

"Oh no. A contest it is, all right. I say I can. You say I cannot. Two people. On opposite sides. Where I come from, that is a contest; no other word will suffice."

"Where you come from is dull," said Emerald, in a put-up-or-shut-up tone.

"Yes, you are probably right," Jael said musingly tone. "Not as dull as Rabelais, of course. All worlds are dull, but some are duller than others. That's why spacing I went, of course. Space is *never* dull."

"Really?" Emerald sat up, interested.

"Space itself . . ." Jael said dreamily, leaning back against Klathur's bulk as though the huge man were a wall. "The universe draped around you like an ever-changing kaleidoscope, the dance of time and dimension, beauty you cannot imagine while shrouded in your atmosphere, so mind-blowing you have to ration yourself, or fall prey to the rapture of the deeps—it happens, you know, people go out in suits, drifting in that endless glory as long as their air lasts."

"Pictures are dull, dull, dull," Emerald interrupted. "You're just trying to get out of proving yourself."

Jael stretched, as much as she could in her chains, and grinned at the pouting girl. "Truth to tell, petkins, I was."

"I knew it." Emerald made a face and sniffed.

"My motives the most altruistic, I swear by the Book of the Guild. I have been thinking as I looked, and the way we set up our contest is unfair."

Emerald made a moue; put into words, it would have been something like *Suck space, worm!*

"To you," Jael finished gently, with a sweet smile.

"To me." Emerald sat up, stared.

"Of a certainty. Not a contest. Odds so much in my favor, be a walkover." Emerald opened her mouth. "They are contracteds. You are their c'holder, I am your guest."

Emerald burst out laughing.

"Sweetheart, proven that is to be, very, very soon. So, officially or unofficially, I am your guest. Stop and think. How react your contracteds to your guests? They please you first, your guests second. So what will hap when go we to a contracted, say he is to be with me for the next few hours. What thinks he? Does not matter what you say, he is trained to please. You can tell him now, this minute, that he is to choose freely, that he need only pleasure himself and me if he wants to, but it will make no difference. He has been trained to *please*. He might even think you were saying it as a joke, or a momentary whim, you will change your mind and be angry if he does not satisfy a guest. We could talk ourselves hoarse, and he might believe, or think he believed, what we said, but in the back of his mind, all those years of 'Please the guests.' It would have to affect him, see you not?"

"Ummmm."

"And to make it a double bane, these here know I am a Navigator. Young you are, too young to know what haps to one who damages a Navigator. Men have died, ugly, for that sin. Who can be sure? Everybody knows about

Navigators, mentally delicate and all . . ." She displayed her teeth in a tiger grin that told all who watched just how *un*delicate she was. "Maybe saying no could damage them." She breathed on her nails, buffed them again on her shirt. "Agony Square beckons." She grinned at Emerald. "So—no contest. Sorry, petkins."

"You're right," Emerald said thoughtfully. "Nobody in this room—"

"No contracteds." Jael said firmly. "A c'holder equal in power to you, otherwise he might be afraid of offending you."

"No c'holders," Emerald snarled. "You aren't a Navigator, and I won't share you."

"That is it, then, petkins. Has to be free choice, or the contest is an abort. Cannot risk that one of your contracteds might decide, whatever you say, what you want is to show hospitality. Tsk. It might have been fun, at that."

"You—choose."

"No. Will not. Has to be a powerful c'holder, or nobody. Anybody else, free contractor, lesser c'holder, and especially contracted, they would just feel obligated to you, just do what they think you want, not what they want. Sorry about that, petkins, a fun idea it could have been, but unfortunately neither of us thought it through."

"You choose—or else."

"Petkins, don't you listen? Camouflage myself I can so I do not look like a Navigator, non-reg I am wearing under my tunic, but a contracted is a contracted is a contracted. No fun. Boring." She picked up her free leg and scratched idly behind her knee.

Emerald sucked in her breath, but Jael just yawned. A sly look came over the spoiled young face. "Suppose he wasn't a contracted."

Jael pursed her lips, looked mildly interested, then sighed. "No good. You said, no powerful c'holders. What is left but contracted?"

"I'd cancel his contract first."

Jael snorted. "What haps to people not protected by contracts here? He will be trading one c'holder for another, and he knows it. There are not so many of you. Like as not he will be pleasing you as someone else's guest next week, and that is simple fact. So he dares not displease you. The only contest would be what he thought would please you most."

"You'd better come up with something, because you're choosing tonight." The *or else* wasn't spoken, just . . . there.

Jael fluttered her fingers. "Let me think. There must be—" A pause, then a smile. "Of course." She strolled over, "Brilliant you are, petkins."

Emerald blinked. "I am?"

"Certainly. You had it when you said you would cancel his contract, you just carried it not far enough. Think. You are a contract-holder, correct?"

Emerald nodded. "Of course."

"Which means you hold many, many contracts, correct again? Not just people. Property. Farms." She hesitated. "Weaveries? Potteries? Inns? Places that produce contracts on their own?"

"Farms, yes. A pottery. A gladiatorial school. Yes."

"That's it, then. You do not just cancel the subject's contract, you assign one of your smaller contracts to him. A farm, say, big enough to feed a man and his family, and enough left over to bring into the city and contract for whatever a man cannot grow for himself. Independence, you see. That way, whoever I pick knows he will never fall back to being a contracted again. Then he does not have to think like a contracted, please somebody else. He will think only of pleasing himself." She stretched. "And that, petkins, is where I shine."

"You're skinny and old." Emerald sniffed.

"I have what it takes, petkins." She chuckled, a rich, merry sound. "I'm not bored now. Eat your words I am going to make you. This is going to be fun."

"We'll see who makes who eats whose words." Emerald sat up. "Fix your costume so it won't look like a Navigator's."

"You make up the contract assignments, petkins. This 'old lady' plans to howl tonight." Her free hand was tugging at the pressure seams in her shoulders.

But as Jael bent over to work on her wrists, her eyes caught Petrik's just for a second. A cocked brow asked the question: *Shall it be you?*

His jaw stiffened. She could see the longing for freedom in his eyes, but he shook his head almost imperceptibly. *Contracts, no! If you choose me, she'll* —A roll of eyes, lifted brows said it all.

Another slight flicker of expression: *Help me choose, then.*

An almost imperceptible nod: *I will!*

He was young, he was about as unhandsome as Emerald allowed her contracteds to be, and he had been under her contract for only a few weeks, obtained after a complicated exchange with several other c'holders. He had been a farm-worker, but then his c'holder had died and he had been passed from c'holder to c'holder. Up to now he had been a washer in Emerald's kitchen.

He was also very lucky.

He kept staring at the witnessed contracts, copies of which had been sent off to be filed in the Adjudicators' records, and blinking. "I don't understand," he mumbled over and over. "I don't understand."

"All you have to understand," Emerald cooed, "is that your contract has been canceled. You are now a minor c'holder yourself, with no obligations to anybody. You are free, you are independent, you may choose whatever you want to do and whoever you want to do it with." She smiled slyly. "I want no gratitude." Her eye glinted at Jael. "No thanks. I always free one contracted every year on my mother's birthday. She"—a tear slipped out—"she would have wanted it so."

He was in his early twenties, and he had spent most of his life under the aegis of a humane c'holder. But the months since his c'holder died had been a revelation and education. "I'm—free."

"Yes." She slithered up to him, ran her fingers up his arm, rubbed against him with all the skill of a kitten who wants to be seductive and doesn't quite know how. "You're free to do whatever you choose. But I—I like you. I hope you choose . . . to go with me." Over his shoulder, she sent Jael a triumphant, malicious glare.

"Go with you?" he repeated. "But—I'm free. I don't have to go with anyone."

"I know. But I like you. That's why I chose you. I wanted you to be free, to be able—I hoped you would come to me freely."

"Freely." He had absorbed enough. He stiffened, stepped back and away from her, his hands held up in an outspread, *Keep away!* gesture. "Given a choice, I'd as soon snuggle up to a viperscorp."

"Ohhhh!" she wailed. Then, clinging to her illusions: "You don't know me, know what I can do, that's all," she said loudly.

He laughed. "Lady, not all the contracts in the world prevent talk. Do you think any *man*'d touch you, if it wasn't a choice between that and the whip, or torment, or emasculation. Eccch!" He spat, carefully missing her embroidered scarlet slippers.

Her lip was trembling. Suddenly she whirled, screamed at Jael. "He didn't choose you, either. He can't, he might as well be a harem guard."

"Is that what this is all about?" the ex-contracted growled. "One of you c'holders' petty little wagers."

Jael stepped forward, smiling. "I am not a c'holder, and you might say it was a wager, though the stakes were not what she thought, nor the contest either. Won I have, man, won *one*, though a small start it is. And should you take the advice of one who wishes you nothing but well, you will walk, not run, to that farm, and not look back."

"I—" Jael had been behind Emerald and the guards, and when she came forward her chains clanked. "I— You're chained. What—I don't—" Suddenly, clutching his precious contract, he dropped to his knees before Jael, buried his face in the now crushed and dirty rose of her blouse. "You did this, somehow. Thank you. If there's anything I can do for you . . ." It was almost a sob. "Please say there's something, anything I can do." He was clutching her around the hips.

She patted the top of his head with a mother's tenderness. "Go," she said gently. "Live. Be happy. If you would pay me back—"

"Oh please!"

"Choose for yourself a life's helpmeet who chooses you, both of you freely. Love her and stay by her and have children by her, and teach them to be proud and free and how to love and share."

"That's all?" He looked up at her, his face a mask of disappointment.

"That is all. Help others whenever you can. Kindness can be contagious; you just have to give it a little start. Now." She leaned over, planted a tender kiss on his cheek, and slapped his shoulder lightly. "Go."

He knew what was unsaid, that his contract would not protect him long, if he stayed by Emerald; she was red with fury. "But you—"

Jael winked. "She cannot hurt me. That is truth."

"I think it is—only—"

"I worked hard for your freedom, my son. Throw not my effort back in my face." A thousand things were said without words. He smiled.

"Yes."

"Go."

"Yes. Someday could I—we—"

"I have chosen, long ago."

"Oh." Then: "For you, there will always be a place—"

"For the last time—go!"

He went.

Jael had bought her time—but the price was far higher than she imagined.

EIGHTEEN

It was more than a hour before the contract copy could be located in the Adjudicators' massive files and brought to the hearing. By then, the audience was restless. Several had gone out to relieve, refresh themselves. But Lachesis sat on the truth dais, an avenging angel with the terrible sword concealed but ready, smiling that knowing, evil smile the whole time.

The Adjudicator tapped the folded, sealed contract unhappily against the podium he was sitting at. "This is the contract you wish entered into the record of this adjudication?"

"Yes."

"You aver you have the right to so enter it, it being a sealed contract?"

"I am one of the signatories."

"Very well. You have so witnessed, and I wish it to be recorded that I am now breaking the seal of the referred-to contract." There was a thin knife on the podium; he used it to slit the seal and unfold the contract. It was shorter than most, a single page, and he frowned down at it. "You wish it read aloud?"

"It will be quicker if you read it to yourself, and then explain its gist and significance to the Navigators. The whole can be appended formally to the record later."

"Does that suit you, Guildmaster? The whole can be read aloud if you wish."

"You think we can understand all your whereases and clauses? We'll take your interpretation, Adjudicator, with the right to hear the whole if necessary."

"Wise." The Adjudicator dropped his gaze to the parchment and began reading. He had read down only a few centimeters when his eyes widened and he rose in his seat, pale and gasping. "Is this true?"

"The captain was green with fear and sweating when we worked out the details of that contract. I had no reason to doubt what he said."

"Sacred con—" His gaze flicked to Estaban, and he flinched back.

"Adjudicator." The Guildmaster rose. "What's amiss?"

The Adjudicator swiped sweat off his forehead, and gulped. "The Navigator Xavier"—his eyes held a mixture of pity—and fear—"has been"—his teeth were chattering—"ex-exposed to Moldr-dravian fever!"

The only people who stayed in their seats were those few Rabelaisians who had never heard of the off-world plague that had ravaged the earlier empire. There was a chorus of screams, and a general stampede of people trying to get out.

The woman's voice, amplified for the truth machine, cut through the hysteria. "Cowards. Count the days. He's safe, he's not infected. He's not a carrier, either!"

"Are you sure?" the Adjudicator snapped.

"Brandy's not showing any of the symptoms, is she?" she asked Estaban, who, unlike the others, had stayed in his seat.

"No."

"If you had been infected, you would have shown the symptoms while still aboard your ship."

"Yes."

"But you might be an immune carrier. So the captain dumped you here, for me to quarantine."

"What was Brandy?" he roared, suddenly furious. "A test case, to see if I was an immune carrier and would infect her?"

She couldn't answer, because the Adjudicator was banging his gong, trying to restore order.

It took a while, but he finally managed to get everybody back into their seats. "If you let anyone out screaming plague," the witness had said sourly, "you'll have a fine panic on your hands."

When all was in order, he barked to the woman to explain herself, in as few words as possible.

"The captain told me that he had gotten a message, just before going into hyper, that the Navigator Xavier had been exposed to Moldravian fever. He said he briefly considered spacing the Navigator, but knew that the other Navigator he had on board would report him and he'd be blacklisted. So he decided to dump his problem into the hands of someone willing to quarantine him, at his next port of call."

"Others of his crew could have been exposed," Estaban growled.

"Some Navigators tend to shun contact, and he said you were one of them. He was hoping to escape, once he had off-loaded you and your gear. I burned it," she added, without being asked.

"Captain Disselhopf and I had had contracts before. I decided the reward was worth the risk. The captain kept Navigator Xavier aboard until I was ready, and notified me when he was likely to be coming ashore. He wasn't expecting trouble, and my men had an off-worlder device that causes unconsciousness to the unprotected against it. My men were doubly protected: against the device and, by covers made of an off-world protective stuff, against the plague. Except for Brandy, everyone who had any contact with the Navigator was so protected. The captain dumped the rest of the Navigator's gear, and, as I said, I burned it, along with the clothes he was wearing and everything he was carrying.

"Then I quarantined him."

"Why didn't you tell me?" Estaban got out between his teeth.

"Which is worse, being held in a small room harmlessly for a time, or being told that there is a possibility—small at that point, true, but still there —that you might die, painfully, within a few days?"

"You—should—have—*told*—me!"

Very cool: "I don't agree with that."

Still between his teeth: "Had I been diseased, or a carrier, my escape would have put dozens, hundreds of innocent people at risk!"

"Yes." She nodded. "A lot of contracts might have been broken by your actions. However, as it happens, they were not."

The Adjudicator had recovered to the point of chiming in, "I'm afraid she has a point, Navigator Xavier. How could she have anticipated your escape? Only a man as intelligent and strong-willed as yourself could have conceived such a possibility, much less carried it through."

"She risked—"

The Guildmaster patted him on the shoulder. "Hush, it's over now."

But Estaban gave the woman calling herself Lachesis a long, hard glare. It was not, as far as he was concerned, *near* over.

"That's about it," she went on. "I waited until the symptoms would have appeared in the Navigator, if they were going to appear at all. When they did not, I put the girl in with him. I had heard that Navigators are more . . . requiring than most men. I intended to leave them together, in as pleasant surroundings as possible, until it was proven that the girl was likewise disease-free. Secondary infections show up more quickly than primary. It would only have been a few days. Only—"

"I escaped first."

"The Navigator escaped. A minor breach of my contract, but I took all precautions I could think of to prevent it, and my fine should be light. Especially considering that I have lost one of my contracteds as a result of it."

Estaban's teeth ground together so loudly that the Adjudicator could hear them. He sent the angry man a helpless look, spread out his hands. "The Navigator is right in one respect," he said sternly. "You should have told him the risk."

"Had he recovered, but been mentally damaged by being told he was probably doomed, what would the Navigators' Guild have required of me then? I recall a man who died on Agony Square for triggering an attack of

Navigator's Syndrome. I knew him well. I have no intention of dying as he did."

The Adjudicator ran his hands over his depilated skull, as though there were still hair there. "I cannot take into account the loss of the contracted, since the Navigators will reimburse you for her contract, if they take it over as they are contractually allowed, as an apprentice to their Guild."

"Come, Adjudicator." She spoke in the practiced whine of a market haggler. "The girl had a great deal of potential. She was worth far, far more to me than the ostensible value of her contract. Losing her, even though I am reimbursed for her contract's value, is still a great loss."

"I'll take that into account," he mumbled, not meeting the Guildmaster's infuriated glare.

"I want it recorded, now, that it is your adjudicatorial opinion that, save for the matter of the Navigator Xavier's escape, which I could not have prevented, and which I shall pay the fine to wipe out—but no more than the worth of the girl contracted Brandy—"

"Twice," he muttered fiercely.

"Twice the worth of the girl contracted Brandy, save for that matter I have done no more and no less than my contractual duty, I have upheld the sanctity of contracts in all respects, I have acted totally and in all ways as a respecter of all contracts should and must act."

It was a familiar formula. "Affirmed," the Adjudicator mumbled.

"Noted and recorded?" she asked sharply.

"Yes, madam contractor," the young apprentice said, "noted and recorded."

"Good. Because I would like to say a few truths to Navigator Xavier, while I am still sitting in this chair which weighs truths."

Estaban knew an enemy when he confronted one, and a weapon when it threatened him. But he had pride as well as honor. "Go ahead, madam who sells her children. Speak all you wish, here and now, in front of me and anyone else who cares to listen. The truth cannot harm me. I have acted always as a man of honor."

"Have you, Estaban Xavier, Navigator, man who prides himself on his honor? But I'm glad you invited me to speak the truth freely. Now, so long as I speak the truth, no matter the result, I cannot be adjudicated against."

"Harm the Navigator—" The Adjudicator knew a trap when he smelled one.

"Will it not harm him to be denied what he has requested so strongly to hear?" A thin smile. "Did you think it was coincidence that I sent the girl Brandy to you, Navigator?"

"Not now," he growled.

"I chose her most carefully. Not one of my other girls would have done."

The smile broadened. "We knew each other once before, Estaban Xavier. Many years ago. I was called Leany then."

"Leany." He shook his head. "Impossible. You're too old."

"My thanks," she said dryly. "Hardships leave marks. Like you left marks on me, Estaban Xavier. You punished me, because I did what your world considers wrong, dishonorable. You made no allowances that my world would not consider what I did so wrong."

"It was wrong and you knew it."

"No. My contract was held by the Innkeeper Zaqanna, not by the Navigators, not by the Lady Jael. You punished me, and I swore that if I ever got the chance, I'd revenge myself on you."

"You imprisoned me. You enjoyed that."

"I did. Every second you paced back and forth, the control you held so strongly, your features so calm on the outside but all seething emotion underneath—pure joy." She smiled ferally. "Appetizer."

He rose slightly in his chair. "If you think to do—"

She laughed, wild manic laughter that echoed in the high ceiling and made more than one of her audience flinch and shudder. "I don't have to do anything more, honorable Estaban Xavier. It's done and cannot be undone." Another burst of hysterical laughter, choked off with a serpent's smile. "Or am I underestimating your virility, after all? Perhaps it was no hardship to deny yourself Brandy, perhaps one of your fellows enjoyed her favors once you had stolen her away, used the Navigators' contracts to take over hers."

"There was no contract involved between myself and Brandy." He bit the words out one by one. "Only free will, two people attracted to each other."

"You alone, or did you share her with your Navigator friends?"

"It was not a question of my sharing. I told you, hers was the choice." Not proudly, matter-of-factly: "She chose me."

The Adjudicator stirred. "This is not germane."

But the woman Leany/Lachesis smiled, looking like her namesake, the Norn who cut threads of life, the destroyer. "You alone have enjoyed the girl Brandy." Another smile. "I thought she would choose you, given the choice. She was . . . most carefully raised." Then: "She's pregnant." The screen stayed blue.

"How can you know?"

"Pregnancy costs. All my girls have an off-worlder device which trips a screen when they get caught. So something can be done quickly, while it is simple. But you—you Navigators and particularly Estaban Xavier—have taken Brandy's contract. She's your responsibility now."

"Quite," the Guildmaster said shortly. "You needn't be concerned, woman."

"I'm not. She's all yours, and the baby will be all yours. Will you abort her? No, your world calls abortion dishonorable, no matter what the cause."

Estaban rose. "You've forfeited all claim to Brandy or her future."

"Fifteen years, Estaban Xavier. Fifteen years. But you came back to Rabelais, and now I have you. Where's your honor now, Estaban Xavier? Brandy's *your* daughter, Estaban Xavier. You took your virgin daughter, and you got her pregnant!"

"Imposs—"

But the screen was blue. Pure blue. "Revenge is sweet. You should have taken her in the cell; at least you could have told yourself you couldn't help it. But not you, not honorable Estaban Xavier. You escaped, and then you took her, of your own free will. Incest, with the fruit of it yet to come."

"You're lying! I always use—"

"Contraceptives. I know. I switched them, when you had me. And dosed your food with a counterchemical, when I had you. I waited fifteen years for you to come back. Fifteen years—and worth every minute of waiting and anticipation. Incest, Estaban Xavier, incest. You've committed incest. Where's your honor now, what worth your honor, you've smirched—"

"I'll kill—" He moved toward her, ponderously, an oak uprooting itself and staggering.

"Go to it," muttered the Guildmaster.

She only laughed, softly. "Favor for favor, Estaban. You penanced me, I brought a penance for you, if you want it. What penance bad enough for incest?" She laughed again, holding out something. "I brought you ugly, painful suicide, if you want."

It happened in seconds. Estaban stood towering over Leany, though she had stood herself, and was facing him unafraid. "Settle the accounts, Estaban," she said.

And he did.

One hand smacked against her neck, and the wet, butcher-shop kr-runk of cleaver splitting carcass echoed through the room. As she went down, his other hand swooped and caught the capsule from the hand going limp, and thrust it in his own mouth and swallowed it.

"Estaban, don't!" the Guildmaster screamed—but it was too late.

Leany continued to fall, her mouth somehow frozen into a smile, and Estaban went to his knees, catching the body, laying it down.

"Sanctity preserve us," the Adjudicator said. "She meant you to do that, all along."

Estaban, kneeling with the woman's body in his arms, said, simply, "Yes."

"Both."

"Yes." It was as though the killing had purged him, somehow. "She wanted me to act as I would never have under any other circumstances, to do what my enemy wanted."

"What was in the capsule?"

A wry smile. "I'll find out—soon enough." He frowned, then, hesitantly, raised his hands to his eyes. "I feel . . . odd. My eyes—I can't—" Looking up at the Adjudicator on his dais: "You look so bright, so bright." He gasped for air, and his breath . . . sparkled, tiny dancing firefly motes glittering near his lips.

"Estaban." The Guildmaster came to kneel beside him, to try to raise him to his feet. "We'll get you to a medic, treat you."

He let her push him up, smiling. "Too late, already." His voice was slurred. "She would have anticipated—so bright—so beautiful. You're the most beautiful thing I've ever seen. I think I love you—so beautiful—"

One of the c'holders frowned, and leaped the row of seats to stand beside Estaban, tilting his chin to stare into his face.

"You're beautiful, too," Estaban said. "So beautiful. I think I love you, too. Why is everything so gloriously shining and beautiful?"

"There's nothing you or any of your off-worlder magics can fix, nothing," the c'holder growled to the Guildmaster. "Kindest thing you can do is cut his throat. Now."

The Adjudicator leaned down. "C'holder Danile, do you know what the Navigator has been given?"

"Poor devil." The man sighed and turned away. "She was right when she said it was the ugliest, most painful form of suicide known."

"But what—"

"Uncut Elysium!"

NINETEEN

The sound of Leany's neck breaking was very loud in the adjudication chambers, unmistakable to one with experience. While most of the audience crowded forward to see what was happening, one man, smiling, scrambled backward over the seats until he could race down the aisle to the exit.

The Sandman had wanted one incident to set off his conflagration. Now he had it. The disciple's mind was racing even as he ran, one arm pumping to help the once brawny body to its top speed. On his other side, the elbow-length stub worked too.

The Hall of the Adjudicators faced one of the entrances to Agony Square, with about two hundred meters from the portals to the fringe of the mob listening to the Sandman.

Perched high as he was, the Sandman saw the running man, his one arm waving frantically, and stopped in mid-syllable, his hands held high for silence. "Firez?" he shouted the one-word question.

The answer rumbled over the heads of the packed mob of contracteds. "An off-worlder killed a c'holder. The adjudication was against his wishes, and he killed her."

A gasp went up from the mob, but the Sandman's face glowed with triumph. "You hear that, brothers and sisters! The off-worlders know the truth. In seven years' time, a person's body replaces itself piece by piece, cell by cell. A new person is born. No contract over seven years old involving a person's body can be enforced. We're all *free!* Contracts involving a human body are *worthless!*"

He had been priming them for weeks, months. Now was the day, the stour, the stecond.

"You're all free! None of your contracts are worth the flames to burn them in!"

A roar went up from the mob.

"No contracts bind you!" He didn't have to say it: Ninety-nine percent of contracteds were contracted from birth. "Nothing stops you! *Do unto your c'holders as they have done unto you!*"

He would have said more, but the trigger had been pulled, the spark set to the fuse. With a mindless, animal roar, the mob split up, began flowing away from Agony Square in all directions. There were three uniformed enforcers on the fringe of the mob. One managed to draw his sword, but the sheer mass of bodies rolled over him.

Quicker than thought, the square was empty except for the Sandman, still standing, arms upraised, a Joshua holding up the sun, and a scatter of trampled bodies, three of whom still wore the remnants of enforcers' uniforms.

An echo of the Sandman's last words seemed to hang in the air like dustmotes: *Do unto c'holders—*

Slowly the dust settled, and Firez, who had had the wisdom to duck into a doorway as soon as he saw the mob start to turn, slid out and stared at the empty scene.

The Sandman smiled down, a terrible smile. "That did it. By nightfall there won't be a c'holder alive in the city." He sat down suddenly, leaned wearily against the gallows, legs dangling limply, arms sprawled like a corpse's. "And bloody few"—he chuckled softly—"*bloody* few free-contractors." He sighed dreamily. "I wonder how long before someone realizes that if the Hall of Adjudicators is burned, along with all contract copies, *no* contracts will be enforceable."

Firez slowly crossed the square until he stood directly under the gallows. "Lysander, that's going too far. I never thought—they won't—*what about after?*"

Lysander—the Sandman—lolled against the gallows, idly rubbing the crooked bone in his right arm with his left hand. He didn't notice that three running figures charged into the Hall of the Adjudicators.

Alizon and Spyro, Rowan just behind them, burst in the adjudication chamber not ten minutes after Firez, the ex-enforcer had left; in those few minutes, outside, a world had changed. But Alizon was aware of nothing but the small tableau in front of the Adjudicator's dais.

"Wheel protect us all," she moaned. "We're too late."

The Adjudicator looked up at the sound of her voice. Most of the c'holders, deciding the amusement was over, had left. But all the Navigators, himself, and a few c'holders were gathered about the long, jerking body sprawled in the narrow space.

"Estaban." Alizon said on a moan. Then: "Spyro." His bulk cleaved a way easily for them both, through those circling the helpless man.

"Estaban," she said again, dropping to her knees over the blank-eyed man trembling epileptically, froth from his lips spraying all around him. "Estaban." Her hands, fingers spread wide, hovered over him, trembling.

"Can you help him?" the Adjudicator asked, while the Guildmaster looked puzzled at the strange face. "Sister?"

"We just landed," Spyro growled.

"Brother?"

"Hush. Let her—"

But she drooped back on her heels, her hands falling in helpless curls on her knees. She looked up, lip trembling, tears dribbling. "I can't." Her voice trembled, too. "I can't. Too late."

Spyro clamped his teeth tight on a curse. He had never, ever, seen his Alizon other than calm, cool, and collected. He squatted, wrapped his arms around her, and rocked in that narrow space murmuring, "We did the best we could, love. We tried."

"Brother?" The Guildmaster said again.

"She's psy," Spyro informed. "She knew. Months ago, on Lotsaluck. We tried to get here, half killed ourselves, only . . ." He sighed, shrugged.

"I see," the Guildmaster said, with a sad little nod. "You tried. I thank you, as I'm sure Brother Xavier would thank—"

Alizon screamed, a keen of such sheer agony of soul that when she stopped only the echoes of that frantic cry against fate were left.

"Love." Spyro had to make the effort to speak after that soul-scarifying scream. "Love, we tried."

"No." She broke out of his arms, stood, sheer will draped in a pale, frail slim form. "No. You don't understand. I didn't understand. *It's not Estaban!*"

"Not—" The Guildmaster glanced down. "An imposter?"

"No, no." She looked around, a general marshaling her troops. "I thought it was Estaban who was in danger, but it's all of us. Blood and fire and savagery, and it's started already, and likely too late to stop it."

"What?" said half a dozen together.

"This world has been trembling at critical mass for years, just waiting to go super," Alizon snapped. "Now it's started. They're out there now, amok, only a few of them, but the madness will spread. A few now, more as the contagion circles out. Within stours—"

The Adjudicator spoke. "You. I remember you. From the other time. You predicted—"

"What's about to—what's happening now. Your people won't be safe here. Get them together. Strip, those clothes will be your death warrant. This place will be a charnel house by nightfall. Guildhall may be safe, if you can make it. Together will be your best chance."

"Yes." He nodded, his lips curled in a small smile as he tore the yellow robe off. "You go now. Don't wait for us; we've many to gather, and records that must be saved."

"Your records or your lives," Spyro snapped.

The gentle smile broadened. "Our records are our lives."

"Adjudicator," a young c'holder asked in a puzzled voice, "what's going on? I don't understand."

"No time to explain, Lady Evelyn." He was down to a loincloth, his thin body bleached-pale and vulnerable-looking. "There is danger and perhaps death waiting. Go with the Navigators, do as they say."

"No." She threw her head back. "No. If there is danger and death . . . Eric is at my villa. I will not go to safety and leave him in danger. We go together"—her voice broke, then went on in calmness—"or not at all."

"Adjudicator." It was the older male c'holder who had first identified Estaban's plight.

"C'holder." The Adjudicator was at the door; he turned. "I go to warn my own. There may be no safety for any of us, anywhere, but if there is, it is with the Navigators. The choice is yours." He went on through the door, leaving his audience staring.

Outside, in the streets, the mob of several hundred that had been listening to the Sandman was scattering, splitting into clots of two or five or ten, running off in as many directions as there were narrow, crooked streets, splitting and resplitting—and gathering new supporters as they went.

Two would become eight, five a dozen, a dozen a score, as contracteds saw the running groups and asked what was happening.

"Contracts are finished!" the contracteds screamed.

"The Sandman has spoken! An off-worlder has proved it! No contracts involving people are binding!"

"Death to c'holders! The Sandman has spoken!"

"Do unto c'holders as they have done unto you!"

"No contract over seven years old is sanctified!"

"Death to c'holders!"

"The off-worlders are killing c'holders, and so are we!"

"No contract is sacred! The Sandman proclaimed it!"

"Kill the c'holders!"

"Kill! Killl! *Killlllll!*"

The girl Evelyn was wriggling through the crowd when Alizon, conferring rapidly with Spyro and the Guildmaster, snapped, "Stop her!"

Three Navigators ringed her, blocking her exit. She pounded small fists on the nearest one's chest, "Let me go—Eric!"

"You can't treat a c'holder like that—" The older male started.

"Hush!" Alizon squeezed to the girl. "That's mild compared to what will be if she gets away." She put a hand on the girl's shoulder. "Listen—" She stopped. Then chuckled. "Well, well." To the girl: "He's psy, he's safe. Now, come with us and save yourself. I'd not like to answer to that one if you aren't."

"You're lying."

"Time's passing. I'm not lying, Sugar Puss."

"Oh, how did you know . . . ?"

"He has a purple birthmark on his left hip, you've a freckle in almost the same spot, you laugh about it, and—"

"Ohhhh!"

"I'm not lying, Sugar Puss. Now, let's go!"

Spyro picked up Estaban's long body and slung him around the broad shoulders like a shawl. A jerk of his head, and the Navigators started to ease down the aisle.

"Formation?" the Guildmaster asked.

Alizon was, for now, their expert on conditions outside. "Tight. Weapons handy but not in hand. We don't want to start anything if we can help it." Louder: "All of you. Imagine you're walking through tigers. They're hungry for blood, yet they don't want to spill their own in a hopeless battle. But if it's a mob, and they're maddened—"

"I don't understand." The male c'holder stood slightly to one side, a pair of bodyguards flanking him. "But I don't like the odds. I've a full squad outside. Will that help?"

"So do I," chimed in an older woman.

"And I." Tamilee, the off-worlder once bonded to the most humane c'holder of them all, had been kneeling to try to aid Estaban however she could. Now she rose, easily, poised and ready.

The first of the Navigators had reached the end of the narrow aisle and were forming up, leaving a hole in the center for Spyro and his burden.

"Is their loyalty to you, or to the contracts?"

"Karolly's folk? To me, always." Tamilee was sure.

"Lord Karolly's people will all be loyal," the male c'holder affirmed with a nod. "But of mine . . . Chris?" A wry smile for the man on his left. "Valjean?"

"Lyall listens too often to the Sandman," the man named Chris growled. "I'll send him away. The rest are safe—or I'll break their necks."

"Good."

"Amory," the older woman quivered to the guard standing easily to her left.

"I'll take care of you, love," he said with a smile. Then, to his opposite number, as a maximum of two were allowed in the actual chamber. "Bryce, take the squad, run to the villa. Pack some food, take the kids and all the 'tracteds you can trust into the hills. Call it a picnic, whatever. Don't come back until you get word from me."

"Right. Take care of our lady. And don't take too long cleaning this up. You're two nights ahead of me already."

"One night, curd-brain. You never could count." The second man was already leaping easily over the bolted-down chairs, heading for a different door from the ones the Navigators were forming at. His voice floated back, "Two, and I intend to have them both."

The one left, Amory, pulled his sword slightly, kissed its hilt at the woman he recognized as temporary general. "Lady?"

"Form square and move as fast as you can. Strip off identifying insignia as we get out of here." To the male c'holder and Tamilee: "You and your men, too. Anyone else?"

There were four or five c'holders left, some with a pair of guards, some not —preferring space to personal safety inside what should have been the sacrosanct hall. Only one moved forward, a sly-faced, portly man with an oily smile.

"Me," he said, working on his own clothes. "But I'm afraid my people be useless. In fact, if you would care to silence these two." He gestured back at his guards, who had been watching mutely, faces mirroring identical, puzzled frowns.

One of the Navigators grinned, and the two men fell. "I may need that later"—he stuffed the paralyzer back in his pockets—"but I figured we couldn't afford a scuffle now."

"Good thinking." The portly man was down to sandals and a pink satin chemise reaching halfway to his knees. "I'll dirty it first chance I get," he informed the world at large.

"Anyone else?" Those left, mouths curled, shook their heads. "Good luck."

Alizon shucked her jacket, draped it around Lady Evelyn, and jerked downward on the elaborate ruffled turquoise skirt. "Sorry. Come on." As they were moving up the aisle: "Your squad safe?"

"I don't understand."

The male c'holder ranged himself alongside them, grinned. "What she asked me." He was struggling out of his own clothes as he moved. "If they think they won't be punished after, will your squad be loyal *now*?"

"Ye," she said automatically, then thought about it. As they reached the end of the aisle, she said slowly, "There are two who . . . envied Eric, for being my favorite, my only favorite. The others—"

"Send them back to your villa." They were through the door. "Tell them you're planning a party, a masquerade."

"Lord Danile." They were moving through the hall now, heading for the main door. "Do you really think there's danger?"

"I don't know. If that odd-colored woman is wrong, we'll be much embarrassed. But . . ." He grimaced. "I'd rather be safe than sorry." A grin. "I just hope a few of them try their tricks at my villa. They'll get a warm welcome."

The word was spreading, almost as fast as a man could run. Mobs were forming, rioting, splitting up, and spreading out, the parts aggregating new members and growing back to their original size, like crystals spreading through supersaturated liquid. The original mob of a few hundred became ten smaller mobs, twenty, a hundred. Those hundred grew and spread, to become more and more.

The word was getting simpler, too.

Contracts are worthless; the Sandman says so.

Revenge! Torment! Kill!

In the street, they formed into a ragged square and started toward the Guildhall.

Alizon slid through the movement and suddenly ran toward the open space called Agony Square.

The Guildmaster turned. "Sister?"

"Go on. Be right with you."

She stopped under the gallows and the single man who leaned against it, leg swinging idly, a dreamy smile on his sand-brown face.

"Lysander. You did this! Why?"

His eyes opened slowly. "Why, it's Lady Alizon, isn't it." His left hand rubbed at the crooked right arm, an old habit, almost instinctive. "You know the why, lady."

"Do I? Tell me. Say it aloud."

He smiled. "Abuse. Torment. Terror. I swore an oath, Lady Alizon."

"Abuse. Torment. Terror." She smiled grimly. "I hope revenge is enough, Lysander. Because of what one man did to you, you call vendetta and pain and death on thousands."

"I hope he's out there, somewhere."

"But you haven't changed anything, except for the worse. History's my avocation, Lysander, and I tell you this: Violence begets violence. You've killed abusers—and innocents—but you've only set up a worse group of abusers in their place."

She'd finally gotten through to him. "What? What are you saying?"

"You think this hasn't happened before, on other worlds? Many times, many, many times. Destroy the structure of society, give some people a taste for blood and power, and you'll wind up with some new form of slavery for the many, and cruelty and lust unbounded for the powerful few."

"No. We'll all be free, once they're dead."

"No. You trusted my equations once, listen now. You've started it, and it can't be stopped, but it might be . . . channeled. If enough of the current power structure is spared, it might serve as a—a bridge, a transition, to a new and better society. It wouldn't need much: the more intelligent, flexible c'holders, the Adjudicators, perhaps the Navigators or other off-worlders who are skilled in governmental theory."

"Too late, Lady Alizon." His sand-brown eyes were fixed over her shoulder.

She whirled. Behind her, filling the street, was a mob of naked or almost naked people, some bloodstained, all holding weapons, swords, rakes, mallets.

The man in the forefront, a bearded giant with whip scars from his neck to his toes, took a step forward. "Hello, lady. Off-worlder." He took another step toward her. "C'holder. C'holder treatment." A sly smile, his nakedness making clear what he intended. "I saw her first."

"No!" Lysander jumped down from his perch.

"Sandman," the giant acknowledged, "you can have her first, then."

"No. Don't touch her."

"Sandman, this is a *c'holder*—or as good as. You don't want your share, step out of the way."

"No. She's not a c'holder, and she's not for you. Go find some real c'holders to revenge yourself on. Not Lady Alizon."

"That choice, is she? All right. I gave you your chance—now step aside."

Lysander stepped in front of Alizon. "You'll have to kill me before you touch her."

The giant took another step, to stand in front of Lysander, his huge sword almost as long as Lysander was tall. "That the way you want it?" He tensed, held the sword two-handed, high over his head. "All right, then."

TWENTY

Brine was waiting at the door, with a blanket unwrapped and ready.

As soon as Petrik appeared, with the helpless Jael in his arms, he began winding it about the long, trembling body. "Warmth for shock," he muttered. Then: "I have you, love. You're safe now."

"She bought you your time," Petrik said.

"I know. Thank you for the medi-machine for Golden."

"How is he— How did you know?"

But Brine had moved to a chair, seated himself, was crooning to the trembling woman in his arms.

"She seemed fine," Petrik informed no one in particular, in a puzzled voice, "until we were through the door. Then she just—"

"I know."

"You do know, just as you knew who sent the healing device. How?"

Brine looked up, smiled. Then he frowned down at the woman whose face was buried in his broad chest. "Hush, love, hush. You couldn't have known."

Muffled: "I saved the boy. But then—then—"

"I know, I know," he soothed. "But it's done and can't be undone. For now, we—" His face changed, from concern to frowning concentration. "Contracts!" he burst out.

Petrik's brows rose, just slightly. He'd suspected the ugly man with too much courage had been a native of Rabelais. Perhaps it was instinct, perhaps recognizing like, perhaps he knew too much of the society and how it thought. Now he was sure. But what he would or could do with the knowledge . . .

Brine stood up and deposited Jael in the startled Petrik's grip, so suddenly that he almost dropped her. Then he was watching, open-mouthed, as Brine strode over the Golden, still lying immobile under the mechanical healer.

Brine stared down at it, then hesitantly began making changes. Petrik frowned. Almost as if someone else were telling him what to do, there was a jerkiness in his motions, as though he did a step and then stopped and listened. Then, as he finished the conversion of the machine to a portable, he spoke. "I assume there is a safe place somewhere in this mausoleum?"

"I, ah—"

"We have minutes at best. It's started."

Petrik felt as if he had somehow missed half the conversation. "It?"

"Anti-C. Riot. Blood flowing like a river. C'holder blood. C'holders and all loyal to them."

Petrik whirled, forgetting that he had Jael in his arms. "Lady Emerald—"

"Run to her," Jael ordered, sliding to out of his arms to land on her feet, her eyes clear and bright.

"Wha—" He stared down at her. Too much, too fast, that the limp, eyes-shut, he'd-thought-unconscious burden was suddenly transformed into this brisk leader of men.

"Needs must." She smiled grimly. "Once the mob gets here, there will be no time. First, give us directions to the safe place. We'll be slower than you, carrying Golden. How many can the place accommodate?"

"For a few hours—dozens, more. For several days—a dozen at most."

"Assume a few days. Choose carefully, those most at risk. If you cannot get to them quickly, don't try. Be thinking as you go." Then, without a pause or a quiver: "Want you to include us three?"

"Jael!" from Brine.

"We are off-worlders and/or officially off-worlders, and so much at risk. But the sanctuary is yours."

Time was at a premium, and he knew it, but he couldn't help asking, though he knew the answer, "May I choose you alone, Lady Jael?"

"Yes!" from Brine.

"No!" from Jael, simultaneously.

Petrik smiled over her shoulder at Brine. "If we all survive . . ." A very male glance at Jael that neither she nor Brine had any trouble interpreting; but a second later he was all business: "Let the man take the golden one's shoulders, lady, and you his feet. That will be quickest. Left when you leave the cell, fifth door on the right, enter, go up until you can go no further, out through the door, left again, and as far as you can. I should meet you there somewhere."

"Up?" Jael asked, puzzled.

Petrik grinned again, threw over his shoulder, "Of course. They always scour the basements and cellars."

Emerald had discovered a glorious new way of spending time and had no intentions of leaving it. Petrik finally lost patience altogether and tossed her over his shoulder, snapping quick orders, including sending one young guard on the run to the pink villa of Lady Medee Oriflamme, the oldest of the Oriflamme family.

Emerald pounded her little clenched fists on his back, but he strode relentlessly up to the sanctuary regardless. If he had the tiniest of doubts about his actions, they didn't show on the grimly determined face, with its glittering blue eyes.

Not that he doubted what the two off-worlders had said. He knew truth when he heard it, and he had heard it in Brine and Jael. Even their reactions when he offered to protect the lady alone fitted what he knew of them both. But how those two, in a cell in a private house, isolated by that rarity in the crowded city, wall and small garden, could know what was going on out-side . . .

But they knew. He believed.

Rowan Reis, freighter-master and unofficial Navigator, ran easily through the crowded, twisted streets of the city of Pantagruel. Two angry minds beat at his, ordering him to go back, but he only smiled, white teeth splitting the dark-red beard.

Mind-linkages were not directional, but there was an instinctual surety as two linked minds came closer to one another. The directions he had gotten from the adjudicators were right after all. All he had to do was follow them. It wasn't easy, in the twisting, stop-and-start alleyways of the inner city, but it was the only way.

Behind him, like a great monster stretching and waking, he could sense the mobs forming and growing.

Under normal conditions he couldn't read minds, though he shared inti-mately with those he was linked to. But sensitized by the years of linkage with mam and his mental kin, he was open to the massive outpourings of savagery of the growing mobs. Bloodlust, violence, and rapine were thunder-ing behind him, and it was with an effort that he armored himself against being overwhelmed by that tidal wave of mindless, instinctive savagery.

Brine and Jael strengthened their linkage, stood mental shoulder to shoul-der with him, and his grin broadened. All an outsider could see was a red-haired man, in a spacer jumpsuit of aquamarine that matched his eyes, run-ning easily along, but in his mind three people ran in unison, all alert, guard-ing each other's backs.

"I'm ahead of it, I think," he muttered.

Not by much. Jael had Golden's feet, and was concentrating hard on going up the steep steps.

And what the c'breaking do you think you'll be able to do when you get here, anyway? Brine's mind grumbled.

"I spy!" Rowan sang it almost, startling a female contracted who was hanging out some glittering white linens over a balcony rail to sun. As on any ordinary day, she was doing her duty; and would, until the mobs rolled out this far.

Rowan almost stopped; she was young, and looked gentle and cared for. But by the time the mobs got this far . . .

There were too many to warn them all. Then he caught his flight on the railing of the balcony she stood on and called up, "Lady, little lady." The truth would take too long. He quickly went on, "There's a ship in the port with a weak bottle that may explode and take the city with it. Warn your c'holder. All of you go down in the cellar and barricade yourselves in and stay there. Or better still, run, get out of the city, stay away for at least three days, a week would be better."

She frowned down, incredulous, disbelieving. "You've spun this tale to no one else, off-worlder."

"I go to warn friends and daren't delay. If I'm caught still out in the open . . ." He made the ancient gesture, running his finger across his throat. "But you're such a pretty little thing, I'd hate to see you torn to bits. Protect yourself, pretty little one." And he ran on.

Behind him, the girl stood for a few seconds, frowning and chewing her lip. Then she ran inside, leaving the half-draped and half-still-crumpled linens flapping in the gentle breeze.

Emerald was bored. There were a dozen people in the room with her, but they were all her favorites, useful, whom she didn't want to waste except in a pinch. And she wasn't to that point yet; she'd be out of here too soon.

Except for the three off-worlders, and she didn't dare touch them—yet— in case the woman's claim turned out to be true.

Her lip hanging down, she glared at the four consulting in low voices in the corner. The three off-worlders and that traitor, Petrik. She'd waste *him* now, all right, except that she wasn't sure the three guard lieutenants could take him, even three on one, and in these close confines, somebody else— she!—might get hurt. She sniffed. Petrik's time of importance was limited to while they stayed here—which had better not be much longer.

Jael was saying just the opposite. "Bad it is out there."

Petrik looked from Jael to Brine to Golden, now emerged, they hoped healed, from the medic. All three had the same calm message in three different-colored eyes. Firmness.

"You keep not much track of history here," Jael said softly. "Other worlds do. Riots like this burn hot for days, even tendays, then burn down. At least—"

"Go on."

"The mob violence burns down, but . . ." She sighed. "If you stress social structure too much, it twists or turns upside down or breaks apart entirely. Then you have— A classic example there is, a world called France, once, an early, First-wave world. Classes it had much like yours, only they called themselves nobles and bourgeoisie and peasants instead of C'holders and free-contractors and contracteds."

"Yes." He glanced at Emerald, read only too well the pouting sullenness on her young face. "So?"

"I've studied some of those tapes myself," Brine said in a low growl. "The parallel is apt. That's what this sociology boils down to. The study of how and why people have acted in the past, and the application of those how and whys to the present."

"What's happening here and now could be very similar to what happened on that long-ago world." Golden spoke for the first time. "Listen, man, and be warned."

"I have not a computer, nor remember the exact equations, but the parallels are so strong." Jael chewed her lip. "Like yourselves, the peasants of France were almost totally in the control of the powerful nobles. Like your free-contractors, the bourgeoisie had some independence, but were muchly under the thumbs of the nobles. The peasants suffered, and the bourgeoisie had hopes and ambitions that the nobles suffocated. The peasants labored, and the nobles enjoyed themselves, and the bourgeoisie plotted.

"Finally, the peasants had suffered enough, and there was a riot in the capital city, Harris. Mobs of peasants ran in the streets, nobles were slaughtered, those who tried to protect them dying with their masters. The original riot lasted for days, then spread through the countryside. Hordes of peasants burned the villas of their masters, often with the masters inside. Women were raped and slaughtered, children, infants. It fed on itself, and grew worse. Crops burned with the villas, and the people starved. Starving mobs roamed the countryside, desperate, the strong grabbing what food there was, the weak falling. In Harris, it was little better. The bourgeoisie thought they had wrested control from the nobles, many of whom were dead, captured, helpless. But anarchy—"

"I think I understand," Petrik said with a slow nod. "Like ligers for the arena. They are born in cages, grow up in cages, are transported to the arena in cages. But once they are released onto the arena sands . . ." He shrugged. "I've done gladiatorial duty. There's no way to get the animal back into the cage. You just keep feeding gladiators to it until one of them kills it."

"Right." Jael nodded. "The bourgeoisie thought they had control of this weapon, this liger, the peasants en mob. But they didn't. Nobles were killed publicly, one by one, amid great shouts of joy. When they ran out of nobles, many of the bourgeoisie were accused of noble ambitions, and likewise fed the great knives and the bloodthirst of the mob. When they ran out of bourgeoisie, peasants, favorites, guards, seamstresses and cooks, they went to quench the mob's blood hunger, too. It was called the terror, and it lasted for styears."

"What stopped it?"

"A man. A dictator. He got enough of the young and strong behind him, then turned he the people's hate and bloodlust outward, into foreign wars. France became the center of a great empire. But his ambitions grew too fast, the worlds he had attacked fought back, others next on the list banded together, and France ended devastated, with those of the nobles who had managed to flee to other planets restored and crueler than ever."

"What's war?" Petrik wanted to know.

"A form of forcing contracts from outside," Brine supplied, when Jael looked as if she couldn't think of a way of putting it. "Like if the people of La Belle came here and said that all our contracts were abrogated, and only those contracts which they authorized would be henceforth enforced."

"That's"—Petrik thought it over—"that's ridiculous, unthinkable. Besides, it's impossible."

"Not when the group of people who want to enforce their contracts on a second group of people have a lot of enforcers to make the second group do their will." He winked at Jael. "For all you've said about our society, love, we have no wars."

"Certain of that, are you?" Jael shot back. "You don't keep much track of your history. I'll wager you've had some contract disputes that were war in all but name."

"Oh." Petrik blinked. "Large-scale contract disputes. I understand that, all right."

"Very large-scale," Golden said. Then: "You're right too often, love, and besides, we're wandering off."

"You." Emerald poked him in the ribs. "You're healed now. Let's see if you're all show and no do."

"Lady—" Petrik warned.

"I'm not ordering him," Emerald whined. "I want to do what's best for him. He can have his pick." She preened. "It's not good for a man to go without. I've heard all about these Navigators and their needs. I'm not having a charge of c'breaking. He needs, let him satisfy his needs." She smirked. "All he wants."

Golden looked at her, his face concealing what he was thinking. There were five women in the room: Jael, Emerald, and three highly skilled contracteds. Emerald preferred men around her, but she also liked the best, so she had a skilled seamstress, a *very* skilled female used in entertainments and offered as a delicacy to male c'holder guests (or females who wanted such), and a female clerk, in reality a member of the Adjudicators' Unity, but assigned to Emerald's use, a silent shadow who wrote and witnessed and (rarely) advised. (Not because her advice was needed rarely, but because Emerald didn't like advice and tended to ignore it, and the woman was shrewd enough to save her energy for the most important issues.) The skilled woman was in her prime, the seamstress older, a woman whose sexuality—if she'd ever had much—had been damped down so long it was a habit. If she attracted the attention of a c'holder it meant rape, and of a contracted, frustration for both, unless they were lucky. Two of the three sat quietly in one corner, the seamstress sewing, hair caught behind a veil, eyes lowered, the slut bluffing her toenails, eyes narrowed and considering.

The adjudicator/assignee, too, was quiet, in her own shadowed corner, working away on parchments she had brought. She didn't even look up. She may or may not have heard what was being said. But if c'holders were used to considering contracteds as furniture, toys for the playing with, the Adjudicator was less and more.

"There's no privacy here," Golden remarked, almost idly. Once he had scheduled sex games in arenas, and participated eagerly himself. But that was before he had gone back to babyhood, and lived through a second childhood and maturing, emerging a much different man.

"Privacy?" Emerald blinked. Privacy, especially for contracteds—and she was still half thinking of him as a contracted—was an uncommon whim of c'holders.

"Privacy." He smiled gently.

"Privacy." She chewed her lip. "Perhaps we could set up barricades." There were blankets, boxes of food stacked about.

"It isn't privacy when others can hear." His voice was still soft, gentle.

Eagerly: "I'll order them not to listen."

"That's not the same." Beside him, Jael was having difficulty keeping a straight face.

Emerald wasn't stupid; her mouth pursed angrily. "If I order, they'd better obey," she spat out. "But if this isn't good enough for you"—Petrik stiffened; he had a good idea what was coming—"then we'll just go back to my rooms. We've sat cowering up here long enough."

"Lady Jael?" Petrik asked.

"Madness," she said tersely. "Were we not so high and so insulated, we'd be hearing the screams now. You and your men would last ten steconds once they break in. Five, if your own contracted join them."

"She's lying." Emerald hauled back and kicked his shin, carefully above the metal-plated greave. He winced but didn't jump to obey orders.

"I said she's lying. Obey me!"

There was sweat around the rim of his helm; the russet locks peeping out were dark with it. "My lady, I cannot. The danger—"

"Kneel." The high, thin voice was vicious. "Turn your back." He obeyed instantly. "Perhaps one of your men can beat some courage into you. Perhaps when he's through, I'll keep you as a guard, though all you're good for is to guard haremliks."

He shuddered. The threat was plain.

"No." Everybody in the room except the clerk blinked and jerked. Though the single word was low-spoken, the command in it cut like the crack of a whip.

Emerald stared at Golden, mouth open. "You dare say no—to me."

His smile was gentle, but something in his expression froze everyone in the room but Emerald. She brought up her hand in a slap that echoed, and her knee a second later. But Golden had moved, and instead of smashing his genitals, Emerald found herself sailing upward, impelled by his own knee, and then held, dangling and helpless. She screeched and struggled, but he was half again her height, and as lithe as a greyhound.

He still smiled, that smile freezing the three guards. Petrik, who had been ordered to his knees, stayed there. "Lady Clerk." Again that soft gentle voice that somehow commanded.

"Yes?" She looked up, apparently became aware of the struggle going on for the first time, and said, softly, "My, my." With a perfectly straight face: "Has she ordered you to do that?"

Jael grinned suddenly. "Dear Golden, so impetuous. Afraid I am he didn't wait for her to express herself verbally."

Emerald's screeches went up in volume. Shorn of obscenities, there were occasional "Put me downs" barely intelligible.

"You are aware," the clerk spoke to Jael, but her words were meant for Golden, "that she is a c'holder of no little contracts. If she has not at least acquiesced—"

Golden dropped to one knee, his other leg straight out and then bent at the knee, his sole firmly planted, so that the thigh presented a convenient ledge.

The clerk's brows went up. "Acquiesced, then you are liable—"

Golden draped Emerald over his thigh and positioned her.

"To a charge of—"

He raised one hand and brought it down with a loud crack; Emerald convulsed and let out a howl like a siren bearing down on a speeder.

"C'breaking," the clerk finished, as Golden spanked Emerald again, even louder.

The three guards broke out of their daze and converged on Golden, who evidently thought if a job's worth doing, it's worth doing well. The pistol-crack of his hand landing cut even through Emerald's cries and screams.

Jael took a step forward. "Stop." She raised a hand to the guards. "Touch him"—she had to raise her voice over the ruckus—"and it's c'breaking."

The three guards looked at her and then, unconsciously, appealed to the authority.

The clerk's face was solemn, but her eyes sparkled with suppressed glee. "C'breaking is an awesome charge. You'd better at least hear her out."

"I know what she's going to say," one of the guards burst out. "She's a Navigator, she claims."

"Ah!" Jael held up a hand to stop him, but Brine caught it. "She's an Adjudicator. As sacrosanct as contracts. Let me."

"Right."

"Are you a Navigator?" It wasn't obvious. Jael in black, with her Navigator's peaked cap, looked all business. But Jael in a rose-pink blouse and black breeches was another matter.

"Yes." Jael and Brine said it together. "A message to Guildhall will confirm my claim," Jael went on, "but the reason we're here is that sending such a message, with the streets as they are . . ." She shrugged.

"The men also, they are Navigators?"

"No. They are merely associates protected under Navigators' contracts."

"I see. Then that does not give him the right to—"

The guards took a step closer; Golden ignored them.

"Guards!" Brine could put order in his tones, too. "Stop. We're not through."

"Yes?" She was sitting on a crate, using a board as a desk. Nonetheless, her spine was erect, her dignity unimpaired. She knew who and what she was, and if an Adjudicator owed all to the Unity and had no individual power, still, her word would be the final law. "You have further argument?"

"Brine—"

"He's only claiming the protection of the Guild, his right as a Navigator's bonded, while his own claims are being established. And once they are—and they *will* be—"

"He will have contracts of his own?" the clerk sounded interested.

"Many." *Very* gleeful: "Petrik—"

"Yes?" He turned, saw the expression on Brine's face, and started to hope.

"Is your contract officially assigned to the Lady Emerald Oriflamme via her aunt, Lady Medee Oriflamme, through her mother, Lady Esme Oriflamme, or as an heirship assignment from the holdings of Lord Golden Singh?"

"I don't know."

Brine winked. He knew. Or rather, Golden did. He had been doing some snooping.

The clerk knew, that was her profession. "The guard captain Petrik's contract has been assigned to the Lady Emerald via probated heirship from the holdings of the Lord Golden Singh."

"Didn't anybody consider that the Lord Singh might object to his holdings being assigned, almost blindly?"

"The Lord Singh is dead, and since he left no chosen heir, his holdings were assigned to his only known child, the Lady Emerald."

"The Lord Singh"—Brine was enjoying himself—"is very much alive and currently spanking the child who's made havoc with his holdings the last fourteen years."

"What!" The clerk dropped her quill. The guards flushed, dropped to their knees, or covered their faces. The women and the studs stared interestedly at the man who might be their new owner.

The clerk licked her lips. "Can you"—she was having trouble breathing—"prove that claim?"

"Eventually." Brine shrugged. "We have to keep him alive until it's proven. But it's truth."

She sucked in a deep breath, actually shuddering. "He looks the part. Except, shouldn't he be . . . older?"

"Gene-altering and technology," Jael informed her. "On other worlds, men of two centuries' age can look like boys if they choose."

"I can't—"

"It may not matter, depending on what happens after this riot," Jael went on. "But Golden Singh he certainly is. You must have some kind of identification."

"Footprints on parchment," Brine supplied aloud.

"He will match."

The clerk covered her mouth with a trembling hand. Even in the dimness —there were only a couple of artificial glowers—she looked pale. A major c'holder, returning to find so many of his contracts assigned or abrogated— even the Adjudicators' Unity might not escape a charge of malicious contract manipulation.

"Now." Golden plucked Emerald off his leg, set her upright, and rose to his feet himself, all in one smooth, easy motion. "You," he said to the girl, voice still soft but with that undertone of command. "Go into the corner, face it until I tell you you can come out."

"You!" She stamped her foot, but had the smarts not to try another slap or knee. "You can't tell me what to do."

His hand shot out, and she was whirled almost before she'd realized he'd moved, one arm twisted painfully behind her as he began marching her toward the corner, talking as he went. "I can, and will. They've mucked you for fair, girl—" He stopped, because Emerald, writhing and screeching, was in the corner he'd pointed to. Holding her there, not even panting, he went on, "But they did it in my name, which makes you my responsibility, and I'm living proof that no one can't be taught better. I know how, and I intend to take that responsibility, starting—" She drowned him out, but he clapped a hand over her mouth and went on.

"You're my responsibility, starting now. You'll learn to do what I say." She writhed, but his hands were firm. "You'll obey me, until you've matured enough to be trusted."

He dropped his hands and stepped back, and she spun, nostrils flaring, eyes with a rim of white showing all around. "You dare—"

He whirled her back to face the corner and smacked her on her already sore bottom. "You'll learn. Face the corner."

She whirled again. "Guards!"

He turned her and added another loud lesson. "Until I say you can come out."

She twisted. "I'll have you—"

He twisted her back, spanked her again. "No. From now on, I and only I give the orders."

She stamped her foot, but didn't turn. "You'll beg—"

He tapped the abused area, not hard, just a reminder. "And be silent. Your whining bores me."

"I'll have you—"

Smack.

"Wait until I can—"

Smack.

"My guards will—"

Smack.

"I hate y—"

Smack.

"Oooooooh!"

Soft smack.

"Aiiiiiyeh!" She screamed, thrashed, suddenly dropped to the floor and rolled, screeching and drumming her heels and pounding with her fists. Her people all screamed and jumped away or quivered and tried to make themselves small. They'd all seen the aftermath of such tantrums.

Golden simply sighed. "You'll learn." He deftly picked her up and held her high in the air, arms and legs flailing. Then somehow he had rotated her so that she was dangling, back to him, from one arm, which made it possible for him, by bending, to attack his chosen target with the other. "Silence." Smack. "Silence." Smack. He wasn't even raising his voice, just calmly punctuating his one-word order with an emphasis that would, sooner or later, despite struggle and screech, get through.

The others all had lost track of the number of "Silence's" he had uttered, in that calm soft voice, when he said it, and—*mirabile dictu!*—there *was* silence.

Almost silence, broken by muffled sniffles.

"Very good," Golden approved. He marched, Emerald still dangling from his hold like a limp banner, back to the corner and set her standing, facing the corner. "Now stay there—silently."

"I'mhungry." All one word, in a little voice.

A light spank. "No you're not. You ate some sweets not an hour ago."

The old Emerald: "I *hate* you."

Another reminder. Boredly: "You've said that. You might at least show some imagination in your insults."

"I ha—" Very fast: "Ineedtorelievemyself."

"Are you sure?"

A long sniff. "I already—"

"Finish the job, then, you know where the pot is. Go, and come back immediately. Don't make me chase you. My hand will last longer than your skin will, and if it wears out, there's bound to be belts. Go."

Stiff-legged, sniffling, glaring, eyes promising *revenge*, she shuffled to the pot, used it, and reluctantly, as slow as she dared, shuffled back to her corner.

Golden sighed, strolled back to the clerk to lean on the board she was using as a desk. "Preliminary depositions, in secrecy for obvious reasons, have already been recorded in the Adjudicators' Hall. A preliminary adjudication has stated that, until I prove my claim one way or another, as little as possible will be done in re all contracts I once held. However, I believe that I can safely claim the guard captain Petrik, for now, don't you think?"

"I—I can't—"

"I merely intend to use him to help protect the Lady Emerald—except against me. Of course, since she just reduced him in rank, there might be difficulties. I, of course, aver my intention to restore him immediately I have the official adjudicatorial authority to do so, but . . ."

It was a nice point. The clerk, with one eye on her erstwhile c'holder, quivering in a corner, prepared to argue it out for hours, days if necessary.

Brine, grinning, strolled over to Petrik and sat them both comfortably and prepared to introduce him, with Jael's kibitzing, to the intricacies of Backgimon, using Petrik's own dice, a board scratched on the floor, and bits flaked off the wall for counters. The three guards and one of the pretty boys got into a gambling game, while the other boy sat between the two contracted women, gently teasing. (A stour or so later, the boy and the slut, looking about to see if anyone was watching, slipped around into a corner shaded by a stack of boxes. Not because either of them had any idea of privacy, but so nobody would tell them no, you can't.)

They were all prepared to wait, as comfortably as possible, until it seemed safe to come out.

Except that about two stours after Emerald had been exiled to her corner, Jael gasped and covered her mouth with one trembling hand, Golden stiffened, and Brine let out a curse.

"Is something wrong?" the clerk asked.

Golden seemed to be breathing deeply, smelling the air. Brine chewed his lip. Jael's head was bowed, her eyes closed.

"Is something wrong?"

"Smell," Golden ordered.

She did. "There's something—"

"Smoke," he informed succinctly. "The air's smoky. There must be a massive fire."

"A fire!"

"Downstairs somewhere." Jael stood up. "We're going to have to get out of here and take our chances. If there's fire down below, we can't stay here, to be trapped and burn!"

"Stone doesn't burn."

"Everything else will, once the fire's caught hold." Golden was checking for weapons. He strapped a sword and scabbard to his own waist, began pulling out others, handed one to Brine, another to Jael. "Can you defend yourself, lady?" he asked the clerk politely.

"Yes." She accepted a sword, strapped it on.

"Any of the rest of you?" He raised his voice, and one of the boys came forward, hand out.

"Is it really . . . that desperate out there?" the clerk asked.

"Worse. No choice, though. We're going to have to risk it." The clerk's eye flashed to the girl in the corner.

"No. Not yet. I'll protect her," said Golden. "Emerald." He snapped it out. "Come here. Stay under my left arm, no matter what."

"Can't we wait?" one of the guards asked, licking his lips, but he was sniffing the air worriedly.

"Only if you want to be roasted." Golden lined up his little band. "All right. Once more into the breach."

Jael sighed. "I taught you too well."

"For all our sakes"—he flashed her a smile—"I hope not."

TWENTY-ONE

Like a strand of wheat bending before the wind, from back to front, the bloodthirsty mob confronting Alizon and the Sandman began to bend, to slither senseless to the ground.

The last to fall, the huge, scarred male in front, looked surprised. The sword he was carrying dropped, missing Lysander by inches.

The two blinked and looked down the street for their rescuers. They were not hard to spot. Marching out of the Adjudicators' Unity and forming up were a mass of people. They were of all ages from child to ancient, men and women, dressed in yellow robes or very little, but all were alike in two respects. They all carried boxes and bundles of rustling parchment or heavy clay tablets, and they all had faces and bodies shouting *Determination.*

"Lady Alizon." A slight older man, his almost naked body pale and fragile-looking, strolled up, as casual as if he were sightseeing. "You waited for us. I said it was unnecessary."

"No." She gestured to the sprawled bodies. "You did this? You have weapons?"

"Yes. They have their limits, of course, but time is precious now." He noticed the Sandman and frowned. "You are the Sandman," he said, not an accusation, but a filing away. Later, if there was a later, would come the adjudication.

"He comes with us. With me, if you prefer," Alizon said hurriedly. The foremost of the Adjudicators was moving, and the rest lining up behind.

Aristide the Adjudicator had fine, pale brows. In the sunlight, they were almost invisible. They went up now, and he smiled. "Lady, 'twas you who brought us warning in time to have a chance to save our records. If you consider him more important than your own safety, of course he comes with us."

"Lysander." He had been standing, stunned by the violence, the savagery he'd unleashed. "Come, Lysander." She caught his hand, drew him toward the group moving slowly away. "You will be needed."

"I—" He came as she pulled, but slowly, unwillingly. "I— You saw. I can't."

"Tomorrow will be different. You will be *needed.*"

The colorless brow went up even higher, as Aristide eased the pair into the slowly moving phalanx of Adjudicators. The inner core consisted of the young and older, loaded down with their precious burdens. The outer rim had burdens, too, but they also had weapons showing, and their hands hovered, their eyes darted around, alert for enemies.

Alizon pushed Lysander into the ranks, farther in, caught a box that was about to topple from a too-high stack a child was struggling with, put it in his arms, filched another from the shoulders of a panting boy who was struggling to balance it, added a third from an older man's burden.

"I'll keep an eye on him." Aristide had come up, clutching his own burden, a stack of something wrapped in an oiled canvas. "You go to the front. Lead. You may be our best weapon."

"It doesn't work for me." Her lip twitched. "But it may for Lysander. I'll do what I can." She began to move through the throng, a slim wraith with a sheaf of pale-pink hair swinging like a banner.

"Um." Aristide stared at Lysander assessingly. The gaunt face and body were a man's, a man who has endured much and survived. But the wide, blank eyes were a child's, a hurt child's. The Adjudicator pursed his lips. He'd seen shock from the unendurable often in his career. But this one was a survivor. What they would have on their hands when the shock wore off . . . ?

He only hoped the Lady Navigator knew what she was doing. He'd rather have a sandcat than this unpredictable, dangerous man. At least with a cat one knew what to expect: violence, viciousness, and constant attack. The worst danger was the sudden turning without warning of what one thought was safe into savagery.

Their journey was nightmare slow, since Alizon insisted on warning folk as they passed. Because the mobs had split up, and were roaming randomly, they moved through large sections that seemed peaceful and undisturbed. They knocked on doors, asked if the c'holder or free-contractor was in, and quickly relayed the message, the messengers coming from the front of the moving line, and then re-joining in the back as they finished, or running around to do the same to a door farther down.

Many of those spoken to disbelieved, but the sight of a large mass of Adjudicators—plus the c'holders and contractors and their favorites who had joined them, carrying hastily gathered jewelry or (the practical ones) food and clothing—was a potent argument.

By the time they were halfway to the Guildhall, they had enough people to frighten off, by sheer numbers, any but the most suicidal of mobs. By then they were starting to pass where the mob had been, and the salt-sweet smell of spilled blood tantalized the air. More and more of the doors didn't answer, and if they were not empty within, there was nothing that could be done.

Several times they startled a small segment of the mob. Each time the smaller group, not quite that insane with bloodlust yet, fled, leaving behind their victims. The dead were left, the still-living carried along.

Medee Oriflamme, unluckily for her, was visiting in the house of a minor c'holder who arranged living amusements of ingenuity for the delectation of his fellow c'holders. Unlucky in two senses: She had not bothered to send a message to her own people when she accepted his invitation on a whim, and the man was notorious; many unfortunate contracteds had passed through his hands, writhed and screamed, been tortured and humiliated for his and his friends' pleasure. Even his guards had little loyalty, because they knew that one mistake, even whim, and they would be in the amusement pit, praying for release. Not death, he was careful about that. All his subjects got traded eventually, as they became hardened to torment.

Half a dozen hot-eyed contracteds slid into the kitchen, told their tale to the workers there. (Some had had their sessions in the amusement pits. All feared them.) Eye met eye, then the kitchen workers were arming themselves —knives, cleavers, pokers, skillets for those who couldn't find anything better.

Down to the basement, where those imprisoned, waiting their turns, were let out, armed.

The contracteds' quarters, where the night crew was sleeping.

A sweeper in the hall was gathered up, his broom head screwed off, the handle making a fine club.

By the time they strode down the wide hall, chanting, "The Sandman has spoken. Contracts are invalid. Kill the c'holders," there were over thirty of them.

There were guards at the entrance, staring at this unprecedented sight.

One of the men in the front rank greeted a guard by name. "Giles, the time has come. The Sandman has proclaimed it. Contracts are invalid."

Giles had had one session in the pit and knew he was due for another soon. "The c'holders—"

"KILL THE C'HOLDERS!" thundered back from a dozen throats.

"Kill C'holder Vessalyn!" Giles spat to his fellow guards.

"Yes," growled another guard gloatingly.

"No." A youngster. "It's not right. Contracts are sacred. I—" His eyes rolled up, his mouth drooped open, and he slid to the floor, tipping slightly sideways to display the hilt sticking up from his back.

The gloater retrieved his knife, wiped it mostly clean on the thick brown pelt of his leg. "Yesssss," he hissed.

The fourth guard didn't know or care if contracts were sacred. He just knew he couldn't stand alone against Giles and the gloater, much less the armed contracteds gazing at the door and almost drooling. "Down with the c'holders!" he shouted hurriedly.

His shout, like those earlier, went through the thick door, muffled, sound but not meaning. Those inside, if they heard it at all, ignored it.

C'holder Vessalyn was frowning. His reputation depended on the subtlety of his entertainments, and this current, even though it was only an intermission while a real entertainment was being prepared, still . . .

The victim wasn't pleading heartrendingly enough. The torturer—actually another victim, that was part of the amusement; watching the expressions, the desperation, on the face of the one knowing that as soon as his action ceased to amuse, *he* (or she) would be worked on—seemed almost apathetic.

"Stop," Lord Vessalyn ordered. The victim went limp. Lord Vessalyn studied both. No, he wouldn't switch them—yet. The victim, bound helpless in a rectangular frame that held him but exposed all his body except wrists and ankles easily, and could be turned and rotated to get him into any position, was a strong young male, who could take a lot more before he either lost consciousness or became too pain-hazed to be amusing. So far little had been done to him, actually. A few strokes of a cane, Lord Vessalyn's name drawn on his back with a tiny hot rod, splinters under his toenails. At the moment water was being forced down his mouth, and even that was coming to a close, as his stomach was dangerously distended, so he looked oddly like a pregnant woman.

"Clamp his nostrils closed," Lord Vessalyn ordered.

Medee Oriflamme tried to suppress a yawn. The entertainment was dull, her personal contracted wasn't enthusiastic enough, and the food was poor. She sighed. Ever since Golden Singh had left, entertainments had been dull. Now, there was a man who could plan an entertainment. She sighed again, remembering, and picked at the piles of sweets set on a handy table.

And sighed yet again. Even the food was tasteless.

Behind the c'holders were a dozen guards, yawning or trying not to look into the pit, according to their natures. No one in the front noticed when Giles opened the door a crack, stuck his head in, and, frowning, gestured two of his fellows to slip out and join him.

In the pit, following instructions, the amateur tormentor had clamped the victim's nose shut and covered his (muffled pleading) mouth with a coarsely woven cloth. The man was gasping and choking. A small wedge prevented him from closing his mouth, and the cloth was shoved deep down into his throat, causing him to gag reflexively and writhe convulsively.

Medee watched, then looked away. Boring. Beside her, Genesis, equally bored, snored, his mouth open.

Below, in the pit, the tormentor had jerked the victim's head back and was slowly pouring water into his mouth. Gagging, choking, convulsing, water and cloth going down his windpipe as he struggled to breathe, the victim was thrashing like a mad thing. But his audience couldn't hear him pleading.

"Pull the cloth out carefully," Vessalyn ordered. "Now, contracted, what do you have to say?"

His throat was raw from the abuse; he choked and gasped, only half conscious.

"Kick him in the belly a couple of times," Medee suggested idly. "See if he'll choke on the yorked-up water."

"Magnificent." Vessalyn applauded softly. "Then we'll try the cloth and water down again."

This time it was one of the guards who had left who stuck his head in, gestured two of his friends out into the corridor.

The second time the water-soaked cloth was pulled from the victim's mouth and throat it was smeared with pinky-red blood and scummed with tissue. The man hung limp, head down, breathing in pain-filled, shuddering gasps.

Vessalyn gestured a pair of his guards into the pit. "Cut him down, put the other up."

"*No*, please!" the to-be-victim screamed.

"Take him to the recovery room, and send out another contracted to work on him."

"Noooooooooo!" But the two guards were already in the pit, working in easy unison, one limp body slithering to the sand, another, struggling and cursing and pleading, going up.

In the back of the room, two of the guards who had left returned. Another pair, puzzled, frowning, went out to see what all the whispering and conferring was about.

"Ajax," Vessalyn ordered, "soften the new one up a bit. The cane or the leather strips, whichever; a light hand now." To Medee: "I can't understand the delay. It's a machine I haven't used before, but it should have been ready long since." A frown. "I'll have to do a little culling among my people." He knew how bored she was, because she didn't ask to see the results of that culling. His frown deepened. "Achilles," he called down sharply, "take that miserable lump out and see what the delay is."

One of the guards who had slipped back in went out again, quickly warned those outside. Nothing was coming because the basement was now empty, except for one protester—an older man who was prized by his master for his ingenious machines—who insisted that contracts were sacred and he for one, didn't intend to— He now lay sprawled on the floor, arms hugging the machine he had been working on, the blood from his slit throat tracing dark rivulets.

Achilles, big, strong, virile, and highly sexed, was a favorite instrument of his master, especially with female victims. But he knew how fickle his master tended to be, so he had the loyalty of a three-days-dead fish. He didn't even give his confronters a chance to ask. "Contracts are worthless?" He dropped his burden. *"Me first!"*

Once they had enough "recruited" guards outside the door, they could call them out in fours instead of twos. Then—

The sleeping Genesis never woke up. One of his own guards slit his throat, laughing maniacally.

A dozen men and women rolled over the Lord Vessalyn, picked him up, threw him into the pit, and jumped in after him.

Ajax, hearing the sudden roar as the door was opened and the mob poured in, looked up in time to see his master sailing down at him, followed by a dozen or more contracted, screaming, laughing, struggling to get close enough to plant a blow on the struggling Vessalyn. Achilles grabbed his partner.

"Our turn now. Let's string *him* up!"

"Wha—"

"Contracts are worthless! *Don't kill him!*" His deep voice, full of years of command, rumbled even over the mob's bloodlust. "Let us show you how."

Vessalyn, unable to adjust from master to victim, was roaring threats. Achilles grinned. Ajax's eyes widened, and he nodded. Working in easy unison, the two untied their original victim and tied up Vessalyn.

Above, Medee's slow reaction time had her barely sitting up before she was surrounded by wild-eyed contracteds. One of them leaped onto her lounge, shoved her flat, and tore up her skirts. He was naked, his condition and intent brutally obvious. She lay back with a sigh. Trust Vessalyn to come up with something new. The entertainment was boring, and her own contracted stud far overdue for replacement. She lifted her great hips, shifted slightly to make his access easier, and prepared to enjoy, sighing contentedly. The old ways are the best. Eventually the contracted was replaced with another, as violently enthusiastic as the first. Medee grinned and ignored the screams that were now coming from the pit. Vessalyn was getting trite, anyway.

It was the third contracted in line who realized that Medee, in her own odd way, was enjoying what was happening. Years of experience, perversions of all sorts, early schooling by a master of vileness—the more he attacked, the more her fingers digging into his back urged him on. When he was through, he glared down into her replete, drowsily smiling face. There had to be something. . . .

His lips twisted in a grin. The small knife he had snatched up in the kitchen was honed to a scalpel's sharpness; it could cut through an entire joint, bones and all. He grabbed her wrists, flattened her fingers. She let him, her other hand fumbling on the sweets table.

He poised the knife over the joint of her little finger.

Medee bucked and screeched, crumbs spewing from her open mouth.

The contracted smiled, tossed his still-bleeding souvenir up and caught it, waved the next man into position, and ostentatiously laid the small knife on the table, ready for its next use. Then he strolled off to see what was going on in the pit, whistling.

In the pit, Ajax and Achilles had organized the contracteds. They had rolled dice for who would have first go, and a thin woman, dressed in a loincloth, which revealed that she had had her nipples cut off at some point and odd jagged scar lines covered her body, had chosen the first. Vessalyn, still screaming, threatening, occasionally cajoling, had been tied to the frame, and now dangled, naked and upside down. At least a dozen fine fishhooks had been inserted at various points of his body, so fine that in only a couple of places was even a drop of bright blood trickling out of the wounds. But the hooks had chains attached; from the chains, shallow bowls dangled. The woman was slowly pouring sand into the bowls, and Vessalyn's threats quickly became interspersed with pleas.

When pouring in sand palled, the contracted began tossing pebbles in.

For Vessalyn, it was going to be a long, long night.

For Medee, not so long. Finger joints, ears, toes—by the time someone sliced off the tip of her nose she wasn't screaming, merely lying limply, eyes shut, breathing stertorously.

By the time one of the contracteds went for a more intimate souvenir, she wasn't breathing at all.

Emerald didn't realize that she was the last living member of the House of Oriflamme. She was too busy beating on a broad golden chest, coughing and choking, as the man who claimed he was not her father but she was his responsibility struggled to carry her down a smoke-filled staircase.

TWENTY-TWO

Coughing and choking, half blind from the smoke pouring up the stairs, Golden and Brine and Jael and Emerald's crew spilled through a doorway into a large room.

"I told you smoke would flush them out," gloated a man's hoarse voice.

"Stand aside." Even with the smoke's hoarseness, fifty years of command in Golden's voice made the contracteds pause. "I don't want to hurt you, but I will if I must."

Automatically, as they'd entered, the armed ones formed a semicircle, the noncombatants—except for Emerald, still draped over Golden's shoulder—in its heart.

Jael blinked, looked around. There might have been twenty or fifty contracteds facing the small, determined band. They had obviously broken into the supply cellar; the remains of a Lucullan feast were scattered about, and the faces of the mob bore greasy witness to their repast. Many of them staggered, and there were half a dozen barrels (wine?) broached and/or tipped over. (One of them had a pair of naked feet sticking up from it. Jael hoped it was empty and the owner of the feet had crawled in for a joke, but from the stillness of the feet, she feared it wasn't.)

"He's got her." A woman slinked up to face Golden. She was tall and thin, her eyes glittering like an animal's, her bony body draped in swaths of tissue-of-gold that Jael, at least, recognized as coming from draperies in Emerald's room. Many of the others were likewise sporting booty.

The gloater was a stocky male, grizzled gray but hard-muscled. "You're contracteds, like us." He was judging from clothing. The contracteds were wearing standard, or standard plus guard leather. Petrik had sent Brine and Golden simple clothing from the contracteds' supplies along with the healer-machine, and Jael's once immaculate rose-pink blouse had been sullied and torn during Emerald's games. "Haven't you heard the word? The Sandman has proclaimed it. Contracts are worthless." He roared a great laugh. "We can do what we want to c'holders. *And I'll tell you just what I want to do to her first.*"

There was a roar from the rest of the contracteds. Evidently most of them were Emerald's, and their only bone of contention was which of them would have the earliest turns.

Forty drunken maniacs, against a dozen, of which five were armed, trained guards, two more—Jael and Golden himself—capable of holding their own against odds, the rest noncombatants or unknown quantities. Nonetheless, Golden adjusted his burden slightly and said loudly and firmly, "Emerald Oriflamme is now my responsibility. Let us pass in peace."

"Leave her." The stocky man was the voice of the mob.

"No. Stand aside."

"You're ten to our fifty. We've no quarrel with contracteds, just her. We're free now, and—" To one of the guards: "Don't you understand, Mandan? We're all free. You don't have to obey her, don't have to do evil to your friends under threat of Agony Square. Mandan—"

It was the worst moment. Invited to join the mob, the guards had no reason to defend their own lives and many reasons, perhaps, to revenge themselves on Emerald. Golden shifted slightly on his feet, laid his hand on his hilt. "I said I meant no hurt to anyone, but if anyone attacks me, I will do whatever I must to defend myself and my responsibility," he said in a cold voice that gave the mob facing him pause. But beside him the man Mandan was hesitating, turning.

"No." It was the Adjudicator, moving to stand between Golden and the guard addressed as Mandan. "No. You know me, I am the Adjudicator Paloma, you know I speak only truth. All contracts still stand, and whatever violence has occurred this day will be paid for, once order is restored."

"Order!" The stocky man jerked.

"And order will be restored," she went on calmly. "Do you think the off-worlders, with contracts of their own to protect, will hesitate to settle things? Tonight, tomorrow, perhaps another day, and there will be an accounting. Contracts—"

"Where do you think we got the idea for the fire?" the stocky man said with a snort. "Contracts can't be enforced if they're destroyed. The Adjudicators' Unity and all contracts within are flames and smoke. All the contracts held here, too. How do you think we smoked you out?"

"*No!*" Paloma staggered, and Golden automatically put an arm to her shoulder to steady her. She looked up at him, lip trembling, shocked to helplessness at such destruction where she had been cool and calm at the threat to her own life. "All the records! No—"

"Adjudicator," the stocky man sneered. "Bad as a c'holder. Leave the two women, contracteds, or stay and join the fun. Last chance."

Golden shoved Paloma backward, sure that Jael was waiting, ready to gather the trembling, shocked woman into soothing arms. Mandan, the guard appealed to, turned toward Golden, his sword sliding out. It crashed back into its sheath as Petrik, on Mandan's right, smashed under his chin with his gloved left hand (the knuckles neat disks of gleaming copper), and the guard crumpled to the floor, forgotten.

Like a beast erupting through an opened cage into the arena, the drunken contracteds charged the small band.

Brine, to Golden's left, fought with half an eye on the guards on either side of him who might or might not switch coats. (Neither had thought of doing so. One was Staven, Petrik's gray-haired second; the other Halvord, the youngster who had been used as lure. But he had liked his opponents, Golden and Brine, admired them. And given his choice, he would have followed Jael anywhere, through any danger, faithful as a puppy and wishful of no more than an occasional pat on the head.) There were trained guards in the mob, but they were hampered by the pushing and shoving of the mass itself. Whereas the defenders simply closed ranks and attacked all close to them.

Jael thrust Paloma into the arms of the nearest noncombatant—the seamstress—and ordered, "Take care of her," before springing for the gap the fallen Mandan had left.

Petrik, almost instinctively, tried to give her what the guard had gotten, but she hissed, "Friend, you ape," and the familiar voice, stopped him. Then he could concentrate on taking out as many as he could of the mob.

In the first seconds, it looked like sheer force of numbers would do the trick, but the fallen piled up, making a small barricade the next ranks had to scramble over. With the pressure of the attack, the thin line compressed, backs against the wall or door or those they protected, and there was no way the mob could get behind them. Had their attackers been even slightly organized, they would have gone down, but as it was, it was like defending against a shark pack: cunning, vicious, bloodthirsty, but not intelligent. No one tried to step back and throw weapons to take out the defenders, and Golden, Brine, and Jael, along with Petrik, the remaining guards, and the young stud, were defending themselves ably.

It was the stud who was having second thoughts. When people charge at you waving weapons, you defend yourself. But all they wanted were the two women. He had nothing against Paloma, who defended the contracteds as much as she could. Emerald, on the other hand . . .

He had more than one score to settle against Miss High-and-Nasty Lady C'holder. If the defense broke, and he helped break it . . .

He wanted to hear her beg.

He wanted to be the one she was begging.

"Ah!" He moaned, doubled over, stepped back. Automatically, one of the guards stepped sideways to defend the sudden gap, and Brine moved to take over some of the space the guard left. The individual fights continued, one or two on one, but there was one less defender. Still bent over, he moved behind the guard, behind Brine. Huddled in the center were the two older women, plus Paloma, her eyes dazed, and the other stud.

"Can I help you?" It was the woman not comforting Paloma, raising her voice to be heard over the animal roar. He shook his head.

He had meant to take out Petrik, but the space was too tight, and the woman and his fellow stud were both watching him. It would have to be Golden. Probably best, anyway; Golden was leading the defense and in the center. Take him out and the others could come in. He straightened, raised the knife he'd been holding—

"Look out behind you!" the boy and the woman screeched together.

Jael twisted, her arm moved, knocking the knife-stroke awry. Not all the way; the hilt thunked lightly against the base of Golden's skull, then the stud wielding the knife was pulled back and thrown down by the sudden allies, the woman and the younger boy.

At the same instant, Jael's opponent struck, his cleaver smashing down on her shoulder, with a wet scrunch and a sharp crack audible over the screams and curses. Jael didn't scream, though her mouth came open. She froze, then crumpled slowly, blood spurting scarlet against the soft rose of her blouse.

"Aiyaaaaa!" Golden went berserker. He had been fighting carefully, his opponents stunned or disabled by flesh wounds. Now he charged forward, his deep voice bellowing obscenities, the sword in his hand swinging like a scythe, mowing down those who faced him.

He cut into the heart of the mob like the grim reaper himself, literally carving a path through the ranks, his sword swinging, growing dark as a severed hand flew in this direction and a chunk of head, brains glistening, in that.

The mob broke and fled. It was too much, the big man, golden from head to toe, the girl forgotten, draped over his left shoulder like a shawl, swinging that sword and fighting fearlessly, as if he couldn't be killed. Maybe he couldn't. A woman screeched in terror, and as that stained sword swung in her direction, threw herself against her neighbors. In seconds, the mob had turned, was fleeing.

"Cowards, come back and fight!" Golden roared after them, almost running. He was nearly at the door when Brine stopped him.

"Golden, she needs us." The voice wouldn't have done the trick, but the mind-link did, shocking him back into sanity.

Golden whirled. Petrik was making sure of his opponents, but using his hilt, not the blade. On the other side, the remaining guards were doing the same, using their blades until a snapped command made them reverse the bloody weapons. The two studs and one of the women were thrashing in the corner, and the other contracted woman, Brine, and Paloma the Adjudicator were bent over Jael's sprawled body.

Golden strode back, remembered Emerald at the last second and urgently dumped her to her feet. "You brainless, worthless thing," he snarled to the wide-eyed girl. "She needs me and you're not worth a scrap of her toenail. But I took responsibility for you, so listen and listen well. Out there right now, being a c'holder won't protect you. If anything, it's a short contract to torture and death. I'll protect you as long as I can. For now, stick close, don't interfere, and obey orders. Or you'll wind up like that." He pointed. One of his victims was twitching spasmodically, dead or dying, final convulsions.

She had seen people die all her short life. But never right next to her, so she smelled the blood, never herself been under attack, held helpless while the gladiatorial contest raged around her. She stared at him without speaking, her lower lip trembling.

"Obey me," he hissed, drawing the flat of his wet blade across her lower face, so that it trailed blood and scum from ear to ear. "Obey me! Petrik!" It was an order.

"Yes." Acceptance of the temporary responsibility.

He threw himself on his knees beside Brine.

In the corner, Staven, the older guard, finishing with the dozen or so unconscious or dead, strode over and grabbed two upper arms, separating the combatants by sheer strength. "What's going on here?"

"He struck at the golden one from behind," the woman accused shrilly. "I cried warning, and the striped-haired woman turned to block the blow. 'Twas how she got hurt, and the line broken."

"That's what happened," the younger boy corroborated.

"Ah!" He turned to the one stud, dropped the other, and pulled out the sword he'd sheathed to stop the fight.

"No." Petrik came up behind him, dragging Emerald by one wrist.

"No? He's a traitor."

"No," Petrik repeated, impaling the trembling youngster on a glance sharper than an épée. "I know he's a traitor, but I know how *they* think. Stun him, bind him, and leave him."

"Please."

"Please?" Petrik raised his sweat-darkened brows. "You could be dead."

"I didn't mean to hurt the lady." His mouth turned down in a scowl. "I wanted to hurt *her.*" He glared at Emerald, still clamped to Petrik's side.

"I'm your c'holder!"

"You're a nothing! You think I liked you, any of us liked you? Playing up to you, you conceited, mindless bitch, was almost worse than Agony Square. I wanted, just once—"

It was just what the other freed contracted had said. "You 'tracted!" She screeched and lunged, fingers out like claws.

Only Petrik's grip on her one wrist saved the youth's eyes. As it was, the nails of her free hand scored deeply down his cheeks, blood spilling in the five channels.

Weirdly, he smiled, his tongue tasting the blood. "I hope they scar," he told her, struggling and shrieking in Petrik's grip. "I hope they scar. Then, no matter what happens, I'll never be expected to please an ugly, witless, nauseating thing like you again."

She screamed again and pounded on Petrik's chest with her free hand, struggling with the other one, writhing and sobbing, "Let me at him, let me at him!"

"Hush!" Petrik had had about as much as he could take, too. He reached back and slapped her, full in the face, with careful force. "Hush," he told her frozen, stunned face, one hand on the slapped cheek. "We've no time for this now. You're not witless, I know. You've just never needed to use the wits you have."

She sniffed, a long, snuffling noise.

"As for beauty or ugly," he went on hurriedly, forgetting for a second his small audience, "the Lady Jael said a thing to me not long since, and I think it's truth. Beauty exists only in the gaze of whoever's looking at you." His mouth twitched. "She was trying to explain why she thought the man Brine beautiful, when I could see he was less than plain." He caught her chin, stared boldly into the lost young eyes. "You could have beauty; you have the potential for it. If you use the wits you were born with, you'll listen to the man Golden and the man Brine and the woman Jael, and any others who can help you develop that beauty."

He had slept with her a dozen, more, times, each time praising her to the skies. Now he spoke bluntly but with the ring of sincere truth. Her lip trembled.

"Captain." From Staven the guard. "What about him?" Nodding to the stud.

Petrik hesitated, then spoke to the youth, standing there with five rivulets of blood trickling down his face. "You said please. Please what?"

His eyes dropped. "Take me with you," he said, low-voiced.

"You'll like be safe enough. We'll leave you tied loose, or someone will come along."

"No. That's not—" He licked his lips. Then, all in a rush: "I want to learn, too."

"Ah." Petrik exchanged glances with Staven, his lieutenant, and Halvord, the remaining guard. (And was a little surprised to see the almost instant understanding in the youngster's eyes.) Then, wryly: "So do I. So how can I refuse you? But one warning, traitor. Turn your blade or your hand against any of us, and I'll slit your weasand on the spot."

"You're going to let him, just like that," the other boy burst out.

Petrik smiled. "I'm learning, too."

The youngster thought it over. "You think they'd be willing to teach me, too."

"I think"—Petrik was suddenly sober—"that they teach just by being what they are, and that they'd turn no one away who wants to learn from them."

"Oh!" The boy smiled brilliantly.

There was the sound of running footsteps, coming from the open doorway at the opposite end of the room.

The thing that impressed Paloma most, herself still half in shock from the thought of the records in the Adjudicators' Unity burning, was the way Golden and Brine worked in unison.

Neither one of them had spoken a word to each other, but as soon as Golden had dropped to his knees beside the sprawled body, his hands swooped out and seconded Brine's.

Not that they didn't talk—to her, to the other woman. But not to each other. It was as if they knew.

She looked down at the partially exposed wound and bit her lip. Could a person live with that much damage?

They had brought a minimum of medical supplies with them, and the men were using them lavishly.

She suddenly noticed that Brine himself had a long, sullenly oozing scratch on his left arm. Waiting until he didn't seem to be using that arm, she swiped it with a cloth soaked in healing lotion.

"Thank you," he said, not looking up from his work.

"More healant," Golden barked, almost at the same minute.

She slapped another plastic pack, its corner torn off, into his hand before answering Brine. "You're welcome. No use getting an infection."

"Infection," he said, and snorted.

Paloma looked down at the patient and chewed on her lip. There was so much blood. She was vaguely aware of the scuffle in the corner, of the subsequent murmur of voices, but mostly she was another pair of hands to try to stop the bleeding, to pack the ghastly, gaping wound.

Once, Brine looked up blindly, and she caught her breath. If his own arm had been hacked off, he wouldn't have had as much pain and rage and fear in his eyes.

She didn't hear the footsteps until the other woman tapped her. The two men remained as they were, and she got up, pulled out her weapon, to protect against this new enemy.

He burst into the room, a red-haired man in a spacer jumpsuit of aquamarine, torn and filthied from tousled head to bare toes. (His boots were strung on his belt. Odd, a part of her mind noted.)

"Outofmyway," he snarled, and kept coming.

She tensed, aimed the point at his midriff.

"Friend, Paloma," Brine barked, and she whirled to see him still bending over the dying woman.

"How do you—"

But he had used her distraction, slapped the blade out of his way and almost literally vaulted over her to land beside the other two, dropping to his knees and reaching to haul a small pack off his back.

"We'll need a container," he was saying, digging into the pack and pulling out some sealed packets.

"Paloma." Brine was still forcing pads into the wound, his hands covered in red. "Water and something to hold it in. Boiled if you can, but anything will do. She's fading fast."

"What—"

It was the newcomer who looked up, explained. "I've supplies, including concentrated plasma to help replace what she's lost. But we need water to dilute it in. Boiled or plain. If we can keep her alive, we'll worry about infection later."

"Right." She stood up, hesitated. For all the time she'd lived in the Oriflamme/Singh holdings, she hadn't the foggiest idea where the kitchens were.

"I'll help." Petrik winked, knowing her problem. "Staven." He handed over Emerald's wrist, his eyes warning the other man. "Guard."

"Yo."

"I'll come, too," the younger stud volunteered. "You'll have to guard, and there might be stuff we can use, left." He looked around the room, sniffed. "If they left anything."

"Me, too," the older woman exclaimed. "I can carry, and"—a swift glance at the scene by the archway—"I know nothing of the healing arts."

A muscle in Petrik's cheek jerked, but he said nothing aloud. He was afraid it was a soul-guider they needed here, not a healer.

"I'm strong, too," the older boy volunteered also.

"Someone should stay here, sentry-watch." Halvord was growing up rapidly.

"Right. Let's go, then."

When they got back, with the water and some carefully selected packs of what had been left after the banquet/orgy, Brine and Staven were constructing a litter. Petrik noted, amused that Staven had solved his prisoner problem the simplest way: Emerald's hands were bound, judging from the color, with her own skirt, and there was at most a foot of slack connecting the bound wrists and Staven's belt. Since he was bent over, working, she was squatting, too. From her expression, she was adding more to the accounts.

"Ha!" The red-haired spacer jumped up, grabbed for the water, and began pouring from the bucket into his odd spacer packet, which began swelling as the water went in, until it was as big as the bucket had been. With quick, skilled movements, he hooked the packet onto some sort of support, planted the support next to her, and began pulling a tube out of the bottom corner of his whatever-it-was. When the tube stretched down long enough, he pushed the end of it against her bent elbow, where it stuck. There was an odd, gurgling noise.

"Come'n," Brine ordered Staven. The two dragged their makeshift litter over next to the wounded woman.

"You can't move her!" Petrik burst out.

Golden looked up, wiping his hands absentmindedly on his short tunic. "We've no choice."

"No choice. She needs a medic, I'll go for one. And—she shouldn't be moved."

"I know." Death looked at him from haunted golden eyes. "But I told you, no choice. She needs care, proper care, now, and—"

Petrik looked down at her, at the ruined shoulder and soaked blouse, made a wordless protest.

"Smell," Golden said, almost calmly. Petrik drew in a breath.

"It still smells smoky."

"Because they left the fire they set to smoke us out unattended. By the time we realized—it's past stopping, even if there were more of us. This whole building will go, and maybe . . . Who knows how far or fast it'll spread."

"Sacred." Petrik's mouth dropped open.

For some reasons, c'holders prized and fought over these high houses built close to the remains of one of the ancient walls. But not far away was the rookery, one of the worst areas of the city. If the fire got into that . . .

"Precisely," Golden Singh said with a nod.

TWENTY-THREE

The city was burning.

During that first night of blood and terror, most people had been too busy defending or revenging themselves to think ahead or notice what was happening. The Hall of the Adjudicators' Unity burned while a mob of contracteds stood and cheered. The wind carried sparks, and they backed away as the heat became more intense.

Many of the watchers had a place they hated most, a gladiatorial pit, a c'holder's manse, a factory, a palace of pleasure. More than one cowering c'holder was smoked out of sanctuary. More than one c'holder was bound or hamstrung, left in the midst of a pile of flammables, or slow-roasted over a hearth fire too big for the hearth.

Mud-brick and stone won't burn, but almost everything else in and of the buildings would, from the straw in the stables to the draperies that were used as room dividers and doors as well as window covers. Once started, the fires grew and spread like ravenous beasts, eating all in their path and growing hungrier.

Many were caught, that first night, sleeping off their drunken stupors; they died, writhing in the flames. Others wakened and fled, some not stopping until they reached the almost dry river, others fleeing into the distant hills. Some were trapped, the very masses of the fleeing folk jamming a narrow way until smoke or flame caught them.

Many of those caught or trapped died; a few were spared by one fluke or another.

The vast spaceport, with its acres of synthi landing surface, was a natural goal for many of the refugees. The native fringe was as vulnerable as the rest of the city, crowded and—with its many storehouses—tinder for the first spark.

But the broad, nonflammable surfaced landing area, and places such as the fortresslike Guildhall, were natural islands of safety, and people headed there instinctively.

The first night, Guildhall had been stuffed to the gills with refugees from the mobs. That night the fires began their toll. By the next day those fighting their way through were fighting mostly the mobs, but some came smoke-blackened.

And by the day after that . . .

The first floor of Guildhall had been taken over as a hospital for the emergency cases. The lesser cases, walking wounded, were either treated and released to the courtyard, or stashed in the higher rooms, wherever space was available.

The second floor was command center. Banks of communicators linked not only the ships and their worried captains and crews, but the bands of men and women—armed against the still-raging mobs—who were out in the city fighting the fires, guided by two tiny hovers contributed by one of the huge luxury liners (they were normally sight-seeing vessels) and all coordinated by the desperate men and women in the small room.

"You can't, you can't!" the white-haired woman was screaming.

Lysander swiped sweat and grime off his forehead. He no longer looked like the desert sand; like all of his squad, strangers two endless days ago, now mates, he was a filthy ash gray. "I'm sorry, Mother, we must."

"No. *No! No!*" She was clutching what looked like an embroidered pillow to her thin chest. "You can't. I bother no one. I have a contract. My c'holder—"

One of the lucky ones, he thought. Pensioned off, with a tiny space of her own and a food contract. "Mother." He made his voice gentle with an effort. "We must." Though the wind was blowing toward where the fire raged, there was dust and smell of scorch in the very air. "Mother, we must. The fire must be stopped. And the only way to do it is to start a counterfire from here."

"You mustn't, you—" She stopped. "You're the Sandman," she squeaked.

"Yes."

Almost a moan: "You must?"

"Yes."

"And—after?"

He'd not thought about after; now he was living in it. "I'll take care of you after, Mother. Unless— Stay with my squad. But if we . . . get separated, or anything, go to the Navigators' Guildhall, to the Lady Alizon, say I sent you and she is to see to you."

"Yes." Worshipful. "Sandman."

Alizon's husband, the Navigator Spyro, was with another squad. But though arms and legs and brain were worrying about a burning city, fleeing people, and moaning victims, underneath he was focused on only one person, his wife Alizon.

The psychic Alizon was heavily sedated and under partial life support. She was not burned, had not been hurt in the one mob attack the band of Adjudicators had had to fend off before reaching the sanctuary of Guildhall.

It was the mob violence that had felled her. Worried about the Navigators and the world, her psychic abilities tuned to their highest pitch, she had been vulnerable to the red blast of bloodlust and fury as the mob had grown and fed. Screaming, as she joined minds with victims and violators, she had been given a light sedative, then heavier and heavier ones. Now she lay unconscious, and frantic healers, with far too many patients, tried to remember to check to see if she needed additional attention.

Spyro tried not to think about her, as he grimly beat at small running flames, or kept a stream of frightened people moving, out away from danger.

Rowan Reis, his red hair and beard a sweat-soaked matted tangle, his eyes a little wild, was working in the bowels of one of the liners. He and three engineers were struggling to cannibalize some ship's supplies to make large portable extinguishers that could be deployed from the air. The small portable extinguishers the ships carried had already been taken and occasionally brought back for refills, but their smallness limited their use. However, if they could jury-rig these pumps and chemicals . . .

Every now and then he paused, as though listening to voices none of his companions could hear, and then, with an oath or a sigh, got back to it.

The two men and a woman working with him were too busy to exchange glances. But they all knew vaguely that he had folk out fighting the fires, and that was a lot to worry about, even if the fires didn't veer and threaten the port itself.

Brine led a squad of mixed Adjudicators, enforcers and grim contracteds, competently, but there were more tears running down his cheeks than could be accounted for by smoke.

Back at the command post, the Guildmaster took advantage of one pause, when nobody was screaming an emergency to ask the Chief Adjudicator, who was manning one of the screens, "The fires will be conquered or die out eventually, Lord Adjudicator. What about after?"

"I've been thinking about that. We're going to need your help."

"You'll have it."

"All you off-worlders' help?"

"You'll have it—or else."

The Adjudicator smiled to himself and turned to a screen where somebody was screaming at him. But despite the worried frown as he listened, his mouth curved in a gentle, Machiavellian smile. The Guildmaster had not thought to ask exactly what kind of help the Adjudicator had in mind.

Brandy was acting as a nurse. The Guildmaster had ordered that—for her own safety—she be kept secure within the walls of the Guildhall, and in all the confusion had never thought to amend that. So Brandy stayed, though she would have volunteered to go out and help fight the fire, even though she thought—nobody had told her all the details of the adjudication because of the confusion—she would be at risk from her mother.

So she walked slowly down the long aisle of moaning or silent people, here checking the life-support as she'd been hurriedly taught of a woman Navigator with a cleaver-ruined shoulder, there checking on a blinded burn victim, farther on slipping her arms under a pair of anonymous shoulders and letting the unfortunate drink.

She had been at the whole routine so long she did it all like a sleepwalker, which is almost what she was. At the end of the hall, she went up a staircase to the room she had shared with Estaban, to knock and peek in. There were dozen or so people in it, mostly refugees sleeping on blankets on the floor. Three children were crowded in the bed. One of them, a little girl with her hair singed off, sat up wild-eyed, but Brandy put her fingers to her lips, whispered, "Just checking, go back to sleep," and shut the door.

She sighed, her shoulders sagging, as she went back to her duties. Strangers. All strangers. Estaban was still—

—Heading up a small squad of dare-alls who were the cutting edge of the firefight. Checking houses in the path of the flames for unconscious but savable victims, using blankets, water, sand, chemicals, anything to gain a few meters of ground, a few minutes to get people out of the path, anything to hold back death until people could be cleared away in front of it.

Once, when they were running from one emergency to the next, the free-contractor who was his second-in-command panted, "Like your off-worlder's hell, isn't it?"

"Always," answered Estaban, in such an odd voice that his cohort turned to stare at him.

For three days the mobs and then the fire held sway, but gradually they both burned out.

In a way, the fire was a blessing, for all the destruction and death it caused, because it stopped the mob violence with a speed that nothing short of some other major disaster—tornado, volcano eruption, earthquake—would have.

Three days of terror, and effort, and agony passed, and on the fourth morning the survivors, soot-blackened and exhausted, looked at each other.

Smoke floated on the air, great swaths of the city were rubble and ash, but the ravening, yellow-eyed, red-fanged monster had fed on itself and died.

After had come.

Small groups of men and women, wearing bands of tricolored braid on their foreheads, yellow, black, and silver, moved through the crowds of weary, frightened hungry refugees. They passed out concentrates—and a message: "Eat and rest. Tomorrow we will all meet and decide."

"Decide what?" the recipients—a woman nursing her baby, a naked man who had seen a life's labor eaten by flame and floating on the wind—might ask.

"After."

TWENTY-FOUR

The worst was over. The city stank of wet ashes and bitter tears. Thousands of refugees huddled on the sleek synthi of the port or on piles of rubble left by the fires or the firebreaks. Weary people dragged themselves about, looking for loved ones who may or may not have survived, or food or shelter. The fire had (mostly) burned out bloodlust along with half the city, and the survivors, if they remembered their just grievances, were too physically and emotionally exhausted to do anything about them.

Not that many c'holders were stupid enough to try to regain what had been their human property. Many contracteds stuck with their c'holders because of affection, respect, or habit, but woe unto one of the cruel kind who snapped out an order without guards to back it up.

In the fortresslike Guildhall, a group of people who were calling themselves the After Committee worked together to design a blueprint for living on the new Rabelais. No one had elected them. No one had appointed them. They were just a group of people who wanted tomorrow to be better than today, and that the terrors of the riot/revolution would never strike again.

They talked mostly, and recorded their discussion. They dragged in any who might have something to contribute—spacers to start with. Some staggering from lack of sleep fighting the fire, but willing to croak on about the system or systems used on their home worlds.

Several of the Navigators—besides Alizon, now recovering from the bestial mob mind—were sociometricists. It was a mathematical discipline, after all, and Navigators were mathematicians to the core, loving all form of mathematical puzzles, diversions, and complexities.

The After Committee was listening to a chief engineer from Algorithm with politeness, but after the endless hours spent together, they knew each other's very expressions so thoroughly that it might as well have been said aloud: A system that depends on every citizen having his own computer, and voting on every minor issue, even whether the medical assessment should be raised to provide a new emergency station to an outlying area, would never work on low-tech Rabelais.

There was a timid knock on the door. The engineer stopped, and people twisted and turned to see what was wrong.

Alizon got up, her pale hair a banner, raised a hand to stop questions, and said loudly, "Come on in."

Brandy, dressed in her apprentice whites, now grimy and creased, stood in the doorway. Behind her was the stocky, gray-haired Brine.

"I beg pardon for interrupting you," she said hesitantly, "but—"

"Have you something to contribute?" barked a spacer captain near the door, known to her crew as Hard-As-Nails, who had come to talk and stayed to add to the discussions.

"No." Brandy flinched from the woman's sternness. "I—I'll go."

"No!" From Brine, and at the same time, Alizon said, "Wait!" Spreading her hands in appeal, she spoke to the others. "We are working for a better future for all. But what kind of future can we possibly build if we start by denying individual need?" She looked around slowly, gathering nods from those whose opinions carried most weight within the group. "You see"—to the young girl and the man—"we're here. What do you want of us?"

Brine was literally swaying on his feet with fatigue, his eyes sunken in a face gray beneath its bronze. "Help!" Then, his eyes focusing on her: "Lady Alizon. Help me. I can't bear to lose them both."

"We've a patient who's dying," Brandy hurriedly explained. "One of the firefighters. When he collapsed, they thought it was exhaustion or the fumes. But it was an unsuspected internal bleeding. When they realized, they brought him in. The medics could fix the wound, prevent further loss of blood. But he's weak, dying, he lost too much blood, and we've none to replace it with. Nothing, it was all used, everything. He's dying. He might live if he had blood given him by somebody who could spare it, but the medics say he has a rare sort of blood, that he'll die for sure if we give him any from those who've already volunteered to give blood."

"I see," the woman captain said with a decisive nod. "You're looking for donors."

"Yes!" said Brandy.

"He's dying. If he doesn't have a transfusion *soon* . . . The medics say he can't even accept the stripped blood they usually use in such a case," said Brine.

"Where do we go to be tested?" Tamilee, off-worlder now Rabelaisian, asked.

"I don't understand," murmured one of the Rabelaisians.

"There's a patient dying, who could be saved by a gift of blood in an amount easily spared from a healthy person," Tamilee explained hurriedly. "But not all blood is exactly the same, and the wrong kind of blood can kill as quickly as poison. These people are looking for a person or persons whose blood can help the man who is dying."

"I still don't understand," the Rabelaisian said with a nod, "but if you'll tell me what to do to prevent this person from dying, I'll be glad to try."

Brine sagged against the doorway. "Thank you!" Then, muttered: "You who made the spinning worlds and Sanctity, save my son!"

The Chief Adjudicator, sitting near the door, recognized the oath and raised a brow. The man might be dressed in spacer garb, but he was Rabelaisian.

"We've test papers." Brandy was handing out thin transparent sheets from a box in her hand. "Peel the top sheet off like this." She demonstrated. "And then put the newly exposed surface against your bare skin. Anywhere, face, back of the hand, as long as it touches your skin." She continued to pass them out.

"Nothing's happened, it's just lying there," the Rabelaisian commented.

"Anybody—has the tester changed?"

Alizon shook her head. "Not me. What have you rigged—"

A man at one end of the long conference table stood up. "Mine's turned bright red. Does that mean . . . ?"

Brine straightened with a sigh of relief that answered the question without words. "Come with me, please—lifesaver."

The man wriggled through the chairs and people to the doorway. "Now?"

"He's dying." Brine grabbed an arm and pulled.

"Anyone else?" Brandy asked. "Did I miss anyone with the testers? Did anyone else's tester change?"

There was a chorus of no's, and heads shook.

"I'll keep looking, Brine." To the committee: "Thank you. I'm sorry to have interrupted, I know how important what you do is, but he's worked so hard, and he's dying." A gentle smile. "I don't even know his name. A spacer."

"Good luck," said the Rabelaisian. "You've found one, you'll find others." It was a dismissal.

"I thank you, ladies, lords." She ducked her head, scurried out, closed the door behind her.

The hospital area was still jammed worse than any ship's emergency lifeboat packed with all, instead of part of, the crew. Despite that, many of the patients had one or more companions, checking equipment as harried nurses had showed them, or talking, or, if the patient was unconscious, simply holding a hand, trying to keep the thread of life going by sheer will.

Brine twisted and squirmed his way through the packed bodies toward a pallet slightly to one side of the hastily converted room. Two people were seated on the narrow pallet, crowding the patient. One was a russet-haired man in the remnants of a guard's uniform, his shallow-eyed gaze frozen to the console perched precariously by the patient's head.

The other, held by a hand clamped tightly around her wrist, as she unconsciously pulled away, her face twisting at the smell and sound of slow death and pain all around her, was a girl who might have been Brandy's age, give or take a few months. But the contrast between them couldn't have been greater, though a general description would have fitted either of them: early adolescent females, long brown hair, still childishly slim. Yet where Emerald's expression was the petulance of long spoiling, Brandy's ordeal and the work in the hospital had matured her immensely. The clear, richly colored eyes were soft with compassion, glowing with inner strength and willingness to give. The heavy shadows beneath them and the paleness smudging her skin were like badges of honor. The russet-haired man had smiled at her with genuine gratitude when they first brought the patient in; instinctively he had recognized that if skill and will and plain hard work and care would bring the patient through, then this tired girl-child could and would supply all but the first, or drop dead from exhaustion.

It was Emerald that Lysander, being half dragged along behind Brine noticed first, mainly because she was straining away from Petrik and facing the door. Instinctively, he dug his heels in. But Brine, thinking he had gotten caught in the tight spaces, only jerked harder on the arm he still held.

"Lady Emerald," Lysander protested.

"No other place to put her, wish there were." Brine dodged around a double bed with half a dozen moaning children squirming on it. "She's willing him dead every second."

"Ah." Lysander relaxed and squirmed after. Any enemy of Emerald's was ipso facto—

"No!" This time he dug in his heels so hard that Brine, despite the disparity in their weights, was jerked to a halt. He turned, mouth dropping open at the expression of sheer hatred distorting the pleasant face of the only man so far they'd found who could give blood and save—

"No!" Lysander repeated. "Not him! Anyone but him!"

"What?" Brine shook his head as though to clear it, with the slowness of a man struggling through a molasses-all-around nightmare. "Why not? He's *dying!*"

Hissed between clenched teeth: "Let him die! That's Golden Singh!"

"For Sanctity's sake!" Petrik had realized that this was the person they had gone to find, the one who could save Golden's life. Now, at the last second, he was refusing. "If he dies, I go back to her."

Emerald snickered, a vicious, triumphant cackle.

"That's only one more reason for letting him die," Lysander bit out. "Nothing's worse than belonging to him. I *know.*"

Petrik's mouth twisted. "You're insane! You don't know her!"

"But you will!" Emerald pointed out gleefully, a threat and a promise.

"I know him," Lysander repeated grimly.

Petrik was shaking his head. "No. Or you'd be pleading to help."

"No is right," said Brine, raising a big fist. "You don't have to be conscious to give your blood."

Lysander knew a trained fighter when he faced one, to say nothing of fanatical determination. Nonetheless he shifted, intending to defend himself as best he could. "Use *me* to help *him*, my greatest enemy."

Anyone could have seen what the outcome of a fight between Brine and Lysander would be, but it wasn't Lysander's pitiful-by-comparison defense that made Brine lower his fist, unclench it with an effort of will reflected in the sheen of sweat along his jaw, the tight muscles in his cheek. "You *slime!* But he says he'd rather die than take the gift of life torn so unwillingly from anyone. You worthless lump of stupidity. My son's worth ten of you."

"Son." Lysander wriggled, got to where he could get a good look at the man on the pallet. The gray-haired Brine was dressed in spacer clothes; perhaps the dying man was a spacer too. Everyone knew that the Singhs had bought their GAing from spacers. So maybe . . .

"Your son." Suspicious: "How can you know what he wants?"

"We're linked. Mind-to-mind sharing. His body's unconscious, but his— his selfness retains some awareness. As you might be asleep, but answer questions aloud sometimes without waking."

While Brine had been talking, Lysander had been staring. The man on the pallet looked young. There were fatigue shadows hollowing the sunken eyes, and he looked as if he had gotten too close to the flames more than once. His lashes were thick but stubby in spots, and the waving golden mane likewise looked as if patches of it had been burned and fallen off. The bone structure was right. It was hard to tell exactly how he'd look with his eyes open, but he looked too young. Men got older as the years passed, not younger.

"He's not Golden Singh, then."

"Oh." Brine had realized what he had, a man who had a personal vendetta against the Singh that was. "That can't be answered simply," he said slowly, incurably honest.

"If he *is* Golden Singh—"

"He was Golden Singh," Brine barked. "He's someone else now."

Emerald managed to stand, wriggled her hips at Lysander. "Promise not to help him," she cooed, "and I'll give you such pleasure."

"Bitch!" Petrik sneered. Habit made it under his breath, but he had been growing through these interminable days, too. "An offer like that would make me give my lifeblood to anybody!" he added, louder.

"You'll beg!" Emerald stuck her tongue out at him childishly. "I've been doing nothing for days but think of how I'll make you pay, you traitor!"

Petrik looked at the console, then back at her. "You'd better start praying for him, bitch. You'll survive him by seconds, and I don't care what they do to me afterward."

"Petrik, no." Brine had been distracted. "He wouldn't want that and you know it."

"I don't care what he would have wanted," Petrik said wildly. "I'll not go back to her!"

Brine, like Jael or the new Golden, was incapable of not helping someone when he could. "You'll not go to her in any case, Petrik. You know he cares. He left a new will, attested before he went out to fight the fires. Do you know the Lady Tamilee Zarkos, she who was bonded to the Lord Karolly Zarkos?"

"Oh." Petrik collapsed.

Lysander blinked. "He left his heirship to the Lady Tamilee Zarkos?" he asked hollowly.

"Among others like her." His eyes checked the console. He caught a scrap of lip between his teeth.

"That's impossible. I know her, she's much like the Lord Karolly, or the blessed Lady Esme Oriflamme. He'd never—"

Brine drew a breath. "I told you he'd changed. The Golden he is now would die himself, gladly, to prevent anyone from suffering under those like her, or like the man he once was."

Bitter: "I don't believe you. No man could change so much."

Equally bitter: "And you the man who talked so much about people renewing themselves every seven years!"

"He is what he was!"

"The man who talked about obligation to common humanity. Well, boy, there it is!" He pointed at Golden, his finger trembling. "There he is, a human being. A human being, dying, that you could save, at no cost to yourself, except a little time that you might be sleeping. Sanctity, you can sleep. A few hours," he pleaded, "and a man will live who would have died."

"Anybody but him!"

Brine caught his shoulders. "You mentioned the blessed Lady Esme. Were she here, what would she think of your selfishness, your refusal to aid a fellow human?"

"I loved her. But I am as he made me."

"The spacers have a word for that," Brine sneered. "They call it a cop-out. An excuse. You're as you made you. We're all responsible for ourselves. In the end, it is every single one of us who makes his or her own choice. Every single one." His lip curled. "Odd, that sounds familiar. I have heard words very like them recently. They sounded sincere, but it seems to be that the man who said them only intended them to apply to others, not himself."

"I don't care. Proclaim it from the height of the wall, if you wish. I won't. You can't make me."

"He's a good man." Petrik suddenly reentered the fray. "She hates him. Doesn't that convince you?"

"They hate each other, the bad ones. It doesn't prove a thing."

Petrik clenched his fists. "If I could give my blood, I would. I know him, I tell you. I'd give all of it, if it would help him."

"So you say."

Petrik suddenly smiled. Still holding Emerald with his left hand, he drew his sword, cautiously for the crowding, and laid it against the side of his neck, the scalpel-sharp point aimed at his jugular. "Shall I prove what I say?" he asked.

"Petrik, no!" Brine cried out.

"He wouldn't want that, I know—but *I* want this. Our world needs him and those like him more than it needs me." He was opposite the pallet from Brine, far enough away that he couldn't reach him in time.

"No!" from Lysander.

Petrik didn't lower the sword. But he didn't thrust it in, either. "You'll give him what he needs."

"I—I'll discuss it."

Petrik smiled. "That's not good enough." He drew his hand back. Brine leaped over the bed. Emerald struggled, fearing the glittering blade so close to her own body.

It was the scream that stopped them all, Petrik poised with the blade starting to slice, Brine vaulting, Emerald jerking away. *"What are you doing!"*

Brandy had come in. She stood a few feet away, separated from the tableau in the corner by two filled pallets. "What are you doing?" she repeated in a broken voice. "Sanctity preserve us, hasn't enough blood been shed, you fool, that you add your own?"

"Did you find someone else?" Petrik barked.

"No." She shook her head. "He's it. What's wrong?"

"He won't," Petrik informed her grimly, while Brine regained his balance and made a grab for the sword. Petrik let him have it. To Brine: "I'm a guard, man. D'you think you'd've stopped me? Do you think I haven't more—"

Brandy had squirmed close enough to put her hand on Lysander's arm. "I don't understand," she said in the hoarse little voice that was all she had left. "You agreed. He's dying. Why won't you help?"

"He's my enemy," Lysander said simply. "I hate him more than I thought possible to hate. Because of him, I brought the whole system down. If you gave me the choice of having my own throat cut or giving blood harmlessly to save him, I would choose my own death."

"You should be made to—" Brandy started, then stopped. "That's what it was all about, individual's choice. But when it's your emotions, versus his life . . . He's dying now. If you change your mind later, not want his death on your conscience—"

"I'll dance in the streets when he goes!"

"It'll be too late." Her shoulders sagged. "It was all for nothing."

"Yes," said Brine grimly.

"What we did, what you did, the deaths, the fire, the hurt and screaming and the lives we struggled to save, all for nothing. It's never going to change, not really. The names, the forms, the outwardness, they may seem to change. But it's all a sham. After is going to be just like before."

"What do you mean?" Lysander barked it out.

"It's all a lie. All of it. All the things the Sandman said, about making tomorrow better than today. People don't change. If anyone, for any reason, can just stand back and let a man die." She looked straight at Lysander, her sunken, richly colored eyes almost serene. "I thought what my mother did to Estaban—giving him the Elysium, worse, destroying his faith in himself, all he held of value—I thought that was the worst a person could do. I guess I was wrong. I guess a lot of us were wrong." Carefully, she laid the small pile of testers on the foot of the bed, and turned.

"Where are you going?" Lysander asked her.

"Out. There must be some who still want to hurt and kill out there somewhere. I'll find them."

"You can't." Petrik had grown, in these few hours, to admire this small, quiet, but fanatically determined girl. "What about what's-his-name? Your Navigator. Lady Alizon told me somewhat. You're all he has left."

"Estaban has nothing left. If he has not what he considers his responsibility to me, perhaps he will finish what my mother started. He lives in pain, let him die in peace." She smiled at Lysander. "Thank you for showing me my mistake. Let this one die too. It's a kindness, after all."

"No!" Lysander caught her arm. "I've nothing against you. Why should you . . . ?" But it was there, in her eyes. Nothing left to fight for. Desperately: "After has to be better!"

Petrik made a smothered noise, somewhere between laughter and a groan. "Sure. And you're the living proof. Moral obligation to help others, eh, Sandman."

"He's Golden Singh!"

"He's a man," Brandy said. "And each and every individual human is important, or he or she is not. There is no middle ground."

"Keep arguing, child," Brine said bitterly. "The point is becoming moot. He's sliding away into death as we speak."

Lysander dropped to his knees, so that his gaze and Brandy's were on a level. "You people—the future—that's what I was fighting for. Must I choose, between that promise of the future . . . and him?"

"But don't you see? They are one and the same."

There was a long silence. Then Lysander rose, his gaze still fixed on hers. "You came to me because you have a patient dying you want to live. You said I could help. I have not seen him; he is just a dying man. What must I do?"

She sagged against him, then straightened, the nurse again. "Sit, however you can, as comfortable as you can, with so little room. You'll be sitting quite a while. Then, just give me your arm."

He lowered himself, back to the pallet, eyes still locked with hers, arranged his legs as best he could, and then, slowly, held out the crooked arm.

"Thank you." Brine came around, watched her neat movements as she connected the flow of life from one man to another.

"I have an enemy, somewhere nearby. I look for him constantly. When I find him, I'll kill him. But fairly, man to man."

Brine tucked himself in beside Lysander somehow, an incredible feat considering the space available and his own stocky bulk. He smiled, relaxed, and shut his eyes. "I don't think so. Your enemy killed himself, years ago. No loss, he was a thoroughly rotten person, though he might have been salvageable as himself, Mam says anyone is, if you're willing to put enough effort into it."

"Salvageable?"

"Um." His efforts were catching up with Brine, his mouth was dropping open. "Changed. Rescued. Turned. Brought to understand and accept what you call moral obligation to common humanity. Good made out of evil. But that's not what happened this time. Your enemy is dead, though his body lived on. That's my son up there now, my son who was born when your enemy died, my son who will live on now, with your blood."

"He can't be your son and my enemy."

Brine swallowed a huge yawn, his eyelids drooped. "Raised him from a blank-minded infant to the man he is now. Did a good job. He's my son." He slumped.

"I don't—"

Petrik jammed himself somehow next to them, slid down, one arm still stretched out, holding Emerald. "Brandy's keeping watch." He yawned, too. "They explained it to me, you know. Funny story. The c'holder, he was trying to catch them, had c'holder games in mind. Only *he* got caught, and somebody played games with him."

Lysander snorted, muttered something.

"The games were meant to help him, make him realize that what he was doing, had done, was wrong. Only his mind broke instead. They had a man's body, with an infant personless mind inside. So they raised him again, as though he were the infant his mind thought it was. Through babyhood, childhood, all the way. It didn't take as long as real growing up would have, but—that's why Brine calls the c'holder his son. Because the Golden Singh that is now is what he and the Lady Jael and the others made."

"I'm not sure I believe you, but I follow what you're saying. If there is any real truth in that, it's why he keeps saying my enemy is dead. The person who was Golden Singh, my enemy, is dead."

Petrik nodded.

Lysander pursed his lips. "Too ridiculous. Impossible. Ludicrous."

"I never met Singh myself. I was traded to the consortium after he left. But I've heard of his reputation. This man is not he. He's caring, compassionate, he's ready to defend any stranger who needs defending, ease pain at his own expense, never give it. I truly believe that he would rather die than take life torn unwillingly from another."

Lysander started chuckling.

Petrik frowned. "What's funny?"

"This whole situation. You see." A nod toward Singh. "I guess it doesn't matter if people know now. He's my father."

"What?"

"Uh-huh. Blood father. Course you know how some c'holders are, think that parenthood just gives them more rights." He shifted, ran his hand over the crooked arm, carefully avoiding the odd leechlike object sucking away near his elbow. "He was responsible for this, and a lot more besides. But if what you say is true—"

"It is!"

"Then this grimy snoring spacer next to me is my grandfather!"

Petrik suddenly clapped his free hand over his mouth, while smothered snickers burst through. "Wait'll you meet your grandmother," he sputtered out, then sobered abruptly. "If she lives."

"Someone else involved in all this. Not—" His eyes slid over to Brandy, who was now watching the console as though if she took her eyes off it for a second, the patient would die.

"No. A Navigator. She's badly hurt, and this mind-linkage of theirs . . . All I understand is, if he dies, she has no chance at all. If he lives—"

"She lives."

"She has a chance," Petrik corrected.

"They should both die." Emerald, still held by Petrik, sneered. "She's a bitch, and he's cruel." She peeked around Petrik, eyes wide and innocent. "He beat me."

"He did?" Lysander raised an eyebrow. "For that he gets some of my blood, with my best wishes."

"I'll beat you too, if you don't keep quiet." Petrik gave her a shake. "He spanked her, as one disciplines a child," he went on to Lysander. "He says even she is—what's the word?—salvageable, and he intended to do so." His mouth twisted. "What do you think?"

"He's bit off a chore for himself."

"If anyone can do it, he can. Of course, he'll have the others to help. Brine, and Lady Jael, and Freighter-Master—"

"What? You mentioned a Navigator. Not *Navigator* Lady *Jael*—"

"Who else? I thought—"

"She dies if he does?"

"Yes. So they told me. This linkage they have—"

"Then he *must* live!"

"We waited long," Brandy spoke above them. "He's gone far."

Lysander shut his eyes and leaned back. He had never prayed in his life, even when he was being tortured. He was praying now.

TWENTY-FIVE

It was a sad, chastened, and quiet throng of people that spread out from the improvised dais over the vast and smoky-smelling great port of Rabelais. It was not all the former population of Pantagruel, not even all the survivors. There were too many hurt and their attendants missing, old and young left wherever they were camped, again with a few to watch over them; there were those who wouldn't come, and those who couldn't come, and those who were coming but hadn't made it yet. But there was a fair fraction of the people of Pantagruel, and they were beginning to show signs of restlessness, and those on the dais decided to begin.

One of the some two dozen on the dais stepped a little forward, fiddled nervously with something around his neck, and a great voice boomed out, "People of Pantagruel, can you hear me?"

There was shock for a minute, then an assortment of yeses and we-can-hear-you's.

"In the back, can you hear me?"

"Yes!"

"Brothers and sisters, After has come. I am the Sandman."

A great roar, mostly approval, some anger and shaking of fists.

His amplified voice rolled out over them. "After has come, I say. The fire was a great tragedy which cannot be undone. The deaths and destruction of the last days and nights cannot be undone. But we must—"

A single voice, a woman's, hysterical, accusing: "It's your fault!"

"Faults and blame and accusations must be put behind us."

Hundreds of voices, men and women's: "I'll not go back to my c'holder!"

Again the amplified voice rolled out. "Brothers and sisters, please be silent and listen. Do not interrupt, as I have much import to say. I ask you, as you have listened and found wisdom in my words before, to be seated, get comfortable, and listen without interruption. After has come, and the rest of our lives depends on what we do and decide this day." He held out his arms. "Brothers and sisters."

There was a silence. Then, from somewhere: "I'll hear your words, Sandman!"

"Tell us what to do!"

"Help us!"

"Sandman!"

Again he held up his arms for silence. "Seat yourselves, and prepare to listen long. Many of us have labored on these words I would say to you. They are the concentrated wisdom of many, many hours and minds. I ask only that you be silent, and listen, and then think hard over what I've said. Can you do this?"

"Yes!"

"Then, let me begin." He took a deep breath, audible over the amplification, and said, "Declaration of the Living. Agreed to by a committee of inhabitants of Rabelais and off-worlders."

He smiled, then began, speaking very slowly. "We hold these truths to be self-evident, that all humans are created equal; that they are invested from their creation with certain inalienable rights, that among these rights are life, liberty, and the pursuit of happiness."

He paused, but there was silence. He looked out on a sea of puzzled faces. They had heard or heard of the Sandman, though. They knew he sometimes spoke of strange things, but that he would then explain so all could understand.

"That to secure these rights, systems of living together are established among humans, deriving their power and sway over those humans by the free and informed consent of those living within the system."

He paused, looked around, saw all eyes focused on him. Here and there a cough, a sniffle broke the silence.

"However, whenever any system of living together becomes destructive of the ends for which it was established, it becomes the right and obligation of the people to alter or abolish it, and to institute a new system of living together, laying its foundation on such principles and organizing its powers on such form as it seems to them most likely to protect their safety and happiness."

There was a great sigh from the crowd, and he waited until there was silence again.

"Experience has shown," he went on, "in many eras and on many worlds, that humankind as a whole is more disposed to suffer evils, while such evils are sufferable, than to right them by abolishing the systems to which they are accustomed. But when a long series of abuses and usurpations evidences a design to imprison them under absolute despotism, then it is their right, their duty, to discard such a system of living, and replace it with new forms for their future security."

"No more c'holders?"

He held up his hands again. "Yes, no, and maybe." When the crowd burst out at that, he silenced them, though it took longer than it had before.

"Listen well. We the committee representing the interests of Rabelais have come to these conclusions. That we do need and must have a new and agreed-on system of living. That we of the committee have neither the knowledge nor the authority to devise such a system. That while such a system is being duly formulated, we of Rabelais need an interim system of living, to sustain us until a permanent system can be provided and agreed on. We would like to put that interim, temporary system before you now for your agreement, as well as a suggestion for how the permanent system is to be worked out."

There was a man in the front row who seemed to be asking the questions. "And if we don't agree?"

Lysander shrugged. "The Adjudicators have rescued many more basic contracts than might have been expected. We could reestablish all contractual obligations."

"NO!"

He waited until the no's died down. "No, brothers and sisters, I did not think that would be your choice. I did not speak myself hoarse in Agony Square, or argue my brains numb with the committee after the fire, to see contractual obligations becoming again the all-emcompassing chains."

"Then what?"

"If the agreement we have worked out is not satisfactory, we will all stay here and try to find a consensus that is. Because the only alternative if we reject contracts is total anarchy, and if the taste of it the last few days is not enough, the off-worlders have informed me that the usual end product of anarchy is total dictatorship, all and everyone controlled by one single person, as though there were only one c'holder and everyone else was contracted. The off-worlders also say that this system is even worse than contracts and many c'holders. We all know that there are some c'holders it is far worse to be contracted to than others. With a dictator, he or she is usually the very worst kind of c'holder and no one is free of agony, because there is no chance to be traded away to a better c'holder.

"If our choice is narrowed to c'holders and a dictator, then my vote—and you know how I feel about c'holders—must be for the c'holders."

"What is this system of living you speak of?"

"We all agree that we need some temporary system, until we have established a permanent one."

"Yes!"

"And we all agree that once that temporary system is set up here we will all abide by it?"

Silence. Lysander spoke slowly. "We will agree here, all of us. Then, once we have all agreed, we will all abide."

Again the spokesperson. "That sounds reasonable!"

It took quite a while to hammer out the details. It was obvious to all that it was going to take a united effort to keep food coming into the city, to care for the many hurt, to provide shelter.

For the food, the off-worlders had contributed the emergency concentrates, but that supply was limited, and they would expect to be repaid eventually, somehow. Lysander made a face. "The off-worlders speak of something they call taxes. I don't understand it, I don't like what I do understand, but I do realize that people are hungry, and with so much food lost in the fire, we need food now, and we'll have to worry about fulfilment of obligations for it—call them contractual or whatever—later."

The folk agreed with that. Nobody wanted to go hungry.

Contracts would, within stringent limits, and temporarily, continue.

That caused almost another riot, but Lysander calmed them down enough to listen to him. "From now on, no c'holder will be able to punish, use, abuse, or order about a contracted. However, by mutual consent, the c'holder will agree to obtain food, shelter for his or her contracted, while the contracteds agree to do whatever work the c'holders order for the common good, such as clearing debris, or raising food. Right now, we must all work together or we will all starve together. Any contractor who tries abusive tactics or willful orders will quickly find him or herself without contracted to abuse or order, because they will have gone to c'holders who care for their contracteds, who are working for all to have a better life. Many of your c'holders are dead. Those contracteds can either come to the unity for work assignments and food, or the Navigators' Guild, or to c'holders they know will take true care of them. We all know that kind of c'holder. There are many of them here today. The other kind will take proper care of their contracteds, their responsibility, or they won't keep them; the good c'holders will get them. And of course, as things settle down, as food supplies are reestablished . . ."

Other details.

"Children will be taken care of by mutual agreement by their parents and their c'holder. If they have been separated from their parents, and their parents cannot be located, the Adjudicators' Unity will act temporarily in loco parentis."

Accurate records would be kept, of work done, food distributed, whatever.

Contracts would be replaced by mutual agreements, as quickly as possible.

Skilled workers would continue to serve in those capacities, especially those whose skills involved the raising, transporting, or preparing of food, hunting or fishing, record keeping, or the like.

A committee would be set up to devise the new system of living. Its final constitution: five members of the Adjudicators' Unity and some fifteen c'holders, suggested from within the crowd and approved or disapproved by voice vote. Plus an equal number of free-contractors, ditto, and, surprisingly, a few contracteds, who were well known for one reason or another. At

Lysander's suggestion, the Navigators' Guild and the representatives of the off-worlders agreed to supply some additional experts in the art of "systems of living," these to have voice in the Council but not a vote in the final decisions of what to offer to the people as a whole.

The people as a whole, again banded, were to have the final say on all systems suggested.

And on and on.

At dusk, the final agreement was reached, and the people began slowly to move away,

Lysander returned to the back of the dais and sank into a chair with a weary sigh, eyes closing. "Thank goodness that's over."

"Is it?" asked the pink-haired woman in Navigator black.

His eyes flew open. "Lady Alizon," he sputtered, "I've done my share."

Her smile broadened. "In every government—system of living, if you prefer—there always has to be a final authority. In a good one, that authority is hedged about with safeguards for the people's sake. In a bad one . . ." She shrugged. "But always, always—"

"Oh no!" He looked around. The dozen-plus by-now-familiar faces of the committee all stared at him.

"Oh *no!*"

Alizon grinned. "The pick stops here." He groaned. "You're picked, Lysander." He looked around; fourteen heads were nodding solemnly.

He glared at her. "You can't make me. None of you."

"Conscience doth make cowards of us all," said the blinded ex-spacer called Will. His voice was compassionate. "You've a conscience, Sandy my man. They want you, and they'll have you."

He put out a trembling hand. "Lady Alizon."

She caught it, squeezed. "It could be worse. There's an old piece of advice for a woman about to be forced. Relax and enjoy it."

EPILOGUE

The world of Star-roads was the most advanced in its sector, and one of its most famous specialties was medicine.

The patient and the physical therapist were both laughing as they wound up their hard-fought game. The scores of both inched up, the advantage now to one, now to the other. The wobbling ball with its internal sac of mercury twisted and danced, flashing through the intermittent holo displays, bouncing and turning as hands, feet, heads connected with it; its path was the wildest of Brownian motions.

Bong!

All the holos went off, the ball dropped as both contestants relaxed, and the PT swiped at her sweatband, rubbing back the cotton-candy-blue nimbus she sported instead of hair. "Good game, lady." A wry smile. "I'd hate to take you on when you *really* wanted to win."

The patient grinned back, wickedly. "When I really want to win, I play by my own rules." An easy kick, and the sport shoe on her left foot sailed upward, and the patient wiggled the long finger-toes it had concealed. Catching the shoe on its downward arc, she sailed the right one upward in the same breath.

Someone applauded, but the applause lasted only a second, as the man stopped to catch the second shoe in mid-flight.

The patient smiled. "Your reflexes haven't slowed, either, I see, Rowan," she said.

He grinned, tossing the shoe lightly up and down. "Oh, I was pretty good at this myself, once upon a time. I expect I could give either of you a challenging match even now." A grin that matched hers. "If you keep your shoes on."

He was a good-looking man in his prime, hair a dark red and eyes a clear aquamarine, and the PT had been attracted to him the first time she saw him. "I'd be glad to give you a match whenever you choose, Freighter-Master Reis," she purred. "On my off-duty hours, of course." Normally, she wouldn't have broken into a pair-bonding, especially when one of the pair was her patient. But over time, she had changed her mind about the relationship between these two. From the beginning, he had been as attentive and considerate as any woman would want her permanent to be. But while he was obviously prepared to defend his lady with his own blood, there was nothing possessive about their relationship, close as it obviously was. Though they looked about as different as two people could and still both be (mostly) unmodified human, they must be closely related, the therapist had decided, and the man's next actions confirmed it. He gave her a long, very male assessment, and smiled slowly.

"I have duties, but when my off-duty time coincides with yours, I would be pleased to . . . match you."

The woman further confirmed it. "Watch out for him, Lady Insouciant," she said with a rich chuckle and a toss of tiger-striped hair. "He knows some very ingenious moves, does our Rowan." Her eyes sparkled with sheer amusement, and there wasn't a particle of jealousy in the sly wink she accompanied the word *ingenious* with.

"I'm sure I know all the counters, even to the most ingenious moves," the PT said, chuckling herself, and the women laughed together.

"Ganging up on me, are you!" The man swooped, so suddenly he had a woman's body under each arm before they could defend themselves. Despite the weight of his captives, he was off and running, over the rise, where a small lake sparkled sapphire in the soft sunshine.

Then two twisting, cursing bodies sailed out and down and, with a mighty splash, in.

At least that was the scenario Rowan had planned. He had forgotten Jael's hand-feet, and the ball-and-socket flexibility of her knees and ankles. As he tossed, she attacked. He lost his balance and toppled after them, three mighty splashes, three people choking and sputtering and laughing and engaging in a childish water-fight.

But nothing could make Rowan angry on this day of days, the day he was sure, with no lingering doubts, that Jael was healed, was back to all she had been.

In another sector of Star-roads, a man lay contentedly smiling. His eyes were bandaged, but this time the bandages covered new eyes, cloned eyes. It would take time, but the medicos assured him that the nerve splices were knitting nicely and he would have new, usable eyes.

It was going to be strange, learning to see all over again, but he was looking forward to it. Then he would go back, back to Rabelais, to help build a new society almost literally over the ashes of the old.

" 'The Lark's on the wing;/The snail's on the thorn:/God's in his heaven —/All's right with the world!' " said Will, to no one in particular.

His monitor, hearing, smiled, but checked all his readouts, just to make sure.

All green. The smile broadened. Success was always gratifying, and success on this scale, healing a crippled fellow human, even more so.

The monitor flicked a switch. "Patient Hotchkiss, since you're awake, I received that new recording of Morgenstern's 'Bridge of Sighs' I mentioned last shift. Would you like me to play the audio portion for you?"

"Thanks, I would." He thought his new eyes were being paid for by a distressed spacer's fund, which they were not. The world called Maze had amassed a large credit on Star-road's files, and the amount needed for his new eyes and after-treatment hardly showed. But no money at all could pay for the personal attention and encouragement he had had from the first. Part of it was due to the nature of the Star-Roadians themselves, and part due to the charismatic smile of the man who had signed him in.

Not that that mattered, either.

This was only an interlude. Soon he'd be healed, and going home.

Home.

Rabelais.

It was an odd docking, but luckily the passengers didn't realize how odd.

The little freighter sped toward a destination that only showed in the screens as an absence, its master humming quietly to himself, not controlling the ship, merely keeping an eye out to be sure that all internal systems were functioning normally.

Once the younger passenger came in, and he jumped and instinctively tried to shield what he wasn't doing, then realized she didn't know enough to know. "Will it be much longer?" she asked, her large, brandy-colored eyes too sad for her young age.

"No, not much." He patted her trembling shoulder gently, his eyes oddly compassionate in his battered space-pirate's face. (He hadn't realized yet that she wasn't fooled by the exterior, the shaggy rust-colored hair and beard, the scar that cut that beard, the crudity of rough features he had never bothered to have bio-sculpted into handsomeness. The softness in his eyes gave him away, and she trusted him wholeheartedly.)

"We'll be there soon, Brandy, very soon."

She worried her lip. "He just . . . lies there. I know—*I know!*—that he wants, needs to scream, to rampage, to curse and struggle and—and—and he won't let himself. He won't even let himself tremble. He just lies there, eyes open, waiting until it's time to feed himself, or sleep or—" A drop of blood welled, satin-ruby, where her teeth dug in too hard.

Even his coarse voice was oddly compassionate. "Has he—has he allowed you to solace him yet?"

"Oh no, Master Reis," Brandy told Rowan's older brother, Hannibal. Infinite sadness: "He says now that he knows, never. He'll let me do whatever I wish for him, except that. And he—he just lies there. And his *eyes* . . ."

"Has he asked for another dose?"

"No."

He patted her shoulder again. "We'll be there soon."

Tears made her eyes glitter before tracking down her newly hollowed cheeks. "What good will it do? What good can anything do? There's no *cure.*"

"No physical cure. But then, it isn't a physical addiction."

"So cruel . . ."

"Trust me. Trust us."

Her lip twitched slightly, but she didn't say it aloud: *Have I a choice?*

The landing came some hours later. Even when he was waiting for it, he could never detect the slight zoop that was a matter-transmitter landing. In one nanosecond they went from here to there, and stopped dead. It was his controls that told him, as they reacted to the change. Since he hadn't had the engines on, they didn't go off, but the artgrav did, as it was replaced by the real thing, or an outside equivalent. He began his checks, humming slightly under his breath. He was home.

Mam was waiting as he opened the port, with the bulk of a huge man beside her, grinning welcome.

"Mam!" He exploded out of the port, his passengers behind him forgotten, and charged down the ramp, to toss the plump motherly figure high in his arms, before enveloping her in a hug that had her tugging at his hair and sputtering, "You naughty lad, put me down, I can't breathe!"

Obediently he put her down, but chucked her under the chin, grinning, "You don't breathe, Mam."

"I do so." She wrinkled her snub nose at him. "I modified myself while you were gone. Listen." Ummm, ahhhh, she made deep, breathing noises.

"Well, it sounds like breathing," he admitted, still grinning. "But do you need to do it?"

Her full lips pouted. "I haven't worked that out yet, son, but I will."

He was already turning to the man at her side. "Ferine, brother, thought you and Damask were off honeymooning again."

"With a little our-business on the side?" The smiling giant grinned back. "He is. I'm not."

"Ah." Hannibal Reis stared way, way up at the duplicate of the man who had become another of his mind-brothers.

"Yup." The giant stretched and wriggled his fingers. "Waste not, want not. With him so far away, the link's attenuated to nothing. I've been developing on my own ever since I was awakened, and will continue to do so. With luck, by the time he gets back, I'll be enough of an individual, with enough of my own memories different than his, that we'll both stay independent, no more linkage than any of the rest of us. I'll be calling myself Secundus, by the way, until I come up with something better."

"You will, dear." Mam wrinkled her nose at him, and Hannibal Reis couldn't help reaching down to tweak its delightful snub.

"Your passengers, dear." Mam said a little later, breaking up the reunion that might have gone on for hours.

They stood at the base of the ramp, a tall man whose hair was not silver with age and whose tawny-amber eyes would have fitted well in a death's skull, and a slight girl-woman with brandy-colored eyes equally sad and lost, and a tiny bulge in her otherwise petite midriff.

"Ah." Hannibal Reis cleared his throat. "Mam, this is Navigator Estaban Xavier y Perdones and his daughter, Lady Brandy Xavier y Leany."

Brandy nodded. Estaban merely blinked, and his proud head lowered, the merest trifle. No one was insulted. It was taking all his massive will to remain standing there, and not beg for what he needed, or run screaming off, amok, berserk under the strain of denial.

"Ser and Lady Xavier." Hann Reis made a slight, proud gesture. "This is Mam." Once, when he had first known her and what she was, he would have said "Mam" as though he said "empress of the universe." Now he knew better. She was, in a sense, empress of his universe. She was also immensely powerful. But she was also and totally Mam, and he loved her for what she was to him, not what she had the power to be to many.

"Welcome to Maze, my children." Mam beamed.

Estaban made that slight, slight inclination of his proud head again. It was Brandy who said softly, "We thank you for your welcome, lady." She hesitated, and Mam held out her arms. Brandy flew into them, sobbing, while Mam stroked her hair and murmured "Dear, dear," and other soothing human things she'd learned from the newest members of her immense family.

"Women" Reis said with a wry twist of the mouth. Then, "Navigator Ser Xavier, this is another of my family, Secundus."

Again the stiff, almost imperceptible nod.

"This all your gear?" Secundus asked cheerfully, reaching for the soft bag that Brandy had dropped in her rush. Without waiting for a reply: "Let's go, then, leave the women for a bit." A wink to Estaban. "Do 'em good."

"Prax?" Reis asked, surprised, having picked up their destination through the linkage.

"Mam's idea," Secundus answered, the bag Brandy had had to drag with both hands tossed casually under one arm. But then, he could have carried Brandy herself as easily.

"Let's go, then," said Reis, and their surroundings . . . changed.

Estaban blinked, and blinked again, his gaze slowly going in a circle as the stiffness oozed out of his body.

"Prax's lair," Secundus informed, proudly.

"It's . . . very nice," Estaban said slowly, his voice hoarse, hesitant as though he hadn't spoken except to scream raw-throatedly for a long, long time.

"We think so," said Secundus casually, as though there wasn't more sheer beauty crowded in that one room than most people enjoyed in a lifetime. "Course, this is only his workroom, crude stuff here. If you want to see his current—" Without waiting for an answer, he caught Estaban's nearest hand in his own free one, and all three men again translated . . . elsewhere.

Estaban took one look around and dropped to his knees, covering his eyes with his hands—Secundus had dropped the hand he was holding as soon as they arrived—and shuddered, sobbing aloud.

"You don't like it?" said a new voice. It belonged to a tall man whose prosthetic arms were works of art in themselves. He strolled toward the new-arrived trio, a disappointed frown marring his smooth, blue-gray forehead.

Estaban sobbed aloud.

Prax dropped to his knees to bring his own face level with the newcomer's and said gently, "I'd hoped you like it, I'd hoped you'd stay here with me. Don't you like it?"

A shudder, then, through sobs: "It's . . . very nice."

Shrewdly: "But not up to what you have with the drug, eh?"

"N-no." A trembling breath. "You know?"

"Of course." Prax smiled. "What one of the family knows, we all know, unless light-years separate us. Even then, if the emotion is strong enough . . ." He sobered. "It is such cruelty and the situations that breed it that we are fighting against, each in their own way," he informed.

"She—" Estaban shook. "She was honest. The cruelest, most painful way of suicide, she said. It was what I wanted."

"She knew you well. It was what you thought you wanted, and yet it is not. A subtle, treacherous cruelty."

He shuddered again, a whole-body tremor, a controlled convulsion that was a faint echo of the chaotic emotions within. "Yes. No matter which way I go, I am—am—"

"I understand. If you continue to take the drug, you will die, quite quickly, but immeasurably content, happy, enthralled and wrapped in visions of paradise. People who take Elysium die of an overdose of beauty."

It was not inaccurate. Elysium was an emotionally addicting drug. The sensations it produced were so overwhelmingly magnificent that the users could not bear the harsh drabness of reality. Most Elysium users took dose after dose, programmed an injector to feed the drug directly into their veins continuously. Eventually their bodies died, even in cases where the bodies were on artificial life support. Elysium users cared nothing for the mundane business of eating and surviving, but their families sometimes cared for them —even if the body was cared for, when its owner did not, the emotional highs produced, one after another, burned the body and brain out. Most Elysium users died—ecstatically happy—within a few weeks of their first dose; those on support lived two or three times as long but no more. No continuous user had ever survived more than half a standard year.

The exceptions were the few, very few, addicts who could control the psychological addiction, bear reality for the prescribed times between each dose. Most of them broke sooner or later, demanded the drug continuously. But while they endured, they suffered unimaginable hell in their own mind, the stark contrast of their drug-hours and the cruel reality.

Estaban had not touched the drug, though it was his for the asking, since he had unknowingly taken the first dose Leany had offered him. The effort was showing. Despite the fact that Brandy had forced him to eat, the sheer tension involved was gnawing away at his flesh. When it had happened, he had been a muscular man, lithe and athletic. Now he was pared down to bone and not much more, losing far more weight than he could afford to get rid of.

"Take the drug, and die quick and happy," Prax said with a nod. "That's not much of a penance, is it?"

Through gritted teeth: "No."

"But if you don't take the drug—"

Very soft: "Hell."

Even softer: "How much hell can any one man be expected to endure, eh, even as a penance."

"I—" Estaban scrambled to his feet, staggered over, and sank onto a soft hummock, head buried in his hands.

"Don't know," Prax finished for him, rose easily, and plumped himself beside the stricken man.

"We had hoped—" Reis took a step toward the two on the hummock, but a quick thought flashed through the linkage caused both him and Secundus to step back. Then, with a wink at the newcomer, Secundus blinked out. Reis followed him with his mind for a second, then, a slight flush spreading beneath the leathery spacer tan and the beard, loosed his concentration. They all made a background in his mind, but Secundus and what he was doing was now a shrouded part of the background.

Prude, sent a female mind through the link, and his flush deepened at the sensation of a soft, sisterly kiss of welcome on his cheek. But the kisses she was sharing with Secundus were far from sisterly, and he hastily added her psyche to the wrappings. A slight giggle echoed in his mind, and he returned his attention to what was happening in front of him.

"We had hoped to be able to help you," Prax was saying, the mental exchange having taken only a few seconds. "We had hoped—but I had hoped for more. I had hoped you could help me."

"Help?" Estaban stared at Prax, a man driven past his limits, holding on to sanity by the frailest of threads.

"Not because you feel obligated, or anything like that, because we are trying to help you. We would have anyway, if we can."

"I know," Estaban muttered, not knowing how he knew, just that he heard truth. These people, on this world, would help their fellows whenever they could.

"But because," Prax went on, "you can help me, and you're the only one who can help me, and because what I'm doing is of untold significance to— to the universe. To generations yet to come."

"Need—penance."

"If you help me, you'll have it, and to spare. I'll not lie to you. You called it hell, but if you do what I want, it'll be even worse than that."

"What kind—" Reis started to explode, but a mental hand on his mouth stopped him. *I know what I'm doing!*

"Explain." Estaban hadn't heard Reis's outburst, he was too intent on Prax.

"It's the drug. It's made you see . . . paradise."

Tormented: "Yes!"

"I'm an artist. Part of my art is to get as close to ultimate beauty as I can, as I have here."

"Yes." He looked around again. "You've come closer than anyone else I've ever seen."

"Thank you," Prax said with a nod. "But not close to what the drug shows you, eh?"

"No. But your work is . . . nice. Nice."

"My thanks." A twist of the lips. "What I was hoping was that you'd be my critic."

"Critic? I know nothing of art."

"No. But you have the drug and its visions. What I want you to tell me is, which of my works is furthest from your perfections, and which parts of each study are furthest."

"Critic." Estaban nodded slowly.

"To do that," Prax said softly, "you'll have to stay alive. And take the drug at intervals, to keep its perfection clear in your mind. And deprive yourself much of the rest of the time, to survive. You wanted penance."

Low: "I don't know if I can."

"Perhaps you'd like to see some of my other creations." Without waiting for an answer, Prax caught one of Estaban's hands, and the two flicked out, like lights shutting off.

Reis stared at where they had been, his face pursed. It might work. He remembered some of Prax's creations, and his face slowly began to brighten. If anybody could pull it off, give the man a reason to endure, it was Prax. He was a planet-class artistic genius, the kind that came along once in centuries. And some of his works . . .

He smiled. Problem not solved, but at least there was light at the end of the tunnel. Prax's genius and the solid results of that genius. Estaban needed beauty, and Prax could supply close to that ultimate.

Up to Prax now. Reis's eyes brightened. His turn for a real welcome home. Like Prax and Estaban, Reis blinked out.

To reappear elsewhere on Maze, step into waiting arms and enjoy *his* welcome.

Emerald set her lips mutinously. "I won't."

Petrik sighed. *How* he had ever let himself be talked into this?

But Golden had decided that his "daughter" needed some time on her own, and it was obvious that neither Golden himself nor Brine, her true father, could be spared.

"No work, no eat," Petrik said grimly, for the nth time. *Golden, old friend, when I get back . . .* he was thinking.

Not that Golden, immensely busy with his work of interfacing the new Rabelais and the rest of the universe, would have worried, had he stopped to consider what his favorite assistant was planning. And Petrik, thinking yearningly about tying certain—unnamed—people up and setting certain other—unnamed—people to filling their golden-skinned ears with whining until they went as teeth-clenchingly frustrated as he was at the moment, knew it.

Golden always could charm a fish into trying to breathe air. But *next* time . . .

Emerald whined again and tried to snatch a collop of delicious-smelling roasting meat from the campfire. Petrik slapped her hand away and repeated his order firmly.

As for that calculating look he had noticed in the shrewd golden eyes lately, as they went from acknowledged daughter to friend and assistant!

Golden, once his mind was made up, could be as unstoppable as an avalanche, but if he (Petrik) convinced Brine that the little spoiled piece was still too young . . .

It would give him time to find a victim—contender!—who was A) more appealing to her and B) approved by both her male parents. Not an easy chore. But desperation—Emerald was whining again—is the mother of a lot more than invention.

With a sigh, the First Administrator of the Independent City-State of Pantagruel on the planet of Rabelais sat down at his desk and called up his calendar for the day on the console. His eyes worked down it; then he groaned and ran his hands through his already rumpled, gray-streaked, sand-colored hair. Behind him, his administrative assistant giggled smugly.

He sucked in a deep breath and whirled. *"Look*—at that!" he snarled, trembling finger pointing to the screen. *"Lookatthat!"*

Paloma grinned.

"You've scheduled every long-winded bottle of hot air, every waffling committee head who chases his own brain in circles, every—" He looked back and shuddered. "Wheel take you, woman. Arturo Pisces of the League of Fire-Recompensing! How *could* you?"

"If you'll excuse me, I've work to do." She slid a printout from the slot in her own machine and got up and turned to the door.

He blocked her escape. "Did I make you angry last night?" he coaxed. "Yesterday? Whatever it is"—he kissed her soulfully on the cheek—"I'll make up for it." His mouth nibbled slowly at one pinkening ear. "Darling."

"We're in the office here," she reminded.

He was busy. *Very* busy.

"We're official here," she said, more sharply.

"Ummm-hummmm." He silenced her the immemorial way.

Five minutes later: "That's enough, Sandy."

"No, it isn't. But will you fix my schedule, anyway, love?"

A low laugh. "Bribe me."

"My first appointment's in five minutes."

"It only takes a minute to go down the stairs."

Five minutes later, with her pushing a little, he was trotting obediently down the stairs. With a grin, she went back to her console and programmed his real appointment calendar.

Every now and then it was good to establish who the real boss was.

ABOUT THE AUTHOR

Jayge Carr started writing on a dare. One evening, angry at what she was reading (let us not Name Names or Point Fingers), she tossed the book across the room and snarled, "I could write a better book than THAT!" Her other half, working at his desk, looked up and said (was he joking?), "Why don't you?" "Because, I'm not a writer," replied she, with great logic. Then he, little knowing—or did he?—what he was unleashing on an unsuspecting world, quoth thus, with greater logic, "How do you know until you try?"

Said trying has produced the books, *Leviathan's Deep* and three in the Jael the Navigator series, *Navigator's Syndrome, The Treasure in the Heart of the Maze,* and RABELAISIAN REPRISE, plus dozens of short stories published in magazines like *Omni* and *Analog,* and more in original and reprint collections, including three BEST OF anthologies.

For those fascinated by statistics, Ms. Carr was born in Houston, is the oldest of four sisters, has a degree in Physics, and worked for NASA as a nuclear physicist, is married, and is now inhabiting a very mundane (until you get into her study) ranch-style house on the wrong side of Lake Pontchartrain from New Orleans (she considers it the right side) with her husband, four cats, and the occasional presence of her two daughters, usually away at college (business/art) and grad school (English/education). (Can't imagine where the latter got her literary leanings from.) In person, Ms. Carr is a stereotypical housefrau, except perhaps for an occasional amused glimpse in her eye and a devilish imagination. The last named of which has produced this book, which she hopes the reader is currently enjoying.